"I got no need of a man."

"I ain't offering to marry you."

Lucy snorted. "That's not exactly what I meant. I meant to escort me to the recitation."

Wade refused to repent. "I still ain't offering." He had been alone for a long time. Preferred it that way.

They reached the schoolroom. Lucy led him to a desk near the front and they crowded in side by side. He noted how nicely she fit next to him.

Again he marveled that a body as pretty and as sweet smelling as Lucy's—like a field of clover in full bloom—could house a heart of coal.

Thankfully it was time for the program to begin. He forced his attention back to the front of the room. Then Lucy rose.

For a moment, he couldn't take his eyes off her, then he forced himself to remember why he was here.

Lucy—with her grey eyes and teasing smile—had succeeded in throwing open all the gates in his thoughts. But he wasn't here to moon over a gal. He cared for only one thing—convincing Lucy to visit her father.

Linda Ford
and
Laurie Kingery

Dakota Cowboy
&
Mail Order Cowboy

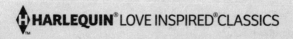
HARLEQUIN® LOVE INSPIRED®CLASSICS

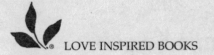 LOVE INSPIRED BOOKS

Recycling programs for this product may not exist in your area.

ISBN-13: 978-1-335-45460-7

Dakota Cowboy & Mail Order Cowboy

Copyright © 2019 by Harlequin Books S.A.

The publisher acknowledges the copyright holders of the individual works as follows:

Dakota Cowboy
Copyright © 2010 by Linda Ford

Mail Order Cowboy
Copyright © 2010 by Laurie A. Kingery

www.Harlequin.com

Printed in U.S.A.

CONTENTS

Linda Ford lives on a ranch in Alberta, Canada, near enough to the Rocky Mountains that she can enjoy them on a daily basis. She and her husband raised fourteen children—four homemade, ten adopted. She currently shares her home and life with her husband, a grown son, a live-in paraplegic client, and a continual (and welcome) stream of kids, kids-in-law, grandkids, and assorted friends and relatives.

Visit the Author Profile page
at Harlequin.com for more titles.

DAKOTA COWBOY

Linda Ford

In thy presence is fulness of joy;
at thy right hand there are pleasures for evermore.
—*Psalms* 16:11

To God be the glory. As Jesus said in John 15:5, "For without me ye can do nothing." I am aware of my limitations every day and grateful for His sufficiency.

Chapter One

Summer 1896, Dry Creek, North Dakota

He looked like any one of the hundred different cowboys who came in pretending they wanted a nice meal in a fancy dining room when what they really wanted was to eyeball the girl serving the food.

Yes, he looked like every other cowboy except for his steady eyes and how quiet and still he held himself, all watchful and calm.

Eighteen-year-old Lucy Hall served dozens of men like him every day—ignoring their invitations to walk her home, smiling at their jokes, ducking away from those who would steal a touch. None of them made her look twice.

Until now.

It was the way he seemed so self-assured, so peaceful with himself that drew her glance to him time after time. Often she caught a little smile on his lips as he overheard something from a nearby table. She wished she could share his amusement, grab hold a bit of his calmness. He gave her the feeling all was right with his world.

Lucy hesitated just a fraction on her way to get his order. No one would have noticed the slight pause if they'd cared to glance up from their meal. Only she knew the way her heart skittered with something akin to the nervousness she'd felt the first day she'd worked in the Dry Creek Hotel dining room.

"Morning, sir, what can I get you?" The words caught on the back of her tongue, but she would not clear her throat and cause any of the patrons to glance her way nor give them reason to tease her.

He smiled. His eyes were blue-green, like pond water on a bright day. He owned an unruly mop of blond curls.

Her cheeks heated as if seared by a July sun.

"You here alone?"

The sunshine threatened to blind her, though she knew the curtains muted the morning light. Her feeling of being shone upon had come from his smile, his eyes. She pulled her thoughts into orderly control and turned her concentration to his question. Was the man joshing? No, she sadly mused. Only like a hundred other cowboys wanting to sweet-talk her. She knew how to handle them. Tease them. Pretend to play along with their nonsense while guarding her words, her thoughts and her emotions. "Let's see. Apart from—" she glanced around the room "—about a dozen others and Harry and Hettie in the kitchen, yup, I'm pretty much alone."

He tipped his head back and laughed. "Guess that was a stupid question. It's just that I was told—I wondered if there was another girl helping you."

Lucy's nerves danced in accompaniment to his

chuckle. She sniffed in air heavy with the smell of bacon and fried potatoes. He was like a hundred others she saw every day.

Only he wasn't. She wished she could put her finger on what made him different—besides the fact he made her nervous and excited all at once.

"I'll have a good-sized breakfast, please and thank you."

Please and thank you. Well, that was different. "Eggs? Sausage? Bacon? Steak? Hash browns?"

"Yup. The works, if you don't mind. I'm feeling just a mite hungry."

She chuckled. "Better bring a pocket full of bills if you ever develop a big hunger."

He favored her with another white-toothed smile. That was different, too. Most cowboys neglected their teeth, allowing the tobacco so many chewed to discolor them in a most atrocious way. "And coffee, please."

Lucy left the table, walked over to the pass-through window and called, "Starving Bachelor's Special."

Hettie snorted. "Pile it high?"

"Man says he's a mite hungry."

"Gotcha."

Lucy reached for a fine-china teacup and saucer. She loved the way so many of the men sputtered when she handed them the dainty things. She'd chuckle and leave them struggling to figure out how to hold the tiny handle. She filled the cup with scalding coffee and took it to the cowboy who picked it up with perfect calmness. Yes, that was different, too. This man was beginning to interest her. Who was he and what was he doing in the Dry Creek dining room?

She refilled a few more customers coffee cups before returning the coffeepot to the stove.

"Bachelor breakfast ready." Hettie wiped her sweaty brow on her wide, white apron.

Lucy grabbed the waiting plate of food and took it to the quiet cowboy.

He dropped his gaze to his plate. She could practically hear the rush of juice in his mouth. He held his fork and knife, poised as if ready to do battle with the teetering pile of food.

She sensed his reluctance to eat while she hovered at his side. "I'll bring more coffee."

"Much appreciated."

Still, she hesitated wanting…she knew not what.

But she had other things to attend to and she took the coffeepot and began to refill cups on other tables.

"Lucy gal, order up," Hettie called in her beefy voice.

"Oh, Lucy gal, you can order me up whenever you want."

Lucy filled the leering man's cup and ducked out of reach.

"Lucy gal, Lucy gal." A row of patrons—all male, all ranchers and rough cowboys—hoisted their cups and leaned over, begging for refills.

Lucy hurried down the line, dancing out of reach, laughing at their teasing. There was a time they had scared her, made her tense and anxious. She soon learned the best way to deal with them was to turn it into a game. That way they all had fun. And if anyone got rowdy or out of line, Harry, Hettie's husband and owner of the dining room, would hustle them out the door so fast they dug ruts in the polished wooden floor.

Harry tolerated no unruly or rude behavior, and Harry was brawny enough that no one argued with his rules.

She took the coffeepot to the hungry cowboy and refilled his cup.

"*You're* Lucy?" he asked.

She tipped her head to one side and planted a finger in the middle of her chin. "Now, I can't imagine how you'd know that. Oh, unless it's because the name has been hooted, bandied about and generally abused for the last ten minutes."

He nodded, his eyes suddenly watchful, guarded even. She couldn't think why he should look at her in such a way. But she didn't have time to wonder for long. Duty called and she got back to work.

After she'd been back to his table to refill his cup a fourth time she stifled a giggle as she glanced at his ears. It wouldn't surprise her none to see twin spouts of brown liquid gushing from each side of his head.

By now, only the coffee-swilling, no-longer-hungry cowboy and an older couple remained in the dining room. Lucy began to wonder if someone had smeared his chair with glue before he sat down. Wouldn't Harry have a conniption if they had?

His presence trickled along her nerves, making her very aware of him as she put fresh white cloths on each of the tables, and set out china and silverware in preparation for the customers who would come for the noon meal.

Harry charged into the room and glanced around. He took note of the lone cowboy before he poured himself a cup of coffee and sat down to read some papers.

He glanced again at the cowboy and slid Lucy an inquiring look. She read his silent message. *Is this fella bothering you?*

She shrugged. How did she explain the way she felt drawn to him? Hoping…for what? That he'd hung about waiting for a chance to speak to her? Lots of the patrons waited for such a chance. If he had something to say, best he come right out and say it.

Not one to play coy games, she grabbed the coffeepot and headed in his direction. He was no different than any of the other cowboys who came and went. Most of them she didn't give a passing glance. A few she favored with a walk out, or accompanied to a play or some activity put on by the cultural society. If this one asked, would she agree to go? Yes, she would because there *was* something different about him. She couldn't put her finger on it. She only knew there was something in the way he *didn't* look at her. His stare was not openly curious and measuring like so many of the cowboys— as if they were checking her for conformity, estimating her hardiness—judging her like she a good beef animal.

"Another refill?"

He pushed away his cup. "No, thank you, ma'am. Mighty fine it was, though." He edged his chair back and looked at her, a hard glint in his eyes.

Lucy hesitated. What had happened to change the softer, kinder look she'd first noticed? But what did it matter? He was only one of hundreds of cowboys she served.

Wade Miller struggled to get his mind around the discovery that this was Lucy Hall—Scout's daughter. At first glance, he had been mesmerized by her bubbly personality that had every pair of eyes in the full dining room following her with amused appreciation. Who would know from the way she acted that beneath the surface lay a heart as cold as river ice? What kind of girl would return her father's letters unread and refuse continued invitations to visit?

He was here to change that.

She hovered at his side with the bottomless coffeepot. He planted his hand firmly over the top of his mug. His eyeballs were already drowning.

"I'm done. Thank you very much."

She nodded and told him the total for his breakfast.

He made to pull the money from his pocket and paused. Slowly, cautiously, he brought his gaze to her. She wore the same amused expression he'd observed throughout the morning.

"Something I can do for you, mister?"

He didn't like tipping his head to talk to her and pushed his chair back so he could gain his feet and full height. That was better. Now she had to tip her head, which set her pale brown hair to quivering. He'd once seen hair that color on an old dog he was particularly fond of. The animal had the smarts of a fox and the heart of a saint. For a dog the fur had been silky enough but he was willing to believe Lucy's hair was a whole lot silkier. And a thousand times sweeter smelling.

He jerked his thoughts back to reality. Nice hair did not change the cruelness of her heart.

"You're Lucy Hall, I take it."

"Where you plan to take it, mister?"

He grinned. She'd given him the perfect opening. "I'd like to take it and you to see your father."

She stepped back and curled her lips like he had a bad smell.

"My father sent you?"

Coming here had been his idea, not Scout's. "He figured you hadn't received his letters."

She planted her hands on her hips. "You tell him I got them just fine. You tell him I don't care to hear from him. You tell him—" She gasped in air like a horse that had been rode too long and too hard.

He wasn't about to give up just because some little filly was all tangled up in some sort of hornets nest. "He's sick. Wants to see you. Seems reasonable enough."

She leaned forward, her chin jutted out, her eyes warning of approaching thunder. "Mister, you had your say. I suggest you move on."

"Trouble, Lucy gal?" The big man Wade took to be the owner breathed down his neck. Every nerve in his body jerked to full alert. He knew better than to mess with a man that size and with that warning note in his voice.

"I'm on my way." But he'd be back.

He left the dining room and swung into the saddle. He rode past a rowdy bar. Knew the cowboys would be filling up the hotel rooms come nighttime. He could buy himself a bed but he was used to his own company. Preferred it to the sort he'd find crawling around town.

He reined his horse toward the thin stand of trees where he intended to set up camp. He unsaddled Two Bit and tossed him a handful of oats. He'd let him roam, picking what he could. The horse would come as soon as he whistled.

After finding a rock to lean his back on, Wade settled down to think. The heat beat at his skin. It caused the landscape to sway like grass in the wind. Nothing blocked his view of the town. A struggling prairie town with high hopes, few trees.

Nothing about this scenery compared to the ranch in the hills, to the west. There, grass grew high as a horse's belly, a house sat in the shade of cottonwoods, and a pretty little creek made a beautiful sound as it washed over rocks. No one could see the ranch without loving it. Not even someone like Lucy. He was equally certain that if she saw Scout she would forget whatever little tiff had made her shut him out of her life.

He could drive a herd of cows and rope a wild mustang but how did a cowboy persuade a reluctant, beautiful woman to go where she didn't want to go?

He intended to find a way. Maybe he could even use some help from God. He hadn't put much stock in the faith his mother had taught him until last winter, but there was no denying God had answered his desperate prayer back then. He wasn't sure if he had the right to ask anything more of the Man up above but figured it wouldn't hurt.

God, Scout looked about to die when I left. He hoped he could fulfill this task he had given himself before the man drew his last breath. *Seems only reasonable that he get the chance to see his daughter before he does. Might help if You show this Lucy gal that she should pay her father a visit.*

He returned to town a few hours later and passed some time nosing about. As the evening shadows lengthened, he thought of riding to the front door of the dining room and going in for supper, but Harry had been a little less than welcoming in his final goodbye.

But having asked around, he knew Lucy would be done as soon as the supper crowd left. He'd not been able to discover where she lived. People tended to be a little suspicious if his questions were too direct.

He decided he'd wait at the back of the Dry Creek dining room and reined his horse in that direction. Sooner or later he'd get a chance to talk to her, persuade her to visit her father. Once she knew the precarious nature of Scout's health, there'd be no way she could refuse.

He slid from Two Bit's back, and let the horse lounge in the shade provided by the board fence at the side of the alley. He leaned back against the rough lumber and got himself comfortable, pulling his hat low to shade his eyes. Anyone seeing him might think he slept on his feet. They'd be wrong. His ears registered every skittering bit of dirt, every creak of the fence, every footfall.

He cracked one eye at the patter of running feet. A small ragamuffin of a boy skidded to a halt fifteen feet away and stared from Wade to Two Bit. He heard the boy's sharply indrawn breath, took note of his sudden wary stiffening and hid a smile as the youngster just as quickly donned a sullen expression and a slouch before he plucked a blade of grass from beside the fence, stuck it in his mouth and swaggered to the door of the dining room to lean back as bold and unconcerned as if he had his name on the deed.

Wade used one finger to tip his hat back. "Howdy."

"Howdy." The boy gave a barely there nod and a bold, uncompromising stare.

Wade lowered his hat again and settled back.

"You waiting for something?" For a youngster so

scrawny Wade could practically count his ribs through his thin shirt, he sure did have a challenging way of talking.

"Just waiting."

"You hoping to see Lucy, ain't ya?"

"It concern you if I am?"

The boy scowled something fierce like a kid used to fighting his way through life. "Lucy don't care for drifters hanging about."

"Can't say as I blame her."

The boy snorted.

Wade shoved his hat back and came off the fence so fast the boy flattened himself to the wall. "Name's Wade. Wade Miller." He shoved his hand toward the boy.

"Roy. Just Roy." He took Wade's outstretched hand. His grip surprisingly firm for such an undernourished-looking body.

"Pleased to make your acquaintance, Roy." He leaned back, studying Roy. "You waiting for Lucy?" Did the boy have some claim on her? Too old to be her son. Maybe a brother, though Scout had never mentioned such.

"Just waiting."

Wade gave him a steady look. He didn't say it but he thought, *Kid, don't bother trying to whitewash the truth with me.*

Roy must have read the unspoken words in Wade's eyes. He rolled the end of the grass around in his mouth to inform Wade he might or might not choose to tell him more. "Lucy gives me a plate of food every night."

Wade ran his gaze over the scrawny kid. "Looks like you could do with a good feeding."

"Lucy says it's impossible to fill a growing boy."

"How old are you, Roy?"

"Ten. But I can do a man's work. I work over at the livery barn. Mr. Peterson gives me a place to sleep in exchange for cleaning the barn and seeing the horses have feed and water." The words came out in a rush as if Roy needed Wade to understand his value.

"Where's your ma and pa?"

Roy's expression grew indifferent. "Ain't got none."

A rattle at the doorknob pulled their attention to the Dry Creek dining room. Lucy stepped out with a plate piled halfway to the roof. "Hettie said there were lots of leftovers today. You'll get a good feed tonight." She ruffled Roy's hair and beamed at him. "I see you washed up."

Roy had his face buried in the food but spared her a pained look. "'Course I did. What you think I am? A…a…?" He couldn't seem to find a fitting word and tilted his head in Wade's direction instead. "Who's he?"

Lucy jerked back, finally realizing his presence. Her expression grew a whole lot less welcoming. "What are you doing here?"

Wade snatched off his hat. "Ma'am, I just want to talk to you."

"I think you already said all I want to hear."

"What's he want?" Roy spoke around a mouth crammed with food.

"Don't talk with your mouth full. He's nobody. Just another cowboy. I see hundreds of them."

Roy wisely ignored her comment and continued shoveling in food but his eyes darted from Lucy to Wade.

"All I ask is that you allow me to explain the whole

thing." Once she knew how desperate the situation was, she'd surely agree to visit the ranch.

Roy paused from inhaling food. "You got no one to take you to the recitation tonight. He could take you."

At the look Lucy gave Roy, Wade wondered if the boy would have singe marks.

"I don't need an escort."

Roy shrugged. "You said you don't like walking home alone after dark."

"You must have misunderstood me."

Roy stopped chewing. He looked like she'd personally called him a liar. Like her approval of him meant more than the food itself. The boy scraped the last of the food into his mouth and ran his tongue over the plate. Well, maybe not more than food. But he was obviously hurt by Lucy's remark.

Lucy saw it, too. Her expression flicked toward regret. "I'll be fine, Roy. Don't you worry about me."

Wade saw his chances of Lucy agreeing to accompany him slipping away. "This here recitation—it's like a meeting thing?"

"Lucy has a poem to say." Roy sounded as proud as a papa.

"It's the literary society." Lucy's tone made it plain that a cowboy wouldn't enjoy such.

"I like recitations." A lifetime ago he'd hovered behind a half-closed door and listened to recitations and music playing in the drawing room of the house where his ma worked. "I'd like to go if it's open to cowboys."

She didn't miss his mocking tone and looked slightly regretful.

"Go with him," Roy urged. "Ain't you the one to always say a person shouldn't be afraid to take a chance now and then?"

Lucy closed her eyes and sighed deeply. "Roy, do you write down everything I say and commit it to memory to quote at the most awkward moments?"

Roy got that hurt look again but Lucy smiled at him and squeezed his shoulder.

"You'll go?"

"Of course I'll go. I'm going to recite."

Roy shook his head. "I mean with him."

Lucy studied Roy a long moment. "I don't see why it's so important to you."

"I want you to be safe."

Lucy ruffled his hair. "For you, I'll do it." She faced Wade, an expression of pure stubbornness on her face. "On one condition." She waited for him to accept.

"Can't hardly agree to something when I don't know what it is."

"You promise not to talk about my father."

He swallowed, weighing his options. His primary reason for wanting to go to the event had been to explain why Lucy must visit her father. But a pack of other reasons overtook that one. It had been a lifetime or two since he'd heard poetry. He imagined Lucy speaking with the laughter in her voice that she seemed to reserve for everyone but him. But poetry and a musical voice mattered not. He had to convince Lucy to visit her father. Perhaps if he bided his time, she would get curious and ask after Scout.

"Deal." Yes, he'd promised not to talk about her father. He hadn't, however, promised not to talk about himself.

Chapter Two

Wade couldn't help but stare at Lucy. When he'd first seen her, serving in the dining room, she'd worn a black skirt, a white top and a crisp white apron with frills along the edges. Her hair had been up in a tight bun although bits of it had come loose. She now wore a dark pink dress with a wide pink ribbon around her tiny waist. A few more strands of hair had also fallen loose from her bun. She looked very pretty. Like some kind of candy.

Wade glanced down at his trousers, suddenly aware he might not be fit to attend a literary society function. But having gained Lucy's agreement to let him accompany her, he wasn't about to let his lack of Sunday-go-to-meeting clothes hinder him.

She tilted her head in the direction they were to go.

He whistled for Two Bit to follow, nodded goodbye to Roy and fell in at Lucy's side.

She waited until they turned from the alley into the street before she spoke. "I'm only doing this for Roy."

Her words were so unnecessary he couldn't help but

laugh. "And all this time I thought it was my irresistible charm. You sure do know how to cut a man down to size."

She looked vaguely troubled by his comment. "I got no need of a man."

"I ain't offering to marry you."

"That's not what I meant. I meant I don't need a man to escort me to the recitation."

"I still ain't offering." He had been alone for a long time. Preferred it that way.

They reached the schoolroom that apparently served as home to the literary society and crowded inside with the others. All the windows had been shoved up and the doors at both ends propped open to let in air. Still, the place was like an oven ready for baking bread. Lucy led him to a desk near the front and they crowded in side by side. It was a tight squeeze. He noted how nicely she fit at his side, her head inches above his shoulder so every time he turned her way he could study how straight and fine her nose was. He could admire the color of her hair again and see how it shone in the slanting light from the open door. He squeezed his hands together to keep from touching her hair, aching to know if it felt as silky as it looked. He realized he still wore his hat and snatched it off to scrunch it to his lap.

Again he marveled that a body as pretty and as sweet-smelling as Lucy's—like a field of clover in full bloom—could house a heart of coal. He tightened his mouth. He'd endure her pressed to his side, tolerate how nice she smelled and ignore the way her hair begged to be touched all for the sake of finding a chance to persuade her to show some human decency and visit her father.

Thankfully, it was soon time for the program to begin and he could concentrate on the proceedings.

A man with a handlebar moustache stood and welcomed everyone. And then the recitations began. Wade laughed at the story of a man searching for his horse and running into all sorts of calamities. His amusement grew by leaps and bounds as he met Lucy's laughing eyes. He forced his attention back to the front of the room as a frail lady recited two Psalms. A young girl did a sweet poem of hope and love. Then Lucy rose. She fairly glowed as she began to speak, putting her heart into every word.

Wade had heard the poem before and knew what to expect, but enjoyed it just as much as the others who alternated between laughter and tears.

Lucy returned to her place at his side amidst clapping, cheering and shouts of "Bully for you, Lucy gal." Twin roses bloomed on her cheeks. She gave Wade a look he could only interpret as triumphant.

For a moment, he couldn't take his eyes off her then he forced himself to remember why he was here and what she was like beneath all that charm and good humor.

Three more recitations and the program ended. Wade bolted to his feet, his chest tight with a nameless anxiety. He had to get Lucy alone so he could talk to her, explain why it was so necessary to make the trek to the ranch.

But before his muddled brain could devise a plan, a black-clad woman called for their attention. "Tea and cake will be served outside. Ten cents each. Remember the money all goes to buying a bell for our church."

"Let's go." Lucy grabbed his arm. "I want to get a piece of Mrs. Adam's chocolate cake."

Seemed everyone had the same idea. A stampede tried to squeeze out the door, pushing Lucy tight to Wade's side. He discovered she not only fit like they were meant for each other, but that it was going to be nearly impossible to keep his thoughts on the purpose of his visit. He grunted as someone elbowed him. "Trouble with being at the front is you're the tail going out," he murmured.

Lucy groaned. "I know all that chocolate cake will be gone."

A young man in a suit and tie, with a complexion the color of biscuit dough, allowed himself to be jostled against Lucy. Wade felt her stiffen, knew she didn't appreciate the boldness of this dandified man. Wade edged forward just enough to push the man away. And then they were through the door, in the open where a person could breathe without inhaling someone else's air. He grabbed Lucy's elbow and hustled her to the table. 'Course he didn't have to do much hustling. He was hard-pressed to keep up to her as she made the hundred-yard dash to the table covered with a selection of cakes. He dropped twenty cents into the plate and got two cups of tea in exchange.

"Look, there's a piece left." She dived for it and emerged crowing with triumph. A thought seemed to choke her pleasure. She glanced from the cake to Wade. Doubt clouded her face. "I could..."

She was considering giving up her cake after wrestling it from the kid behind her who now glared daggers at her. "You'd never forgive me." He did not need her to hold a grudge over some cake. And to prove his point, he scooped up a large piece of spice cake with brown sugar icing, followed her away from the table to one of the benches and sat down.

Lucy ate the cake like it was a matter of life and death. She licked her fingers. Barely resisted licking the plate. He was so fascinated with her enthusiasm he forgot to test his own piece of cake.

She must have seen the wonder in his expression. "You have no idea how delicious it is."

"Was."

She eyed her plate.

"You ate the whole thing."

"I offered it to you."

"Yup." He took a bite of his own selection. "This ain't half bad either."

"Like comparing beans and peaches. Both good but—" She shrugged, letting him know he got the beans but she wasn't a bit regretful.

He mused about how best to bring up the topic of the ranch without mentioning her father. "I heard that poem before. My ma used to work in a house where they had literary gatherings. She loved that poem. Guess that's why I like it."

"You mean the poem I recited?" She grinned. "Or the one about chasing the horse?"

Far as he was concerned, only one poem stood out as being worthy of mention. "Yours. It made me miss her."

"Where is she?"

"Died some years ago."

"I'm sorry. My ma is dead, too."

Another thing Scout neglected to tell him. "I guess you never stop missing your ma." Though he'd started missing his ma long before she died. Once she started working for the Collins family after Pa's untimely death, she'd never had time for him.

Lucy nodded. "I don't expect I'll ever forget my ma or the lessons I learned from her."

He wanted to talk to her, ask her about her mother, tell her about the ranch but a continual string of people came by to say howdy-do to Lucy. She laughed and joked with them all. She had an easy way about her, as if life fit her well.

Someone came by and picked up the empty cups and plates.

Lucy sprang to her feet. "I could of done that. I'll help with the dishes."

The lady, the same black-garbed woman who had announced the refreshments, tittered and batted her eyes at Wade. "No, no, dear. You enjoy your beau."

"My beau?" Lucy sputtered so hard Wade whacked her between the shoulder blades. True, he did so a little harder than necessary but the way she had said beau, as if he had as much appeal as a seven-day rash, kind of rubbed him the wrong way. He *could* be her beau if he wanted.

She stopped sputtering and shifted away from his patting, giving him a look fit to fry his brain.

"Wouldn't want you to choke to death," he said.

"I was in more danger of having a rib broke than choking." She moved with the determination of a filly eager for freedom. "I'm leaving now."

She didn't need to go away in a huff. He hadn't patted her *that* hard. He glanced around and realized the yard was emptying out. Lucy was already headed for the gate. Did she think to leave him standing in the middle of a vacant pen? He charged after her. "I'll see you home."

"I know the way. Probably better than you."

"I might be nothing but a rough, tough cowboy, but I'm gentleman enough to see a lady home."

"Perhaps you ought to go find yourself a lady, then."

He laughed. "You'll do."

She stopped so sharp he ploughed into her, staggered to keep his balance and steady her, too.

She spun about.

He winced back at the fiery light in her eyes. Had he said something offensive?

"I'll do? I'll do?" Her voice rose with every word.

"You don't think so?" How could she object to that? He'd meant it as admiration.

She clamped her lips together and continued down the street. Wade lifted his hands in confusion. Give him cows or horses any day over womenfolk. Who could understand them?

She stopped in front of the Dry Creek dining room. "This is where we part ways."

"You're going back to work?"

"No. I'm going to bed."

"In the dining room?"

She rolled her eyes. "I have a room in the back." She squinted at him as if suspecting shenanigans from him. "Right next to the room where Harry and Hettie sleep."

He grinned. "I had no plan to search out your sleeping quarters."

Her cheeks reddened. "I didn't suggest you did."

He kind of liked seeing her flustered. He shepherded his thoughts back to the reason he had looked her up. "I only want one thing from you."

She opened the door and stepped inside. "Good night." The door closed.

He raised his voice. "Don't you want to know why it's so important?"

Her muffled voice came through the wood. "There aren't enough words in the world to make me change my mind."

He stared at the closed door for some time before he whistled for the patient Two Bit and rode to his camp. A man with an ounce of sense would admit defeat and ride away, but he had made himself a promise to pay back Scout's kindness by bringing his daughter to visit. He wasn't about to give up. Lucy needed some persuading was all. And he was a patient man. He just hoped he wouldn't have to be too patient. He'd like to get back in time to see Scout before his friend departed this life.

He wondered how Scout was doing. Wade had arranged for an old cowboy friend to stay with Scout when he'd left to find Lucy. But Wade didn't figure Scout had many days left in him. He needed to hurry along Lucy's change of mind. He again prayed—a still unfamiliar activity. *God, help me accomplish the task I've chosen.*

Lucy shut her bedroom door and began to prepare for bed.

She didn't want to know anything more about her

father. She'd spent too many pointless years waiting and hoping for him to do more than flit in and out of her life. She'd seen far too clearly how her mother had pined after a man who had made promises he never kept. After her mother died, still hoping for her father to make good on his promises, Lucy had sworn never to need or want anything more from her father. Nothing Wade could say or do would change that.

She sat cross-legged on her bed and opened her Bible. It had been her mother's. In the front were the family history pages. Lucy stared at them. Her name and birth date entered by her mother. Her mother's death in Lucy's handwriting. The births and dates of death of her mother's parents and her mother's brother who had died when he was only three months old. She turned to the conspicuously empty page for registering marriages. No marriage between her parents had ever been entered because her father failed to marry her mother and make an honest woman out of her, despite his many promises to do so.

Lucy sighed. It was old news. She no longer cared. Turning the pages carefully, she paused at the bookmark and read a chapter before gently replacing the Bible in its place of honor on her bedside table. She said her prayers as she'd done from her earliest remembrance. She knew—because her mother told her often—there had been a time when their lives didn't include churchgoing, Bible reading and prayer. A time when her mother had been a rebel and a runaway. But she thankfully did not recall that period. Her father was part of her mother's BC time—Before Christ—and Lucy did not want any share of it.

She lay staring at the narrow window high in the wall opposite her bed. Often she wished she could see outside without standing on her tiptoes, but Harry and Hettie were more than generous to provide her a room. She had only to think about Roy to realize her life without family might be a whole lot worse.

Thinking of Roy brought her thoughts round to Wade. No doubt after her rude dismissal he'd ridden out for wherever it was he headed. Made no difference to her. He was like a hundred other cowboys she saw.

Only—she regretfully admitted—no other cowboy had insisted on accompanying her to a recitation, nor admitted bold-faced how he missed his ma and her favorite poem.

She would doubtless never see him again and that, she told herself, was a good thing.

The next day was Sunday and Lucy headed out to church. Hettie and Harry had never asked her to work on Sunday. They had another gal come in to handle the Sunday crowd.

As she sat enjoying the organ music before the service began, someone slipped into the pew beside her. Wade!

She couldn't tell him to move along—not in church. Not that she didn't want to. But she feared she would incur the wrath of God if she acted on her unkind thoughts, so she gave him a smile that went no further than the corners of her mouth. Indeed, her lips said, "Good morning." But her eyes said something entirely different.

"Nice to see you at church," he whispered.

"You thought me a heathen, did you?"

He quirked an eyebrow. "Now why would you think such a thing?"

Why, indeed? But her conscience smote her. She'd been rude and dismissive. And him being a stranger in town. Hadn't the Lord commanded them to be careful to entertain strangers? A grin filled her mouth as she thought of the rest of the verse—entertaining angels unawares. She had her doubts about Wade being any sort of an angel.

"Care to share the cause of your amusement?" he whispered as the pews filled up around them.

She couldn't restrain herself and told him about the verse. She then added, "It doesn't say what those who aren't angels turn out to be."

He managed to look sad even though his eyes shone with amusement. "I would not expect anyone to consider me an angel. But I guess that means you're obligated to entertain me this afternoon."

Obligated?

Her mind said no—she wanted nothing to do with a cowboy who knew her father and expected she would be glad to pay him a visit.

Her heart said otherwise. Obligation, cowboy, father—none of it mattered. The idea of an afternoon in this man's company sounded fine.

Her mouth said, "I guess I'm obligated."

He grinned. "I guess I am, too. No cowboy in his right mind would turn down such a generous invitation."

Knowing he realized as much as she that it had not been one bit generous, they both laughed. Seems he didn't mind the obligation any more than she, which was somehow all wrong. This man had made his intention perfectly clear—he only cared about spending time with her in order to persuade her to visit her father.

Just as she'd made it clear as a spring morning she wouldn't be persuaded. So, what harm was there in spending a sunny afternoon with him? It wasn't as if she was about to let this man, or any man, share anything but fragments of time. She had no need nor desire to give a man the right to twist her life into disarray as her father had done to her mother.

And herself.

She managed to postpone how she would deal with the afternoon until the service was over and she turned to see Wade grinning at her, his eyes dancing with amusement. She got the feeling he knew she'd boxed herself into a tight corner and he was enjoying her discomfort far too much for her liking.

She lifted her head. This was nothing she couldn't handle. "Let's get some lunch from the dining room." Hettie would willingly give them a portable lunch. Lucy thought she'd take him to the park where the young people tended to congregate on Sunday afternoons. Safety in numbers.

When they arrived at the dining room and she told Hettie what she wanted, the woman practically crowed. "Off to courting corner, are you?"

Lucy gave her a look of devout distaste, grateful Wade had waited outside, out of hearing distance. "I'm not interested in courting, only in having lots of people around so I don't have to personally amuse him."

Hettie chortled. "I suppose that's why all the other young people go there, too?"

"I wouldn't know."

"Now, don't get all prickly with me, Lucy gal. I recall a time or two you've been there with some anxious young man."

"I don't need a man."

"So you say. You'll change your mind soon enough when the right one comes along." She handed Lucy a basket full of food. "Now, off you go. Have fun. Who knows? This might be the right one."

Lucy thanked Hettie and waited until she was almost out the door to add, "Not in a million years." She'd never trust her happiness and future to any man.

Thanks to Hettie's comments, she felt conspicuous as she led Wade to the park where she was certain everyone she met had the same sly look in their eyes, and similar thoughts in their heads.

At least Wade had no idea how people viewed a harmless little jaunt to the park.

She saw a spot under a sprawling group of trees where several others she knew gathered. Mr. and Mrs. Nolan sat by themselves on a nearby bench. With three daughters of courting age, they usually spent the afternoon at the park, providing proper supervision.

"Over there." Lucy pointed toward the group.

"They your friends?" Wade looked toward a more secluded spot where an umbrella of branches provided an alarming amount of privacy. "It's quieter over there."

"They'll be glad to let us join them." She didn't give him a chance to say yea or nay. She had no intention of being shepherded to a place where they would be alone, knowing he would likely consider it an opportunity to tell her how she ought to visit her father. She led him to her choice of location and introduced him to the group—most of whom had been at church earlier. After a round of greetings, she found a roomy spot and allowed Wade to spread the blanket Hettie had put in the basket.

The afternoon heat made everyone mellow. Lucy was glad no one prodded her with questions about Wade. She didn't want to talk about him. She didn't want to explain who he was, what he was doing here.

Hettie had packed fried chicken and fresh buns for Lucy, which they'd both enjoyed. Lucy took out a plate of cookies and offered it to Wade.

He took one. "I see there are certain advantages to working in a dining room." He slanted an amused look toward the next couple who'd had only syrup sandwiches.

"I don't think they noticed." It was the youngest Nolan girl and a farm boy.

"If they did, they didn't seem to care." Wade leaned close. "I think they're more interested in their sparking."

His breath warmed her cheeks, filling her with a curious sense of longing.

She pushed away the idea. Only thing she longed for was her self-sufficiency. Life was meant to be lived, enjoyed, embraced, not spent clasping hopeless dreams based on empty promises from a man.

She would not be like her mother.

Wade still leaned close, his gaze warm as sun flashing on a quiet lake, his expression curiously watchful, as if wanting something from her.

She shifted away, turned to gather the remnants of their lunch into the basket. She knew what he wanted—for her to visit her father. But she wouldn't do it. She'd already given her father too many chances, wasted too many hopes and dreams on him.

Lawrence, a young man who seemed to escort a different gal to the park every week, picked up his guitar and began to pluck out a tune. He had a liking for popular ballads, which made him a hit with both sexes. He began to sing "Oh! Susanna." Soon, more young people crowded around, joining their voices to his as he went from one popular tune to another.

Lucy loved the songs and joined right in. She didn't have to look directly at Wade to see he wasn't singing. At first she thought he didn't know the newer songs, but even when they sang some old hymns he didn't join. She tried to remember if he'd sung at church, but she'd been too busy mentally kicking herself for agreeing to spend the afternoon with him to pay attention.

She focused on the next song, and tried not to think of Wade sitting there quietly. He shifted, stretched out his legs, and leaned back on his right elbow. Was he bored? Restless? Through some perverse idea that God wanted her to entertain this stranger, she'd volunteered her afternoon. If Wade chose to be not entertained by the music, that wasn't her problem. She'd done all that could be expected of her.

He sat up straight and pulled his knees to his chin. She didn't miss how he shuffled about so he could stare at her.

"An angel wouldn't stare," she whispered.

"You've known a few, have you?"

"No. But I know they wouldn't."

"Well, see, I'm not so sure. I think they watch us all the time."

She rolled her eyes to signify how silly she considered this conversation.

"Let's go for a walk." He bounced to his feet and held out a hand before she could refuse. She automatically let him pull her to her feet but withdrew from his grasp before they had gone two steps.

They headed past Mr. and Mrs. Nolan. Mrs. Nolan was writing a letter. Mr. Nolan was lying in the shade, his hat pulled over his eyes.

Lucy waited until they were far enough away from the music to be able to converse easily before she spoke. "I noticed you didn't sing."

"If you heard me you'd know for sure I was no angel." His tone carried a hint of self-mockery. "Cowboys normally sing to the cattle at night to calm them. I tried it once. The cows all signed a petition requesting I stop."

She laughed at the idea of cows signing a piece of paper. "Did they read it for you, too?"

"Read it myself but the head cow stepped on my foot to emphasize the point." He paused to rub at the toe of his boot as if his foot still hurt.

She laughed harder at his silliness. "It can't be that bad."

"Oh, yes it can."

Now she wanted nothing more than to hear and judge for herself. "Show me."

He held up his hands as if warning her. "I don't want the afternoon to end on a sour note. Or a flat one."

"You think I'd run home if I heard you sing?"

"I know you would, with your ears covered, begging me to stop."

He kept a deadpan expression so she couldn't know for sure how serious he was but she couldn't believe he meant all he said.

She held a hand up as if swearing honesty before a court of law. "I vow I would not run away if you sang."

Their gazes locked and for one still moment, nothing existed apart from the two of them and the promise of something exciting between them.

"Would you run for some other reason?" His words were low and soft, teasing.

She tried to find an answer to his question. "I can't say." At that moment, she could think of nothing that would send her running. Not when her heart had developed a sudden ache to know more about him.

He took her hand.

She let him.

They reached the edge of the park but didn't turn around. Instead, they crossed the street, walked the half block to the edge of town and continued along the dusty road bordered by yellowed grass swaying in the breeze.

"This country is as flat as pie dough rolled out," he said.

"Great for farming, they say. Best number one hard wheat grown right here. Much of it on bonanza farms. Can you imagine one farm with thousands of acres under crop? I'd like to see that some day." Why was she running over at the mouth about farming? Only thing she knew about it was what she overheard at the dining room where some of the big landowners met with bankers and investors to discuss things.

Wade made a dismissive noise. "Farming is okay. But for real pretty scenery you should see ranching country. When I see the hills and trees and vast stretches of grass, I just want to put down roots like a big old cottonwood tree and never leave."

Lucy turned to stare at him. "I never knew a cowboy who wanted to settle down."

Wade gave an embarrassed grin and shrugged. "Never thought about it like that but now you mention it, the idea sounds kind of nice. But the ranch I mean belongs to your father."

She pulled her hand from his grasp.

"Lucy, he's sick. Near death. All you have to do is visit him. How hard can that be?"

She backed away with every word he uttered. Her eyes felt overheated, the air too heavy to breathe. "I will never visit him."

"Why not?"

"Because when my mother died I decided I would no longer allow him any part of my life. He hurt her time and again with empty promises. I won't let him do the same thing to me."

"Just a little visit."

"Never."

Wade's jaw muscles flexed. "He's very sick."

"I'm sorry." She headed back to town like she was trying to outrun a thunderstorm.

He easily caught up to her. "I'll not leave until you change your mind."

"It will never happen." She mentally kicked herself all the way back to the dining room and slipped into her room. How many times had she vowed not to let her heart yearn for any man—not her father, and certainly not a run-of-the-mill cowboy? She wouldn't let herself care if the King of Spain showed up to court her. No. Her heart belonged to no one. Ever. She'd witnessed the incredible pain and suffering in her mother's life and would have no part of it.

Yet she'd let her conscience, her duty, the warm sun and a pair of bright blue eyes momentarily make her forget.

Well, not again. Besides, Wade was only spending time with her in hopes of talking her into visiting her father. Wade said he was sick, dying even. But he'd been dead to her for years so what did it matter? Any little pang of remorse she felt was only for what she had once wanted.

And never had.

Chapter Three

Wade alternately stared at the ashes of his campfire and the dusty toes of his boots. Three days. Three long days he'd hung about trying to convince Lucy to do her duty as a daughter and a decent human being and visit her father before he died.

Wade had haunted the dining room waiting for opportunities to talk to Lucy until Harry had stomped out with a spoon the size of a bucket hanging from his ham-hock fists and ordered him to leave Lucy alone.

Wade had no desire to come to blows with the larger man or any of his primitive kitchen utensils, so he'd waited for an opportunity to speak to Lucy away from the eagle eyes of Harry.

He'd found such opportunity when he watched her and Roy settle on a rough plank bench in the shade of the livery stable. He followed at a distance, undetected, and slipped around the barn until he could listen and watch unobserved. It took him a moment to realize Lucy and Roy were bent over a book, their heads almost touching as Lucy taught the boy to read.

Huh. Wade sank back on his heels. Why would she spend that much time with Roy yet refuse to visit Scout—her own flesh and blood?

He moseyed around the corner and confronted the pair.

Roy glowered at him. "She don't want to see you. Thought she made that plain."

Wade wanted to laugh at the boy's belligerence. He posed no threat, carried no oversize kitchen spoon but he was every bit as protective of Lucy as Harry was. Having no desire to mock the boy's spirit, Wade kept his face expressionless. "I think she owes me a chance to explain."

Roy jumped to his feet, fists curled at his side and donned a scowl fit to curdle Wade's supper.

Lucy rose to Roy's side and dropped an arm across the boy's shoulders. "Let it be, Roy. I can defend myself." The way she stuck out her chin and gave Wade a look fit to set his hair on fire made him squirm.

"No need to get all prickly around me. I mean no harm."

"Just going to make a nuisance of yourself because you won't take no for an answer."

He thought some on that. Finally, he let out a long-suffering sigh. "I guess there's no point in hanging around any longer. 'Sides, I'd like to see Scout before he passes. You'll find me camped in that piddly patch of trees on the other side of town if you change your mind or decide you want to hear why I think the man deserves a visit from you." He purposely waited, hoping she'd be curious to know why he owed the man this, but she just stared.

"Fine." He spun around and marched away without a backward look, without saying all the hot words that pushed at the top of his head. The woman was a lost cause. Too bad for Scout, but perhaps it was best the man yearn after a girl he remembered as sweet and loving rather than face the truth about her coldheartedness.

He'd ride out first light. Or maybe he'd endure a train ride as he'd planned to do when he figured to have Lucy with him. He wanted to make it back in time to bid Scout farewell.

Though he hated to face the man and admit he'd failed to get Lucy to accompany him.

Even though he'd prayed. Guess a man couldn't expect God to jump to do his bidding. Being rescued by prayer once was more than most ever experienced and he would never forget the occasion, nor how it had made his faith in God grow like desert flowers after rain.

It was an experience that meant a lot to him. He might have shared the details with Lucy in the hopes it would convince her to visit Scout.

God, I know I ain't got the right to ask for more than what You've already given, but if You could do something to prod Lucy to consider allowing Scout to see her once more before he dies...

He returned to his campsite and settled back against one of the puny trees. He'd wait until morning to leave. Give Lucy a chance to reconsider. Give God a chance to do something to persuade her.

Dusk turned the street gray and darkened the shadows along the buildings to indigo. Grasshoppers and crickets sought to outdo each other in their creaky nightly chorus. Birds settled in for the night, calling to each other one last time.

Lucy and Roy leaned against the livery stable wall. The worn wood hoarded the heat of the day and baked their backs, but they were too content to move. She'd been reluctant to return to her solitary room after the way Wade had stalked off, anger evident in every step. Her heart clenched. Seems Wade had found friendship, perhaps belonging, maybe even a home with her father—something she had wanted most of her life. But her wanting had brought her nothing but disappointment and pain. She would not let Wade's insistence and pleading trick her into walking headlong into a repeat of those emotions.

She should return to her room. If Harry and Hettie knew she was out alone after dark they would both scold her. But she wasn't exactly alone. Roy had no place to go but the corner of the loft where he slept, so he willingly kept her company.

They had no need to talk but sat in companionable silence listening to the night and bits of conversation floating on the still air.

A harsher, louder sound caused them both to jolt upright.

"It's just the door into the barn," Lucy said.

Angry voices rose and fell. She made out a few words. "Cheat." "Pay back."

Curious as to what it was about, Lucy looked around, saw a tiny circle of yellow light and pressed her eye to the hole in the wall. Roy found another spot. From her spy hole Lucy got a clear view of Smitty. She resisted the urge to spit. Smitty was a scoundrel and the town could well do without him. He bullied and threatened his way around, acting like he owned the town and its inhabitants. He spent time in jail on a semiregular basis for minor offenses. Too bad someone couldn't prove one of the many bigger things they suspected him of.

Another man faced Smitty, someone Lucy had seen only a time or two. She'd noticed the man had eyes that seemed to see everything, yet reveal nothing. But he sure looked scared right now. He held his hands out toward Smitty.

"I got no gun."

That's when Lucy saw that Smitty held a pistol aimed straight at the other man's heart.

Her breath stalled halfway to her lungs and she clawed for Roy's hand but found nothing but raw, slivered boards. She should leave. Run as far and fast as she could but she seemed tacked to the wall watching the two men, their forms wavering uncertainly in the flickering lamplight.

Smitty's teeth gleamed in a sneer. "Dead men tell no tales." Light flared from the end of his pistol and the noise of a gunshot rattled against the walls.

The second man clutched at his chest. He stared at his blood-covered hands, then gave Smitty a look of surprise before he pitched to the ground.

"Is he dead?" Roy whispered.

Smitty, who had leaned over to put a second gun in the fallen man's hand, glanced toward them.

"Shh." Lucy didn't dare move for fear of giving away their presence.

Smitty stepped back, turned to a third man that Lucy hadn't seen until this point. She recognized him, too. Smitty's half-brained sidekick, Louie. The man wore a perpetual smile that revealed a whole lot more mean-ness than humor.

Smitty spoke to the man and nodded toward Lucy and Roy's position. Louie jerked his head in compli-ance and strode for the door.

Lucy's blood burned through her body. "They know we're here." She turned, grabbed Roy's hand in a death grip, held her skirts with her other hand and ran like her life depended on it, which she was quite sure it did. They didn't stop until they crossed behind the black-smith shop where they pressed to the wall. Lucy held her breath hoping they hadn't been spotted. She hoped they were invisible. She prayed the men might think they'd been mistaken in thinking someone had seen them.

"Who's there?" Louie called.

Lucy clutched at Roy's hand knowing he was as scared as she.

"Maybe I seen a kid and maybe someone else. Thought it was a woman."

Lucy's heart rattled against her ribs. *Please, God, let them think they made a mistake.*

"It's that kid who sleeps here," Smitty grumbled. "And I know who the girl is. Only one person spends any time with the kid. Never mind them now. We know where to find them. We'll get you later," he called.

Lucy knew he meant the words for them just as surely as she knew he wouldn't hesitate to do to them the same thing he'd done to that man in the barn.

Other voices called. She recognized the sheriff's voice asking what happened.

She leaned over her knees and tried to catch her breath.

"What we gonna do?"

"Let me think." They had a few minutes while the sheriff investigated, but she knew Smitty had set it up to look like self-defense when it was clear and simple murder. Only Roy and Lucy knew the truth. And Louie, who would never tell. He'd probably been cheering in the background when Smitty shot the unarmed man.

Her heart rate spiked again. Smitty wouldn't hesitate to get rid of anyone who could testify against him.

How long would it take for everyone to accept Smitty's version of what transpired? How long did it give her to come up with a plan of escape?

"Come on." She practically dragged Roy toward the dining room. They couldn't stay there. It would be the first place Smitty would look. All he had to do was wait for her to…

Her heart climbed up her throat and clawed at the back of her mouth.

"Hurry. We have to find someplace to hide." She burst into her room and grabbed up her Bible, which held her meager life savings in an envelope. She grabbed a battered valise Hettie had given her and randomly threw some articles of clothing on top of her Bible having no idea where she would go. She only knew that it wasn't safe here.

She headed for the door, paused. She didn't want Hettie and Harry to worry so she scribbled a note and left it on her pillow. "Went to visit my father. Will contact you later."

It was an excuse they would believe.

"What are we gonna do?" Roy's voice thinned with fear.

She grabbed his hand. "Follow me." She had no plan except escape.

They slipped out of her room and clung to the black shadows as they made their way to the edge of town opposite the livery barn. A commotion indicated the sheriff was still investigating along with every curious citizen who had come running at the sound of a gunshot.

Smitty wouldn't be able to look for them until that was settled.

Roy yanked away. "If we're leaving, I'm taking Queenie." Mr. Peterson had given Roy an old nag of a horse. Roy diligently tethered her where she could nibble grass and faithfully carried water to her.

"Roy, we don't have time."

"We could ride her."

There was something to that. "Where is she?"

He named a place and they head in that direction. "We'll stop and get her."

They just might get away in time.

Two Bit whinnied.

"What is it, boy?" Wade tipped his head and listened. He heard it a minute later—the sound of an approaching rider.

He scooped up his rifle and lounged with deceptive casualness. In his experience only trouble came riding into camp before dawn.

"Wade, are you there?"

His heart skidded sideways and crashed into his ribs. "Lucy, is that you?" What was she doing out before the sky had begun to lighten?

She rode up to him.

He grabbed the bridle of her horse, all the time alert for signs of danger. When he saw none, he relaxed.

"You've decided to come with me?" he teased. She'd made it abundantly clear wild horses and six mad bulls wouldn't drag her to the ranch.

"On one condition."

He wished he could see her better. Assure himself she was teasing because, plain and simple, he didn't believe she meant it.

"Yeah." His voice dripped with sarcasm.

"Wade, I mean it. I'll go with you to see my father if you agree—" She glanced over her shoulder. Roy peeked around her arm. "You agree to take Roy."

Wade wasn't much for fancy talk. Sometimes he had to search for words. It came from spending most of his waking hours with nothing but cows, horses and equally untalkative cowboys. But for the life of him he couldn't find even one word in his surprised brain. Not one word to say to this gal who had changed her mind faster than Dakota weather.

"Wade, we'll go with you. But we have to hurry." Her urgent tone caused his brain to burst into a gallop.

"What's the rush?" He could feel the nervous tension vibrating from the pair. No way was he taking a step anywhere until he knew what was going on.

"I'll tell you everything on the way."

No mistaking the way her voice quivered. He guessed it was fear or nervousness. "What's the hurry?"

"Smitty is after us."

He knew about Smitty. Anyone who had been in town more than a few hours knew of the man. Either by word of mouth or by encounter. Wade had seen him in the store a couple of days ago. Had been forced to witness the man blatantly threaten a farmer over some disputed fence line. From what Wade gathered, the farmer was within his rights but it was plain as dirt on a white shirt that Smitty didn't care about what was right. And certainly didn't intend to let it interfere with his plans.

After the pair left, he asked the store owner why the sheriff didn't do something. The man said, "He'd like to, but so far no one will testify against Smitty."

"He's gonna kill us." Roy's voice shook. All the kid's bravado had vanished.

Roy's fear sent Wade's nerves into full alert. "Why?"

"Smitty killed a man in cold blood. We saw him. Smitty doesn't want any witnesses." Lucy's voice trembled so bad he wanted to scoop her from the horse and hold her tight, assure her he'd keep her safe.

"You going to help or just stare at the horse's nostrils?"

Wade laughed. "Lucy gal, you sure do have a sweet way of asking."

"Phweet. If I'd known you expected sweet talk I'd give it, but right now I think urgency is a little more important."

"Why don't we just to tell the sheriff the truth?"

"You don't know Smitty." Her voice was tight, signaling her fear. "He'll convince everyone the shooting was self-defense. He'll already have half a dozen men as nasty as him watching for us. We wouldn't make it two steps in town before he or one of them would grab us. We wouldn't get anywhere near the sheriff." Her words grew more urgent. "The best thing we can do is go somewhere and hide."

"I expect you're right. Good thing I was ready to go." He settled the saddle on Two Bit, stuck his rifle in the boot and swung up. He paused to have a good look at the other horse in the gray light. "Where did you find that old nag?"

"She's a good old horse." Roy sounded a whole lot more like himself as he defended the bag of bones.

"Emphasis on old," Wade muttered. "Come on, let's make tracks." The "good old horse" would have found Roy a load let alone the pair of them. She probably found her skin almost more'n she could handle. He edged up beside Lucy. "Roy, get on behind me. We'll have to take turns carrying you."

Just a few hours ago Wade had asked God to melt Lucy's stubbornness. Little did he expect things to turn around so suddenly or in such an alarming fashion. He scanned the horizon, saw no sign of pursuit and prayed for God's protection. He briefly considered his options. Seems he had only two—head for the train, or ride west. Riding left them exposed and vulnerable. He could likely outride and outmaneuver any pursuers, but doubted Lucy or Roy were up to the challenge. Certainly not on the old nag they had brought along.

On the other hand, he'd picked a campsite on the far side of town away from the rail station. Didn't make any sense to ride through town.

He made up his mind. They'd head for the railway but not through town.

"Let's ride." He urged Two Bit into an easy lope. They rode from the shelter of the trees and headed west. A few minutes later, he glanced over his shoulder to check Lucy's progress.

She kicked at the old horse's side and slapped at the

animal with the end of the reins. The horse managed what might pass for a jog.

"I can walk faster than that." Someone had not gotten a good bargain on horseflesh.

He waited for the struggling pair to catch up. Lucy looked about ready to chew a handful of nails for breakfast. "Where did you get that old hay burner?"

The look she shot him made him winch. "Mr. Peterson gave her to Roy."

He sputtered with surprise then the humor of it hit him and he roared with laughter. Two Bit perked up his ears and danced sideways. Roy clung to his waist. Wade wiped his eyes and continued laughing despite Lucy's pinched look.

"Did you think we stole her?" she demanded.

Wade managed to choke back his enjoyment of the idea of someone persuading Roy he was doing him a favor though he couldn't stop it from circling his words as he spoke. "Mr. Peterson saved himself the price of a bullet and left Roy with the responsibility of feeding the old thing. Got to admire a man with such business savvy." Even free was too much for this sorry piece of horseflesh. He whooped with laughter.

Lucy fixed him with a hard, unyielding frown.

Wade forced himself to put on a sober face, though inside he continued to chortle. "If we hurry we might make the rail station by nightfall." He reined toward his destination, knowing now he could hope for nothing more than a plodding walk.

The pair of them seemed to think a walking glue factory was a wondrous gift. It amazed him. Delighted him. Filled him with admiration for the kind of spunk his Lucy showed.

His? Was his brain addled from surprise and too much laughter? She wasn't his. Never would be. She had only agreed to accompany him because she needed to get away from Smitty. Would she stay on the ranch any longer than it took to say "Hello, Father. Goodbye, Father.?" Then reality hit him square between his eyes. Lucy couldn't ride away after a hurried goodbye. Not until Smitty had been locked behind bars. The idea of that man posing a threat to Lucy or Roy made his fists coil.

They inched across the flat prairie. Although he took a circuitous route that kept him away from town, he felt as exposed as the sun. His skin itched at how easy it would be for someone to spot them and ride after them. Running from pursuers was impossible. But getting back to Dry Creek and catching the train was equally impossible. By the time they got there, Smitty would have every way in and out of town guarded by one of his cohorts.

He pulled up. "This ain't going to work."

Lucy's shoulders drew back. "Where there's a will, there's a way."

He chuckled at her determination. "You planning to push that nag all the way across Dakota?"

Her eyes sparkled. "Now, how gentlemanly would that be? If someone is to push…" She left the rest unsaid. But he understood her message. If anyone had to do the pushing, she expected it to be him.

He eyed the tired old horse. "I could try riding her. Maybe I could convince her to go a little faster. Otherwise, we'll be spending the winter out in the open plain."

Lucy scowled. "You'd whip her, I suppose?"

Roy dropped to the ground and rushed to the old nag's side. "You can't hit her. She can't help if she's old."

"Don't suppose either of you thought to bring wheels?"

Two pairs of eyes regarded him suspiciously.

"The way I see it…" He pushed his hat back on his head and leaned over the saddle horn as if contemplating one of the universe's darkest mysteries. "Either we plan to inch across the prairie—easy for anybody to see us, easier for them to chase us down—or we put wheels under that thing and I'll drag her."

"'Course we didn't bring any wheels."

He sighed. "I feared that might be your answer. Like I said, this isn't going to work."

They all stared at the horse.

"She happen to have a name?" Somehow, it might be easier to deal with her if she was more than a nameless pile of skin draped over protruding bones.

Roy wrapped his arm around the sorry animal's head. "'Course she has a name. It's Queenie. 'Cause she's like a queen." His tone dared Wade to question the name.

In order to restrain his laughter, Wade drew his lips in tight hoping he looked thoughtful. He slanted a look at Lucy and when he saw her eyes brimming with merriment, he had to bite the inside of his lip.

But their lack of speed was no laughing matter. They had to find some other way of getting across this open land. He studied the landscape trying to come up with a solution. Wheels were not the answer. Unless…he stared southwest. "We'll go that way."

"We aren't going back, are we?"

"Lucy, we're going to find some wheels."

"Who's going to push?"

"The iron horse."

"A train?"

"Yup." He'd planned on catching the new SOO line that was direct to Minot and from there they would ride. But if he dropped down to the Northern Pacific line and the less direct route, it might serve their purpose even better, make it a little harder for any pursuers to know for sure where they were headed. And the line was considerably closer if his reckoning was right.

Lucy brightened faster than the sun that now sat several degrees above the horizon, promising another searing day.

Wade eyed the flat land. Being out on the unprotected prairie didn't seem like the best plan a man could devise. "Come on, Roy. Climb on." He reached out a hand.

"Will we get breakfast when we get there? I'm awfully hungry."

"Roy, you're always hungry." Lucy's tone warned him not to complain.

Wade lifted the boy to the back of his horse. "I'm feeling kind of hollow myself. I'm sure we'll be able to rustle up something." If he was correct they should connect about the same place as the little town of Anders. They'd find food there. Plus water and relief from the unrelenting heat.

Three hours later, the heat shimmered unmercifully

and between them they had downed his entire supply of water.

Wade began to wonder if they'd missed the line entirely and were doomed to wither into nothingness in the baked grass.

Chapter Four

The hat Lucy wore did little to provide adequate shade. The sun was unrelenting, threatening to bake the three of them. She'd watched Roy swallow the last of the water what seemed an hour ago but was likely only a few minutes. Roy had long since stopped complaining about hunger. He no longer mentioned the heat. In fact, he looked about ready to perish. And she felt the same. Did Wade have any idea where they were or was he, as she suspected, only guessing? She kicked Queenie mercilessly until she rode at Wade's side. "How much farther?"

"Can't be far."

"Seems I heard that a time or two already."

"It's closer than last time you asked."

She sighed mightily, too hot to hide her worry. "So is Christmas. I'm wondering which will get here first."

"I 'spect we would have been there by now except we have to move at a snail's pace thanks to Queenie there." Sarcasm edged his words. "A mistake if I ever saw one."

"Would you suggest we should have hung around making detailed plans until Smitty found us?"

"'Course not. But next time steal a fast horse."

Roy tipped sideways and Wade caught him. "Hang on, Roy, we're almost there."

"We're already *there*." Lucy's lips pursed as she spoke. "Which is where? Lost in the middle of no-where. Going round in circles waiting for the buzzards to find us."

"We ain't lost. We ain't going in circles."

"I suppose you mean that to be comforting? It's not."

"Look yonder." He pointed.

She squinted into the distance. "Nothing but more heat waves and endless grass."

"Right down on the horizon. See. A water tower. It's our destination."

She finally located it. Her whole insides kicked with new hope. She checked over her shoulder and allowed herself to relax when she saw no dust trailing in their direction. "Roy, hear that? We're almost there. Thank God."

Roy stirred himself. "I'm thirsty."

Wade patted Roy's leg. "There'll be water there. And food."

Now that her inner knot of concern had relaxed, Lu-cy's conscience smote her. Wade had led them to safety. And she'd been snippy about how long it took when really she had only one party to blame—Queenie, the slowest moving horse this side of eternity. "Wade, I'm sorry for being impatient."

He slowed so they rode side by side and gave her a

look of wide-eyed surprise. "Why Lucy, I hardly noticed."

Her heart kicked up its pace at his teasing.

"Besides, I intend to get you safely to the ranch."

His words effectively reminded her he had only one reason to care about her safety—his own feelings for a man she didn't want to see. His concern wasn't personal at all, much as her fickle brain hoped for just a fraction of a second it was. Which was stupid. She'd long ago learned not to pin her hopes and heart on expecting anything from a man.

And now she had to face the reality of seeing the one person she'd vowed to never speak to again—her father. She looked at Roy, now alert and peering toward the approaching town. She hadn't been able to see an alternative in the predawn hours. After a moment's thought she could still find none.

Somehow she'd survive the visit and return to her familiar world and her own plans. She only hoped it would be with her emotions unscathed. But as she allowed herself a fleeting glance at Wade who continued to study the horizon with a mixture of relief and concern, Lucy knew walking away with her heart intact may well be impossible. Not only would her father shred it yet again, she feared Wade would, as well.

It took them another hour to reach the town. They went directly to the low building that served as the train station and learned the next train would arrive in half an hour. That gave them enough time to hustle up some food and drink.

Half an hour later, their thirst quenched and hunger

demands met, she and Roy stepped into the puffing, smoke-belching train.

Lucy heaved a sigh of relief as she sank down on a stiff green leather seat. Roy guarded the sack of sandwiches wrapped in brown paper Wade had ordered for the trip. He didn't intend to let anything happen to their food supply. She glanced out the window and allowed a bit of tension to ease from her muscles. So far there'd been no sign of Smitty. He didn't appear to have followed them on horseback or he would have overtaken them.

Not that she was foolish enough to expect he'd forget she and Roy were witnesses to his murderous act.

Wade had been seeing to the horses and now joined them.

She spread her dusty skirts and hugged the middle of the bench. As if reading her reluctance and finding it amusing, Wade grinned, pushed aside her skirts and planted himself beside her. She shifted over and pressed against the window trying to convince herself she had no reason to be annoyed at him. After all, he had readily agreed to protect them. Of course, she knew it was only because he had gotten what he came for.

No, the reason she was annoyed was because she'd agreed to go with him after days of vowing nothing would drag her out to the beautiful ranch. But she had only his word that it wasn't a spit-dry piece of land with nothing to break the monotony of the endless prairie.

She had only hours before she came face-to-face with her father.

As if sensing her regret at being in the very position

she'd vowed to avoid, Wade leaned close. "Relax, Lucy. Enjoy the journey."

Annoyed because he'd read her thoughts, she jerked back and faced him. "It's a little difficult knowing what's at the end."

He considered her for a moment then a slow smile filled his eyes with sunshine. "Lucy, you might be surprised at what you find."

She wanted to argue but he stared out the window, a dreamy look on his face and spoke before she could gather her thoughts.

"It's a real pretty place and there's lots of room to roam. No need to spend time in anyone's company unless you chose to. There's one place— You ride up this slope that seems like nothing more than a ripple in the prairie. But when you reach the top you realize you've climbed a small mountain. You can see for miles and miles. They say the Indians used it as a place to spot game and enemies." He sucked in air like a man deprived of it for most of a day. "You can't help but be impressed. When we get there I'll show you."

She wondered what it would be like to have such a view. And something inside her reached for the experience.

Then he met her watchful, wondering gaze and gave a self-deprecating chuckle. "I do go on, don't I?"

She nodded. "You sound like a man in love."

He lowered his gaze. "Guess you could say I am." Slowly he faced her again. "I thank you for agreeing to come."

"It's only to get away from Smitty. I still don't want to see my father."

He nodded, his expression regretful and then glanced across to the facing seat. "Roy boy has fallen asleep."

They smiled at the boy who was curled up, his dark lashes resting on his cheeks, his fists still tightly clutching the bag of sandwiches.

All morning, under the hot sun, Wade had kept his thoughts centered on getting them to safety. He hadn't allowed himself to think past the immediate need to reach the rail line.

Now he couldn't keep his fears and anger at bay as he pictured Smitty trying to chase down Lucy and Roy. Hoping to disguise his concern, he stretched his legs under the seat where Roy slept and crossed his arms as if nothing mattered more than enjoying the trip.

"When did you see this—?" He left the question unfinished having no desire to scratch any itchy ears of the nearby passengers. "Where did you spend the night?"

"It was already dark when…it happened."

What was she doing out after dark? A woman with a speck of sense would be home safe and sound at that time. But he refrained from saying so, knowing Lucy would get all prickly and defensive and likely not tell him the things he wanted to know.

"I knew Smitty would look for us at the dining room. So we couldn't stay there." Despite the heat, she shivered.

It was all he could do to keep his arms crossed instead of reaching for her and pulling her against his chest. She didn't deserve to be involved in Smitty's messy schemes. Nor did Roy.

"Roy wouldn't leave Queenie behind." She chuckled. "I know she's no prize—"

"You could say that again with all honesty."

"But it's about the only thing Roy has ever owned. It makes him feel special to have a horse."

Wade understood that. Roy didn't have much reason to feel valued. A man had to be something at least in his own mind. Guess owning a horse—no matter how sorry—did that for Roy.

"We went to where Queenie was tethered and led her farther from town then sat down to catch our breath and try to think. Only thing I could think of was joining up with you." She slid him a sideways glance and a tiny smile tugged at the corner of her lips.

The look said so many things; her regret at having no other choice, and maybe—if he let himself push the meaning of her smile—just a hint of gladness that she didn't.

He forced his gaze to the window across the aisle and watched the prairie slip by broken only by the occasional settler's shack. He wanted her to be glad but had no reason at all to believe she was. He'd been her only option. Nothing more.

"Wade, what's to stop Smitty from checking who got on the train? Wouldn't take more than a question or two to locate us."

He gladly reined his thoughts back to a situation where he had some hope of making a difference. "I've thought of that. If we head to Minot there will be lots of different routes we can take. Maybe we'll get on a train and let him think we headed one direction then get off and backtrack before we head for the ranch." Pretty hard to completely hide their activities, but with a bit of good fortune and some help from the Mighty Lord they might slip away.

"You'll be safe," Wade promised. "Both of you." This could get pricey. It was a good thing he'd brought a fat wallet.

She shifted so she could give him a hard look. "Don't make promises you can't keep. Smitty is an evil man who won't easily let us get away." She shivered and jerked back to stare out the window.

Wade curled fists into his armpits.

"Still, I won't stay any longer than I need to," she murmured.

He knew she referred to her visit to the ranch and Scout. "You won't be safe back in Dry Creek. Not while Smitty is walking about a free man. No, Lucy, you'll have to hole up at the ranch until it's safe to leave." He slouched lower in the seat happy to have settled the matter satisfactorily in his mind.

She stifled a groan. "Don't see why you're looking so happy about it. My life has been turned inside out."

For a moment he didn't answer as he sought for words that would say all the things he felt in his heart. "Sometimes change is good. Surprises can turn into prizes."

"Don't get all philosophical on me, Wade Miller."

He bristled and pulled himself upright. "Don't you go getting all prickly."

"Prickly? Me?" Even as she spoke, her defensive barriers came up.

"You got something against men in general or just your pa?" He knew the question would turn her into a porcupine but he was past caring. Past trying to avoid the topics he wanted most to talk about.

"Neither." Her voice growled with denial. Then she laughed. "Maybe both."

"Maybe it's time you got over it."

They dueled with their eyes. Hers flashed lightning. He guessed his reflected it back with added vigor. "You got no reason to resent me. Didn't I just save your skin? Didn't I just promise to protect you?"

She glowered.

"And no matter what Scout did to start this silent war of yours, he deserves a visit from you at the very least. After all, he is your father."

"He never married my mother," she mumbled.

"Huh?" Scout had forgotten to mention that little detail. What else had he left out? "Don't change the fact he's your pa."

"My father," she corrected as if there was a vast difference.

"When did you last see him?"

She shifted and stared out the window, her eyes narrowed as she squinted against the bright sun. He guessed it wasn't the sun that made her pull her lips into a tight line. "He didn't even bother coming to my mother's funeral."

"Likely he didn't know." Scout hadn't said so just as he'd never mentioned he hadn't married Lucy's mother and he guessed he must have known that for sure.

"I sent a wire. He knew. He just didn't care enough to stir himself and make a trip. He only came when and if it suited him."

Wade tried to think what would make the man decide

to visit or not. What constituted something suitable? For the life of him he couldn't think what would keep a man away from his family. Why if he had a little girl like Lucy or—he licked his lips and tried to stall the thought but it came without pause—a wife like Lucy, he couldn't imagine what could keep him away.

He shifted his thoughts back to Scout and safer territory. What she said about Scout simply did not fit with what he knew of the man. "Maybe he's changed."

She gave another sound of disbelief. Between the way her eyes flashed and the expressive sounds she made, Lucy had no need of words. He read her message loud and clear.

"My mother died when I was fourteen. How old were you?" He wanted to talk of things that didn't bring out the prickles in her.

"I was sixteen."

"What did you do?"

"I was a mother's helper for a couple of years then I met a friend of Hettie's and she arranged for me to work for Harry and Hettie."

He didn't like to think of her all alone especially when she had family who wanted her. Didn't seem right. "I barely remember my pa. He was killed in an accident when I was eight." He widened his eyes to keep from closing them where he knew he would see the pictures of that day branded on the inside of his eyelids. "They brought him home strapped over the back of a horse." His voice cracked and he stopped. Forced his eyes to see the passing scenery out the window across the aisle.

A warm hand touched his elbow. "Wade, it sounds awful. I'm sorry."

She withdrew her hand but her touch lingered in his pores, in his thoughts, bringing with it a breath of comfort.

"So, you were alone at fourteen. What did you do?"

"I was used to being alone by then."

"But your mother—?"

He hadn't meant to say that. It sounded as if he didn't miss Ma. He had. He did. "Ma had to work after Pa died. She got a job as housekeeper but the people didn't want a dirty little boy hanging about."

Lucy bristled up as if poked by a stick. "I'm sure you weren't dirty."

Seeing her all defensive on his behalf spread sugar over the mean comments he'd endured from the Collins family. "Ma scrubbed me with a brush and washed my clothes within an inch of survival."

"There you go. You weren't a dirty little boy at all."

His grin spread like butter on hot bread. "Nope. But I learned to stay out of sight. Unless they needed me to run an errand. Then suddenly I was Wade, the useful boy." He raised his voice in a high mimic of Mrs. Collins who said that very thing when she needed him.

Lucy widened her eyes. "They sound like a delightful family." Then she giggled. "Sorry for my sarcasm. Hettie is always telling me it isn't an attractive attribute in a young woman."

Wade couldn't stop staring. Couldn't stop thinking how good it felt to share his past with Lucy. "I guess it's like dynamite. Good in small doses."

She laughed outright at that and something sweeter than sugar edged across his heart. "I'll have to keep that in mind." She turned to look out the window again.

Wade slowly eased his world back toward normal but before he reached that state she jerked back to face him. "So, what did you do? All alone. Really alone."

"Found work. I spent some time working in a store. Worked on a farm then got on driving cows. Sure saw some pretty country doing that."

"Yeah?" Her eyes widened. "Like what?"

He told her about Texas, about the Canadian foothills. "It's real pretty up in the British Territories. Snow caps on the mountains most of the year."

She drank in his words as if she saw the things he described.

He liked the way she shifted to watch him. He liked the way her eyes sparkled as he talked about the scenery he'd seen. He especially liked the way she held his gaze as if every word he spoke meant more than gold to her. "Late last fall I was on my way south. Hoped to cross the prairie and make it to Texas before winter. But I was barely into the Dakotas when the temperature dropped like a rock. I could feel snow in the air and looked around for shelter." He chuckled. "Couldn't find myself so much as a tree to cling to. So I kept riding. Hoping I'd run into something. All I ran into was a snowstorm." He paused to enjoy the way her eyes widened. "I was lost for sure. About to freeze to death."

"What happened?"

"Well, come about Christmastime someone noticed this snow-covered mound in the middle of nowhere and they dug me out still sitting on my horse. They found some wood and built a fire around me. Took 'til spring to thaw me out." He grinned as her startled expression gave way to surprise and then she laughed.

"The cowboys must love to have you spin tall tales around the campfire. That's a really tall one."

He nodded, pleased with having amused her. "Been practicing it for a few months. You're the first one I got to tell it to."

"Best practice a bit more before you tell a bunch of tough cowboys."

They both laughed as their gazes caught like they'd been lassoed in the same coil of rope.

She pulled away first. "So, what really happened?"

"I prayed." He settled back as he recalled the day. "My mother had taught me about God. I believed but didn't think God really cared much about a dirty little boy." He gave a lopsided grin as he realized he used the same words to describe himself as a man as he'd used to describe himself as a boy. "But I didn't have a lot of options so decided to see if God could really hear and answer my prayer."

"And?"

"Maybe it wasn't really a prayer because I think I yelled something like 'God, help me.'"

"What happened?" Her voice was breathless with anticipation and made him feel as if every word he uttered was precious.

"Nothing. It got colder. The snow got worse. I knew I was going to die. I didn't even realize Two Bit had stopped moving. Suddenly, someone grabbed me, dragged me from the saddle and into a warm place." He considered how to tell the rest.

"That man—I'm guessing it was a man—saved your life."

"Yes, he did. He wrapped me in blankets, warmed

me slowly. Took care of my fingers and feet so I didn't lose any to frostbite. I was sick for a couple weeks and he fed me like a baby. I owe that man my life."

She sat back. "That's an amazing story. God certainly heard and answered your prayers."

"Yup." He could wait to tell her it was Scout that rescued him, Scout he owed so much to. "I'm still learning to pray, still wondering when it's okay to ask, and still wondering if God is really going to listen to a dirty little boy."

She laughed. "You aren't a dirty little boy. As a child of God you are loved and precious."

Would he ever feel loved and precious? Didn't seem like he would, but her words eased across his mind seeking out crevasses and cracks and pouring in a bit of warm honey.

"It was Scout who found me. I owe him."

Her expression changed so quickly he could hardly believe it. The sunshine went from her eyes, her brows drew together in a harsh vee. "Now you can pay him back." She gave him a good view of her back as she stared out the window.

"Lucy, can't you give him a chance?"

"I gave him plenty. Keep in mind I'm only going because Roy and I need to get away from Smitty."

Gouges dug into his mind and hot water scalded his thoughts. For just a moment he had forgotten he was only a means to an end for her.

Chapter Five

Lucy turned her back to Wade and stared out the window though she saw none of the passing scenery; anger blinded her. Why had she let herself forget why she and Wade and the sleeping Roy were together? It had nothing to do with how Wade made her laugh, how he touched a tender spot in her heart with his description of himself as a dirty little boy. She struggled to ignore the lingering ache as she thought how terrible it was a child should be made to feel that way. And that a man should carry the remnants of such an emotion.

Best she concentrate on the fact she was only an obligation, a means to repay the kindness her father had shown Wade. How ironic her father could stir himself to rescue Wade but not to visit his daughter. So many years she had waited for a visit, clinging to his promise to return within a few weeks.

With fists of steel she punched back her regret and disappointment. She would seek shelter at her father's ranch only because she had no other choice.

But she would not let her father or Wade beguile her into thinking she'd find anything more while there.

Her neck cramped from twisting it so hard to keep her eyes trained out the window and not at the man beside her. There was nothing to see but mile after mile of flat prairie.

She finally turned and studied the other occupants in the semi-full car. A couple of business-looking men sat a few benches away. Both held newspapers in front of them so she got only a glance as they lowered the papers to turn the pages.

At the far end of the car a man slouched low in the seat, his cowboy hat pulled over his face, his booted feet propped on the facing seat. A cowboy sleeping it off, Lucy decided and shifted her gaze to the man and woman across the aisle from the cowboy. They sat prim and proper facing straight ahead. Neither blinked. They could have been made of wax for all the life they showed. Lucy decided they were probably a married couple who'd had a row about something.

Across from the couple sat a woman alone, dressed in black except for a white lace collar making a shy appearance at her neck. Noticing Lucy's gaze the woman gave an overeager smile. Having no wish to engage in conversation with a stranger, Lucy nodded hello and brought her gaze to her hands curled in her lap. If only she'd brought a book but somehow the idea hadn't intruded on her hurried plans. Her only concern had been to escape Smitty. It was still her number-one concern. She'd simply deal with everything else that crossed her path as the necessity arose.

"I think I'll go check on the horses," Wade murmured. "Sweet Queenie put up quite a fuss at being tied up in the car."

Lucy nodded as he slipped away. She looked longingly at Roy curled up and wished she could do the same. She covered a yawn.

"It's a long trip." The black-dressed woman slid closer and leaned forward, eager for conversation. She tittered and ducked her head. "Of course, I suppose that would depend on where you're going."

Lucy had no intention of telling anyone her destination nor where she'd come from. "Where are you headed, ma'am?"

"To Seattle. To see my brother and his wife. Margery—that's his wife—has been ill so they need my help." Her taffeta skirts rustled as she smoothed them. "I never married so I'm grateful when someone offers me a home even if it's only my labor they want." She raised watery blue eyes. "You're so fortunate to have a husband and child."

"I—" Why bother correcting her? If anyone—like Smitty and his friends—asked if a woman and child were on the train, this woman would only remember a family. "I'm glad they need you."

"My brother is my closest relative. I guess he feels obligated to take care of me."

Lucy ground her teeth together to keep her words from bursting out. She would never let herself be so dependent on a man. There were lots of ways an unmarried woman could take care of herself.

She had a job in the dining room that offered her as much independence as she cared for.

"I'm supposing you are heading back to your home."

Lucy let her suppose whatever she wanted.

"You look like a very happy family. It does my heart good to watch you."

A clatter at the end of the car brought a frightened look to the woman and drew Lucy's eyes in alarm. The cowboy who had lounged in the corner seemed to have fallen off the bench. He now righted himself and fumbled in his pocket. He pulled out a flask and tipped it to his mouth.

"Tsk," the woman in black said. "Public drunkenness is so appalling." She shrank back against the window.

Lucy knew enough to mind her own business and looked out at the passing scenery.

The cowboy staggered to his feet, mumbling to himself. He headed down the aisle, lurching from one bench to the next. He would have to pass Lucy. She kept her gaze pointedly turned away.

He drew closer, still mumbling. He fell into an empty seat, laughed and managed to regain his feet.

She could smell the alcohol on him mixed with rancid sweat. Lucy held her breath and waited for him to safely navigate the next few yards, praying he would pass without incident.

The woman in the opposite seat tsked again, loudly, her disapproval as obvious as a shovel full of dirt.

The cowboy stopped, swaying to stay upright. "Old bat. Dried-up prune."

The woman sucked in air, shocked, no doubt, by the names spewing from the man's mouth.

Lucy didn't allow so much as a twitch to reveal her anxiety.

The train swayed. The cowboy tipped sideways and

landed practically in Lucy's lap. She jumped up and perched on the edge of the opposite bench, sharing the space with Roy's feet.

The cowboy peered at her bleary-eyed. His mouth parted in a sloppy grin. "Hey, it's Lucy gal. Whatcha doing here?" He hiccoughed. "Why ain't you serving all them hungry folk back to…to…well, shoot, you know what I mean."

She didn't recognize him. But then hundreds of cowboys ate at the dining room.

The cowboy leaned closer and she shifted back, barely able to keep from pressing her hand to her nose.

"I don't recall seeing you when I got on the train."

Perhaps she could divert him. "Where you headed, mister?"

"Seattle." The word came out so slurred she only guessed that's what he said. He pulled himself as close to upright as he seemed capable. "Say, did you hear some guy was shot in the barn?" His gaze shifted to Roy as if trying to place him.

Lucy prepared to defend the boy but Roy was dead to the world. He hadn't even sighed at the racket.

The black-clad woman made more disapproving noises and the cowboy's eyes narrowed momentarily. Lucy sensed his annoyance with the woman. "I hope they found the killer," the woman said with a sniff.

"Self-defense." The cowboy managed to mangle the word.

"Were you going to check on your horse or perhaps get a drink?"

"Can't remember. Don't care. You never gave me so much as a smile back at the—" His train of thought derailed. He paused, seemed to search his mind for where he meant to go with the conversation. "Now we're traveling companions." He leered in a most disgusting way. "Come and sit by me, Lucy gal." He patted the seat beside him.

When she made no move, he reached for her. The effort tipped him off balance and he fell toward her.

Wade's insides boiled as the drunk fell toward Lucy. His fists clenched as pure, undiluted anger rolled through him. He closed the distance in three strides and grabbed the man by the shoulder, deriving a certain amount of satisfaction from the way he flinched. He hoped there'd be a bruise for weeks to remind the man of the consequence of his inappropriate behavior.

He jerked the man upright, yanked at his belt and rushed him out the door and into the baggage car, dropping him into a mound of hay. "Don't come back. You can sleep it off out here." It required a great deal of self-control to keep from laying a thrashing on him.

He paused several minutes before heading back to the passenger car, waiting for his heart to resume a regular beat.

If Lucy was hurt he might yet use his fists to teach the man a lesson. He didn't expect this was one of the times God would say to turn the other cheek.

His blood still surged through his veins with unusual heat when he reached Lucy's side. "Did he hurt you?"

"I'm all right."

"Glad I got here before he could harm you."

She fixed him with stormy gray eyes. He didn't

blame her for being upset. He should never have left her alone, unprotected.

"I could have taken care of myself."

He blinked in surprise that she would object to his help, but then she was used to defending herself against the advances of the many cowboys who took their meals at the dining room. "You don't need to. I'll protect you. I promise you'll always be safe with me." He felt a prick of worry that he couldn't protect her after she returned to Dry Creek if she chose to do so.

"Don't make promises." Her low words carried a note of steel. "I don't trust promises. I learned a long time ago there's no point in looking for a hero. I take care of myself."

He studied her determined expression for a moment. She might as well have painted a sign on her saying "no trespassing." She'd just as effectively created invisible walls.

"I used to think I could manage on my own. This past winter taught me how valuable other people can be."

"I suppose you mean my father."

He sat beside her, ignoring the way she skittered as far away as possible. "Yup."

She gave him a disbelieving look. "Don't expect me to feel the same way."

Lucy obviously did not want to continue the conversation. She kept her face resolutely toward the window, no doubt drinking in the fascinating scenery—the vast miles of nothing but grass, wheat fields and farms clustered close to the tracks.

He rearranged himself, stretching his legs down the aisle. Even if the drunk cowboy returned, he'd have to climb over Wade to get close to Lucy and that wasn't going to happen. Wade let his head hang down, his chin almost on his chest and allowed sleep to come.

He slept lightly, something a man learned to do on the trail. So he noticed right away when Lucy sighed and straightened to face forward. Guess she got tired of the fascinating scenery. He knew the moment the monotony of the landscape and the clack of the train numbed her brain. Her head fell forward and she followed suit, jolting upright just before she melted to her knees. It was only a matter of time and he waited for the moment, adjusting his height in preparation. It came on angel wings—the peace of sleep. He caught her as she tilted forward and angled her toward him letting her head fall against his shoulder. With a deep sigh of contentment, he settled back and relaxed. She might hate him when she woke but at least she would be able to get a few hours sleep.

An hour or more passed. Roy jerked awake and sat up.

Wade stole a look from under his eyelashes.

Roy's eyes ate up his face as he looked around the entire car. When he saw no danger he let out a rush of relief. Then another fear seemed to hit him and he scrambled to find the sack holding the lunch they'd picked up.

Wade kept his head down not letting on he was awake. He didn't want to disturb Lucy. Roy however, had no such qualms.

"Lucy," he whispered fiercely. "Wake up."

Lucy sighed and rubbed her cheek along Wade's shoulder.

He buried a smile deep in his heart. It was one of those moments he would hang on his wall of remembrance.

Slept left her in stages. First the nuzzle, then a protesting sigh, followed by shocked stillness as she realized where she was, that she was snuggled up to Wade.

He didn't allow his eyelids to flicker as she bolted upright. Even with his eyes closed he felt her glare sear his skin. When she believed him asleep, she relaxed.

"When did you wake up?" she asked Roy.

"Just now. I'm hungry. Can we eat?"

"We should wait for Wade, don't you think?"

"He might sleep a long time." Roy's voice edged toward panic.

"Roy, you won't starve."

"How do you know? I'm a growing boy, ain't I?"

"Try growing a little patience."

Roy nudged Wade's leg rather sharply. Wade figured he'd done it intentionally, determined to waken him.

"Let him sleep."

Lucy's defense of him was more satisfying than any food he'd eaten.

"How long?"

Lucy sighed. "He's been good enough to drag us along. You might be taking that into consideration."

Wade knew he should let them know he was awake but listening to this conversation was too enjoyable— though being reminded that she'd only come out of desperation nipped at the edges of his enjoyment.

"We're going to your pa?"

Without opening his eyes Wade knew Lucy bristled. "We're going to a ranch farther west. Smitty won't have any way of knowing where we've gone. That's about all we need to know."

"I don't remember my pa."

The boy sure did know how to turn his words into a wistful song.

"Could be your good fortune. Might be he was a scoundrel."

"I wouldn't care. I'd still love him."

Wade tensed, waiting for a reply from Lucy.

"You should be cautious or you'll end up feeling like a kicked dog."

She'd been hurt bad by Scout. Perhaps by some other man, as well. It had left an oozing wound.

"I don't care. I'd still love him." His foot banged against Wade's shin, emphasizing every word. It hurt.

Wade jerked his leg away and opened his eyes. He blinked and yawned as if slowly finding consciousness. "What time is it?"

None of them having a timepiece, they all looked out the window. Roy had his own internal sense of time. "It's way past dinnertime."

"I 'spect it is at that. Wonder where we could get us something to eat?"

Roy rattled the sack. "We got a lunch packed before we got on the train. Did you forget?"

"Why that's right. Is there any left?"

Roy nodded hard. The little towhead needed a haircut. Wade rubbed his neck. He did, too. Maybe when they got to the ranch he'd find a pair of scissors and see what he could do.

"I never touched them. We were waiting for you."

"Well. Let's get at it."

Roy hesitated, halfheartedly offering the sack to Wade.

"You be in charge."

Before Roy could pull anything out, Lucy touched his hand. "Let's say grace." She gave Wade a questioning look as if asking if he would do the praying.

He hesitated. Not because he didn't want to thank the good Lord for food and protection and His many blessings, but because he'd never prayed aloud before others.

Lucy smiled. "Go ahead." She bowed her head.

Wade glanced at Roy. He clutched the bag, his head bowed, his eyes squeezed shut.

Lord God, thank You— He realized he spoke the words inside his head and started over. "Lord God, thank You for Your many blessings and Your love and protection. Amen."

Roy handed Lucy a sandwich, practically tossed one at Wade then unwrapped his own and bit into it. He ate with the gusto only a growing boy or a starving man could bring to the task.

Three thick sandwiches later, Roy slowed down enough to glance out the window. "Are we almost there?"

"It's not far now. Once we get to Minot, we'll change trains."

"How far to the ranch?" Roy persisted, shifting restlessly on the bench.

"Not so far if we go direct, but we won't. Got to hide our tracks, don't you think?"

Roy grew still, his eyes wide as he remembered why they were on this trip. "He won't be able to find us, will he?"

"Not if I have anything to do with it." He'd do his best to make it impossible to guess where they'd gone.

"We going to live at the ranch?"

"Don't see you have a lot of choice right now. Wouldn't want Smitty to find you, would you?" It wasn't Roy he watched for a reaction. It was Lucy. He'd never given much thought to his future past the next job, the next destination. Now he thought of what it would be like to share it with someone whose eyes went from calm gray to a thunderstorm in a flash, someone who teased him and laughed with him, someone as stubborn as an old oak tree. He decided to test the waters. "'Course, you might all decide to stay."

Lucy's eyes grew brittle. "I prefer to make plans to return to Dry Creek or perhaps a job in some other town where we can forget Smitty and where I depend on no one but myself. Besides, what am I supposed to do on a ranch?"

"You could cook if you want. That'd be a great help."

She tipped her chin upward. "Of course. I intend to pay my way however I can." A sparkle lit her eyes. "Though I know nothing about how to manage on a ranch. You might regret my efforts."

He tried not to imagine her in the kitchen cooking meals and washing the dishes—two jobs he detested. "So long as you don't feed us poison mushrooms I don't think there's much to fear."

"But where does one get supplies? Who provides meat?"

"I will supply the meat and there's a good store of supplies at the ranch. Besides, we aren't beyond civilization. Lark is the nearest town and quite adequate. Anything you need you can get there."

"Good."

At the talk of food, Roy checked the empty lunch bag for crumbs. There were none. It would be way past supper time when they reached the ranch. They'd have to scare up something to eat before then or Roy would surely expire.

The miles clacked away. Heat filled the car relieved only slightly by the ash-laden air coming in the windows. He tried a time or two to make conversation but it required a great deal of effort on his part—Lucy seemed to have sunk into a heat-induced stupor.

The conductor swung through the car. "Minot, next stop, folks."

Lucy looked like someone had thrown water on her best dress with her in it.

He understood her concerns about hiding their tracks but perhaps it was the idea of seeing her father that filled her with apprehension. He couldn't understand it. Scout was a great guy. Hardworking, honest and generous. He'd treated Wade like a son.

He had no more time to mull over the future, nor wonder about Lucy's past as the train ground to a halt. He grabbed their bags from the overhead shelf.

He led them to a slice of shade on the narrow platform. "Wait here while I get the horses."

Roy dropped the empty sandwich bag and raced after Wade. "How long do we stay here?"

"About an hour."

"Smitty don't know where we are, does he?"

"Don't see how he could." The cowboy still sleeping

in the hay might pose a threat. But Lucy had said he was
bound for Seattle. "You'll be safe on the ranch," he told
the boy as he unloaded their two horses.

"You'll be there, won't you?" Roy asked.

He understood the boy's worry. "I'll be there and so
will Mr. Hall and Lucy." He led them down the ramp.
Queenie hung her head like an old hound dog. She rolled
her eyes to make sure Wade understood how tired she
was.

"Why don't Lucy like her pa?"

"Roy, I couldn't say." He glanced in Lucy's direction.
She stared down the tracks, her shoulders set in rigid
defiance. "Might be wise not to ask her."

"She don't know how lucky she is to have a father."

"That's a fact." But it didn't change how things were.

Roy looked about. "Don't suppose there's a dining
room in this town."

"I don't suppose you could be hungry again?"

"A little."

Wade scrubbed his chin, pretended to be in deep
thought. They had less than an hour before the next train
on the Northern Pacific line. The ranch lay to the north,
fifteen miles from the town of Lark along the SOO line
but he figured to head west, get off down the line and
then ride back. It was circuitous, but meant to be. He
hoped it would confuse Smitty if he tried to find them.

"Don't suppose you could miss this one meal?"

Roy hung his head, a perfect match for old Queenie.
Maybe the pair had been spending too much time together. Both seemed to have a healthy interest in food.
He'd noticed the horse developed the sprightly step of a
young colt when he tossed out oats for the horses. He'd

had to push her away from Two Bit's share. That gave him an idea. He might be able to put her greedy appetite to good use.

"You ain't got some old biscuits or a can of beans?" Roy persisted. "I like cold beans right from the tin."

Wade guessed he liked anything out of the tin—cold or otherwise. "Fact is I do have two tins. You think Lucy would like cold beans?"

Roy spared Lucy a considering look. "Maybe not. She's a mite fussy about her food." Misery weighed his shoulders down.

Wade decided to stop teasing the boy. "I think we might find something at that hotel down there." He pointed.

And just like Queenie when she caught the scent of oats, Roy perked right up.

A short time later, Wade felt a lot better having filled up on a generous portion of stew and fresh bread. Lucy barely picked at her food but it wasn't wasted. Roy cleaned up what she didn't eat.

"You sure you don't have a hollow leg?" he asked the boy.

"I'm growing."

Wade laughed. "Roy boy, you keep eating like that and you'll be as big as a house." He glanced at Lucy expecting her to share his amusement but Lucy wore a strained look and gripped her fork so hard her knuckles were white.

After loading the horses onto another train they sat quietly as it pulled from the station. Wade tipped his hat low and tried to be invisible. Lucy sat so stiff and upright that her back didn't touch the bench.

"Relax," he whispered. "No one has noticed us. We're just a family headed west so far as they're concerned."

"I wish I could relax," she whispered back. "But I feel like I'm stuck between a rock and...." She shrugged and didn't finish.

He didn't need her to.

Twenty minutes later they slipped off the train and gathered the horses. Then headed south away from the ranch, Queenie acting put upon because she was expected to move faster than a caterpillar without legs. Wade paused and opened the bag of oats. He put a layer in his hat and held it out. Sure enough, sad, worn-out Queenie perked her ears and trotted toward him. He gave his hat to Roy. "Keep shaking it but don't let her reach it."

"I see you aren't above a little trickery." Lucy's words were drummed out of her by Queenie's rough trot.

"I like to think I'm smarter than an animal." They made a few miles. He hated to keep Lucy at that pace. She'd be beat to pieces by the time they got to the ranch. But if he slowed, the horse would grab the oats. He urged Two Bit to a lope. Queenie whinnied a protest then settled back into her plodding walk. "I guess she's not up for a challenge."

"She can't run that fast." Roy defended his pet.

The title of pet suited her better than that of saddle-horse. They managed a few more erratic miles with Queenie dashing for the oats if he allowed Two Bit to slow, and then slowing to a crawl if Two Bit sped up.

"Remind Queenie of the oats."

Roy shook the hat. "Come on, Queenie. Here's something to eat."

Wade could almost hear Lucy's teeth rattle as Queenie trotted toward the treat. He tensed his jaw. He couldn't stand to watch Lucy shook up like that. "Watch the oats." He jumped from the saddle and grabbed Queenie's reins before she could knock Roy off Two Bit's back. "We're going to change places," he told Lucy and reached up for her.

She tried to swing off the saddle but her skirts caught and she tumbled into his arms. He felt her galloping heartbeat thud through her body, no doubt jolted into such a pace by Queenie's rough gait. She clutched her arms around his neck and hung on like she'd found home sweet home. He held her tight both to calm her shudders and to still the blessed lurch of pleasure at the weight of her in his grasp; the alarming, unfamiliar way his heart swelled against his ribs as if it were reaching toward *her* heart to calm it. To hold it. To cherish it.

What had been in that stew? Whatever strange ingredient, it certainly had affected his ability to think straight. He swung Lucy toward Two Bit. "You ride my horse. Otherwise, I can see us riding all night to get a few miles."

She scrambled into the saddle. Roy clung to her waist. Wade allowed himself a quick glance, noting the pink in Lucy's cheeks. He'd embarrassed her and chewed on the thought a moment. He regretted making her uncomfortable, but decided if he said anything he'd further discomfort them both. Grinding down on his molars in disgust at himself and his stupid reaction, he swung onto Queenie's back. "Keep the oats where she can see them." He faced straight ahead. "Keep a good pace. Whatever's comfortable. We'll keep up."

"I don't know where I'm going."

Her words blazed across his brain. He didn't know where he was going either. "Just head down the trail. Two Bit knows the way." He'd gotten all twisted up with thoughts of sweet little Lucy—a woman who said time and time again she had no use for a man, no faith in promises and had made it clear she would not trust another.

But none of that mattered more than a heap of straw. He only wanted to take her to Scout before the man died. He owed him that much.

Chapter Six

Throughout the train ride and as they left behind the tracks to wander from one direction to another, Lucy worried how she'd face meeting her father again. Now, after what seemed like hours on horseback, her muscles cried out for relief and she no longer cared who or what waited for them at the end of the trail. All she wanted was to get out of this saddle and find a soft place to stretch out and give her body a chance to relax.

Roy had long ago stuck the hat of oats between them and leaned his head against her back. She wouldn't wonder if he'd fallen asleep.

Wade fought Queenie every step of the way.

Lucy turned to check on their progress. The old horse amazed her. Where did she get the energy to keep fighting? Talk about stubborn. Maybe she was part mule.

Wade noticed her watching and widened his mouth in a gesture as much grimace as smile. He had the look of a man pushed way beyond his level of patience. And she grinned, just a tiny bit pleased at his struggle. Somehow it felt like justice to see him having to cope with a stubborn animal and his frustration drained some of hers.

Roy slumped to one side.

She reached back and steadied him. "Stay awake or you'll fall off."

He mumbled something and righted himself.

Darkness crept in, gray and gentle. Pink tinted the western sky and ribbons of purple, orange and red crossed it, too. Then the gray deepened. Lucy struggled to keep her eyes open and prayed they would arrive soon, before she and Roy both fell off and decided to spend the night sleeping on the prairie.

Wade took the reins from her, and she realized they'd stopped moving.

"We're here." He lifted Roy from the horse and put him on the ground where he crumpled into a ball, asleep.

"Thank God." Gratitude rounded her words as much as fatigue. "But where exactly is *here?*"

"The ranch." He offered his hand to help her down.

She hesitated. Her heart, which moments before had slowed to sleep mode, kicked into a gallop as she remembered falling into his arms a short time after they started this torturous ride. She'd embarrassed them both with the way she clung to him even though it was only because she shook clear through from riding Queenie. That was her excuse and she didn't intend to allow any other reason to intrude. But the idea of a repeat performance both tempted and frightened her.

"This is the ranch?" She strained to see anything in the darkness, using the time to get her feelings under control. "I don't see anything."

"We're at the corrals. There's a low barn to your right."

She followed the line of wooden fence to a building. "I see it."

"You can't see the house in the dark, but it's over there." He pointed to the left then reached for her again.

She allowed him to take her hand and slowly eased down, determined she would not throw herself into his arms this time.

Her legs buckled as they took her weight and she clung to his hand as longing surged up her throat. Why had she thought she didn't want to find security against his solid chest?

Because she did not, would not, could not ever let herself pin her hopes and dreams on a man. Nor could she afford to forget that he wanted her here for only one reason—his obligation to Scout. She forced steel into her legs and released his hand. "Thank you."

"Wait with Roy while I turn the horses into the corral." His voice sounded faintly amused with just a pinch of regret, as if he'd read her thoughts.

She leaned against the fence. She would have liked to curl up beside Roy but knew if she did, she would never be able to get up and make the journey to the house. Peering into the darkness, she made out the faint shape of a building beneath the limbs of a big tree. Was it the house? But wouldn't the house have a light burning?

She turned her gaze away and tried to tear her thoughts from what lay ahead. In a few minutes she would come face-to-face with the father she'd never been able to count on. The entire long weary day she'd dreaded this moment, wondered what she'd say. *Lord, hold me up through this. Let me not be disappointed again.*

"Are you ready?" Wade asked.

She hadn't heard him and jumped. "Yes." *No.* How could she be ready for something she didn't want and had promised to never again put herself through? She used to eagerly run to the window when someone entered the yard, wondering if her papa had come. She'd stood at the same window, washing it with her tears when he left. As he always did. Leaving behind a little girl who wanted so much for her papa to notice her enough to do more than say hello.

Her heart filled with angry determination. She would not let him hurt her again.

Wade scooped Roy into his arms and she followed him across the yard toward the darkened building she'd studied.

A low growl stopped her in her tracks. The skin on the back of her neck tingled. "What's that?" she croaked.

"It's Bear," Wade said. "He's just warning us in case we're up to some mischief."

"Bear?" That's all she needed. A pet bear. Of course, he hadn't said it was a pet. She began to back up.

"He won't hurt you unless—"

"I don't want to know what's *unless*." Her whisper scratched from her throat.

Wade's boots echoed on wood. She guessed he had reached the steps but she didn't join him. A few minutes ago, she'd been so tired she could barely walk, but now she had the urge to run into the dark. Only uncertainty of what lay out there stopped her.

"Hey, Hunter. It's me, Wade. Call off your dog."

Wade's loud voice jerked across Lucy's tense nerves, and she pressed her hands to her chest as she tried to calm her heart.

Dog? Was Bear a dog? Something creaked. A door opening?

"That you, Wade?"

"Yes. Give us some light, man."

A match flared. The smell of sulfur filled the air. Then a lamp glowed yellow revealing a wizened, bewhiskered man and a hairy dog at his side almost as tall as the man. The dog stood with his hackles raised and white fangs bared.

Lucy's heart kicked against her palm. She backed up several more steps, stumbled and righted herself.

"Yup. It's you all right. Bear, settle down."

The dog stopped growling.

The fact did nothing to ease Lucy's fears.

"I got company," Wade said. "Scout's daughter and a young lad who refuses to wake up."

"Come in the house. I want to get back to me bed."

Wade headed for the door. "Come on, Lucy. We're home." He glanced over his shoulder. "What are you doing way back there?"

She didn't spare him a look, couldn't take her eyes off that animal, certain the moment she did it would rumble from the house and attack her. She didn't want Wade to realize her fear and tried to make her feet move, tried to force a calm word from her throat. All she managed was a squeak.

"You afraid of Bear?" His voice said it all. Amazement, surprise, and a generous dollop of pity.

But she still couldn't make her feet move.

"Hunter, take the boy." The man set the lamp on a stand and Wade shifted Roy's weight to his arms then strode back to Lucy. "Come on. I'll protect you."

She didn't miss the humor lacing his words. Normally she would have resented him suggesting she needed protecting, but somehow her pride had deflated at the sight of the large dog.

Wade wrapped an arm around her shoulders and led her to the step. Hunter and his dog moved aside to let them pass.

She swallowed hard as they made it safely into the house and tried not to think of the dog only inches from her. An impossible task when she could smell him with every tight breath. Surely, he wasn't allowed to sleep indoors.

Warmth crept up her throat as she realized she stood pressed to Wade's side and she eased away, though not too far. He provided her only protection if the dog lurched at her.

"How's Scout?" Wade kept his voice low.

Roy mumbled and squirmed. Hunter set him on his feet. The boy practically melted to the floor then found the door frame and propped himself against it.

"Scout's still hanging on. Sleeping now, of course. Don't think you want to disturb him, do ya?"

Wade shook his head. "Of course not. Besides, we're all about ready for some shut-eye ourselves."

Lucy could make out little of the house—just enough to see they stood in a kitchen of sorts with a cookstove and a few cupboards. A round table across the room was piled high with unidentifiable objects. Past the table she made out a doorway but couldn't tell what lay beyond.

"Scout still in the living room?"

"Yup."

"You're sleeping in the loft?"

"Yup. Plenty of room for ya'll."

Lucy made out a ladder beside the table, leading to

an area with a half wall. She stared at it. Was she expected to sleep there with the men?

Wade touched her elbow. "I have a place for you. Come."

She hesitated. "What about Roy?"

"I'll take care of him."

She still didn't move, concerned for the boy. But her fears subsided as she realized Wade had done a fine job of seeing to them so far. She allowed him to lead her across the room.

He lit another lamp and led her to a door she hadn't noticed beyond the stove. She stepped into a narrow room, just wide enough for a cot with an open cupboard crammed in at the foot of the bed. Not that she had anything to put into it. Her belongings fit into the rather small bag that Wade dropped on the floor.

The place smelled of flour and coffee.

Wade lit a lantern by the door where he hovered. "It used to be the pantry but I figured if you came, you'd need a place of your own. This is it. Good night." He gave her a short nod then closed the door with haste.

Through the dim light, Lucy took in the bed covered with a Hudson Bay blanket. A green blind covered the one narrow window. Lucy rubbed her palms up and down her arms trying to drive away a chill that went deep into her soul and would not be relieved by warming her skin. Her father apparently slept a few feet away, separated by mere lathe and plaster walls. She would not be able to avoid seeing him within the next few hours. The idea caught at her heart, whipping it into a frenzy not unlike her reaction to the big dog. This time she could not find strength in Wade's touch.

Her heart gave a vicious lurch against her ribs as she

thought how she'd practically glued herself to Wade's side. So much for proving she needed no one.

Determination gave momentum to her limbs. She needed no one. She would face whatever this decision required of her and she would come out unscathed from it. Even if she had to nail boards over her thoughts and emotions.

Having established the ground rules for her stay here, she checked the door to make sure it was firmly closed, blew out the lamp, then climbed into bed where she lay shivering under the covers even though the room was warm.

Lucy struggled from sleep as a strange noise woke her. The room was already brightly lit. A fly buzzed against the window. She turned to squint at the window and sat bolt upright when she saw it now went from ceiling to elbow height. Then she remembered. She wasn't in her little room in Dry Creek. She was at her father's ranch.

Falling back onto the cot, she closed her eyes and groaned. Not much chance she could avoid seeing him today.

She listened to the clack clack of a dog's nails as it crossed the floor. The outer door opened and a voice said, "Out."

"Lucy," Roy called.

"Let her sleep. She was pretty tired."

Hearing Wade's voice, she grinned. So, he thought to let her sleep, did he? The idea made her feel a little spoiled, as if she deserved to be given special regard.

"I'm awfully hungry."

Her grin grew wider. Roy was always hungry.

"Who's going to make breakfast?"

"I can cook," Wade answered.

"Like Miss Hettie?"

"'Fraid not."

"Then maybe we should wake Lucy up so she can cook."

Then she remembered that she'd agreed to cook while she was staying at the ranch. Breakfast depended on her. Might as well get up and face the day, her responsibilities and—when he could no longer be avoided—her father.

She pulled on her clothes, ignoring the way her legs ached from so many hours on horseback. She smoothed her hair. As soon as possible, she would slip out to the facilities. She paused at the door, not sure how to deal with what lay on the other side.

Lord God, guide me. Give me strength. Her world righted as she centered her thoughts on God's love and care. She'd learned to trust Him. Being here didn't change that.

The door opened quietly, not alerting any of the others to her presence. Roy sat at the table examining the contents of used cups as if hoping to find sustenance, pushing them aside with a deep sigh when they yielded none. Wade's attention was on filling a kettle from a bucket of water.

Hunter was missing as was, thankfully, his huge dog.

"How long before she wakes up?" Roy sounded desperate.

"I'm awake."

Wade spun around to face her.

She'd cleaned up as best she could. She normally

pinned her hair into a roll but discovered most of her pins had disappeared so she'd braided it into a long plait that hung down her back.

Wade's gaze lingered on her hair and his eyes widened, making her blush. Did he think her hair inappropriate? She tilted her chin slightly. She had done the best she could. No one could expect more.

Then he met her eyes, correctly reading the challenge in them. He grinned. "Morning, Lucy. You look refreshed so I'm guessing you slept well. Last night you seemed a little—" His grin widened and she had the sneaky suspicion he recalled her seeking shelter at his side. "You seemed a little shaky."

"It was a long day." She wouldn't think of that incident or the way her heart had done a slow swoop when she woke on the train with her face pressed to his shoulder. She had feigned sleep several seconds as she'd examined her reaction. He'd felt so solid. So comforting.

She shifted her thoughts back to reality. They were here only to hide from Smitty. Only to fulfill what Wade considered to be an obligation to her father. In that equation there bode no room for silly weaknesses. Not that she would allow them in any case. Last night had been an exception.

She turned to Roy, his eyes widening as he silently pleaded for food. Only she couldn't run into the kitchen and beg a plateful from Hettie. She'd have to find the makings and cook the food before any of them could eat. "Show me where you keep your supplies and I'll start breakfast before Roy fades away to a shadow."

Wade chuckled. "He's been on the verge for several minutes." He pointed to a door in the floor by the table.

"Our supplies are in the cellar. There's lots of things like oatmeal, flour, cornmeal—"

"Can you make corn bread?" Roy asked with such eagerness Lucy glanced at Wade and they both laughed.

She ducked away from the mirth in Wade's eyes, eyes that seemed to offer her so many things. She ground down on her back teeth. She knew the pain and futility of waiting for anyone else to provide what she needed. She found her belonging in God alone and His love. How could she be forgetting her hard-won lessons when her father lay only a few feet away?

Her gaze slid toward the next room.

Wade misinterpreted the action. "I suppose you're anxious to see Scout?"

She half shook her head but until she dealt with this, it would hang over her head like a doomsday ball ready to drop. "Is he awake?"

"Yup. I spoke to him a few minutes ago. He'll be anxious to see you."

Lucy noticed Wade didn't say her father had actually *said* he was anxious to see her. Likely Wade simply assumed it. "How is he?" She'd heard him cough several times during the night and tried not to feel anything but normal concern—one human for another.

"He's weak but—"

She nodded, her gaze stuck at the doorway, her mouth wooden so she couldn't talk. This shouldn't be a big deal. She'd long ago mentally said goodbye, yet…

Hope and regret, dreams and reality clashed so violently, she shuddered.

Again Wade misinterpreted her action. "Don't worry.

He's well enough to see you. Come." He stepped toward the doorway.

Her legs refused to move as she remembered the many times she'd run to other doors, in other houses, anxious for a glimpse of her father. The few times he came, it had been for fleeting visits. His whole visit seemed to revolve around fixing things for Mama. Lucy had hovered in the background aching for recognition, a kind word, anything. The most he ever gave was an awkward pat to her head and perhaps a piece of penny candy.

His leaving had left her wallowing in regret and denial. He'd be back. He'd said he would and she'd believed him and believed that when he returned he'd spend time with her. Only he never came back when he said he would. Sometimes it was months, even years. She forced that memory to the forefront. This was a man who made promises but didn't keep them, who didn't see how deep her need had been for a real father.

Wade waited expectantly, his expression eager.

Wade's only reason for bringing her, for taking care of her and Roy was to meet his own sense of obligation. She pushed that realization to the front, too.

Stiffening her resolve, she followed Wade into the other room, stopping just past the door to look around. A fireplace dominated a long wall in the untidy room. Chairs and a writing table stood at the far end. At last, when there was no more option, she let her gaze slide to the sofa at the far end of the room where someone lay covered by a gray woolen blanket.

"Hello, Lucy. I see you made it." Her father's voice

set off familiar memories. He sounded the same. She expected he was the same in other respects, too.

"Hello, Father." Seems she should be able to think of something more to say but only accusations and questions came to mind and she had no intention of voicing them.

To save them both further discomfort, Lucy shifted her gaze to Wade. He watched her as if hoping for more from her, wondering at the stiffness between her and Scout. But Wade couldn't begin to understand how it felt to have a father who had never managed to give her more than a passing glance during his fleeting visits.

Wade and Roy were both orphans. They knew why their fathers didn't have a role in their lives.

Her father simply chose not to be part of hers.

Roy sidled into the room.

"Who is this young fella?" Scout asked.

Lucy decided his voice was weaker than she remembered. He certainly looked smaller under the covers. Guess being sick could do that to a man. He was paler, too. Last time she'd seen him she'd thought he looked especially handsome with his bronzed skin.

Wade answered Scout's question. "This is Roy. A friend of Lucy's."

"Glad to have you join us, Roy," her father said.

He hadn't said he was glad to see Lucy nor sounded half as welcoming. Rather than think further along that line, she forced herself to look out the window and note the bright sky, the rolling prairie.

After another awkward moment she said, "I suppose I better start breakfast."

That got Roy's attention and he raced back to the

kitchen to stand staring at the cellar trapdoor. "Can I go down?"

Wade laughed and explained to Scout, "Roy is a growing boy who seems to need to eat all the time."

Scout grinned. "Best see to it then." He coughed.

Lucy waited, hoping for more, but Scout lay back against the pillows and closed his eyes. She ground around on her heels and followed Wade back to the kitchen. Anger at herself as much as at anyone else churned through her.

"I guess we're safe from Smitty for now. For that I should be grateful." Her words came out clipped as bullets.

Caution filled his eyes. "You sound anything but."

"I am. Now where's the food?"

He studied her a moment then lifted the trapdoor. "Let's have a look."

Roy scampered down. Wade followed and waited at the bottom of the ladder to help Lucy. She ignored him and made her own way.

The storeroom was cool. Lots of canned and dry goods but no fresh produce. No eggs. Only tinned milk. She could see cooking might be a challenge.

"I think we'll settle for griddle cakes this morning. Maybe some tinned peaches." She let Roy carry the items up to the kitchen.

As she mixed the batter hoping it would be edible without an egg, Roy watched her every move. From the meals he'd taken at the dining room she knew Wade liked coffee so she made a pot.

Hunter stepped inside, his dog waiting on the step. Good place for a dog. Even from there, she could smell the animal. "Now you all are back, I'se heading back to my place."

"You're welcome to stay for breakfast," Wade said.

But the man shook his head. "Got to go."

"Thanks for staying with Scout."

Relief gusted from Lucy's lungs as the man stomped off, the huge dog at his side.

She cleaned soiled dishes from the table, cleared it of assorted tools and papers and scrubbed it until it was fit to eat off. Then she served the griddle cakes, peaches and for Wade, coffee.

When she stood back waiting for them to eat, Wade pulled out a third chair. "You ain't waiting tables here. Sit down with us and eat."

For a moment she wanted to refuse. It was easier to keep a protective barrier around herself if she kept the lines clearly drawn. She was here seeking protection and paying her keep by cooking. Sitting at the table, sharing the meal, blurred the lines.

"We aren't going to eat while you stand there."

At Wade's announcement, Roy swallowed so hard she almost laughed.

"Come on, Lucy. Ain't you always saying we should remember to act like family when we get the chance?"

"Roy, someday I'm going to teach you to remember my remarks when it's for your enlightenment, not mine."

He looked offended. "Well, you did say it, didn't you?"

"I did, but I meant—" What did it matter that she had been trying to teach him how normal people functioned?

Her gaze went unbidden to the living room door. Did she take food to her father or...

Wade touched the back of her hand, sending tingles through her veins. It was about all she could do not to turn her palm to his and hang on for dear life. Instead, she jerked away telling herself she didn't care that his eyes narrowed and hoarded a look of pain.

"He's sleeping," Wade said. "You can take him something later. In the meantime, you might as well enjoy breakfast with us."

Compared to sharing the meal with her father—trying to make conversation when they had nothing to connect them except her mother—Wade's invitation seemed rather pleasant. "Very well." She got herself a plate and silverware and sat in the chair Wade pulled out.

"Thank you. This is better. Shall I say grace?"

She'd noticed his hesitation on the train, guessed praying out loud was something new for him so his offer diffused her annoyance, replacing it with something akin to pleasure.

The three of them bowed their heads as Wade said a simple grace, then Roy attacked the food.

Wade drained his cup but when Lucy started to get up to refill it, he pressed his hand to her shoulder. "I can do it. You enjoy your breakfast." He poured a second cup of coffee and returned to the table.

She ducked her head to hide her hot cheeks. His consideration did something warm and fuzzy to her. For a moment she could forget her father lay in the other room—the only reason Wade cared whether or not she was here.

Chapter Seven

The stove belched out heat. The kitchen grew impossibly warm even though a breeze blew through the open door and windows. Lucy washed the breakfast dishes plus others she'd gathered up around the room. Wade had told her Scout would call when he woke up. So far he hadn't; though she'd heard him cough several times.

And she was grateful for the reprieve. Somehow, she had to find a way to keep her boundaries firmly fixed. Not that it was as hard with her father as it seemed to be with Wade.

She stared out the window. Wade and Roy had left after breakfast to tend to chores. She'd seen them a couple of times carrying things from one spot to another. Each time her heart did a swoop and then climbed like a bird set free to soar the winds. It had taken a firm hand to clip her heart's wings.

When would she ever learn to stop aching after attention and acknowledgment? She'd diverted her futile longings from her father only, apparently, to settle them on Wade.

God help me be wise. I need no one but You. You are my all in all.

"Hunter? Are you there?" Her father's voice came from the other room, ending on a cough.

She had to face him.

Gathering up her strength, remembering her prayer for wisdom, she went to the living room. "Hunter has gone home. I'm here. Can I get you something to eat?"

"What do you have?"

She ignored the feeling that she should whip out an order book and pencil to write down his selection. "Griddle cakes and peaches. Would you like coffee?"

"Sounds fine." He barely looked at her.

She took the water glass from the table at his side and returned to the kitchen. She could do this. It was no different than the work she'd done back at the Dry Creek dining room. Take orders, dish up food, refill cups.

Only back there it had been fun.

So, why not make this fun? Just because it was her father and he treated her like she was invisible didn't mean she had to act any differently than if he was a rowdy cowboy.

She turned her attention to the stove to set the griddle over the heat. Wisps of smoke came from the fat burning off it. The fire snapped.

She spooned batter to the hot griddle and smiled. At first it felt forced. Then she nodded. "Lucy gal here to serve you, sir." She tried a little laugh and swayed her hips as if avoiding an overeager cowboy. "Coffee coming up." She giggled as she imagined Harry hovering in the background ready to straighten out her father.

* * *

Wade stood a few feet from the open doorway, staring as he watched Lucy sway and talk to herself. Something about bringing coffee. He settled back on his heels, enjoying her smile and laugh. Her reaction to her father this morning had baffled him. The pair seemed as strained as strangers forced together in tight quarters. Of course he knew they hadn't seen each other in some time. But to see her relaxed now and enjoying herself like the first time he'd seen her eased his concerns. Her tautness was gone.

He'd done the right thing bringing her here. Right for Scout and right for her. Right for him, too? He couldn't say just yet but he sure did like to see her dancing about the kitchen. "Nice to see you happy."

She jumped a good eight inches and grabbed at her chest. Her expression lost all joy. "You ought to know better than to sneak up on people and scare them."

"I just wanted a drink."

"How long were you standing there?" Her eyes narrowed with suspicion. "You been spying?"

He felt his eyes crinkle, knew they gave away the truth, not only that he'd seen but enjoyed watching her. "Nice dance."

She sniffed.

For a moment he thought she was going to blast him with anger, then the storm in her eyes fled before the sunshine of her smile and she giggled. "I was practicing."

"Yeah? For what?"

She turned her attention to flipping the griddle cakes

but not before he saw how she sobered. He wondered at the cause.

Then she faced him, her jaw set determinedly. "To wait on my father."

"Huh?" That made not one speck of sense. Shouldn't she be happy to do so? Then he knew he could no longer deny the fact she wasn't here because of any affection for her father. She'd only come with him to escape Smitty. The tension in his jaw grew so fierce he figured it might take a pry bar to force it open. No reason he should think how much he'd like for her to stay. He just wished he could figure out why Lucy was so unforgiving toward her father.

She must have sensed his questions coming because she shrugged. "I'm just being silly. What's the harm in that?"

"Nothing. I guess." Still, her words didn't sit quite right with him. As if she had to practice being nice to Scout. Didn't make sense. But then not much about her feelings for her father did.

She flipped the cakes to a plate, spooned on peaches, filled a cup with coffee and stood facing the living room but making no move in that direction. Then she swung her head, sending her long plait dancing and it seemed she forced a smile to her lips. "Want to grab a coffee for yourself and bring it along?"

He'd only intended to have a cup of cold water but he couldn't resist her invitation. Besides, he wanted to see the two of them together again. He filled a cup and followed her.

Scout sat up on the couch with a piece of wood across his lap to use as a tray. He must have been hungry because he didn't even glance up as Lucy put the food before him. He ate slowly, but he ate it all.

That was good. Last time Wade had been there to take food to Scout he had turned away from it. Of course, his cooking didn't hold a candle to Lucy's.

Yes, siree, having Lucy here was going to be good for Scout.

Scout turned his attention to his coffee. "How are the cows?" he asked Wade.

"Haven't had a chance to ride out and check them yet."

"Didn't you bring a boy with you? Where is he?"

"Out exploring."

Scout grinned. "Bet he'll like the open spaces as much as we do." The man's gaze skittered past Lucy without pausing.

Wade resisted an urge to sigh. Of course, it would take time for both Scout and Lucy to feel relaxed around each other. Likely they'd have lots of time because while Smitty roamed free there wasn't any place much safer than right here.

Scout finished and pushed his dishes aside.

Lucy gathered them up and headed for the kitchen.

Neither daughter nor father had spoken a word to each other.

As Lucy dumped the dishes into the dishpan, Wade thought he heard her mutter, "You're welcome."

How strange. Scout hadn't even thanked her for breakfast.

This pair had a long way to go.

He followed Lucy back to the kitchen and watched her washing dishes, her thick braid following every movement of her hands. "I'm sure he's grateful even though he didn't say so."

She glanced over her shoulder.

Relief eased his chest muscles when he saw that she smiled.

"No, you're grateful. But it doesn't matter. I've had lots of experience waiting on customers."

So, that's what she'd been doing while he'd watched through the open door—practicing waiting on customers. But why should she think it was her role with her father? The idea stung clear through to his cowboy boots. It would take time. That was all, he assured himself, ignoring the way he ached to pull her close and tell her she was so much more than a serving girl.

"Thanks for the coffee." He strode across the yard with the hurry of a man fleeing the hounds of a posse. Only in his case it was the barking of his own confused thoughts that chased him. He'd more than half fallen in love with Lucy before they left Dry Creek. On the trip to the ranch, he'd come dangerously close to leaving the halfway mark in the dust even though he knew how foolish it was. But seeing Lucy with her golden-brown braid dangling down her back swinging with every movement, seeing her in the house and remembering the pleasure of sitting at a meal she'd prepared threatened his last grasp on sensibility. There was no point in getting any foolish thought in his head—not when she viewed him with the same mistrust she eye-balled Scout with. As if just by being a man, he could not be trusted.

Seems she'd have to solve some problems with her

pa before she'd see him as anything more than a man to avoid.

He reached the corrals and paused to study the surrounding landscape. *God, seems I'm always asking for favors 'cause here I am with another one. Could You please change Lucy's mind about men in general but especially about Scout...and maybe about me?*

Lucy closed her eyes as anger threatened to fuel a burst of hurtful words. She knew better than to expect anything different from her father. For years she'd protected herself from his hurtful behavior by not seeing him or corresponding with him. But all that had been changed by Smitty. She'd been able to find no other option but to come here. Which didn't mean she had to let the past hurt her even though it lay on the sofa in the other room, a very real presence.

She cleaned up the last of the dishes and tried to bring some sort of harmony to her thoughts but they were a tangle of hope and despair regarding her father, worry over her and Roy's safety, and anticipation over Wade. She shook her head at her foolishness. Anticipation of what? It wasn't like he wanted her here for any reason except her father's kindness to him. Besides, she reminded herself firmly, she didn't intend to place her happiness on the shoulders of anyone apart from herself and her assurance of God's love.

That thought righted her instantly. She'd learned to trust God's love and it had proved more than adequate.

That dealt with, it was time to earn her keep.

She opened the cupboard door and groaned. The dishes inside were spotted as if they'd had no more than a passing acquaintance with hot water. She scraped filth off the shelves with her fingernail. Her work was cut out for her.

The kitchen was hot enough to bake fluffy biscuits, too hot to work in. She went out to the wide step that ran the length of the cabin. A lean-to roof sheltered it and the breeze swept around the walls of the house. It was reasonably cool here and a bench stood close to the kitchen door. She carried the dishpan outside and washed dishes for an hour, changing the water twice. Before she returned them to the cupboard, she scrubbed it with a brush she found tucked away unused. That done, she attacked the windows and floor.

"Could I have fresh water?" Scout called.

She pushed to her feet, wiped her brow on the towel and filled a shining clean cup.

He struggled up on one elbow as he took the cup and drained the contents then handed it back to her. "Where's Wade and that young fella?"

Not a word of acknowledgment. As it had always been. Why? What had she done wrong? Where had she failed? She fought back the questions. She would ask them no more—not of herself and never of her father. That was the past. She cared only about the future. As soon as it was safe she would return to Dry Creek or move on to something new. She knew how to work. She intended to be self-sufficient.

"Last time I saw them they were out nailing a plank on a fence."

"Good man, Wade is. Proved himself a number of times this past winter. Did he tell you how I found him in a snowstorm?"

She nodded. Realized he wasn't looking at her. As if it somehow hurt him to even see her. "Yes, he told me."

"'Spect they'll be in for dinner soon. You got something ready?"

Lord, give me patience. Protect my heart.

"I'll get right at it." She spun around and hurried back to the kitchen where she stood gasping for air and realized she'd held her breath the whole time she was in the other room.

Why did she still let her father affect her so?

Suddenly, she realized if she didn't hurry, Wade and Roy would be stuck eating who knows what—probably cold tinned beans, which gave her an idea for dinner. She whipped up a huge batch of corn bread, hoping it would be moist without the benefit of eggs and stuck it in the oven. If there were leftovers she could fry them for supper. She opened several tins of beans and put them to heat. If only she had a few more supplies— like vegetables and fruit. Dessert would round out the meal enough to fill a hungry man. But what could she make? She poked through the supplies in the cellar, found some hard raisins. She covered them with boiling water and set them to soak. Thankfully, there was a good supply of flour. She mixed up sweet dumplings and dropped them in the boiling raisin mixture. They would be ready before dinner was over.

A few minutes later she had the table set amidst a sparkling clean kitchen. When she heard boots on the wooden porch floor, she took a deep breath. Preparing the meal had been fun. She'd enjoyed playing house. In her pretense, she'd allowed a few thoughts as to how Wade would be pleased.

Enough. She didn't need his approval or recognition any more than she needed or expected her father's. She'd long ago outgrown such childish notions. She was a strong woman on her own. God loved her and that was all she needed. She had a job—or at least had had one. If she couldn't return to Dry Creek she would find work elsewhere. She would be independent.

The way Wade always said please and thank-you brought him to mind.

But she knew she was only a thank-you to Scout for rescuing him.

Before she could firmly rearrange her thoughts, Wade strode through the door. She hoped the embarrassment tightening her cheeks wouldn't show.

Wade stopped and looked around. A smile started on his lips, flashed to his eyes and landed with a gentle plop in the middle of her heart.

So much for not taking his acknowledgment personally.

"You've cleaned the place. Looks good. I had no idea the floor was so brown."

She was pleased at his praise despite all the silent admonitions she'd barely finished delivering. All that foolishness about not caring.

"My mother taught me well." And her father had taught her even more thoroughly the futility of letting what someone thought matter.

Roy skidded in behind Wade. Dirt freckled his face. He'd found an old gray cap somewhere and it sat at a jaunty angle, his straw-colored hair poking out six ways to Sunday. He fair bubbled with excitement. "You should see all the lumber. Stacks of it. Wade says Scout plans to build a new barn. Wade is going to stay and help do it. I helped stake out where the new barn is going."

It was great to see Roy being included in the work and being under the leadership of someone like Wade. She darted a glance at Wade, caught him studying her, a pensive look in his eyes. She held his gaze a moment, wondering at how he searched past the surface.

What did he hope to see? To discover?

There were no deep dark secrets in her life. At least none that she cared to share.

She shifted her attention back to Roy. "My ma would scrub your skin raw if she saw that dirty face."

Roy gave her a look full of wariness as if he feared she would do the same.

She laughed. "Good thing for you I'm not so inclined. I'll let you do your own scouring." She pointed to the washbasin. Only when he ducked to splash water over his face did she return her gaze to Wade. He still wore that probing look that sent nervous tremors skittering one way and then the other across her chest.

"I fear I haven't lived up to my training. Ma wouldn't have stopped cleaning until every spider had packed its bag and headed north to Alaska."

"Your ma didn't tolerate dirt well." Her father's voice from the living room ended on a cough. But she'd detected his note of annoyance.

All the enjoyment she'd gotten from Wade noticing her work instantly evaporated. Ma had been far too complacent about Scout's empty promises. Lucy told her time and again to forget him and accept the interest of one of the many men who wanted to call on her—

good, decent, churchgoing men. But Ma always said
Pa had promised to marry her and she had agreed. She
wouldn't back out on her word. "Ma didn't tolerate a
dirty house but she was maybe too tolerant of people."

Her father didn't answer. How could he? There was
no excuse, no defense for getting a woman with child
out of wedlock and then not marrying her. It had taken
Lucy a long time to get over the stigma associated with
that. In fact, she'd had to move away from her home-
town, though once Ma died that was no hardship. In
Dry Creek, where no one knew her shameful past, she'd
found acceptance. She'd discovered her own strength,
and through letting God's love heal her past, her own
worth.

She wouldn't let having to find shelter at her father's
ranch rob her of that.

Wade's glance shifted. Lucy felt his wariness and
maybe even a touch of reproach.

It stung that he'd witnessed this exchange between
her father and herself. No doubt she sounded like a
mean-spirited daughter. How little he knew of the situation. Mentally, she shrugged. She was here to hide
from Smitty and had agreed to housekeeping duties
while they remained. How difficult could it be for all
of them to do their own thing without intruding into
each other's lives?

She flashed Wade a grin, determined to keep things
rolling along on the clear path set before her. "Well,
cowboy, I hope you aren't fussy about your food. I did
the best I could but I gotta say your pantry isn't as well-
stocked as Hettie's. Could be she takes her cooking a
little more seriously than you do, among other things."

She gave a wide-eyed look around the room silently suggesting Hettie would never allow such neglect.

Something flicked through Wade's eyes as if he had to shift horses in full stride to follow her comments. He looked around the room, stopped at the table and smiled. "Seems to me I recall white table-cloths and tall glasses courtesy of Hettie."

She looked at the odd assortment of dishes and the scrubbed wooden tabletop and shrugged. "A person is sometimes limited by the environment."

Wade chuckled as he turned his steady blue gaze to her. "I'd say the environment has improved considerably since last night."

Warmth crept up her cheeks at the way he looked at her as if her very presence made the house, the ranch and even the whole world a better place. She reminded herself how foolish such thoughts were, how stupid she was to build false hopes and expectations. But she failed to completely eradicate the sense of being appreciated and even admired.

"Thanks for cleaning the place." He cupped her shoulder making the feeling even more irrepressible.

The gesture was short-lived. She could almost believe she'd imagined it except for the way her nerves reacted, plucking at her heartstrings with such teasing insistence.

He stepped away to take his turn at the washbasin then headed for the table where Roy sat anxiously awaiting the food.

She'd set a place for herself after a brief struggle as her pride did battle with her wariness and won. She would not allow her feelings to dictate her actions. She served the meal and sat across from Wade, Roy to one side. She glanced at Wade and he nodded. "I'll ask the blessing."

His prayer grew more confident each time. Suddenly, she wondered about his past. How could he be so confident and calm when he, of his own admission, had been made to feel like a nuisance, a dirty little boy as he put it? Had his mother managed to teach him to be strong in his faith despite their situation, or had he come to that strength later during the years he was on his own?

Did Scout fill a need in Wade's life that he failed to fill in Lucy's?

To keep her questions at bay, she passed the food, setting a serving aside to take to her father later.

Roy kept the conversation centered on the plans for the new barn, effectively leaving her to manage her confusion. Between comments, Roy devoured his food.

Wade ate a generous helping and took seconds and thirds. There would be no leftover corn bread for supper.

Roy eyed the pot she'd dished dessert from. "Can I lick the pot?"

"With your tongue?"

She felt especially pleased when Wade laughed.

"My tongue isn't long enough." No missing the regret in his tone.

"That's fine. I can wash it clean." She chuckled at his look of horror.

"It will be easier to wash if I clean it out good first."

"There's that. Sure, go ahead and clean it for me. I could use the help. But use the spoon on the cupboard.

You'll get syrup all over your hair if you stick you head in the pot."

He jumped up and grabbed the pot, returning to his place. "I know you're teasing me but I don't care."

Wade laughed. "You're one smart lad."

Roy spared a moment to flash him a grin then gave his complete attention to cleaning the pot of every speck of syrup.

Lucy met Wade's gaze. They studied each other a moment. He gave a slow, steady smile so full of unexpected kindness that her mental reservations melted like butter in the sun. She could almost forget her vow to remain unemotional about this whole arrangement.

She jerked her attention to the empty bowl in the middle of the table. Her arms feeling wooden, she grabbed it and headed for the dishpan. She had work to do. That would keep her busy enough she wouldn't be able to waste her time dreaming about things that couldn't—wouldn't—be.

She took the plate of food to her father and returned immediately.

Roy and Wade pushed away from the table.

"Thank you for the great meal. Much appreciated. You did a good job." Wade sounded sincere like it was more than polite words.

She nodded. "You're welcome. Kind of you to say so."

He stood there, turning his hat round and round.

"Did I forget something?" She patted her hair as if searching for a mistake then glanced over her wardrobe. "Seems everything is in place."

She'd meant to be amusing but Wade didn't smile. "Lucy, you might try giving your father a chance."

Anger roared through her. She swallowed hard to control it, contain it. When she had it under control, she forced a grin to her mouth. "Cowboy, I suggest you throw your rope around someone else's affairs."

His expression hardened but not before she caught a glimpse of something. Be it disappointment or shock she couldn't say. She only knew it sent shame and remorse through her.

He slammed his hat on his head and headed for the door.

Chapter Eight

Wade grabbed the rifle from over the door as he hurried outside, away from Lucy. He'd ride out and find fresh meat. They could all use a good feed.

And he could use time to straighten out his thoughts.

He'd only been trying to help sort things between Lucy and Scout. She had no call to get snippy with him.

He saddled Two Bit and rode straight toward the bluffs. He reached his favorite spot and reined in to let his gaze sweep the vista before him. He could see for miles, clear to yesterday on one side, and all the way to tomorrow on the other. The sprawling view never failed to calm him and slowly his tension eased. He waited for the usual sensation that all was right with the world. No reason he should let Lucy get under his skin.

He sighed causing Two Bit to snort.

Lucy was already under his skin. The question was, what did he intend to do about it?

He sat staring into the distance. Seemed his options were pretty limited. They were stuck living in the same house as long as Smitty wandered free. After that…well, he wouldn't let himself consider what happened. 'Course it could be a long time before Smitty got corralled for one of his lawless deeds. Seems no one wanted to risk the man's anger by offering to testify against him.

In the meantime he was free to roam around intimidating people. It wasn't right. But he wasn't about to make Lucy and Roy the sacrificial witnesses. So that meant Lucy might be here awhile.

The idea sidled through him like sweet, refreshing water.

Lord, perhaps You could see fit to let her see me with a dose of kindness.

God had answered prayers before. Why, just a few days ago he'd asked for God to change Lucy's mind about coming to see Scout and look how quickly that prayer had been answered.

His mind clouded. A man had been shot. Lucy and Roy had been forced to run for their lives.

Maybe he should be careful about praying for things he wanted.

Something moved in the distance and he squinted to see it clearer. He could barely make out two tiny black objects, little puffs of dust convincing him they actually moved toward the south.

South. Toward the ranch. Could it be Smitty and one of his sidekicks? What was he thinking, leaving Lucy unprotected?

He reined around and bending low, galloped for home.

He barely waited for Two Bit to skid to a halt a few

feet from the back door before rushing up the steps into the house. The kitchen was empty. "Lucy?" No answer.

He dashed into the living room. Scout lay snoring on the couch but a glance revealed no Lucy there either.

Where was she? Had they gotten here before him? It was impossible yet his heart beat double time as he raced back out the door and looked around. He saw his horse, the corrals, the low barn that was about to be replaced with a proper structure...but no Lucy. No Roy.

"Lucy," he bellowed. Did he hear voices toward the creek? He tipped his head. Was that Roy talking? He strode down the path through the little grove of trees. He broke through into the bright sunshine reflecting off the clear water where, pant legs rolled up, Roy waded in the creek.

He still didn't see Lucy. Wade's breath twisted in his throat before he finally spotted her hidden in the shadows, sitting with her back against a thin aspen. His chest heaved with relief.

What was she thinking? His insides steamed as he strode toward her. "What do you think you're doing?"

She tipped her head up and smiled though her eyes carried a hint of caution. She'd have to be dumb as the dirt at her feet to miss his anger. "Sitting in the shade?"

"Look around you. What's to stop someone from riding up unannounced? And you're..." He waved his hand. "Here."

"So I am. Enjoying the cooler air." She tipped her head back against the tree trunk clearly informing him she intended to continue her enjoyment.

Well, he knew how to end that. "I saw two riders headed this way."

The only sign she gave that it mattered was she opened her eyes. "Haven't seen them."

"Look, Lucy." Anger gave way to impatience. "How safe do you think it is to be sitting out here?"

"Look, Wade."

Her mocking imitation did nothing to ease his impatience.

"I guess I'm about as safe here as I am at the house. After all, there's you and my father to protect me."

Sure didn't sound like she thought they were protecting her. Sounded more like they were annoying her.

"Sit down, you're giving me a crick in my neck."

Sit? Why he'd sooner...

He sat, hunched over his knees, a few inches from Lucy.

"How far can you see in any given direction?" she asked.

Even from the shelter of the trees he could see for miles. But he didn't answer her. He knew where she was going with this conversation and he didn't want any part of it.

She continued, her voice lazy. "I'm guessing about three days. Right?"

He gave a noncommittal sound. Let her decide if it was agreement or argument.

"So, I'm thinking if I don't walk around with my head in the dust at my feet, I should see any approaching riders in plenty of time to—" she shrugged "—well, do whatever. Right?" She nudged him in his ribs.

He shifted away and immediately regretted it. She was right. He'd overreacted. But he didn't like admitting it nor having her see it.

"There they are." He pointed to the pair of riders. "It's a couple of Indians."

She bolted to her feet. "Roy, get over here."

Wade laughed and caught her hand before she could tear away. "They won't hurt you. I recognize them. Usually they ride on by. Sometimes they come for a drink of water or coffee if there's any made. Hope you never have any corn bread lying about though. If they ever discover how good it is, they'll beat a path to your door."

She gave a strained laugh. "I'll never make corn bread again."

"I'm not suggesting that."

The riders looked toward the house but didn't turn away from their southerly journey.

"I expect they're headed for Lark." He tugged on Lucy's hand. "You're safe." She'd always be safe while he had anything to say about it.

A sigh rippled from her and she sank to the ground. "That scared me."

She still held his hand, erasing remnants of his anger and impatience. They sat in peaceful calm as Roy returned to playing in the water.

"Do you think there's any way Smitty can find us?" Her voice trembled and he knew she was truly worried when she let him pull her close to his side. Her head came to chin height. He had but to turn his face to feel wayward strands of hair touch his cheek and he closed his eyes at the sweet torture. He ached to rest his chin on the top of her head, press his hand to her hair and discover its silkiness. He swallowed hard and pulled his thoughts back to her concerns.

"I expect if he wants to bad enough he can find us. He just has to ask the right people the right questions."

"You certainly know how to drive away my fears."

Her dry tone tickled him. "I can only promise to be on guard and protect you to the best of my ability."

She nodded, the movement brushing her hair against his cheek and—oh, mercy—driving all rational thought from his mind. If only they could sit here undisturbed by rational thoughts, unruffled by threats from Smitty, just peaceful and happy.

"I'm glad you don't make impossible promises." She shifted. "Did you bring any game?"

"Game?" His mind was as blank as the cloudless sky.

She jerked back to stare at him. "Didn't you go hunting? I was hoping for something to eat besides beans."

He scrambled to his feet, jeering at his complacent thoughts. "I hurried back when I saw the Indians. Didn't know—" He broke off. His eyes burned as he remembered his fear that something might harm Lucy. He tried to tell himself the fear didn't still linger in the dark corners of his heart. But knowing Smitty was out there somewhere, would likely persist until he found Lucy and Roy, would not allow the feeling to rest. It wouldn't until Smitty was locked up.

Lord, please give someone the courage to testify against him so Lucy will be safe.

Again he warned himself he should be careful what he prayed for. But no, God loved him. God loved Lucy and Roy. He could trust God to do what was best.

Tension slid out his body. "I'll go find some sage hens." He ducked through the trees. Two Bit stood patiently waiting. "Sorry, boy. Forgot about you." He led the horse to water and let him drink before he rode out to find some birds for supper.

Lucy stood in the shadows watching Wade. He'd come back, forgetting even his reason for riding out, just to make sure she was safe. To warn her to be watchful. The knowledge filled her with a sweet, fierce sensation. He was different than the other men she'd met and spent time with. But it didn't change the fact she only mattered to Wade because she was Scout's daughter.

She pushed aside regrets and longings. "Let's go back to the house, Roy." She waited for the boy to plow from the water and race toward her.

"This is sure a nice place. Guess we could do worse than stay here, don't you think?"

Stay. Here. With Wade. With her father. "It's not possible. Sooner or later we have to stop hiding and start living a real life."

Roy bounced around until he faced her. "You just don't want to stay because you're mad at Scout. How come, Lucy?"

She looked past Roy. What did she say to a boy who longed for family? Who craved attention so badly he lapped up the slightest kindness? She remembered feeling much the same way. Only she had Mama. And her faith. "Roy, people are never what we wish they could be. Best not to expect they will change. Like I told you before, God loves us and that's more than enough."

"No, it's not. I want someone I can hear and see. Someone with hands to touch me. Don't see God doing that, now, do ya? I expect that's why He made people. To do the stuff we can see and feel." He glowered at her a moment then raced off toward the barn to wave goodbye to Wade.

She wanted to call him back, warn him to guard his heart against wanting people to fill that need.

But he yelled something at Wade and waved until Wade was far out on the prairie.

She could only pray Roy wouldn't be hurt. And while she was at it, she prayed the same for herself. Her cheeks stung as she recalled how she'd let Wade hold her hand and promise to protect her. Her mouth twisted in disgust. As if she needed anyone to take care of her. Yet, she'd come perilously close to forgetting the fact.

Life settled into a routine of sorts. Scout was safely tucked away in the front room where she could, for the most part, ignore him. But all that had ended three days ago when her father insisted he was going to get up. It required Wade at his side to make it to the porch where he sat on a chair. "Sun feels good," he murmured, his eyes closed.

Roy hung about, his eyes wide and hungry, watching Scout. When he saw Lucy's warning look, he'd favored her with a scowl before he raced off to see what Wade was up to.

Lucy had returned to the kitchen feeling as if she was trapped. She didn't want to work on the porch with Scout out there. He made her feel too small.

Nor did she want to tackle cleaning the living room even though it desperately needed it. She didn't expect her father would want to sit up long and she didn't want to be caught on her hands and knees when he returned.

She'd mixed biscuits for supper. Wade had brought

in more birds. The meat was welcome. She'd made stew with the old potatoes she found lingering in the cellar.

Two days ago, her father insisted he would join them for meals.

Lucy's nerves had tightened at the idea. But she could hardly refuse to eat with the men and Roy. So, she sat with Wade at her right side, her father at her left and tried not to wish—

She wouldn't let her thoughts go in that direction.

She had a life. She was content. This was only an interlude until Smitty could…what?

She could ride to Lark if Queenie would go that far and send a telegram to Dry Creek informing the sheriff of what she'd seen. Only when Smitty was locked up or hung would it be safe to return.

But she'd been around Dry Creek long enough to know Smitty had ways of finding out what he wanted to know. He would be watching the telegraph office. He would be after her before the sheriff read her message.

She'd have to run again.

On her own. She shuddered and glanced about to make sure she was alone.

Perhaps at some point she'd be ready to take that risk.

But not yet.

She wasn't ready to. And if she allowed herself even a fragment of honesty, she would be forced to admit it had nothing to do with the threat of Smitty finding her.

Not that she would admit she harbored forbidden dreams of having her father acknowledge her in a positive sort of way.

But even more honestly, she didn't want to walk away from Wade.

She sighed. Enough of this foolish rambling.

Today Scout had insisted he would go outside with Wade and Roy and inspect the preliminary work on the barn. While he was gone she intended to start cleaning the living room.

She scrubbed the floor within an inch of its life. Still, Scout didn't return so she made dinner. It was ready when the male members of this odd household returned.

"I'm hungry," Roy said as he rushed inside.

"Yup. Guessed you were." Wade laughed.

Scout scrubbed his hand over Roy's head. "A hearty appetite is a good thing."

Roy's food consumption must have triggered a sudden growth spurt because he seemed to grow six inches taller. His expression glowed with satisfaction as he beamed at Scout.

Lucy closed her eyes and prayed for patience to speak only kind words when anger threatened to fuel a burst of hurtful things. Roy was ripe for trusting, hungry for affirmation. He would do well to seek it from someone besides Scout.

The men ate quickly then pushed aside their plates and finished their coffee. Roy ate twice as much as anyone else but still managed to finish at the same time.

"Good meal," Wade said. "Thanks."

Scout pushed to his feet. "I think I'll watch you lay out the timbers."

"You sure you're up to it?" Wade asked.

"I can sit as well there as in here." Her father headed straight for the door but Wade paused at Lucy's side. "We'll be out all afternoon but back for supper."

It both surprised and pleased her that he thought to

inform her. Just as he always spoke a word of thanks. She smiled. Her appreciation at his thoughtfulness sent a bolt of gladness to her lips. She didn't realize how eager she must look until Wade paused, his eyes wide, his gaze shifting from her mouth to her eyes and back.

Roy skidded after Scout. "Can I help?"

Wade dragged his gaze from Lucy. She felt an instant sense of relief. Or was it regret? He studied Roy. Roy had followed Wade everywhere since they first arrived so why he thought he should ask now...

Scout grinned at Roy. "We can always use an eager young fella."

Roy whooped, grabbed his hat and followed Scout outside.

"You'll be in the house alone," Wade said.

Again, his concern was such a marked contrast to Scout's unconcern that a smile settled in her insides even as it settled on her mouth. "I'll be fine."

He squeezed her shoulder before he followed Scout and Roy outside.

His touch remained, warm and steadying, after he left and she hummed as she gathered up the dishes.

A few minutes later Wade returned catching her still thinking of him. Her cheeks stung with embarrassed heat. "I thought you'd left."

"I have something for you." He grabbed her hand and led her to the back door and pointed to a triangle of metal he'd fastened to the corner of the eaves. "You need anything, you ring this." He handed her a length of metal. "Ring it until someone comes."

He'd thought of her long enough to make a way for her to signal him. She wanted to create a little room in her heart where the feeling she had this moment could last forever. She pushed reality to the forefront of her thoughts. "You think Smitty will track us down?"

"It's something we need to consider."

"I suppose it is. You keep an eye on Roy." She wished she could think of a way for him to signal her if he encountered trouble. But that was silly. He surely knew how to take care of himself.

He still stood on the open porch.

Slowly, first giving herself time to hide her concern or at least make it obvious it was only about Roy, she met his gaze. "Take care, hear?"

He brushed her cheek with the back of his finger. "You, too. Keep watch." He jumped off the porch and jogged to the low shed that served as the current barn.

She stared in the direction of the corrals, though her thoughts had gone on a trip that had nothing to do with horses or new barns. Something beckoned her heart. Something alluring and full of promise. She sniffed, realized she'd pressed her fingertips to the spot on her face Wade had touched and jerked her hand away. The only promises she believed were the ones in the Bible. What did the scriptures say? *Was God a man that He should speak and not do?* Even God knew the futility of trusting words given by a man.

Chapter Nine

Their days settled into an uneasy pattern. Lucy cooked and cleaned, did the laundry and every now and then found time to wander down to the creek drawn by the murmur of the running water and the cool breeze.

Scout had taken to going out every day and supervising the barn construction. "He does more than I think he should," Wade commented several times.

Lucy didn't bother to say that from her experience, Scout did far less than she thought he should. But then they were talking about entirely different things. Wade meant work and health; she meant time and interest. Again, she reminded herself, the past was gone. Done. She had only the future to consider but it seemed life was on hold—waiting for whatever came next. She wished she knew what it might be. She knew her future was in God's hands, but still she often felt a restless stirring deep inside as if there was more and she was somehow missing it.

She sighed. It was only because being here reminded her too keenly of the pain of her childhood and made her forget the strength she'd found as an adult. *God, help me keep my eyes on You and what You promise.* The words of a familiar verse came to mind, "Jesus Christ, the same yesterday, and today, and forever." And she was comforted and strengthened to face the uncertain future.

It had been a few days since Wade brought in meat. He'd been busy working on the new barn. She missed the fresh addition to the meals. The limited supplies in the cellar hampered what she could make. But she wasn't about to complain about the hospitality offered.

Wade and Roy had come to the house for a drink of water.

Scout came from the corrals. Lucy had noted how thin he was—the aftermath of his illness. Over the past few days his color had lost its pastiness and his step had grown steadier. "Hey, Roy, I've been looking for you. Thought we'd go hunting together."

Roy jumped off the porch so fast Lucy feared he might break something. He raced to Scout's side, bouncing up and down on the balls of his feet. "Can I shoot the gun?"

Scout grinned. "We'll see. You want to help saddle my horse? We'll ride double."

The pair headed for the corrals, Scout tipping his head to catch every word Roy said. Scout's attention was good for Roy. Lucy didn't resent it a bit. She only wished she'd had even a fraction of her father's attention when she was a child.

She turned away and met Wade's quiet look. Quickly she shuttered her regrets and hurts. It was the past. It had nothing to do with who she was today. Or what she needed. She corrected herself. She needed nothing except a place to temporarily hide from Smitty. Last night she'd made up her mind to see how things lay in that direction and had written Hettie, hoping to post the letter in the near future.

"I planned to go to town." Wade sounded regretful.

That's what she needed most right now—to restock the pantry and post her letter. "I could sure use some supplies. The way the three of you eat, the pantry is emptying out real fast."

He sat down on the edge of the porch. "Can't go now."

"Why not?"

"Can't leave you here alone."

She didn't have to ask why. Smitty might track them here. Or the Indians might visit. She wanted to say she could look after herself but truth was, she didn't fancy encountering Smitty or any of his cohorts while alone or otherwise. As to the Indians, Wade's assurance that they were harmless failed to ease her nervousness at being alone should they come calling.

Wade sat in dejected contemplation.

"I wouldn't mind a trip to town." In fact, it sounded like the best idea since cold water. She and Wade on a trip together. *Stop. You know why you're here and so does he.*

"It's not a good idea for too many folks to know you're here."

She suddenly wanted to go to town so bad she could taste the dust of the trail. "I can be very discreet."

He sighed. "I need to get a few more things before we can go ahead with the barn. I don't want to wait until tomorrow."

She knew he was thinking out loud and let him come to the only reasonable conclusion.

"I guess if we don't advertise your presence too

much you should be okay. You might enjoy meeting the woman who helps her husband run the store."

"Give me a minute to get ready." She rushed inside to get her letter. She told Harry and Hettie the whole story and knew they would keep her whereabouts a secret. They would also let her know if Smitty should move on or be arrested. If it was safe to return to Dry Creek.

She grabbed the only bonnet she'd brought and hurried out to wait for Wade who'd gone to get the horses. Only he pulled up in a wagon. Of course, he'd need something to carry supplies home in.

"I get to ride in style," she murmured as he helped her to the seat.

"I expect it will be better than Queenie."

She felt compelled to defend the faithful old horse. "I don't mind riding her."

"So long as you're not in a hurry."

She laughed and squirmed into a more comfortable position. No need to tell him she was in no hurry. This was the first time she'd been alone with him and she bubbled with anticipation. Perhaps they could talk about what they really wanted from life. Might be he wanted the same things as she.

Again, she drew a line across the path her thoughts headed down. She would not ever pin her hopes and dreams on what a man wanted or expected. Her father had taught her well the pain of doing so.

She sat up primly and faced forward turning her thoughts to the anticipation of a visit to town. "Tell me about the young woman at the mercantile."

He told her the couple had moved in and started the store six months ago, then he continued to describe the various businesses in town. She learned there was a supply store that brought in larger equipment from the east and lumber from the west. A school had been built the year before. She wished Roy had a proper home and could attend school. She'd fallen behind in teaching him to read and write and promised herself to tackle the job again.

They fell into pleasant conversation about barn building and the horses. They talked a bit about Roy. Wade wondered what happened to his parents.

"I don't think he remembers. Mr. Peterson got him from an orphanage to help with the work but he seems content to let Roy run wild so long as he does the chores. He doesn't feed him overly well or buy him clothes. Hettie found the pants he's been wearing and gave them to him."

"He needs a proper home."

On that she'd give no argument. But what a person needed and what they got were not always one and the same thing.

The conversation switched directions and nothing more was said about Roy's needs.

They drove into Lark. It was the first time she saw the town as they'd avoided it on their escape to the ranch. Now she had a good look. Two other wagons were tied at the side of the street as were several horses. Three men in conversation glanced up and nodded as they passed. She hoped they wouldn't take undue note of her presence.

The schoolhouse still looked raw and new. A scattering of houses stood behind the businesses. A new building gleamed white and fresh at the far end. "What's that?"

"Well, I'll be. Looks like the church got built. I wonder if they've started to hold services."

She promised herself she would find out and if she was still here come Sunday, she'd attend. Already she could hear the protests about keeping their presence a secret. But she didn't intend to be tied by a short lead rope. Not even for the likes of Smitty. What could he possibly do in front of a crowd of churchgoers? She shivered thinking of how alone she was at the ranch on many occasions.

But she would not let any man—not even an evil one like Smitty—make her afraid to live her life.

Wade pulled up in front of Lark Mercantile and helped her down. He escorted her inside and introduced her to Mrs. Styles. "Miss Hall is visiting her father."

He murmured low for her ears alone. "You stay here until I come back. Try not to talk to anyone else." His breath caressed her cheek and for a moment she forgot why he wanted her to be cautious, forgot they were not alone. She looked into his warning glance but for the life of her she couldn't get past how special it made her feel to have him want to protect her.

Then he was gone and she began to lecture herself for being so foolish. She didn't get a chance to finish as the woman he introduced came around the counter and took Lucy's hand. "Call me Marnie."

"And I'm not Miss Hall. I'm Lucy."

"How long are you here for? I hope you intend to stay. There are far too few women my age around."

She rushed on so fast Lucy didn't feel any need to answer her original question.

"Now what can I get you?"

Lucy produced her list and the letter to Hettie. Marnie talked nonstop as she filled the order. Within minutes, Lucy knew more about Marnie and her husband,

Ernest, than she knew about just about anyone else in the world.

Marnie ground to a halt and started laughing. "You can tell I've been missing company of a woman my age. Now tell me about yourself. Where are you visiting from?" This time Marnie waited for Lucy to reply.

Lucy chose a vague answer. "From the east."

Marnie asked several more questions then she repeated her earlier one. "How long did you say you were staying?"

Lucy simply said, "It's a short visit. I see you have a new church."

"Oh, yes. How exciting. This coming Sunday is the first service. We still don't have a minister of our own but a preacher is coming for the service. I'm so excited. We haven't had regular church since we moved here in February. Why you'll still be here, won't you? You'll have to come."

"I'd love to if it's possible."

"Surely they'll both come."

Lucy blinked. She hadn't mentioned Roy. Then she realized Marnie meant Scout and Wade. She didn't say anything about Roy. Best if no one knew he was there. Someone asking after a woman and boy wouldn't care about a woman alone. So she only had to convince Wade that the two of them could go without sparking any interest.

"Tell me what you think of the countryside?"

Lucy smiled. "It's amazing. I feel like my heart expands just to encompass all the space."

"Some find it lonesome but I see you're a true prairie spirit."

Lucy sobered. She would soon be leaving these parts behind and returning to town life.

"How is Scout's barn coming along?"

"I heard them talking about bracing the walls and something about a ramp to lift the rafters."

Boots sounded on the wooden platform in front of the store.

"It's Wade." Marnie giggled. "If I wasn't married to a very nice man I might be jealous of you."

"Why on earth?"

Marnie rolled her eyes. "He's such a good man and so dreamy." She leaned closer. "And I see the way he's looking at you."

Lucy had turned to watch Wade approach but at Marnie's words found a sudden need to study the display under glass before her. "You're embarrassing me," she whispered.

Marnie only laughed. "I'll behave myself."

Wade stepped through the door. "Are you ready to go home?"

Home? The word grabbed at her heart and squeezed. She drew in a long breath and told herself home was back in Dry Creek, not on the ranch with Wade where the wind blew through the house and the scent of wildflowers filled her day. "I've gotten all I need for the pantry."

"I'll get a few things." He went to the men's ready-made wear and pointed out a few items to Marnie. She added them to the order.

On the way home, the wagon groaned under a load that included more lumber and a healthy amount of food supplies including two dozen precious eggs that

Marnie had explained with a laugh were as scarce as hen's teeth. "You ought to get some hens of your own."

Lucy didn't bother to say she hoped to be gone before the two dozen eggs were used up. And she determinedly ignored the little tug she felt at the idea. Forcing her thoughts to other matters, she turned to Wade. "They're having their first church service on Sunday."

"That's good news."

"I'd like to go."

He gave her a startled look. "Do you think that's wise?"

"I thought about it. I figure if Roy and Scout stay home no one will think twice about Scout Hall having a visitor."

He swallowed hard. "So, just the two of us go to church?"

Did he anticipate the idea as much as she? "Can't leave Roy home alone."

"No, 'course not."

She couldn't explain why it meant so much but it did. She loved going to church. She needed to attend to center herself again.

"I'll talk to Scout about it. If he agrees…"

She resisted an urge to hug his arm.

It was Saturday and if Wade wanted to escort Lucy to church he had to talk to Scout about it. Perhaps the man would object, stating the obvious—too many people knowing she was here put her at risk.

He watched Roy and Scout. Roy had sure taken to Scout and—for that matter—Scout to Roy. The older man seemed to delight in spending time with the boy, teaching him all sorts of things like how to ride a "real" horse. That brought a chuckle from Wade and he couldn't wait to tell Lucy her father's evaluation of Queenie. Her gaze had drilled into his with amusement and something he could only take as resistance.

"Lucy, why are you so suspicious of everything your father does?"

"I don't want to see Roy hurt or disappointed."

"Don't see how having Scout spend time with him should do that."

She shrugged and started to turn away then spun back, her eyes blazing. "You've known my father what? Ten months? Give me credit that I might know more about him than you do."

A hundred arguments sprang to Wade's mind but he bit them back. He allowed only one to find words. "Seems to me recent knowledge outweighs the past."

She stared lead bullets at him but he refused to flinch or turn away. "What happens when Scout decides he's had enough of Roy?"

"What sort of answer do you expect? That Roy will suffer for it? Or will he be better for the time he's spent with Scout? Lucy, there are no guarantees in life. You just have to take it as it comes."

She gave him a look of pure disbelief. "Is that what you do? Just take what life hands out and never complain? I suppose that's what you did when your mother's employers called you a dirty little boy? Just accept it. Well, I don't intend to sit around waiting for people—or life—to hand me what they choose. I'll make my own way, thank you very much."

He stalked away. She made him sound like a scaredy-cat shivering in the shadows meowing a squeaky protest over unkind treatment.

Out of sight of the house and Lucy's snooping gaze, he ground to a halt. He did his best to avoid trouble. What was wrong with that? Did she see that as running from problems? He didn't figure they were the same thing. Not even close. A fool rushed in with fists bunched at every imagined slight. A wise man avoided confrontation.

He leaned against the rail of the corral fence as a pain shafted through him. She'd made it clear she needed no one. That included him. He hung his head and waited for the agony to pass. Finally, it relented leaving his mind cleansed so he saw things clearly.

He wanted a chance to explain to Lucy how being unobtrusive had worked in the past but he would never stand quietly by if she needed him for anything. He would give his life for her if necessary. No, that might not be a good thing to say seeing as she emphatically needed no one. But perhaps going to church together would give them a chance to heal the rift caused by their spat.

So he must talk to Scout. Hopefully, the man wouldn't object too fiercely.

He found Scout with Roy, showing the boy how to measure and cut a perfect forty-five-degree angle.

"Hey, Scout, can I talk to you a minute?"

"Sure thing." He turned back to Roy. "Finish what I've shown you and I'll be back." He followed Wade into the shade of the old barn. "What's the problem?"

"No problem. Tomorrow is Sunday and the church is finished in Lark. I thought I'd take Lucy to the service." He waited, expecting an argument.

"Roy?"

"I figure if no one knows he's here it will draw less attention to them. Thought you wouldn't mind staying home with him."

"Roy will be safe with me."

"That's settled then."

Scout nodded and hurried back to Roy who waited for him to check and approve his work. Wade stared after him, something vague and troubling scratching at the back of his mind. He couldn't bring it close enough to identify and with a shake of his head abandoned the nagging feeling.

Now all he had to do was announce to Lucy that he intended to take her to church.

He waited until after supper but before he could find the right words to say, Lucy collared Roy. "It's Saturday and you need a bath."

He looked liked she'd thrown a squirming snake at him. On second thought, he probably would have found that less disturbing. "Me and Scout have things to do."

"Fine. But before bedtime, a bath." She tipped her head and studied him. "And a haircut."

"I've got just the thing for you," Wade said, and retrieved a parcel from the loft.

Roy unwrapped the overalls and shirt Wade had purchased in Lark. His eyes grew wide. "For me?"

Wade nodded.

"They're brand-new." The kid sounded like the pockets were full of gold dust. "Thanks."

"You can wear them after your bath."

A rush of exasperation crossed Roy's teeth. "You sure do drive a hard bargain." And before Wade could do more than stare in surprise, Roy backed off the step, paused to give Lucy a fearful look then chased after Scout as if his life depended on it.

"That was very generous of you." Lucy's soft words of appreciation filled Wade with a mixture of sweetness and fear as he contemplated his next step. He needed a haircut as bad as Roy. Maybe Lucy would do him the honor.

The idea of Lucy cutting his hair filled him with a delicious sort of dreadful anticipation. He strode for the door and ducked outside before she could notice the sweat beading on his forehead. Getting her to cut his mop would provide a perfect opportunity to talk to her... though he couldn't think what they would talk about.

But he needed to clean up if he intended to go to the church service tomorrow. And he fully intended to. He looked forward with uncommon eagerness that to his shame had less to do with the fact they now had a church and a whole lot more to do with the idea of spending time with Lucy without Roy and Scout in attendance.

He snagged a bar of soap from the washstand Lucy had set up on the step and headed for the pump house. Realizing he needed clean clothes, he went back to the house. Lucy seemed busy in her bedroom and he slipped inside and up the ladder to get a clean outfit without her notice. He'd prefer to sit in a tub but the idea of stripping naked in the house went beyond his sense of modesty. There was no way he could assure himself of privacy with Lucy nearby, so he filled a bucket and stood in the crowded well shack to soap up from head to toe. He shivered as he poured bucket after bucket of icy water over him until such time as he deemed himself clean.

He'd heard Roy and Scout head out presumably to hunt. The pair of them spent an inordinate amount of time traipsing around the countryside but he understood their enjoyment of freedom. Besides, it provided him opportunity to talk to Lucy.

He heard her humming as he returned to the house and toweled the water off the ends of his hair and finger combed it into place before hanging the wet towel over the bushes. He made a great clatter on the stoop to announce his return.

She stood at the counter slathering icing on a chocolate cake.

"You sure put those eggs to good use."

She jumped. "Marnie said the ladies were all bringing something on Sunday so everyone could enjoy a celebration feast afterward." She paused. "I didn't know if we were going but figured the cake wouldn't be wasted in any case."

She finished the task and set aside the icing bowl. "I'll save this for Roy to lick out." She faced him directly, skimmed her gaze over him, and smiled as a drop of water made its way down his earlobe.

He swiped it away. "I heard you mention something about a haircut."

"Roy is in need of one."

"Maybe you could cut mine, too? I'd like to look decent if we're to go to church." His throat dried so badly he almost choked before he finished the sentence. Then it threatened to close off entirely when he saw pink color flood up her neck clear to her hairline.

She didn't answer.

He wondered if she had the same throat problem he

did. Perhaps it was something in the air. But he knew it was his heart causing the problem—he longed for her touch yet he feared how deep his feelings for her might go.

She sucked in air. "I've got no experience."

He assumed she meant at cutting hair. But he wished she meant at loving. He wanted to be her first love. Her last love. Her only love for as long as he lived. "I can hardly go to church looking like this."

She nodded, studying the hair at his collar with a great deal of fascination as if she couldn't bear to meet his eyes. "I can give it a try."

"Good." He looked around, unable to think what to do next.

"Grab a chair and park yourself on the porch while I get the scissors."

He took a chair outside and straddled it backwards, hitching himself to the rungs like they were all that kept him from drowning.

She came out wielding a huge pair of scissors.

"I don't remember seeing those before."

"Don't suppose you would. I found them with some cleaning supplies." The way she said it and the grin she flashed informed him that anything associated with cleaning would not have garnered his attention.

He laughed. "Guess we neglected the house some."

"*Some* must have a different meaning in your vocabulary than in mine." She spread a tea towel around his shoulders, patting it into place.

He closed his eyes wondering if he could bear the sweet torture long enough to get a complete haircut.

"You praying?"

He chose to let her think so. "I think I'm going to need divine help."

She waved the huge shears. "You aren't in any danger physically…" The scissors flashed like a sword. "But I did warn you about my lack of experience. But then I guess everyone has to start somewhere." And she grabbed a chunk of hair and snipped.

His nerves jolted at her touch. He shuddered.

"Oh, come on. You'll live. If it's too bad, you can wear a hat."

"Not in church."

"I guess not." Another touch. Another snip. He gritted his teeth. This haircut business was not one of his better ideas. He grasped at something else to focus on. Anything else. The price of tea in China. The number of steps to walk from here to Lark and back. How many spikes it would require to put the barn together.

She edged around to cut the front.

He lowered his gaze but nothing but closing his eyes blocked her from his view. Closing his eyes did not stop his awareness but spared him the strain of watching her.

Her fingers brushed his forehead, filling him with such longing he didn't know if he could bear it much longer.

Her touch teased as she grasped bits of hair and snipped. He tried to concentrate on the pieces trickling across his face.

"There. It's about as good as I can get it." She scooped off the towel and flicked it over the edge of the stoop.

He tried to pull his senses into order with very little success. Tried to think of one sane thing to say. He glanced at her, fearful she would misinterpret his silence but she stared away from the house, so still he wondered if she saw something. Smitty?

"What is it?" He leapt to his feet, sending the chair dancing across the wooden platform. He rushed to the corner to study the landscape. He saw nothing amiss, not so much as a skitter of dust that might suggest a rider. "Did you see something?" Nothing out of place so far as he could see. Only Roy and Scout together in the trees.

She nodded, her gaze riveted to the pair. "Looks like they're building a tree house."

He wondered at the way her words choked out and studied her more closely.

Her eyes had a faraway look, the skin around her mouth white.

He wanted to touch her, bring her back from wherever she'd gone but something about her posture warned him how fragile she was and he hesitated for fear of frightening her.

"I remember—" She swallowed hard. "A tiny window I found discarded in a back alley." She fell back a step, her hand pressed to her throat. "Papa was visiting."

He blinked at hearing her call Scout Papa.

"Mama was so happy. Happier than she'd been in a long time, laughing and joking, making special dishes for Papa. I figured he must be very important to merit this kind of attention."

"Lucy?" He reached out and touched her.

She drew back another step.

Regret filled his lungs, making it impossible to breathe. He told himself she was lost in another world, another time but his rationalization did not open his airway.

"I was seven," she continued, her eyes wide and unfocused. "And shy in front of the man I adored. I showed him the window I'd found and he said, 'Lucy Loo, how about we build you a playhouse?'"

She jerked her head and fixed him with a look that seared across his brain.

"I didn't care if he built an upside-down outhouse if it meant he'd spend time with me." She looked past him allowing him to suck in hot unrefreshing air.

"I waited for him to find time. I gathered up scraps of wood. I planned how I would decorate my house. How he would join me for tea parties. Every morning I rushed to the kitchen to see if Papa was up. I hung back waiting for him to announce this was the day he would work on the playhouse. But he didn't even see me. And then one morning he threw his saddlebags over his shoulder and said, 'I'm on my way.'"

Her chest rose and fell rapidly as if she were chasing after her father.

"What about your playhouse?"

She shrugged. "It never happened." For just a moment she met his gaze, let him see the unshed tears, the childhood pain and then her gaze hardened. "Now he's building a tree house for Roy."

She sighed. "Not that I care. It's too late for a playhouse. It's too late for tea parties. I no longer need or want one. I don't need—"

He watched the anger fade away to confusion. What had she been about to say? That she didn't need anyone? Hadn't she said as much already? And where did that leave him? "Thanks for the haircut. I think I'll look around."

He walked the perimeter of the yard to assure himself no one hung about.

Lucy called Roy and he and Scout tramped toward the house, Roy protesting all the way about the waste of water for taking a bath.

Scout ruffled Roy's hair and laughed. "Can't see it's going to hurt you any." Both he and Scout went inside.

Wade went to the tree house under construction. Had Lucy's ability to trust ended when her hopes and expectations had been dashed so many years ago? He couldn't believe it had. Wouldn't believe it. She only needed to see Scout had changed. And even if she didn't accept that, surely she could see she could trust him—Wade Miller. He never made promises he didn't intend to keep. Somehow, she must have seen evidence of that.

Wade remained among the trees, not wanting to face the others. He longed to see a change in the relationship between Scout and Lucy. For his sake as much as theirs. Perhaps going to church would push her on her journey.

He let anticipation smooth his thoughts. A whole day for just the two of them. He intended to use his time well. *Lord, speak to her. Help her learn to trust so she can see love is waiting for her.*

Chapter Ten

Lucy carefully avoided looking at Scout as he and Roy came inside. "Your bath is ready," she told Roy.

"Aww. Do I have to?"

Scout laughed. "A good soaking never hurt anyone."

"You gonna have a bath?"

"Not in here. I'm heading for the creek." Scout snaggled a bit of soap and a towel and strode out of the house.

Lucy's shoulders dropped three inches and she sucked in air.

Roy launched himself after Scout. "I want to bathe in the creek, too."

Lucy caught him and turned him about. "Maybe when you're older. Tonight you're going to scrub right here and I'm going to cut your hair."

Roy grumbled the whole time she scrubbed him. Once he was dried, and wore the new clothing Wade had bought, she sat him on the chair outside and tackled his hair. At least she could relax as she snipped his hair. Not like cutting Wade's curls, which had proved sweet torture. The rough texture of it, the warmth of his skin, the teasing awareness of his closeness.

Just remembering set her heart tattooing against her ribs. For a few delicious moments she'd forgotten her vow to need and want no one. Then she'd seen Scout with Roy and it all came to a sudden halt. Now her insides were as knotted as neglected yarn.

She finished the haircut and let Roy run off to find Scout. As she cleaned up the bath things, she wished it were Sunday already. Perhaps in church she would find peace.

Later, the house quiet and she in her room, she pulled out her mother's Bible. She wouldn't be able to sleep until she'd put to rest the myriad emotions tangling her mind. *Lord, speak to me. You have promised peace that passeth understanding. I could sure use some of that right now.*

She turned the thin India paper pages and tried to think where she could find what she needed. But not even knowing what it was she sought, she couldn't begin to guess where to look.

Closing the Bible and shutting her eyes, she paused, aching for the Lord to speak comfort to her soul. Then she let the pages fall open and lowered her gaze. She read Psalm one hundred and eighteen. At verse twenty-four, she stalled. *This is the day which the Lord hath made; we will rejoice and be glad in it.*

"Thank you, God," she murmured. This was what she needed to keep in mind. The past was over. Gone. Done with. It could hurt her only if she dwelt in it. Today was full of good things.

She was an independent young woman.

She and Roy were safe.

They were in a pleasant setting. She let her thoughts drift to her favorite spot by the creek, let them go further to the endless spaces of the prairie.

She had a friend in Wade and best of all—she gave a secret smile—she and Wade were going to church tomorrow.

She rose the next morning, eager for the outing. Not even the fact Scout didn't bother to glance at her, or note how she'd done her hair up with pins she'd purchased at the store dampened her enthusiasm. Long ago she'd accepted he didn't notice or acknowledge her. The fact had lost its power to sting especially when she saw the eager light in Wade's eyes.

Yes, this was going to be a good day.

We will rejoice and be glad in it.

A cool breeze and a cloudless sky promised a beautiful Sunday morning as Wade helped Lucy onto the wagon. He took his place at her side and smiled at her. She looked fine indeed. She wore a dress he'd seen before—a pretty red print with full sleeves and a lace-trimmed collar. He realized she had only three dresses with her yet she always looked as fresh as a newly blossomed flower. She wore her customary braid only she'd pinned it into a circle around her face that made her look elegant as a princess.

As she returned his smile the sun touched her cheeks with faint pink. "I'm ready."

He grabbed the reins. He'd been staring at her long enough to cause her both amusement and embarrassment. They rode several minutes before he could pull his thoughts into some semblance of intelligence. It wasn't that he didn't have things he wanted to say but his thoughts rushed the gate in general disarray.

"Nice day." It wasn't one of the things crowding to be said. It was a stupid, pointless comment. What other reply could she give besides yes or no? It got him not one inch closer to expressing the things crowding his heart. "I expect there will be a good turnout for church." And how did that help? He restrained a desire to punch the side of his head. *Think before you speak, man.* "Hope we don't have to stand outside." He stifled a groan. When had he become so thickheaded? He scraped his teeth over his tongue. It felt like his but it acted like he'd borrowed it from a dull stranger.

"I don't care so long as we can join in the singing and hear the sermon. I really feel in need of both."

He chortled. "Don't think you want to include me in the singing. I'll be content to listen."

She flashed him a sunny smile. "I can't believe you sing as bad as you say."

"Believe it."

"Someday I'll get a chance to judge for myself."

Their gazes locked at the promise of someday. His heart filled with expectation. Then she seemed to realize what she had said. Her expression tightened and she faced forward.

"Someday might never come." He tried to keep his tone light as if still joking about his singing but his thoughts had shifted to so much more than that and he guessed from her reaction hers had as well.

Again, he tried to corral his thoughts, chase them to the gate in an orderly fashion. There were so many things he wanted to say, ask, discover but he couldn't sort his thoughts into a row. Finally, one question surfaced. "What do you think of the prairie?"

"Lived on prairie most of my life but always in town. Never gave it much study until I came here. There's something about living where you can see for miles in every direction."

"You like it?"

"Yeah. I do. It makes me feel... I don't know. It's hard to explain. I guess I feel bigger, freer." She sighed expansively. "When I go back to Dry Creek I will miss looking out the window and seeing the openness. I can't even see out my window at Harry and Hettie's. It's way up toward the ceiling."

One anxious thought settled back in relief. He'd heard of women who hated the wide-open spaces. But Lucy gal would miss them. He hoped she'd miss a few other things, as well. Like maybe a certain cowboy.

"You don't have to go back." There. He'd brought it out in the open. His lungs refused to work as he waited for her reaction.

She laughed. "I have a job back there I like very much."

He sucked air over his teeth. That wasn't the answer he hoped for. He decided to push the idea a bit further. "Scout could use a full-time housekeeper. I guess you saw that soon enough." He barely stopped a groan. He didn't want her to stay to be a housekeeper for Scout. That wasn't his wish at all.

She studied him a full moment, her eyes steady and searching.

He let her look, let her gaze go deep into his soul

hoping, praying she'd see what he wanted to give her even though he had neglected to say it clearly.

She blinked and shook her head. "I can't stay."

"Because of Scout?"

She stared straight ahead. "Because of me. Because I will never let myself—"

He waited for her to finish but she sighed and said no more. After a few minutes he settled into glum silence.

Soon other wagons of various sorts as well as men on horseback filled the road. He hung back several yards from the nearest wagon to avoid breathing the dust getting kicked up.

He joined the parade down the main street of Lark to the church. "Where did all these people come from?" He had no idea there were so many in the area.

He found a place to leave the wagon and helped Lucy down. She carried the cake as she glanced around, her eyes bright as she took in the people hurrying toward the church. They made their way to the door, pausing often to meet and greet neighbors and friendly strangers. Someone took the cake from her and carried it away.

Inside the church, they squeezed into a pew. The few empty places filled up quickly. As Wade expected, latecomers would be left standing outside.

A very young man stood and introduced himself as the preacher from over at Big Springs. They had no organ or piano so they sang without the aid of instruments. Wade enjoyed the blend of voices—especially Lucy's clear sweet tones.

She shot him a teasing look as he sat silent, listening. The way she wiggled her eyebrows as if daring him to join in almost made him laugh. She'd regret it if he let out so much as one sour note.

The young preacher boy stood to deliver the sermon. Wade didn't expect the preacher had enough experience to have anything of value to say but within five minutes he realized his mistake. The man spoke of hardship and disappointments. He'd obviously had his share of both.

"They can make us bitter or make us better. We have the power to decide which. Don't let your problems drive a wedge between you and your loved ones. Between you and God. Choose forgiveness. Choose love."

Wade vowed he'd never let things make him bitter. *What if Lucy returns to Dry Creek and you never see her again?*

A deep bone-crunching loneliness hit him at the mere idea. *Lord God, may these words speak to her heart. Help her find a way to choose forgiveness.*

The service ended and the congregation moved outdoors where plank tables had been set up.

The men gathered in little knots as the women hurried to put out the food.

The young preacher called for their attention and offered up a prayer of gratitude for God's many blessings. Wade murmured, "Amen." God's blessings were beyond measure. And if God so chose, the blessings would continue.

His gaze sought and found Lucy, surrounded by a gaggle of women. He could enjoy seeing her every day of his life.

What would it take to convince her to stay?

Or perhaps he could find contentment at a job in some town for he knew despite her claims to a home and job in Dry Creek, she could not return while Smitty walked free.

But he knew it wasn't Smitty or the place he chose to live that created the barrier between them.

It was the feelings she'd stored up from her past— hurts and misunderstandings Scout had inflicted.

If only she and Scout could forgive the past.

Lord, show them the way.

As families with young children were urged to the front of the line, Lucy came and stood at his side. He ached for the right to touch her, pull her near, lean close and smell the honey scent of her hair.

But he didn't have the right and would not act inappropriately, shaming them both.

They filled their plates from the bounty. He made sure he got a piece of Lucy's chocolate cake then they found a place near one of the trees, clinging to the meager shade. Conversation lulled as people concentrated on the food.

Wade devoured Lucy's chocolate cake. "Mmm. Good."

"I doubt it's as good as Mrs. Adam's."

He remembered the cake she'd raved about at the literary evening back in Dry Creek. "I wouldn't know, having never had so much as a taste." He gave her a pained look reminding her how she'd hoarded the whole thing.

She giggled. "You'll have to take my word for it."

He sobered suddenly, reminded sharply of the issue of trust. "Lucy, if you say Mrs. Adam's cake beats this, I believe you. Maybe if I say this is the best I've ever tasted you'll believe me. Can you take my word for it?"

If she did it was a step toward trusting him on other things—like love.

She tipped her head and her eyes sparkled with mischief. "I guess I'd be willing to believe you haven't eaten a whole lot of chocolate cake."

He understood her qualified agreement. She could believe only a little bit. It was a start. He wished he felt better knowing it.

A gust of wind tore across the yard, picking up hats and bonnets and baby blankets. A black bonnet skittered by. Wade leapt after it at the same time as Lucy. They banged heads as they reached for it.

Wade grabbed his forehead. "Ouch."

Lucy grunted. "You have a hard head." She stumbled backward.

Wade grabbed her shoulder and steadied her. "Are you hurt?"

"I don't think so." She clung to his arm as the wind whipped about them tugging her braid free, sending pins scattering.

"Oh, no. I've already lost most of my pins."

He searched for them, found four and handed them to her. Their fingers brushed. He forgot the others. "Lucy—"

"My bonnet." An elderly lady hustled toward them. "You stopped it. Thank you." She fluttered her hands toward Wade. "Why you must be the young man who is working with Mr. Hall."

"Wade Miller, ma'am."

"I'm Mrs. Thomas. Widow Thomas. And this young lady is your wife?"

Lucy backed up in alarm. "Oh, no, ma'am. I'm Scout Hall's daughter. Just visiting for a few days."

Wade's feelings dropped into a bottomless cave. Did Lucy have to act like the idea of being his wife was a fate worse than hanging?

Widow Thomas narrowed her eyes and squinted at Lucy. "You're going to be married soon?"

"No, ma'am. I'm just visiting." She emphasized each word with a shake of her head. "I'll soon be gone."

Mrs. Thomas fixed a beady look on Wade. "I expect you'll persuade her otherwise."

"Yes, ma'am," he said. It was his heart's intention.

"No, ma'am," Lucy said.

The widow Thomas smiled at Lucy and patted her hand. "Welcome to the community. I'm sure you'll like it here." She donned her hat and marched off.

Lucy chuckled. "I don't think she got it sorted out at all."

"Guess not."

"What's wrong?"

"Did you have to make it sound like I have a dreadful disease or something?"

"I didn't."

Others were leaving. "Get your things."

She hesitated then went to the table.

He waited, took the empty cake plate and the eating utensils she'd brought and led the way to the wagon. He'd had other plans for the afternoon but now he couldn't wait to get home.

She settled on the seat and waved goodbye to the others. They headed out of town. "Wade, I was only trying to make her understand the truth."

"You did a good job." She might as well have signed and sealed his doom. Obviously, the idea of being his wife sat like a splash of sour milk in her thoughts.

She touched the back of his hand. "I didn't mean to hurt your feelings."

"Of course you didn't." She just didn't see past her own mistrust of commitment. "Do you plan to be single all your life?"

His question seemed to startle her. She started to speak and then paused as if she needed to consider the answer.

"I—I don't know."

At the catch in her voice, he reconsidered his plans. Perhaps she was in a mood to discuss things. He badly wanted to deal with the way things were between them though he wondered if the sweet tension he felt was one-sided.

He turned off at a side trail. She seemed not to notice. His anger melted at the misery in her posture. "Lucy gal, a person can get mighty lonely by themselves."

She huffed. "Guess you forget how many people come into the dining room each day. I don't foresee being alone a problem."

"How many of them keep you company in the evenings? How many care how you're feeling? Who takes time to listen to your concerns? Lucy gal, who holds you when you need it?"

The way she sucked her lips in, he knew he'd touched a raw nerve. He wasn't sure he liked it and reached for her hand. At first, she stiffened and acted like she would jerk away and then she settled into letting him hold it.

It felt as good and right as rain on a Saturday afternoon after the week's work was done.

"I'm not meaning to upset you. I only want you to see where your choices are taking you."

They neared the river and she sat up and looked about. "Never mind where *I'm* taking me. Where are *you* taking me?"

"To the river. Is that all right?"

"Don't suppose there's any need to rush back. The place got along without me before I came and will get along just fine after I leave."

It wasn't exactly the message he wanted to hear but he let it go as he pulled up by the trees and jumped down. She readily let him lift her down, apparently all discord forgotten in her eagerness to explore.

He took her hand and led her through the cottonwoods to the edge of the river.

She breathed deeply. "I love the sound of running water. Can we walk?"

There was no path but the grassy embankment allowed easy navigation. She continued to let him hold her hand and he simply enjoyed the moment. They came to a fallen tree. He planned to assist her over but she sat down.

"This is a really nice place."

"I agree." He was glad he'd chosen to come here. There was that word again—choice. Seems it had been a theme throughout the morning. "Did you enjoy the church service?"

"Immensely. You?"

"Very much. I wondered what such a young fellow would have to say but he delivered a good message."

"I agree."

He laughed at her imitation of his earlier response. "It's sobering to realize how profoundly our choices can affect our lives."

"What sort of choices did you think about?"

"One that came to mind for me was the one I made to live as my mother taught me even when I was among those who mocked my choices. I didn't go into town and spend my wages on drinking and carousing. I didn't buy silly things. I suppose in some ways that choice kept me out of trouble. I didn't mind the ribbing of the other cowboys not even when they called me a Goody Two-shoes."

She squeezed his fingers. "They teased you? About what?"

He shrugged. "I wouldn't swear. And I preferred to go to church instead of to the saloon."

"I guess the teasing must have hurt."

"At first. Then I suppose I got used to it. I did think a couple of times about pretending I wasn't a Christian but I always thought of how disappointed my ma would be and thought better of it. But still my faith seemed secondhand until this winter when I prayed and God rescued me. Now I'm learning to choose to trust God in my life." He turned her hand over and examined it, running his finger along each finger to her wrist. "You know when that preacher talked about choices, I thought of you."

She would have jerked her hand away except he suspected she'd try and tightened his grip.

"Are you going to try and change my mind about

going back to Dry Creek?" Her voice carried a challenge.

"Could I?"

Her gaze darted away from his then returned and remained, seeking answers.

He didn't know if he had them.

He read her confusion, her hesitation and her hurt then she shook her head and turned her gaze toward the water. He dragged air over his teeth and continued. "Because if I could persuade you, I would." How desperately he wanted to keep her with him forever.

Her lips parted but she didn't speak.

"Lucy gal, you know I want you to stay. Because I care about you." He'd said it plain. She'd have no mistake in understanding his feelings.

She held so still, so quiet he wondered if she searched for a way to avoid his words. Then she lifted her head and her eyes shone with what could be surprise or happiness. Either worked for him.

His gaze slipped to her lips. He lowered his head, didn't hide his intention to kiss her; gave her lots of time to stop him. She didn't. In fact, he knew he wasn't imagining how she leaned forward to meet him.

The kiss was short. It filled his heart with unfamiliar sweetness that rolled up his throat and flooded his brain. He couldn't stop smiling as he pulled back.

Her eyes were wide, full of surprise and delight to equal his own.

Then she gave a strangled cry and jumped to her feet.

Chapter Eleven

Lucy tried to run. The grass caught at her feet. She would have fallen except Wade caught her and spun her around to face him.

"What's wrong?"

She rolled her head back and forth. "I can't stay." She couldn't fall in love. She couldn't give the care and keeping of her heart to another. She knew too well the cost. Wade wasn't Scout but it made no difference. Loving, trusting, hoping, led to hurting and heartache.

"I'll take you home."

She didn't care if he thought she meant she had to leave the river or if he knew she meant the ranch. All that mattered was getting away from this intimate place. Only it wasn't Wade she needed to escape. It was her foolish heart. How could she have let herself slide into such a precarious state that she'd actually considered what it would be like to stay with Wade? She had even gone so far as to welcome his words. *I care for you.*

It was Widow Thomas's fault for going on about being his wife.

Only it wasn't. Her own foolish heart found something in Wade that she'd wanted all her life.

She wouldn't allow herself to think what it was.

Wade held her elbow as they retraced their steps. She would have to be in a semiconscious stupor to not notice she'd displeased him. She didn't care for his anger any more than his confession of love. She corrected herself. He hadn't said he loved her. Only that he cared. Well, no doubt he cared about his horse, too. She didn't need to read too much into it. Nevertheless, she wanted to put things back on a less emotional basis.

"Roy will fear he might starve if I'm not back to make supper."

Wade stopped moving and his grasp on her elbow stopped her, as well. "This has nothing to do with Roy."

"What are you talking about?"

"You're afraid to trust. You blame Scout because he disappointed you but the truth is it's like the preacher said—you've made choices and you cling to them."

She pursed her lips as anger surged through her. She sucked in air until she felt in control. "Well, Mr. Know-It-All, exactly what sort of choices do you think I've made?"

He leaned closer so they were almost nose to nose.

She would not retreat.

"Lucy gal, you decided to never trust another person—or maybe just another man. You decided you wouldn't allow anyone to get close for fear they might hurt you."

His words were so accurate she gasped and then pressed her lips together lest he guess he'd struck the bull's-eye.

He nodded. "And you haven't stopped to think it's keeping you from all sorts of wonderful things."

"Huh. Like what?"

"Like a chance to enjoy having a pa. Like a chance to be loved." He grunted and stalked away.

She stared after him. "Who says I want to be loved?"

He glared over his shoulder. "Everyone does."

She wanted to dispute his assurance but she couldn't speak as longing welled up inside her so insistent, so overwhelming she couldn't move.

He strode onward.

She pulled herself together and hurried after him. "Sometimes," she muttered, "a person has to learn to live without love."

She hadn't meant for him to hear and drew to a stop when he turned.

"No, a person chooses to live without love. And it's a mighty lonely life, if you ask me."

So, who asked you? She kept the thought inside her head.

His anger faded. He reached for her.

She knew she should back away, not allow his touch. It would upset her resolve. But she couldn't deny herself the contact. She'd learned to lock her emotions into a secure room but there were times she wanted things she'd denied herself, times when she simply ached to belong to someone.

"Lucy gal." His soft words almost broke down the locks on her secret room. "I must respect your choice. I can only pray something will change your mind."

Let him pray all he wanted. She couldn't see how it would change anything. Sometimes a person just had to live with what they were. But never before had she even considered she might need to change, let alone be able to.

Wade smiled and took her hand. "Come on. Let's go home."

Wade lingered at the table. Since their Sunday outing last week, he'd looked for every opportunity to be near her. He sensed a delicate change between them as if his words had challenged her carefully constructed fences.

She stood in the open door. He slipped over to stand behind her, needing to be as close to her as possible even though she'd done nothing, said nothing to encourage him.

He followed the direction of her gaze to where Roy and Scout worked on the tree house.

His glance at Lucy revealed exactly what he expected to see—hurt and confusion. He wished he could erase it with a touch or a kiss. "The barn is coming along great. The walls are about ready to go up."

She nodded.

"Scout knows his way around a hammer and a piece of wood."

Another nod. But he felt her careful attention as she tried to guess where he was going with this conversation.

"I'm learning lots from him. He's teaching Roy as they work on the tree house. The boy will at least know how to cut a piece of wood and nail it straight when they're done."

She didn't say anything but he felt her tension as if she wanted to and waited, giving her lots of time to speak her mind. And he prayed for God to open her heart to the good things about Scout.

Finally, she sighed. "I hope all he gets is some practical skills." Turning, she came face-to-face with Wade and her eyes widened.

If he wasn't mistaken it wasn't only surprise that filled her eyes. He was certain it was more when her gaze darted to his lips and her breath caught audibly. She swayed toward him.

He caught her shoulders and steadied her although he wanted nothing more than to pull her against his chest and promise her his love, his fidelity, his protection— everything he had and was. Caution stopped him. He understood she was dealing with choices made in childhood, realized they were hard to change. He didn't want to rush her as he had last Sunday by the river.

Perhaps if they could have gone to church again....

But without a preacher of their own, services were only scheduled for once a month.

Determination hardened her eyes and tightened her mouth. She stepped away. "I need to set the yeast for lightbread." She mashed the potatoes as if they deserved all her frustration and confusion, added warm water, two cakes of dry yeast and flour enough to make a runny mixture.

He'd seen his ma do this many times and knew Lucy would stir the bubbles down before bed and in the morning add enough flour to make bread dough.

Contentment seeped through his troubled thoughts as he watched her. Life should be like this—a quiet sharing of daily tasks, enjoying each other's company.

Roy raced into the house and guzzled a dipper full of water. "I'm going to put on the roof tomorrow."

Scout followed at a more sedate pace. "I'll have to go to town and buy some more five-penny nails for Roy."

Lucy's head jerked up. Her gaze bored into Wade, alive with relief.

Did she find Scout's presence so difficult to bear or—he licked suddenly dry lips—was she anticipating having Wade to herself? Roy couldn't go to town but one could count on him spending hours at his tree house.

Scout left early the next morning. Lucy watched him go without any regret. So long as he hung about, larger than life, his voice carrying to her from different areas of the yard, she could not put him from her troubled mind. Since she had attended church with Wade she'd fought hard for peace of mind. Her inability to trust her father—who had proved over and over he didn't want or deserve her trust—did battle with the things Wade had said about making choices that shut others out. And it warred mightily with the feelings harbored in secret places at Wade's kiss.

Since Sunday, Wade had seemed to forget they'd argued—for which she was grateful. He also seemed to have forgotten he'd kissed her. She didn't find that quite so acceptable.

Perhaps if they could spend some time together she might sort out her confusion.

She'd expected Roy to be occupied with his tree house. Instead, he produced a bat and ball.

"Where did you get that?" she asked.

"They're Scout's. He said we could play with them."

"We? Play?" Wasn't exactly what she had in mind.

"Sure. The three of us." He looked from Wade to Lucy, his expression eager.

Lucy glanced at Wade. Did she see the same hesitation she felt? Had he, too, hoped for a chance to be alone, to talk, perhaps kiss?

Roy rushed on. "We can play scrub, can't we? I seen some boys playing it in an empty lot back at Dry Creek. I wanted to join in but they didn't let me."

Lucy knew she couldn't say no after that.

Wade sent her a regretful look and shrugged. "We'll play with you." He caught Lucy's elbow as they headed to a level area a few yards from the house. "Do you know how to play?"

She laughed. "I know how to play jacks, jump rope, hide-'n-seek...." She trailed off after mentioning girlie games. "But I have also played ball a time or two in school."

"Good."

"Just remember how long ago it was."

"Oh, indeed. Years and years."

She giggled. "Seems like years ago. So much has happened." She draped her forearm across her forehead in a dramatic gesture.

"Now that's more like the Lucy gal I first saw." He caught her hand and swung their joined arms.

She scowled. "Are you saying I've grown sour and grumpy?"

He pressed his palm to his chest. "My dear, why ever would you accuse me of such a horrible thing? You've been the perfect model of sweetness."

"Huh." She didn't need him to point out that if not sour and grumpy, she'd been quieter than normal. But today would be different. She could relax with Scout gone.

Roy raced ahead and placed a piece of wood for the batter's plate and another for first. He tossed the ball overhead and swung the bat in an arc that went downward.

"I think the boy could use some coaching," Wade murmured. "Why don't you pitch and I'll show him how to bat?"

"I'll try but be warned that I throw like a girl."

His grin threatened to split his cheeks. "Can't hardly imagine why."

Laughing, she scooped up the ball and faced Roy. Wade stood behind Roy, wrapped his arms around Roy and grasped the bat, showing Roy how to hold it.

Lucy's first pitch was perfect—if Roy was ten feet tall. The next one better suited a grasshopper.

Wade straightened and tipped his hat back to scratch his head. "Here's the batter." He patted Roy's hat.

"I know." She scowled.

"Was wondering, is all. Seems you might of mistook something else seeing as your pitches were…a little wild."

"Watch this one." She narrowed her eyes and focused on the target area, determined not to let Roy's wide-eyed fright nor Wade's chuckle distract her. She threw the ball and it came within reach of Roy's bat. Wade helped him swing and the bat connected with the ball.

"Run," Wade yelled. "Go for first."

Lucy scrambled for the ball, waited until she was certain Roy would make it safely to the base then tossed it to Wade.

"You're safe. Now wait until I hit a fly ball and you can run home."

Lucy gave a long-suffering sigh. "I can see I'm going to be here a long time trying to get the pair of you out."

Roy giggled. Lucy winked at Wade letting him know she didn't mind one bit so long as Roy had fun.

Wade rolled his eyes. "You have to play to win."

"Oh, yeah." She threw the ball as hard as she could. A bit wild. In fact, it would have hit him if he hadn't jumped back and swung the bat at the same time. The ball went straight up and she ran to catch it. Play to win? She'd show him she could.

Wade ran toward first, hollering at Roy to run for home.

Her gaze on the soaring ball, she ran toward the batter's plate, crashing into Wade. He grabbed her, staggering as he kept them both from falling to the ground.

Her breath raced in and out more from the way Wade's arms felt around her than from her run. She forced herself to take slow easy breaths as her fear tangled with her reaction.

She could not, would not risk her heart. Even if she felt tempted otherwise. The pain was not worth the pleasure.

She pulled herself away from his grasp and returned to the game. They played until they were hot and sweaty then headed for the pump to cool off and get a drink.

Roy swiped his arm across his mouth. "That was fun. If we stayed here I think we could always find a way to have fun."

Lucy grabbed his shoulder. "We aren't staying. Once it's safe, we'll go back to Dry Creek or some place else." The words came by rote. Somehow she couldn't make them mean as much as they once had.

"I ain't going back. You can't make me."

"No, I guess I can't." Any more than she could prevent him from building impossible dreams based on what he might get from Scout. "But I'm not staying."

Roy turned to Wade. "I'm going to make her change her mind."

Wade chuckled. "How you going to do that?"

"She likes it here. I know she does. I seen the way she smiles when she looks out the window or stands at the door." Roy tipped his head as if studying the matter. "Guess I could do something to make her see what she'd be missing if she left." His face brightened. "Like bring her flowers. She loves the wildflowers."

Wade stared at the boy with respect. "Why, Roy I believe you've hit on an idea. You'll make someone a fine husband some day."

Roy backed away, a look of horror on his face. "I ain't never getting married."

Wade laughed. His gaze sought Lucy's, full of warmth and promise and—

She jerked away. "Can't live on dreams, Roy."

"Guess I can if I want. You the one what told me we all need to be loved. Well, I guess this is as close as I ever been." He stomped off toward the tree house.

Lucy wanted to call after him, warn him how he could be hurt. She turned to Wade thinking to explain her reasons but Wade picked up the bat and ball and headed for the house. He stored the equipment behind the door then leaned against the door frame and studied her.

She didn't move. Couldn't move as her thoughts zigzagged across her brain.

We all need love. Hadn't Wade said something like that? And hadn't she stubbornly insisted she didn't? Only it wasn't so much she didn't need or want love. It was she had so long denied her feelings she didn't know if she could change what she'd become.

Did that mean she had opened her heart to the possibility?

Lucy scrubbed at her eyes. If only she could go back and adjust her choices.

She wanted Wade to understand. "I don't want him hurt. Children don't have the wisdom of adults so they make choices that seem right in their inexperience. Later, they begin to see the foolishness of their choice. But sometimes it's too late to change."

She felt his careful consideration of her statement and appreciated he didn't immediately dismiss it.

"I understand how that could happen. A child thinks as a child. But an adult needs to put away childish things and reason as an adult."

His words both gave her hope and sent long fingers of fear into her bones making them ache. "Isn't that from the Bible?"

He gave a lopsided grin at her. "Loosely."

"Isn't that like asking a zebra to leave his stripes behind and become a donkey?"

"Not if he's a donkey in the first place and only thinks he's a zebra."

"We aren't really talking about donkeys, are we?"

"No, Lucy gal. We're talking about people." His eyes crinkled at the corners in gentle affection. "I think we're talking about you."

She wanted to deny it. "I don't know if I'm a donkey or a zebra."

His smile edged between her worries and her hope, blocking the former and allowing the latter to thrive. "You are a beautiful woman with a heart capable of loving and trusting. But you've locked that big heart of yours behind walls of fear and mistrust."

Beautiful? Big heart? Did he really believe that? "It's the only way I know."

"But you no longer need those walls."

At the way he smiled, silently promising so much, she sensed a crack threatening her secure walls. Was it possible for them to crumble? She recalled his words on their journey to the ranch, promising he would always be there for her. Were his words enough to enable her to demolish the walls? What happened if she let the barriers down only to find he didn't give anything more than her father had? From the depths of her soul she knew Wade did not deserve to be slipped into the same slot as her father.

"Lucy gal, you are an adult now. You can reason things through and change how you look at them."

"Is it possible to change?" Her whisper came from a secret place that still hoped and still ached for love.

Wade took her hands. "I wish I could tell you what you need to do in order to change but I don't know what you need. I pray you will find the way." He brushed his fingers over her cheek, pulling an errant strand of hair off her face.

She leaned into his touch as inside grew a shimmering sensation of possibility.

He kissed her forehead.

She closed her eyes. With his encouragement, she could face anything. Even her fears. But it wasn't enough. If she let down her barriers, she had to be able to face the consequences with or without his strength. Was she strong enough?

She kept her head tipped. She couldn't meet his gaze, couldn't let him see how vulnerable she was at the moment. It would take very little urging on his part to push her past the confines of her secure boundaries.

Chapter Twelve

Wade wanted to kiss away all her fears, get her to confess she didn't need a blitz of attention from Scout in order to realize she wanted to stay. He wanted to be the reason. He wanted to be enough. His thoughts jolted against his skull. He had always wanted to be enough. It wasn't as Lucy suggested—that he avoided confrontation. No. He simply wanted someone to value him enough that he didn't have to strive for recognition.

Only now the someone had a name—Lucy Hall. He wanted her to care enough about him that she didn't need a reason, no flowers, though he had no objection to that, no need for protection though he would gladly provide it.

He intended to protect her from Smitty should the need arise, even though Lucy quite certainly would say all this hiding and secrecy was only to protect Roy. She'd insist she could take care of herself. He chuckled.

She backed away and darted him a look. "What's so funny?"

He shrugged. "Everything about us. We enjoy each other's company, don't we?"

Her cheeks captured the heat of the afternoon in a flush of pink. She ducked her head. "I guess so." Then the Lucy he knew pulled herself tall, faced him straight on. "Yes. We do."

He glowed with victory at her confession and wondered if his face turned as pink as hers. "Yet we—" He jerked around at the sound of a horse approaching at a furious pace. Smitty? Had he found them? "Where's Roy?"

"At the tree house, I think."

He grabbed her arm and rushed her to her bedroom. "Stay here and don't come out until I say it's safe." He pulled the door closed and turned around.

To her credit she didn't argue but called through the door. "Be careful. Don't take any chances."

He stalled halfway through a stride. Her concern had been for him. She cared about him. He tucked the knowledge away in the back corner of his thoughts, grabbed the rifle off the wall and ran out the door. A glimpse to the trees. Roy safe in the tree house. "Stay there and be quiet." He strained toward the approaching rider. The horse was familiar. The rider, too. Scout? "What's wrong?" The man couldn't hear above the thudding of the hooves.

Wade raced to meet him, grabbing the halter to stop the horse as Scout jerked back on the reins. His mount was lathered, sides heaving. He'd been rode hard. "What's wrong?"

Scout swung his leg over the horse and ignoring the stirrups, landed on both feet with the strength and vigor of a younger man. No one would guess he was on the verge of death just a few short weeks ago.

"Where's Roy?" He didn't wait for an answer. "Roy," he bellowed.

Roy slid down the tree so fast Wade suspected he would have skid marks on his palms. He galloped to Scout's side. "I'm here."

Scout squatted and grabbed Roy by both shoulders, shaking him gently as if to assure himself he was in one piece. "Good boy."

"Scout?" Something had sent this man into a frenzied ride. Wade wanted to know what.

Scout ran his glance over Roy and scrubbed his hand across the boy's hair. Finally satisfied, he straightened and faced Wade. "Miz Styles at the mercantile says some men have been snooping around asking after a young woman and a ten-year-old boy named Roy."

Wade's insides exploded in hot fury. He'd been so busy thinking of a future with Lucy he'd plumb forgot the present dangers. "Smitty?"

"Can't say, having never met the man but Miz Styles said the one man was big with a mean look—"

Roy made a rude noise in the back of his throat. "That's Smitty, for sure. And probably Louie."

"I expect they've figured out where you are." Scout glanced at Wade. "Let's get this young 'un to safety." He nodded toward his horse, signaling Wade to bring him along. "I thought we could hide him back in the hills or—"

Wade didn't move. "Haven't you forgotten something?"

Scout continued on. "Hurry up, Wade. Who knows how much time we have."

"Scout, Roy isn't the only one needing to be protected from these men. You have a daughter who is equally at risk."

Scout ground to a halt. Slowly, he turned around. "I guess I forgot about her."

A sharp gasp drew their attention to Lucy standing on the step. Her eyes were wide and as dark as a thunderstorm. Her skin had lost all the pretty color of a few minutes ago. She must have heard every word.

Wade dropped the reins and took a step toward her. "Lucy—" He wanted to provide an acceptable reason for Scout's forgetfulness but what excuse could he have? The man thought of Roy but forgot his own flesh and blood. Wade recalled all the times he wondered if Lucy's perceptions were from misunderstood childhood hurts.

This proved they weren't.

He hurt clear through at all her years of pain. No wonder she was so cautious around Scout.

Lucy held up a hand. "Doesn't matter. I'm used to it. This is the way it's always been. I don't exist in his mind."

Scout shuffled his feet, glanced over his shoulder as if expecting Smitty and Louie at any moment. "It was only a mistake," he mumbled.

"Guess that makes me a mistake." She turned and stepped inside, closing the door quietly behind her.

Wade scrubbed at his chin. He wanted to hurry in and assure her she was no mistake. She was perfect in every way and especially perfect for him.

Scout jerked at the reins. "No time to deal with this right now. We have to be prepared for those men."

"Right. Do you have a plan?"

"I was going to hide Roy." He didn't go on. Plainly the man had no real plan.

"Look after your horse then come to the house," Wade said. "We'll discuss plans with Lucy."

"And me," Roy said.

Wade smiled. "For sure. This concerns you, too." He headed for the house as Scout turned toward the barn. What could he say to erase Scout's thoughtlessness? *Lord, show me if there's a way I can help her.*

He opened the door and stepped inside. He didn't see Lucy and called her name.

"I'll be right there." She called from her bedroom, and emerged a few minutes later, her eyes clear, her head held high. If she'd been crying she showed no evidence.

He sensed her fierce pride—protection against Scout's neglect. "I'm sorry."

She quirked her eyebrows. "Why? What did you do?"

"I'm sorry you heard that. It must hurt."

She wilted. "I wish I could say it doesn't. You'd think after all these years...." She didn't finish. Didn't need to. "So it looks like Smitty caught up to us."

"The man needs to be locked up." He couldn't understand why such a villain wandered free while good people ran for their lives. "Let's ask God to protect us."

"I'd like that. I don't mind admitting I'm a little scared."

He met her halfway across the floor and took her hands. They bowed their heads and he prayed aloud. "Our heavenly Father, we need Your protection today as we do every day but more so with Smitty looking for Lucy and Roy. Give us wisdom to outsmart the man."

He paused. He wanted to ask the Lord for something more. "Please heal Lucy's hurt. Amen." He opened his eyes.

She kept her head down. Her fingers squeezed his. Holding on. Taking something from him. Something he freely offered—his protection, his care. His love. He sucked back air. He would do everything he could to end this Smitty threat. Anything he could to help her get past the way Scout treated her.

For a moment, anger surged through his thoughts. How could Scout be so unfeeling? He intended to get an answer from the man. But first, they had to deal with Smitty.

Scout and Roy burst through the door. Lucy slipped her hands from Wade's and stepped back. He wanted to pull her to his side, hold her close but he sensed she wasn't ready to let anyone past her boundaries after what Scout had done.

Roy rushed to Lucy's side. "Smitty caught up to us."

She cupped his shoulder and smiled. "I know. But we'll be fine. So what's the plan?" The smile she gave Wade filled him with pride. She was willing to trust him, accept his help, admit she needed him.

Scout spoke. "You could hide somewhere." His gaze shifted to the trapdoor. "Maybe down there."

"Likely be the first place they look." Wade considered the idea. "Unless we throw a rug over it."

Roy stood in the midst of them, his fists clenched. "I ain't going be locked up. I was before. Didn't care for it."

The three adults stared at him in surprise. Wade glanced at Lucy, saw her concern. He spared Scout a quick look, saw concern and something more—perhaps sorrow?

Wade was sure all three adults were consumed with curiosity and sadness at Roy's announcement but it was Lucy who knelt before him.

"Roy, what happened?"

"It was a long time ago. Before Mr. Peterson took me. Some mean man locked me up at night to keep me from running away."

A moment of silence followed his explanation.

"I guess the cellar is out," Scout said for them all.

Lucy grabbed Roy's hand and they faced Scout and Wade as a team. "I'm through with running. Let Smitty come. We'll be ready."

Tough talk, Wade thought. "What if Smitty waits until we aren't ready?"

"Smitty isn't all that smart. He's just big and mean."

Wade wished he could believe Lucy but he'd met big mean men before and they had a cunning that defied reason.

"We need a plan." Unfortunately, nothing came to mind. There was no place to hide. Running would be futile. Smitty would just follow. He could give Lucy a pistol to carry but would she be able to shoot a man if necessary? It wasn't as easy as it sounded. He'd never been able to do it even though he'd felt the need a time or two.

He slowly turned full circle, considering all his options then came to a halt facing the other three, their gazes on him, waiting, expecting perhaps some sort of solution.

He found none. Mentally, he explored the options—

the loft perhaps? Too obvious. The barn? Again, too obvious. "Seems the best thing is to be prepared and confront them."

Lucy nodded. "My idea exactly. I'm not going to spend the rest of my life looking over my shoulder, afraid to go out in public."

Brave words. He admired her spirit but until Smitty was put away for good they would all live in fear.

"Hello the house. Anyone home?" A voice called from a distance away.

Roy jumped like he'd been attacked by the horns of an angry cow.

Lucy pressed her hand to her mouth, her eyes wide.

Scout reached for Roy and pulled him to his side.

Wade scowled at the man. Still worried more about Roy than his own daughter. "Don't think Smitty would be announcing himself like that. You all wait here while I have a look." He cradled the rifle in his arm ready for use and went to the door. A hundred yards down the trail a man sat on his horse waiting to be welcomed or not. "It's an old man."

The rider coughed fit to choke an ox. When he could speak he gasped, "Could you spare me a drink of water?"

Wade lowered the rifle. "Pump's over there."

The man rode wearily to the well, dropped to the ground as if it required his last ounce of energy. It seemed to take all he had to pump some water. He drank heartily then filled his canteen. "Much obliged."

"Where you from?"

The man wiped his arm across his forehead. "Heading for Canada. Heard there's places where the air is so clear it's like a mirror. I figure to get me some rest. Maybe get over this lung problem."

Wade felt Lucy crowding in behind him. "Poor man looks about spent. Could you use some victuals?" she called.

Wade struggled between sympathy for the weariness of the man and caution about inviting strangers into the house.

"We are instructed to entertain strangers," she murmured in his ear.

Remembering when she'd applied the admonition to herself and the delightful afternoon that followed, Wade relented. "You're welcome to come in."

"I thank you." The man left his horse at the corral fence and fair dragged himself to the house.

Lucy sliced bread thick, spread a generous amount of bacon fat on the slices and filled a cup with water. There were molasses cookies and she set the jar on the table, then stood back as the man sank to the chair.

"May you be rewarded for your kindness," he murmured before he tackled the food.

They stood back watching him. Wade figured the old man was harmless but his nerves twitched knowing not all strangers were so.

The man had another coughing spell. He drained the cup of water and still gasped. He held the cup out to Lucy. "Ma'am, I could sure use another drink."

"Of course." She stepped forward to take the cup.

With the slickness of a snake, he grabbed her wrist and leapt to his feet, all evidence of his weakened state gone. Before Wade could react, the man twisted Lucy's arm and yanked her against his chest. He pulled a gun from under his shirt and pressed it to Lucy's ear.

Wade growled as he surged forward.

Scout grabbed Roy and pulled back toward the stove.

"Hold it. Anyone move and she dies." The kindly old man had turned into a vicious thug.

Wade ground to a halt, his insides roaring with anger.

The man leered at Lucy, setting Wade's heart on fire. "Who are you?" she whispered.

"John Smith. Guess you know my brother, Eldon Smith, though you might better know him as Smitty."

Lucy gasped.

John Smith chuckled, a sound as menacing as a growl. "I told him we'd get you and that kid and then no one could say he acted other than in self-defense."

"He killed the man in cold blood. He's a coward." Lucy's voice rang with loathing and disgust.

"Lucy." Wade wanted to caution her to guard her words.

Smith jerked her arm hard making her groan. "You're in no position to be sneering."

Wade forced himself to remain still. He needed to think. Figure out how to deal with Smith. The man edged toward the door, keeping Lucy pressed to his chest. Wade eased after them.

"Hold it, mister."

Wade ground to a halt as Smith pressed the gun to Lucy's temple hard enough to make her wince. Her pain shafted through him like a double-edged sword.

Smith reached the door and kicked on it. "Come on, little brother."

Smirking, Smitty strode into the room, a pistol in his

hand. He looked around. "Nice job, Johnny boy. Very convincing old man." He squinted toward Scout. "Send the boy over here."

Scout shook his head. "He's just a kid. Leave him be."

Smitty grunted. "Ain't leaving no kid to spread lies about me."

Roy started to sputter. Scout silenced him with a touch.

Wade's mind raced. The odds were stacked against them but he would not let this pair take Lucy one step farther. What he needed was a diversion. *Lord, help us.*

He held Lucy's gaze sending silent messages of assurance. Hoping she read his love, his promise to stop these men. Her eyelids flickered. She darted her gaze to one side, widened her eyes and looked expectant.

What was she trying to tell him?

Again her gaze jerked to his right, down toward his feet then returned, eyes wide and demanding.

He didn't move but slowly shifted his eyes to the spot she indicated. A length of yarn went from the chair leg beside him. It was taut, leading toward Lucy's room.

He met her gaze again, saw that this was what she wanted him to see. Silently, slowly, cautiously he shifted his gaze toward Scout and tipped his eyeballs toward the yarn. Scout saw the yarn and indicated with a flick of his eyelids that he saw it.

Wade hesitated. He didn't know what Lucy had in mind but he knew when he moved all of them would be in danger.

"Give me the kid." Smitty reached past his brother.

Now was the time to act. He caught his boot on the yarn and kicked. A great clatter sounded in the bedroom and both the Smiths jerked their attention toward the noise.

It was all the distraction Wade needed. He leapt across the room and caught Lucy who had used the moment to escape her captor.

Wade grabbed the rifle where he'd left it when he invited the "old" man in and ducked out the door all in one movement.

He'd caught a glimpse of Scout moving, hoped he managed to relieve Smitty of his gun.

The Smiths roared in unison, a sound that tingled the skin on the back of Wade's neck and made Lucy tremble. He pulled her close. "I've got you." The way she held on, he wondered if she didn't have him.

They pressed to the warm boards of the wall and edged along the wall. A gunshot rang out.

Lucy gasped.

They reached the window and Wade eased over the ledge to have a look. He couldn't see well enough and pressed closer.

Just then, Lucy gave him an almighty shove tumbling him clean off the stoop. A shot rang out. Then another.

"Lucy," he roared as he rolled to his stomach and bolted to his feet. "Lucy."

She lay faceup on the stoop.

Both Smith men came from the door, Scout holding the men's own pistols at their backs.

Wade rushed to Lucy's side, bent over, afraid to touch her. He skimmed his gaze over her body, saw no blood. "Lucy." The word tore flesh from his throat as he forced it out.

She groaned. "Help me sit up."

He sat because his legs had gone weak as butter and pulled her up facing him. "Are you hurt?"

Leaning forward, she gasped for air. "Knocked my breath out." She blinked and rubbed the back of her head. "Oww."

Relief left him weak, then surged through him in waves of foreign emotion. "Why did you push me? Were you trying to kill me?"

Scout chuckled. "Think she might have saved your life. This old codger was all set to shoot you. Good thing he ain't too quick or he might have hit something besides the roof."

Wade glanced up and saw the bullet hole over his head. That would be the first shot he heard.

"Good thing I was quick enough to get Smitty's gun. I stopped him from getting off another shot."

"You shot my hand." Smith groaned in pain but Wade felt no sympathy.

He turned to Lucy. "You fool woman. You might have been killed."

Her grin was very wobbly. "It never crossed my mind. I only thought of him shooting you."

His insides melted. Her only concern had been for him. She cared about him. His nose stung, his throat tightened. His heart pounding against his ribs, he pulled her into his arms.

"Save that for later," Scout growled. "I could use some help getting this pair into town."

"Riders coming," Roy called from inside the house.

Wade sighed. "Used to be a quiet little ranch."

Lucy giggled. "You mean before I came?"

He allowed himself to run his hand over her hair and

along her cheek, all the time looking deep into eyes as gray as morning fog across the plains. He kissed her sweet little nose then pulled her to her feet. "Guess I better see who it is."

He rescued the rifle and strode around the corner of the house. "It's the marshal and some men," he called to the others. When the knot of men reined to a halt before him, the marshal nodded. "You happen to see a couple of strangers around here? Smith by name?"

"As a matter of fact…" He indicated over his shoulder.

"Everything all right?" the marshal asked.

Wade grinned. "We're all safe."

"I'll take those two off your hands." He signaled a couple of the riders who dismounted and roughly grabbed the Smiths.

The marshal dismounted slowly. "Care to tell me what happened here?"

"We'll be glad to," Wade said. And then he could turn his attention back to Lucy—his sweet, brave Lucy.

Chapter Thirteen

Lucy wanted to make coffee and serve the marshal as he sat at the table but every time she stood, her legs buckled.

Wade pressed his hand to her shoulder. "Sit. I'll make coffee."

"I doubt your statement will be needed but just in case.…" The marshal signaled for paper and pencil from one of the many deputies. "Seems his accomplice, Louie, was getting nervous. Hinted to the sheriff he might have valuable information in exchange for an easy sentence. And then he was shot. Smitty didn't know there was a witness which is why he was after the two of you, wanting to make sure there was no one alive to testify against him."

Her hand unsteady, Lucy wrote out a statement of what she'd seen. Roy insisted he would do so as well.

Then the marshal wanted to know how they had captured the pair.

Wade laughed, his gaze warm and admiring as he told of the yarn Lucy had fastened to the table leg. "What made you think to do that?"

She shrugged. "I only wanted a way to signal you if they showed up and I couldn't get to the triangle. I didn't intend to let them take me without a fight."

"It saved all our hides."

"You sound like a spunky woman," the marshal said. "We could use the likes of you in the country." He folded the finished papers and tucked them into the inside pocket of his vest. "I think that will be the last you hear of them."

He left with his posse, the Smiths securely escorted.

Wade, Scout and Lucy sat at the table sagging with relief.

"Glad that's over," Wade said. He ached inside and out. He wondered if his heart would ever stop rattling against his ribs.

"Can I go out to the tree house?" Roy asked.

The three waved him away.

Lucy sighed. "Wish I had the energy to run and play."

"How's your head?"

She rubbed it gingerly. "It's fine. The emotional stuff has left me drained though. You know, being so scared and so…" She shrugged.

He guessed from the way she avoided looking at Scout that she meant the words she'd overheard. Seems from what was said then and probably on other occasions that the words and deeds had built brick after brick. No wonder Lucy had such thick walls around her heart.

And he didn't want them there. He wanted nothing separating him from her caring spirit he had glimpsed in the way she dealt with Roy, the way she laughed at

life and especially—his heart picked up pace again—
the way she had so readily risked her life for him.

Seems it was time to probe the wound and pull out
the festering thorn. "Scout." He gave the man a steady,
no-punches-pulled look. "You plumb forgot Lucy when
you came from town."

Scout stared at his hands hanging between his knees.
"It was a mistake," he mumbled.

Lucy's hands clenched together. "Leave it, Wade.
You can't change history."

Wade shook his head. "At the very least you deserve
an explanation." He stared hard enough at Scout to light
a fire on the top of his head, which was all he could see
as the man hunched over his lap. "Scout, is Lucy right?
Do you consider her a mistake?"

The man didn't move and the silence hung between
them like a dirty, smelly rag.

"Don't you think she deserves more of an explanation than you made a mistake?"

Still no response and Wade waited, determined the
man would give Lucy some sort of answer. Then Scout
shuddered. "It was her mother's fault."

"Tell her. Not me."

Scout shifted so slightly a person could have missed
it. As if it hurt him to actually face her. Had he always
treated her this way?

Lucy did not want to hear this. He'd provide excuses
which would only make her feel worse, not better. The
past was done. She wished she could cover her ears and
block out his words. *Lord, You can make deaf ears hear,*

*please make my hearing ears deaf. Guard my heart
from the hurt he'll give.*

Scout continued, totally unaware she didn't want to
hear anything he had to say. "That woman was always
pushing at me. Wanting things I couldn't give her. She
used to be a wild as…." He shrugged as if he didn't
want to remember or perhaps didn't want to tell Lucy
the truth.

"She always said she had a life before Christ that
she wasn't proud of."

He nodded. "She wanted to get married. Figured if
she tricked me into making a baby with her, I would.
That's how you was born."

"So, I was a mistake. At least Mama had the decency
not to tell me so." She couldn't keep the bitter note from
her voice and when Wade reached across the table for
her hands, she pulled them to her lap. She needed no
one's pity. She'd faced the shame of being born out of
wedlock long ago. "Good thing God sees me with eyes
of love not condemnation or regret." There were times
she'd doubted that, but lately she had grown more certain of it.

"It wasn't because of you exactly," Scout murmured,
still not able to look at her. "I just wasn't ready to settle
down. I wasn't ready to be a husband, let alone a father."

Lucy said nothing. No need to tell her that. He'd
made it as plain as the dirt on which they walked every
day.

"Then one day I realized I was."

"Was what?"

"Ready to be a husband and father. I found this
place. Built this house. Even got myself some cows."

He looked at Wade who watched them with a certain caution as if he wondered at the tension between them.

She would never be able to adequately explain how it felt to wonder if her father even saw her, and now to have it confirmed that he considered her a mistake… well, it burned all the way down her insides until it stung the soles of her feet.

Scout sighed. "Then I heard that Margaret had died. I realized I'd waited too long to get myself ready."

"You never came to the funeral."

"'Twas too late when I heard and I couldn't face my failures. Seems I've built my life on them."

She stared at her father. He had regrets?

"I guess I mourned Margaret for about six months then I realized my plans didn't have to end. I had a daughter. I figured I would get you to come and give you the home I never had."

"It was way too late. Besides, why would I even consider the idea? You never saw me when I was a child. Or perhaps—" She thought of his recent words. "Perhaps you saw me as a mistake. Seems you can't look at me, see me any more now than you could when I was growing up."

His head jerked up. "I saw you. I memorized every detail of you. Why, I remember the way your hair hung down in twin braids that flipped against your back when you ran. Seems you ran everywhere."

He sure had a strange way of showing his notice. "You hardly spoke to me. Never even said goodbye when you rode out. Did you know I used to stand with my nose pressed to the window, my tears fogging the glass, wishing, hoping, waiting for you to just once turn around and wave?"

"I had nothing to give you. Just as I had nothing to give your mother. That's why I wanted to get this house and ranch into shape before I sent for her—and you."

Lucy sent a silent appeal to Wade. Hearing her father confess his feelings of inadequacy, seeing the defeat in his eyes left her floundering for solid ground. How did she deal with this?

Wade smiled so gently, so kindly she felt even further off-kilter.

"I didn't know how to deal with a little girl. Skirts and bonnets and pretty shoes. I couldn't face you because I knew I failed you. I guess it became a habit."

Fury as pure and unfettered as the prairie wind raged through her turning up debris of her past, boulders of the present. "Habit," she spat out the word. "Please don't excuse your neglect as habit. It was hurtful. Still is." She sprang to her feet. "Look at me. Really look at me."

Scout did so.

She felt Wade's surprised stare as well, but she held Scout's gaze in a demanding lock.

"See me. Do I look like you or my mother? Am I plain or pretty?" She closed her eyes. "What color are my eyes?"

She gave him a second to answer and when he didn't, she opened them again and blazed him with a mixture of fury and sorrow. "I'm real. I'm a person. Not a mistake. Pinch me, I hurt. Treat me like I don't exist and I hurt." Her breathing became ragged. "I deserve to be seen and acknowledged." Her anger fled, leaving her weak and teary. She would not let one single tear escape. She would not reveal a bit of weakness.

Letting out a huff of air, she turned and headed toward the stove. She'd cook. That would relieve some tension but she didn't make two steps before Scout caught her hand.

"You have your mother's eyes. They're gray though they darken to almost black when you are angry. Like right now. But you have my chin and my temper. Heaven help us both. I have avoided you because I know how big a failure I am but when I thought Smith had shot you… Well, I realized if I didn't change, it would always be too late for us just like it is for your mother and me."

Lucy stared. "You know you spoke more words to me in that little speech than in my entire life."

His smile was tenuous. "I can't make any promises but perhaps you'd give me a chance to try again?"

She studied him for one full minute, searching for sincerity in his gaze. She thought she found it but she wasn't prepared to throw caution out the door. "I'll try, but I've been disappointed so many times."

"That's all I ask." He pushed to his feet and headed outdoors, his gait slow and measured as if he suddenly felt sick.

She could only hope the realization of how his treatment had hurt her would have some affect on him. Then she remembered Wade and turned to him.

"It's a start," he said. "It's up to both of you to make it work."

She studied him a long time remembering his protective arms around her, how she'd clung to him. From the way heat stole up her neck, she knew her cheeks blazed with color and she ducked away.

He'd cared enough to protect her. He'd cared enough to try and resolve the strain between her and Scout.

He cared. Sure he'd said it already but his actions had more than proved it.

She didn't know where to look. Couldn't meet his eyes. Couldn't let him see how she glowed inside. Couldn't let him guess the reason.

He headed for the door. "I better go check on the horses." He squeezed her shoulder as he left, and he might as well have squeezed her heart the way it blasted blood through her veins.

The feeling around the table as they gathered for supper rang with victory. Smitty would no longer haunt their thoughts. They had all lived through the ordeal. And Lucy had learned some things about Scout she hoped would make it easier for them to be father and daughter.

She felt a bit of strain as she watched him across the table. But when he looked at her of his own accord for the first time in her life, she felt like she was truly his daughter.

She returned his smile then shifted her gaze to Wade. He smiled as if he shared her well-being.

She owed him for helping them to this fragile place. Somehow, she'd find a way to thank him.

Roy gobbled up his food with his usual gusto then shoved from the table and dashed outside before she served dessert.

"Are you sick, Roy?" she called.

He raced back inside with an armload of wildflowers that he placed in her lap. "For you."

"Why, thank you." She buried her nose in the lovely bouquet.

Wade laughed. "You don't waste any time, do you?"

What an odd comment. "What do you mean?" Then she remembered how Roy planned to persuade her to stay here with gifts and burst out laughing.

"Is this a secret joke?" Scout asked, confused why they should laugh at a handful of wildflowers.

Wade and Roy explained Roy's plan.

Lucy kept her face buried in the flowers. There was no reason not to return to Dry Creek now but she didn't want to go. She and Scout were just beginning to discover what they'd never had and then there was Wade. She wanted to see what would happen to this tender feeling between them.

Something had shifted in the last few hours in her feelings for Wade. He cared. She knew it, believed it. But she wasn't quite sure she was ready to let down all the barriers around her heart.

Next morning, Wade stared out across the corral fence. He had promised to help Scout with the construction of the barn. It would soon be completed. After that he had no reason to stay. But he didn't want to leave. He'd fallen in love with the land. He hadn't thought much about settling down until recently, but now he couldn't imagine continuing his nomad way of life.

He wanted a farm of his own. He thought of the few dollars he'd managed to save and knew he would not be purchasing land. He'd have to homestead. Maybe he'd see if he could find land close to Scout so Lucy and her father could learn to appreciate each other.

Whoa there, cowboy. How had he gone from thinking of being a landowner, to building a home for Lucy?

But that's what he wanted.

He'd fallen in love with Lucy and wanted to make a home and share it with her.

Roy, too. He had no objection to making the boy part of their family.

Wade knew Lucy cared for him. She'd made that plain enough. But whether or not she was ready to trust her heart to the love of another person—specifically Wade Miller—was another question entirely. And the answer might not come immediately.

He caught a glimpse of movement and turned to watch Roy scrounging for more flowers. The boy had the right idea in trying to convince her to stay.

Wade leaned more heavily on his arms. He could bring flowers. But he wanted to show her his love of the land. Create in her a need to share that love, share his love, build a home together.

He thought of his favorite place. "I'll show her that and she'll for sure want to stay."

He wandered into the house to speak to her. Her braid flew as she hurried to the stove to tend a pot.

His mouth dried, his intentions wilted. What if she didn't want to ride to the hill? Didn't want to spend her life with a rancher or—if he must homestead to get land—a farmer? He grabbed a drink of water.

She smiled at him, setting his heart to racing. "Supper will be about an hour. I'll ring the triangle when it's ready."

He carried her smile under his heart as he returned to work. He almost hummed but knowing how the sound affected both man and beast, he contented himself with smiling as he worked on the barn.

Scout had disappeared on some mysterious errand and Roy still picked wildflowers so Wade could enjoy his pleasure privately without anyone commenting on his foolish grin.

The hour seemed like three. He glanced at the house every few minutes wondering why she didn't ring the triangle. Instead, he watched her dart in and out, tossing water to the grass, draping tea towels over some low bushes and generally flirting with his thoughts.

Knowing she was safe now that Smitty and his brother were guarded by the marshal and several deputies made his pleasure grow.

But wanting to spend every minute with her formed a much larger, more demanding urgency. He tackled a spike, driving it home in bone-shuddering blows. Wouldn't be wise to build dreams as big as this barn until he knew if Lucy gal loved him and shared his hopes for the future.

When the triangle finally clanged, Wade threw down his hammer and, restraining his stride to a quick walk, headed for the house. Scout had returned a few minutes ago and fell in beside him. Roy skipped toward the house, his arms full of flowers.

Lucy fed them another fine meal. Her biscuits and browned gravy certainly filled lots of empty corners in his belly. But as his stomach filled, his heart grew hungrier. He wanted to speak of his feelings. Yet, every time he thought of it he almost choked.

Roy ate six biscuits drowned in gravy before he came up for air. "Lucy's a good cook, ain't she?" He didn't wait for the obvious answer. "I'll bet you wish she could stay here forever."

Wade dare not look at anyone for fear they would see his longing. But he felt Scout's surprise. The man sucked in air for a full twenty seconds. When he spoke, his voice had a deeper than usual tone. "Sure could use a woman's touch around here," he managed. "Besides, I always figured this would be her home."

Lucy laughed. Wade thought she sounded more surprised than amused. "I'd say more than a touch is needed. Try good old-fashioned lye soap and a generous amount of elbow grease. I practically worked the skin off my fingers scrubbing everything." She held out her hands for inspection. "Look. I'm still wrinkled like a prune."

One glance. Just at her hands. That's all he'd allow himself. If he looked at her laughing eyes, her teasing smile, he feared he'd embarrass them all by blurting out the words blazing across his mind. *Stay, Lucy gal. Stay. Let me marry you and make you a part of my life forever. I know I could make you happy. You sure do make me happy.*

Wade busied himself swiping up the last of the gravy with a bit of biscuit. He sat back and smacked his lips before he raised his eyes to glance at her hands. Despite his decision to limit it to that, his stubborn eyes did what they ached to do—they sought her face.

She smiled at him. Teasing? Maybe. But maybe something more. Something that flooded his heart with hope. "Lucy gal—" He stopped his mouth before the secret words erupted.

She watched, waiting for him to finish.

He swallowed hard, grabbed his glass and downed water like he'd stepped from the heat of a burning building. *Say something, man. Don't act like such a dolt.* "Lucy gal, I promised I'd show you the big hill. I'll saddle the horses and take you there this evening." There, he'd managed to say the words without making a fool of himself.

Her eyes flashed. She smiled. "I'd like that."

He hoped his grin was the only outward sign he gave of how happy her agreement made him.

"I'll have to do dishes first."

He'd always hated doing dishes but it suddenly seemed like the best job in the world. "I'll help."

She produced a pudding for dessert.

Roy spoke for all of them as he gobbled his down. "This tastes real good. Is it all gone?"

Lucy laughed. "One thing about you, Roy. You never complain about food of any sort. You'll be glad to know I saved the pot for you to clean out."

Roy rushed to the cupboard and tackled the job.

Wade grinned at Lucy. "You probably won't have to wash it when he's done." His heart forgot to beat as Lucy's amused gaze caught his. It took every ounce of inner strength to turn away before he did something foolish like blurt out his deepest desire—to be able to show her his love for the rest of their lives.

Roy ran his finger around the pot one more time and licked off every bit of flavor. "I guess there ain't no more."

Scout scraped his chair back. "Soon as you're done there, young Roy, we'll go see if we can scare up some meat."

Roy immediately brightened. "I'm done already." He hurried to the stoop and waited.

Scout took the rifle from its mount. Lucy gathered up a handful of dishes. Scout paused at her side. He seemed to search for what he wanted to say.

Lucy waited, keeping her gaze on the plates she held.

"Lucy, your ma would be proud to see how you've grown up." And then he was gone.

Lucy stood motionless until the clatter of boots died away and then sighed and headed to the stoop and the dishpan.

Did she find Scout's faint approval satisfying or hurtful? Wade could guess until the cows came home but only Lucy knew. He followed her to the stoop, his arms full of dirty dishes. He snagged a towel off the bushes and dried as she washed.

He felt her tension, knew to mention it would likely make it worse. A person needed time to gather up hurt and disappointment and put it into perspective. He waited for her to break the silence if she so chose. He didn't mind if they talked or not, her company was enough for him.

He dried the dishes as she washed then flipped the towel back to the bush to dry. "I'll get the horses."

As he saddled Two Bit and a reluctant Queenie, he prayed. For healing the rift between Lucy and her pa, for wisdom and patience to let God do His work. God knew better than he how much she needed to sort this out so she could learn to trust another man—not just any man, of course. Only him.

He led the horses back to the stoop where she waited. She looked so pretty in her brown cotton dress. His heart kicked into a gallop as he led her toward Queenie, her hand in his—cool and soft. He caught her around the waist and half lifted her into the saddle. For a heart-beat he considered forgetting about the horse, the saddle, even the ride, wanting to pull her into his arms instead. Thankfully, his arms obeyed his head rather than his heart and he released her as she settled and took up Queenie's reins.

He promised himself he would be sure to lift her down when they got home. And if she happened to tumble into his arms it wouldn't be his fault. He'd find it unobjectionable in every way.

He swung onto Two Bit's back and, ignoring the way his horse tossed his head in protest, kept him to a pace that matched Queenie's lumbering gait so he could ride at Lucy's side. His heart flooded with feelings and longings for which he could not find words. Probably a good thing. Instead, he spoke of the things he found familiar and safe.

"The grass here looks dried but it's full of nutrition. Cows do well on it."

"Seems so dry. Where do the animals get water?"

"The creek, plus there are several springs that Scout dug out so we get a nice flow."

She looked about in interest. "Lots of wildflowers."

He hadn't paid any attention before being mostly interested in grass and game but now he looked and sure enough, bits of color dotted the prairie.

She pointed out every new type she saw.

Seeing her pleasure filled him with such sweetness he felt like he breathed in honey.

They didn't take a direct route to their destination.

He wanted her to see everything, but eventually he angled toward the highest point on the ranch.

"You can't tell we're climbing, can you?"

She laughed. "Queenie makes every step feel like she's scaling a mountain."

"She's rough all right. Do you want me to ride her?"

"Oh, I'm not uncomfortable. I only meant she acts like such a martyr, but thanks for offering." The look she gave him made the sun seem more golden.

He guessed he looked as pleased as Roy did leaving with Scout and turned his attention to the scenery.

A few minutes later they reached the crest of the hill. A rocky butte stood at the very top and he reined in there. He jumped down and before she could make a move to dismount, he lifted her from the saddle. She stood inches from him, her face turned down as she brushed her skirts. He waited, wanting to see more than the top of her head. Probably surprised that he remained so close, she pulled her gaze to him, her eyes round with mysterious depths. Her lips parted as if she meant to speak and then she closed her mouth and stepped back. "So, this is the place?"

He reined his thoughts into order. "This is it."

She looked. "You're right. You can see for miles."

"You ain't seen nothing yet."

He reached for her hand, pleased when she allowed him to take it without protest.

She laughed as he pulled her past the rocks. Twenty feet farther the view opened up like someone had cut it with a can opener.

She gasped and squeezed his hand. "Oh, my."

Her reaction filled him with pride as if he owned

the view. He let her drink in the sight for several minutes without saying anything then he pointed. "Look, you can see Lark."

She squinted. "Where?"

"Follow the horizon from right to left until you see a little rise."

She shook her head in frustration. "I can't see."

"Here." He pulled her in front of him and pressed her to his chest so he could put his head close to hers. His senses flooded with her nearness and he suddenly couldn't speak. She smelled like the warm prairie, a mixture of sweet and spice. From the first time he saw her he'd wanted to touch her hair and assess it's silkiness. He'd touched it several times but still hadn't satisfied his curiosity.

Her braid hung down her back and he picked it up and lifted it over her shoulder. Its weight surprised him and its texture—silkier than anything he'd ever felt. The only thing that he could think that seemed close was the tender petals on the wild roses.

"I still can't see it."

Her words pulled him back to the reason he held her in his arms. He rested one hand on her shoulder, and with the other pointed toward Lark. She followed his finger. "Lower. Just above the horizon."

"I see it." She grabbed his pointing hand and squeezed. "How far is it?"

"I estimate it to be fifteen or twenty miles."

"I feel like I can see forever."

He turned her slightly. "What do you see over there?" He touched her chin with his free hand and turned her face. Telling himself he needed to make sure she focused in the correct direction, he kept his fingers on her chin. It took more self-control than he knew he was capable of to resist turning her into his arms.

"What am I looking for?"

"The ranch." He hoped she couldn't hear the husky longing in his voice.

"Is that it?" She pointed but continued to hold his hand.

"That's it."

"Look. Isn't that Pa and Roy?"

He saw the pair, no bigger than ants, heading toward a dark spot he knew to be some bushes. "Looking for prairie chicken."

She slipped from his arms and sat a few feet away.

He waited for his disappointment to seep out in degrees, then sat down keeping a generous four inches between them. He wanted less but guessed she would want more.

"Lucy, you like the prairies, don't you?"

"They're beautiful."

"Would you want to live here?"

She turned slowly to stare at him. "You're sounding like Roy."

"Roy wants you to stay."

"I guess so."

God help me find the words. Help me not to rush her and scare her off.

"Well, cowboy, exactly what do you have in mind?" Her voice deepened, vibrating across his senses. The look she gave him searched deep into his soul, seeking something she could trust. He met her look with quiet confidence. What he offered would never change, never falter; he'd never forget a promise spoken or unspoken. He loved her and he wanted her to know it, trust it.

"Lucy, you must know how I feel about you. I love you. I want to share my life with you."

Her eyes flared. He let himself think she welcomed the idea. Then her gaze drifted toward the ranch and her shoulders crept toward her ears.

He couldn't guess what troubled her.

He slid closer until they sat shoulder to shoulder. "Lucy, remember when you said I ran from life or hid from it, letting people say things about me but not caring. I cared. But it seemed no one ever saw me as anything but a convenience or inconvenience. They didn't see me as me."

She took his hand, her touch robbing those feelings of their power. "I see you as more than a convenience." She giggled. "Or even an inconvenience." She turned and smiled at him, the glow of the descending sun catching her in her eyes, filling his heart with gold.

"I know you do."

"But—"

"I hate buts."

She nodded, her expression regretful. "I feel like I've just been thrown into the rushing waters of a deep river. Scout's words, Smitty's capture...well, my thoughts are in such a turmoil I don't even know what I think."

"Of course." He had to be patient. Give her time to see that he would never treat her with the same carelessness Scout had. "Promise me you'll think about it."

She still held his hand and squeezed it. "I promise."

Chapter Fourteen

Think about Wade's proposal? She didn't need to promise. In the days that followed, his words filled every space in Lucy's thoughts to the exclusion of all else.

Roy had almost every can and jug in the house full of flowers. "You'll erase every trace of wildflowers from the country if you keep it up," she'd warned him a few days ago and made him promise to pick only one bouquet a week.

She knew how badly he wanted to stay. This was the first bit of family he'd ever enjoyed. Of course he wanted to stay.

Did she?

Wade loved her.

She loved him.

The admission sang through her like the voice of a thousand angels.

But he'd said nothing about where he wanted to live. Did he think to live here with Scout? She wasn't sure she wanted that. Yes, Scout had made an effort to mend the rift between them but her feelings were still new and raw concerning him. Perhaps they would never be what they should be or could have been.

If Wade were to suggest a place of their own…

Was she ready to trust her whole life into the hands of a man after her disappointment with Scout?

Everything was so confusing.

She ducked into her bedroom and opened her Bible. *Lord, speak to me.* She turned to Psalm one hundred and eighteen where she had found direction only a few days ago. She read the entire chapter but the only words that seemed especially directed to her were those in verse eight, *It is better to trust in the Lord than to put confidence in man.*

It wasn't what she wanted to hear even though she had lived most of her life by those words.

She stared out the window. The words didn't give peace because they didn't reach the truth deep in her heart.

She loved Wade. She wanted to feel confident to share his life.

Lord, give me a sign that I can trust my heart to him.

God had been with her all her life, her friend and guide. She would wait for Him to answer that prayer.

A day passed. Two. She tried to ignore her impatience. She watched and listened carefully, looking for a sign from God. But the sky seemed empty.

She stood on the step, the damp tea towel in her hands and looked about. It was a pleasant place. She'd grown fond of it. The kitchen bore the mark of her hard work. Meals were satisfying to make. She enjoyed letting her gaze wander across the landscape, zeroing in on tiny details. The creek offered a pleasant retreat throughout the day.

But she didn't want to be the housekeeper. The cook. Nor only Scout's daughter.

She wanted a life of her own—shared with Wade.

God, I'm waiting for a sign. But I confess I am impatient.

The sound of hammering drew her attention to a spot behind the corrals where Scout and Roy were busy. *I wonder what they're up to.* Then she turned to put things away.

Over supper, Roy gobbled his food with more haste than usual. "What's your hurry?" Lucy asked.

He stopped and made an effort to slow down. Still, he finished well before the rest of them and refused seconds. "Are you almost done?" he asked Scout.

Pa swirled gravy through his potatoes and arranged them into a tidy circle seemingly oblivious to Roy's impatience.

Lucy ducked her head to hide her smile. He must have promised to take Roy hunting for him to be so impatient.

Slowly Scout ate his potatoes, took his time at picking each morsel from his plate while Roy fidgeted and sighed.

Finally, Scout pushed his plate away. "Guess I'm done."

"Now?" Roy asked, almost bouncing from his chair.

Scout nodded. "Now."

Roy rushed to Lucy and grabbed her hand. "We got a surprise for you. Come on."

"Me?" This excitement was on her behalf? She shot

Scout a look. He grinned at her just as she'd always dreamed he would, which only served to further confuse her. She wasn't sure how to deal with a father who actually saw her.

"Come on." Roy dragged her toward the door.

Scout followed looking as pleased as all get-out.

"You coming?" she asked Wade, suddenly afraid to face this alone.

He sprang to his feet. "Wouldn't miss it for the world."

She could barely keep up with Roy as he pulled her across the yard. Behind the corrals a high chicken-wire fence created a yard around the small building. Did she hear the murmur of hens?

They drew to a halt at the wood-framed gate. "See how you open it." Roy unhooked the wire and shepherded her inside. He rushed over and threw open the door and four hens rushed out clucking.

"Chickens?" She sounded as surprised as she felt.

"I asked around and the Perrys said they could spare a few." He reached inside the building, pulled out a wire basket and handed it to Lucy.

"Four eggs."

"Mrs. Perry says they're good layers." He touched her elbow. "Look inside."

She did so and saw a little pen with a clucking hen.

"She's setting a dozen eggs. You could have a nice-sized flock in another year."

Lucy stared at the hen. Slowly shifted her gaze to stare at Scout. "Next year? You're wanting me to stay?"

A wary look came to his eyes. "They're yours, Lucy. Wherever you go, you take them."

She understood his caution and something inside her

fortressed heart cracked open. "Thanks. I'll get some food for them." She took the eggs to the house and returned with a bucket full of kitchen scraps.

They watched the hens dive after the food as if the whole thing was worth charging admission.

"I better do the dishes," she said finally.

Next day, her afternoon chores complete, Lucy paced the floor pausing to look out the window.

She went to the porch and studied the yard. The hens clucked and scratched inside their pen. It still amazed her that Scout had brought her chickens—an unusual gift. And perhaps that's why it confused her. What did he intend it to mean?

Never mind. Eggs were more than welcome. She grabbed the pan of scraps she'd saved and headed out to the new chicken house.

She made sure the setting hen had food and water then left the pen. The air was so calm and peaceful every sound seemed magnified—from the ducks murmuring on the creek, to the grasshoppers sawing on the grass, to the crow wings combing the air overhead.

In fact, she could pinpoint where Scout and Wade were. There'd been hammering a few minutes ago but now she heard their voices and could make out each word.

Scout was saying something about the ranch. She didn't intentionally eavesdrop, but the warm still air and her uncertain thoughts created a sort of inertia and she didn't have the energy to move. Besides, she couldn't imagine they'd say anything she shouldn't overhear.

"You can have the ranch when I die. In the meantime, I'll make you my partner." Scout's voice came clear

as the sky overhead. "It's what I owe you for bringing
Lucy. I know you said you would but I never thought
you'd succeed."

"That's right generous of you."

Lucy's thoughts skidded to a shocked halt. Wade
had come for her simply to get the ranch? What did his
words of love mean? Why did he want her to stay? Was
it only because the place needed a housekeeper? It had
been mentioned often enough but she'd given the suggestion little thought. She didn't want to be a housekeeper. She wanted far more.

She spun away from the fence and rushed for the
house.

*Oh, God, this is not the sign I wanted but I cannot
ignore it.*

Her mind whirled with denials and accusations. She
should have known better than to follow her foolish
heart seeking the approval she'd wanted all her life.

She ran up and down the cellar ladder bringing up
things to make—she didn't have any idea what she
planned. All she knew was she must work, keep her
thoughts locked behind busyness so the hurt wouldn't
consume her.

But working at a furious pace didn't shake the awful
feeling she was falling through space.

She'd trusted Wade, believed his words. Thought he
could give her what Scout hadn't. Whatever that was.
She no longer knew.

The house crowded her. She needed space. She knew
where she could find it. On the hill where Wade had
taken her.

Fleeing her tortured thoughts she slipped out to the

corrals. Hammering came from the new barn. They would never notice her riding away on Queenie and she'd be back before they even realized she was gone.

Bitterness colored her thoughts in stark colors. So long as she had the meals ready on time she doubted they'd even notice if she disappeared for hours.

Queenie leaned against the corral fence, one leg lifted. She tossed her head and dug in her hooves at being asked to leave her pleasant nap.

"Don't be difficult. I'm in no mood for it."

The horse pricked up her ears and seemed to jerk to attention.

"Forget the dramatics. You and I are going for a ride. And I'll put up with none of your nonsense today."

The saddle was in the old barn. She didn't want to risk being seen and having anyone demand to know what she was up to in order to get it. "We rode all the way here bareback. I'll do it again." She scowled at Queenie as the horse shied away. "Stop acting up."

Lucy opened the gate and led Queenie out then pulled herself onto the horse's back and kicked her sides.

Queenie snorted a protest but didn't lift one of her four feet.

"Now." Lucy kicked her again and this time she made it plain she meant business. With all the hurt air of a slighted dowager, Queenie plodded across the yard.

Lucy could see the hill in the distance and pointed the horse in that direction. The other day when she and Wade had made this ride, it seemed to take only a few minutes but today Queenie's pace made it take forever.

"Let's hurry it up a bit. I want to be there before snow falls." But her constant urging only made Queenie more uncooperative. "I wouldn't have believed it possible for you to get any worse. What is the matter with you?"

But finally they started to climb.

Another reason for Queenie to complain. She snuffled and grunted.

"Stop whining. We're almost there." Lucy didn't know who was more relieved when they reached the top. She dropped to the ground and looked about for something to secure Queenie's halter to. The best she could do was a low bush. But Queenie wasn't likely to run off. It took too much effort.

Lucy returned to the place where she and Wade had sat and settled herself. She studied the landscape spread out before her. So peaceful. So serene.

Why couldn't she feel as calm?

Why had God sent her here? Yes, she and Scout had perhaps mended some broken areas, though she wasn't about to throw herself unreservedly into the relationship.

It was a good place for Roy. No reason he couldn't stay.

She knew she skirted the thing that bothered her most.

Her feelings for Wade.

Why had she allowed herself to fall in love with him?

The verse the Lord had given her blazoned across her mind and she spoke the words aloud. "It is better to trust in the Lord than to put confidence in man." She'd certainly learned the truth of those words.

Why, God? Why?

Why did the men she cared about always let her down? Why couldn't she find one who would value her for herself and not see her as either a mistake or a means to an end?

Remembering how Wade thought of himself as a convenience or an inconvenience, she sniffed. They were more alike in this regard than she cared to admit.

How had she responded to his admission?

By assuring him she saw him as neither. What did she see him as?

After overhearing the words indicating she was only a way to get the ranch, she no longer knew.

Wade. Scout. The pair twisted through her thoughts.

And hens. Why had Scout given her hens? Did he hope to convince her to stay? Did he want her to? Would she if he did?

How could she trust any of them?

It is better to trust in the Lord than to put confidence in man.

She sighed. Yes, she could trust God but sometimes she felt like Roy. She wanted someone with a face and arms right here on earth to trust.

Better to trust in the Lord.

Better? Better. An idea budded. Of course trusting God was better. But—the idea slowly unfolded as if touched by unseen hands—that didn't mean it was wrong, or foolish, or impossible to trust man.

She thought of how she held up a yardstick for Scout, wanting, needing to make him measure up. How he fell short of the mark.

And now she was doing the same to Wade. Judging a conversation she'd overheard without asking for an explanation.

Perhaps she only needed to trust man as imperfect.

Not unkind. Not unfaithful. Just not able to measure up to the impossible expectations she had.

Only God would never disappoint.

If she wanted love and relationship, family and belonging here on earth she had to accept it from people who would make mistakes.

She contemplated the idea a bit longer, asking God to insert things into her mind to help her sort out her discovery. The whole idea grew defined. Clear. She could trust those close to her but ultimately, they would fail. Only God would never let her down. She thought of a verse her ma had often quoted. Couldn't say where it was in the Bible. *God will not fail thee nor forsake thee.*

She'd give Scout another chance accepting that he would sometimes fail, sometimes disappoint but whatever he offered her was worth taking.

She'd ask Wade to explain the conversation. And she'd tell him she loved him. And if he still loved her, accepted her with her flaws…well, perhaps they could start anew and with her new willingness to accept an imperfect love, they might do all right.

Lord, is this what you've been trying to tell me? Is this why You brought me here? To show me this truth?

She would forever be grateful He had.

Now when she looked around, the peace of her surroundings echoed inside her. She breathed in the scents—sage, wild roses, the heat lifting the smell of a thousand years from the soil.

Now wasn't she getting fanciful? She laughed out loud. At the sudden noise, a rabbit skittered from a nearby clump of grass and zigzagged a crazy path for several feet then crouched down, perfectly still. And as visible as a picture.

Queenie snorted.

"It's only a rabbit."

The horse whinnied and jerked her head. She yanked away from the feeble bush and turned, kicked her heels once and headed down the hill.

Lucy bolted to her feet. "Stop."

Queenie didn't stop. She ran—the horse could run? She'd certainly hidden the fact until now.

Lucy raced after her but Queenie quickly outpaced her. "You stupid horse." Lucy staggered to a halt. So, now she walked.

Pausing, she took her bearings. The ranch lay to the east too shadowed for her to pick out in the distance.

Shadows?

She faced west. The sun hung low in the sky. How long had she been gone? A trickle of fear shivered through her. It would be dark before she could get back to the ranch. How would she find her way? She scanned the entire horizon. What if Indians found her?

God, help me.

She started to run, stumbled and caught herself before she fell facedown on the ground. Have to be careful. Don't want to break anything. Would Wade or Scout come looking for her?

She walked on, mindful of the rocks and hole she could trip on. It had been a long ride on Queenie's back.

It would be a much longer walk on her own two feet.

The shadows lengthened and sucked the light from the ground. It would soon be too dark to see where she planted each foot.

Lord, keep me safe.

Lord, I put my confidence in You.

I trust Wade to be concerned about me when I don't return.

Scout, too?

She remembered how Scout had forgotten about her when he suspected Smitty was on the prowl. Perhaps she wasn't prepared to trust Scout that much just yet.

But surely Wade would find her. *Oh, please let him find me.*

Chapter Fifteen

Wade ducked into the house for a drink. "Lucy?" No answer. She must have gone down to the creek. For a moment he considered going after her and spending the rest of the afternoon in her sweet company. But Scout wanted to finish a wall today. And so did he.

He wiped his mouth and headed back to barn building.

Something bothered him as he crossed the yard. Something out of place but he couldn't quite put his finger on it.

But as he drove in spikes, the something tugged at his mind. "Isn't it about supper time?" he asked a little later. Lucy hadn't rung the triangle but he was more than ready to quit. "Let's head on in."

"Fine by me," Scout said as he put away the tools. "Roy, supper."

The boy jumped up from playing with the scraps of lumber and the three of them headed for the house.

Wade burst through first, the something he couldn't identify making him uneasy. He skidded to a halt. No food smells greeted them. Lucy did not stand at the stove tending a pot. The table was not set. "She isn't here."

Roy and Scout pushed past him.

"Lucy," Scout called. "Where are you, girl?"

"She's not here," Wade insisted. He didn't need to look to know it. He felt it in every pore.

Scout threw open her bedroom door. "Not here."

The something began to take shape. Wade spun around, raced for the corrals. Two Bit was grazing calmly nearby. Farther away the other horses fed. Except Queenie. "Where's your horse?" he asked Roy who, along with Scout, had followed him.

"She was here this morning."

"Likely nosing around to see if she can find some free oats." Wade vaulted the fence and ducked inside the barn. But no Queenie.

"Lucy must have gone out riding," Scout said. "'Spect she'll be back shortly."

"'Spect so." Wade agreed. But Lucy had never gone riding on her own before.

He couldn't shake the feeling something was wrong.

Scout and Roy returned to the house to await the meal but Wade stood in the middle of the yard, peering into the distance hoping to glimpse a twist of dust, a dark shuffling shape to indicate Queenie and a rider.

He strained for a sound. Nothing but the chirp of a nearby grasshopper and a snort from one of the horses.

Never had the prairies been so empty.

Wait. He heard a muffled thud and turned toward the sound. A horse. Queenie and Lucy? The animal drew closer and he recognized the lumbering gait. It was Queenie. He raced toward the horse. Within three steps he saw she carried no rider. "Lucy?" His voice brought a flurry of noise from the prairie as birds fluttered in protest of the sound.

Queenie jerked back at his roar and acted as if she might turn tail and run.

Wade forced himself to stop. To suck in air. Something had happened to Lucy and the only clue was this horse. He waited for the animal to edge closer and caught her. Sweated up. Had to have run a distance.

He snorted. A good hard run for Queenie was two hundred yards.

"My horse." Roy clattered off the step and ran toward them.

Wade gladly turned the animal over to him. "Better cool her down and brush her."

Scout waited on the step. "So, what's your take?"

"Either Lucy fell off, got tossed off or the stupid horse ran off and left her stranded."

"Either way she's out there somewhere and it will soon be dark."

Wade didn't need Scout to point out the obvious. "I'm going looking." He whistled for Two Bit and did a hundred yard dash to the corrals. The horse met him at the barn. In a few minutes Wade had the saddle on. Before he could swing up, Scout joined him.

"What direction are you going?"

Wade thought. "I can't imagine where she's gone." Or why? His heart thudded so hard it hurt his ribs. Sweat beaded his brow as he imagined Lucy hurt out in the vast prairie. "How will we find her?"

Scout gripped his shoulder. "We'll find her."

It registered that Scout offered to help.

"I haven't found my daughter only to lose her again."

Wade nodded. "And I haven't found the woman I want to spend the rest of my life with only to lose her."

Scout gave him a hard look as if realizing he'd found his daughter only to lose her to Wade if Wade got his way. Wade returned his look, resolve for resolve.

"I'll ride toward the big hill." Wade swung to his saddle.

"I'll head toward town."

"Roy?"

"I'll take him."

He accepted that Scout would always see Roy as a boy needing his attention. That was just fine with Wade. He was prepared to give Lucy all the attention she needed and wanted. "If you find her, fire off three shots. I'll do the same."

"Right."

"And leave a note in case she makes it back before we do."

Wade didn't wait for a reply. He galloped out of the yard. As he rode, he scanned the ground before him, squinted into the distance for anything that could be Lucy. Every few minutes, he paused to call her name and listened for a response. Listened for a moan. Or even a whisper.

Never had the prairies seemed so vast. So silent.

Darkness clutched at his shoulders. He shuddered. If Lucy were hurt, unable to call, he would never find her. He could ride past a few feet away and not know she was there.

Oh, God. You have answered so many of my prayers

in the past. Too often I've looked at the answers for evidence of Your love. I know how foolish that is. I know you love me. I don't need any special signs and wonders. And today I am not asking for myself but for Lucy. Help me find her. Even if she never returns my love. Pain caused his arms to spasm at the thought. He shook his hands. Even if she never returned his love he wanted to see her safe.

Darkness deepened. He fought back despair. God would help him find her.

His plan had been to ride to the hill where he could see for miles but now he would see nothing. Still, it might be the best place to hear if she called. He kept Two Bit on a steady course toward the hill. He started to climb. Paused to call, "Lucy." His voice growing thick and strained with every passing hoofbeat.

A whisper came on the night air. Perhaps only a bird shuffling in protest to this unfamiliar noisy interruption.

It came again, stronger. More formed. About to move onward, he stopped. "Lucy?"

He turned his head trying to catch the sound. There. There it was. Definitely not a bird.

"Lucy, is that you? Keep calling."

He followed the sound until he made out the word, "Here."

His ribs tightened so hard he gasped. Lucy. Where was she? He called again, listened for her response.

"Here. Keep coming."

And then he could make out her shape against the gray sky. She stood upright. His breath whooshed out. At least she wasn't injured—he hoped. He dropped from his horse and picked his way across the rough ground, controlling his urge to fly to her side. "Are you hurt?"

"No. Just mad because Queenie ran off. Didn't know she had it in her."

He grinned at the angry regret in her voice. "She was all lathered up when she got home." He closed the distance between them and grabbed her shoulders. "You're sure you're fine?"

"Now that you're here, I am good. Really really good."

He pulled her into his arms and held her like fragile china. "You scared me some, I don't mind admitting."

"I don't mind at all that you do." Although her voice was muffled against his shirtfront, he detected a smile and let his hopes soar that she was pleased about more than being rescued. He'd ask her just as soon as he could be certain of speaking without his voice cracking.

He couldn't seem to let her go and noticed she made no effort to withdraw from his embrace.

"I was just a tiny bit scared that no one would come looking for me," she whispered.

His arms tightened even as his heart squeezed with painful realization that it would take her a long time to overcome her feelings of being overlooked. He pressed his cheek to her hair, reveling in the texture. As long as he lived, he hoped and prayed he could enjoy this privilege. "Lucy, I would have looked for you day and night until I found you."

She nodded against his chest. "I know."

Her confession tore away any residual doubt that she could ever trust him because of Scout. He grinned into the darkness. *Thank You, God.* "Scout is out looking for you, too. I better signal him." But it required he release her and get the rifle from the boot on the saddle. He couldn't make himself do so just yet.

"Are you sending him smoke signals I can't see?"

He chuckled. "I have to fire off three shots."

"Oh." She understood he must move but her arms slipped around his waist and he knew she couldn't bear the thought of letting go any more than he could. His heart practically flew from his chest. "Lucy gal, I don't think I'll let you out of my sight for a good long time." And if he had his way, not more than a few feet and a few minutes.

"Sounds like a promise."

"It is. It's my promise to love you and keep you and protect you all my life. If you'll let me."

She shifted to look into his face. In the darkness he could barely make out her features though he had no need for the light to know the color and shape and size of every one of them. "I should have let you know where I was going but I was… I guess mostly hurt and a little angry."

He searched his thoughts for a reason. Found none. "I don't understand."

"I overheard Scout saying he'd make you a partner because you succeeded in getting me to come here."

"Yeah. Surprised me some." The man had never so much as suggested such a thing. "Shows just how much he appreciates having you come."

She sighed. "I didn't want the reason you brought me here to be so you'd get part of the ranch. I wanted…"

He held her within the circle of his arms, wanting to keep her there forever. Only closer. Right against his heart. "Lucy, what did you want?"

"I wanted there to be no selfish reason."

Ahh. He saw now. She thought he'd expected some reward for bringing her. "You're overlooking one small thing. I only brought you because you were trying to avoid Smitty."

She stiffened but still didn't pull out of his arms. "That worked out rather well for you, I'd say."

"I'd say so, too. I only wanted to repay Scout for his kindness. At least at first. But after I saw you in the dining room laughing and teasing and so full of life, I wanted you to come for my sake." Slowly, giving her lots of chance to resist, he pulled her closer until he breathed in her warm breath. "I hoped against hope that somehow, someday I would persuade you to come with me wherever I went."

"I think you might have succeeded."

Overflowing with love, he lowered his head, found her mouth and gave her the gentlest of kisses. When she responded by splaying her hands on his back, a gesture that sent sweet responses thrilling through him, he allowed himself a deeper, claiming kiss. Restraining his urge to kiss her for the rest of the night, he eased back. "I love you, Lucy Hall."

"I love you, Wade Miller."

"Now I better signal Scout." He pulled the rifle out and fired the three shots. "Let's get back to the house."

Lucy sat behind Wade, clinging to his back as they rode toward home. She pressed her face into the warmth of his shirt. Home. This was home. Wherever Wade was. His love had taught her where she belonged—with those who loved her and showed it as best they could.

Someday she would tell him how her perceptions had changed while on his hilltop. For now, she wanted only to share her newfound way of looking at life with those who mattered most to her.

They arrived back at the house. Wade lifted her down and left Two Bit standing at the corrals. The fact that he showed more concern for her safe journey into the house than for his horse's care brought a smile of contentment to her face.

"Wait here while I light a lamp." He made her stand at the door until a golden glow filled the room, then he drew her close to the light. With fingers as gentle as the brush of cat fur he examined her cheeks, her chin, her forehead. "I want to make sure you're fine."

Smiling so hard her eyes felt glittery, she lifted her face and let him find out for himself just how fine she was. "I am better than fine. I am better than good. Life is full of sweet promise thanks to you."

"Me?" His eyes crinkled at the corners as he frowned. "What do you mean?"

It would take the rest of her life to tell him all the ways because she knew she could continually find more things to appreciate about him. "You brought me here. You showed me how constant love could be. And you—" Her voice caught. "You showed Scout and I how to start over."

He kissed her nose. "You would have figured it out without my help."

She wondered if they would. "Do you want to be a partner with him?"

He shrugged. "I haven't thought of it but I would like to settle down and I think it would be great if we could live close to Scout so you two could be a family. But none of that is important right now. Tell me you'll marry me and make me the happiest man in the world."

"I will marry you and I will be the happiest woman anywhere. And I will live with you wherever you want."

They kissed then.

The door burst open and Roy rushed in. He skidded to a stop. "You're kissing." His voice rang with disgust.

Wade and Lucy laughed, their gazes holding each other, their eyes filled with secret joys.

Scout followed after Roy. "You're safe." He crossed the room and hugged Lucy. "Praise God." He looked slightly embarrassed as he released her.

It was the first hug she'd ever had from her father and she knew she would cherish it in a special place in her heart forever. However, she vowed it would not be the last time.

He shook Wade's hand, pumping it hard. "I hope you won't mind sharing her with me. We have a lot of years to catch up."

Wade caught Lucy's hand and pulled her close. "What do you think, Lucy?"

His smile filled her with sweet delight and courage. Then she turned to Scout. "I think I'd like that, Pa." The word came out slowly, hesitantly but she meant it wholly.

Scout's eyes filled with tears. He swiped them away.

Roy watched them, his eyes narrowed, his lips tight as he rocked back and forth. Lucy understood his concern. Knew he wondered if he had been forgotten. She held out a hand. "Come here, Roy."

He hesitated, wanting them all to know he didn't need them.

Lucy guessed the others knew as well as she that he needed them and wanted them. "Come over here."

He shuffled forward until she could reach down and capture his hand. She pulled him to her side. "Anyone here object to Roy being part of this family?"

Wade and Scout spoke together. "Nope."

Wade opened his arms to pull Roy to Lucy's side. He wrapped his other arm around Scout's shoulders. Lucy pressed to Wade's side. "I'm not much for praying out loud," Wade said. "But this seems to be an occasion that calls for thanking God. So if none of you object...."

For answer, Scout and Roy bowed their heads.

Lucy held Wade's gaze just long enough to mouth the words, "I love you," before she, too, bowed.

"God, I thank You for bringing us all together and for answering so many of my prayers. I know You will continue to bless us and teach us. Above all I thank You for teaching us how to love. And I especially want to thank You for Lucy's love. Amen."

Lucy's heart filled with joy as she lifted her gaze to Wade and drank in his love.

Epilogue

Three months later, Lucy stood in the still-new church facing Lark's new preacher. She wore a pale gray gown that she knew brought out the gray in her eyes—though she needed nothing to help reveal the sparkle of happiness there. The past weeks had been a blur of joy. Wade, confident of her love, had surprised her with the many ways he found to show his love and appreciation. She knew in the passing years their love would grow sweeter and more dear.

At her side stood Wade. He looked extremely handsome in his black suit jacket. The look he gave her filled her with delight. Today they would become man and wife.

He hadn't wanted to wait but Pa had insisted he would build a smaller house for himself and Roy. "I will always think of this house as yours," he'd said to Lucy. With each passing day she grew more confident of her father's love and her years of feeling he didn't see her or want her began to heal.

Roy would be nurtured under Pa's care, with Lucy and Wade's love, as well.

The preacher began, "Dearly beloved, we are here to witness the joining of this man and this woman in the bonds of matrimony. A union designed by God for our mutual enjoyment."

Lucy blinked back tears of joy.

Thanks to God's faithfulness, she had learned how to trust and in response, she would soon enjoy the state of marriage.

A few minutes later, the preacher called for the ring. As Scout searched for it, Wade leaned close and whispered in her ear. "I will thank God every day of my life for your love."

She whispered back, "And I for yours."

He placed the ring on her finger then kissed her with his promise on his lips.

And then the preacher announced, "Mr. and Mrs. Miller."

Roy sighed loudly. "Now can we eat? I'm starved."

* * * * *

Laurie Kingery is a Texas transplant to Ohio who writes romance set in post–Civil War Texas. She was nominated for a Carol Award for her second Love Inspired Historical novel, *The Outlaw's Lady*, and has written a series about mail-order grooms in a small town in the Texas Hill Country.

Books by Laurie Kingery

Love Inspired Historical

Hill Country Christmas
The Outlaw's Lady

Bridegroom Brothers

The Preacher's Bride Claim

Brides of Simpson Creek

Mail Order Cowboy
The Doctor Takes a Wife
The Sheriff's Sweetheart
The Rancher's Courtship
The Preacher's Bride
Hill Country Cattleman
A Hero in the Making
Hill Country Courtship
Lawman in Disguise

Visit the Author Profile page at Harlequin.com.

MAIL ORDER COWBOY

Laurie Kingery

What doth the Lord require of thee, but to do justly, and to love mercy, and to walk humbly with thy God?
—*Micah* 6:8

To my wonderful editor, Melissa Endlich, who always makes me strive to be the best writer I can be, and always, to my husband, Tom

Prologue

Simpson Creek, Texas, July 1865

"The problem, as I see it," Millicent Matthews announced in her forthright way, looking around the edges of the quilt at the members of the Ladies Aid Society, "is that we unmarried ladies are likely to remain so, given the absolute lack of single men who've come home to Simpson Creek from the war. The few men who did return were already married, and while I'm very happy for their wives, of course—" she added quickly as one of the town's matrons looked up "—the rest of us will have to leave or remain single unless Decisive Action is Taken."

"Oh, I don't know, Milly," said her sister Sarah, staring down at the Wedding Ring pattern as if it held the answer to their dilemma. "Perhaps not all of our men are able to travel yet from wherever they were when the war ended. They might be recovering from wounds, or the effects of confinement in northern prisons…"

Milly felt a rush of compassion for Sarah, whom she

knew was still holding out hope that her beau would yet return, despite the fact he had been reported missing in action late last year. Since then, they'd heard nothing more.

"Sarah, it's *July*," she pointed out gently but firmly. "The war was over in April. We've seen the casualty lists. All the other Simpson Creek men have been accounted for, one way or the other. The ones who survived have managed to make it to Texas. If Jesse was still recovering elsewhere, surely he would have sent word by now." She let the statement hang in the air.

Sarah's gaze fell to her lap and her lip quivered. "I… I know you're right, Milly. I just keep hoping…"

Across from them, Mrs. Detwiler pursed her lips.

Milly laid a hand comfortingly on her sister's shoulder. She was sure the color of Sarah's dove-gray dress was a concession to her uncertainty as to whether she was mourning or waiting.

Milly was just about to say "Jesse would want you to move on" when Mrs. Detwiler cleared her throat.

"We need to accept the lot in life that the Lord sees fit to give us," the woman said heavily, clutching the mourning brooch on her bodice. "I lost my own dear George ten years ago, God rest his soul, and I have learned to resign myself to my widowhood, even—dare I say it—*treasure* my single state." Her expression indicated Sarah would do well to be so wise.

"Mrs. Detwiler, I admire the way you've adapted to your loss," Milly began tactfully, not wanting to offend the widow of the town's previous preacher. "But you had many happy years with Mr. Detwiler, and raised several children."

"Seven, to be exact." Mrs. Detwiler sniffed, and raised her eyes heavenward.

"Seven," Milly echoed. "But Sarah and I and several others here—" she saw furtive nods around the quilt frame "—are young, and have never been married. We'd like to become wives and raise children, too. And there are others who were widowed by the war and left with children to raise and land to work or businesses to manage. They need to find good husbands again."

"In my opinion, you would do better to devote yourselves to prayer and good works, Miss Matthews, and let the good Lord send you a husband if He wishes you to have one."

Milly could feel Sarah tensing beside her. Sarah never liked confrontations. But Milly had seen the spark of interest and approval in the eyes of half a dozen young ladies plying their needles on the quilt, and their silent support emboldened her.

"I agree that prayer and good works are important to every Christian, of course, and I *have* been praying about the matter. Sometimes I think the Lord helps those who help themselves."

At this point Mrs. Detwiler cleared her throat again. Loudly. "I hardly think this is the time or place to discuss such a frivolous topic." From her pocket, she pulled out a gold watch, a legacy of her dear departed George. "I must return home soon, and we have not yet discussed the raffle to be held for the Benefit of the Deserving Poor of San Saba County. If we don't stop chattering and keep stitching, ladies, this quilt will not be ready to be raffled off at the event."

Milly tucked an errant lock of dark hair that had

escaped the neat knot at the nape of her neck and bit back a sigh of frustration. As president of the Ladies Aid Society, Mrs. Detwiler had an obligation to keep the meetings on track, but she suspected the widow was all too happy to have an excuse to stifle the discussion.

"You're right, Mrs. Detwiler, of course. I'm sorry if I spoke out of turn," she said in the meekest tone she could manage. "Perhaps it *would* be best to discuss this subject at another time, with only those concerned present. So why don't the unmarried ladies who are interested meet back here again tomorrow, say at four o'clock? We'll serve lemonade and cookies."

Chapter One

"Sarah, thank you again for making the cookies and the lemonade," Milly whispered as the ladies began to arrive in the Simpson Creek Church social hall. It must have been the dozenth time she'd thanked her sister since volunteering to supply refreshments, knowing it would be Sarah who actually made the cookies. Milly's baking efforts always ended up overbrowned, if not completely charred.

"I told you, you're welcome," Sarah whispered back, smiling. "I couldn't run a meeting the way you're about to. We all have our gifts."

Milly was none too sure she had any gifts worth boasting of, but what she was about to propose to these ladies *had* been her idea.

"Sarah, we're going to need more chairs," she whispered again, this time in pleased astonishment as women kept filing in. They had set out only half a dozen, including the ones for her and Sarah. The next few minutes were a busy bustle of carrying chairs and making a bigger circle. Finally, in all, there were ten never-married ladies and two widows, plus the mother of Prissy Gilmore, who probably wanted to keep a careful eye on what Milly Matthews was proposing—especially because Prissy's father was the mayor.

"Ladies, I want to thank you all for coming," Milly said, pitching her voice louder than the buzz of conversation as everyone settled themselves in their chairs and greeted one another. "I'd like to open this meeting with prayer." She waited a moment while everyone quieted and bowed their heads.

"Our heavenly Father," Milly began, "we ask You would bless us this day and direct our efforts as we seek to find an answer to a problem. Guide us and bless us, and keep us in the center of Your will. Amen." She raised her head, and as the others raised theirs and opened their eyes, she saw them looking expectantly at her.

Milly took a deep breath. "As I was saying two days ago as we worked on the quilt, we single women in Simpson Creek face a problem now that the war is over and there are no single men here—"

"So what are you proposing we do, Milly?" interrupted Prissy Gilmore impatiently. "Become mail order brides and leave Simpson Creek?"

Milly laughed. "Merciful heavens, no! *I'm* not going to, anyway. I love this town. I don't want to leave it and Sarah and go marry, sight unseen, some prospector in Nevada Territory or a widower farmer with a passel of children in Nebraska. I want a husband who can run the ranch Papa left us and defend it against the Comanches if they come raiding. Y'all know Sarah and I have been coping—" barely, she thought "—with only our foreman, old Josh, and his nephew Bobby to help us."

Josh and Bobby weren't enough, she knew. Once, the Matthews bunkhouse had housed six other cowhands, with more hired at roundup time. Josh was old and becoming more and more crippled with rheumatism, while Bobby wasn't even shaving yet.

Josh had taken her aside only the night before and explained that if they didn't find a way to make the ranch productive again, they might lose it to taxes. They were already losing cattle left and right to thieving Indians and rustlers, but there was no way an old man and a young boy could protect the place.

"Maybe y'ought to sell out and move into town, Miss Milly," Josh had said. "Don't worry 'bout me 'n the boy. We'll find a place somewhere." But who would hire such an old cowboy and a boy still wet behind the ears?

"I'm sure you could interest some Yankee soldier or his carpetbagger friend in your ranch," Martha Gilmore, Prissy's mother, suggested with a smirk. "They'd be only too willing to marry you to get their hands on a good piece of Texas ranch property."

Several of the young ladies looked dismayed. "Y-you wouldn't do something like that, would you, Milly?" asked Jane Jeffries, a young widow who still wore black despite losing her husband midway through the war.

"Of course not, Jane," Milly assured her. "I'm looking for a good Texas man, or at the very least, a Southerner. I do realize there are *some* things worse than being an old maid. Marrying a Yankee soldier or a carpetbagger certainly falls into that category."

"I'm relieved to hear you say so," Emily Thompson said from across the circle. "So what course of action *did* you have in mind?"

Milly stared out the open window of the church social hall. "I thought perhaps we could place an advertisement in a newspaper, not the *Simpson Creek News,* of course, but a larger city's newspaper such as the *Houston Telegraph.* It just so happens our Uncle William is the editor of that paper, so I'm sure he'd help us." She smiled at the other ladies. "We'll include a post office address where interested bachelors could reply. Of course they'd be required to send references, and a picture, if at all possible."

"You mean," asked Martha Gilmore, "to enlist mail order *grooms?*"

Milly blinked, startled to hear her idea summed up that way, as several around the circle tittered. She considered the phrase. "Yes, I suppose you could call them that."

"Oh, Milly, I don't know…" Sarah murmured uneasily.

Milly pretended she hadn't heard. Sarah was always apprehensive about daring new ideas. "Who's with me?" she asked, making eye contact with each in turn—Prissy Gilmore, Jane Jeffries, Ada Spencer, Maude Harkey, Emily Thompson, Caroline Wallace, Hannah Kennedy, Bess Lassiter, Polly Shackleford, Faith Bennett. And they met her gaze, some shyly, some boldly, but all with interest.

"How would such an ad read, Milly?" asked Ada Spencer curiously.

Milly thought back to what she had begun composing in her mind at the meeting once Mrs. Detwiler had redirected the conversation. "I'm open to suggestions, of course, but here's what I had so far," she said, pulling a folded sheet of paper from her reticule. "Wanted: Marriage-Minded Bachelors," she read aloud. "Quality Christian gentlemen who desire to make the acquaintance of refined, genteel young ladies with a view to

matrimony are requested to send a letter to—and here
we would need a name for our group, ladies—References
are required, and those sending photographs will
be given preference. Drunkards, Yankees, Carpetbaggers
and other riffraff need not apply."

"I think that's excellent, Milly!" Maude Harkey cried,
clapping. "Bravo! You've certainly covered everything."

Some of Milly's apprehension left her in the face of
Maude's enthusiasm and the approving glances of several
ladies around the circle. "Thanks, Maude," Milly
said. "But we need a name for this group. What shall
we call our organization? The Marriageable Misses?
The Wedding Club?"

Mrs. Gilmore looked as if she wanted to say something
but she held her peace.

"How about The Simpson Creek Society for Promotion
of Marriage?" Caroline Wallace suggested.

It was a more formal name than Milly would have
preferred, but she wanted each lady to feel she had a
say in the formation of their organization, and everyone
seemed to like this one.

"All right, that seems to be the consensus," Milly
said. "That's what we'll call ourselves. The rest of the
advertisement could read, 'Inquiries should be directed
to the Simpson Creek Society for the Promotion of Marriage
at post office box number—' Caroline, can we
arrange for a post office box before we leave town so I
know what number to put in the ad?"

Caroline, the daughter of the postmaster, nodded.
"I happen to know number seventeen is empty. I'll tell
Papa."

"Will you need any money for the advertisement,

Milly?" asked Jane Jeffries. Several of the ladies' faces registered dismay. If there was one other thing the unwed ladies of Simpson Creek lacked, it was ready cash.

"I don't think so," Milly said, and hoped it was true. "I'll write to my uncle this very day, sending our advertisement copy." She was counting on Uncle William to run the advertisement gratis, or at the very least run it at a discount.

"Well, I think that went well, don't you?" Milly said, after the last of the ladies had gone home and she and Sarah were alone in the social hall. She munched on one of the few cookies that hadn't been devoured by the Simpson Creek Society for the Promotion of Marriage.

"Yes…yes, it did," Sarah said, her tone thoughtful as she scooped up the plates and cups filled with crumbs and remains of the lemonade. "They all seemed very excited about your ideas."

"But what about *you,* Sarah?" Milly asked. She hadn't been able to gauge Sarah's reaction during the meeting. "Are you going to be one of us, or do you think it's a foolish idea? Would you rather I hadn't suggested it?"

Sarah's green eyes lost focus. "I… I don't know. Won't it look as if we're somewhat…oh, I don't know…*fast?*"

"Oh, I don't think so, not if the advertisement is worded properly, as I believe it is," Milly said. She had been very satisfied when the group agreed that the words she had composed in her head were perfect as they stood. "We'll be able to tell by the tone of their letters if they've gotten the wrong impression, I should think, and we simply won't extend an invitation to come and meet us."

"I suppose you're right…" Sarah said, but her tone was far from certain. "But Milly, what if—what if the men who answer the advertisement lie about their qualifications? What if they turn out to be men of bad character? Why, a man could say anything about himself on paper, and turn out to be quite the opposite," Sarah said, twisting a fold of her apron. "Why, he could be an outlaw, or a cardsharp—or a *Yankee!*"

"That's true," Milly admitted frankly. "But if we find that to be the case, we'll send them packing. And you know, there are no guarantees when one meets a man in the usual way either," she pointed out.

Sarah looked puzzled. "Whatever do you mean?"

"Just look at that woman in Goliad we heard about, Bertha McPherson," Milly said, with a wave of her hand, as if the woman stood before them. "She married that fellow from Goliad who courted her for six months, and once they tied the knot, she found out he still had a living wife back in St. Louis."

Sarah sighed. "I always thought we'd marry boys from Simpson Creek, boys we'd known all our lives."

"I know…" Milly had thought so, too. Just as she had believed the brave talk of the boys who'd marched off to war, promising they'd be back, victorious, in six months. "Yes, what we're doing is a leap of faith," she admitted. "But would you rather take a chance, or die an old maid? *I* don't want to be called 'Old Maid Milly Matthews,' thank you very much."

"They're already calling you 'Marrying Milly'," Sarah said, then put a hand over her mouth as if she hadn't meant to say it.

Milly blinked. "Who's 'they'?"

"Folks in town," Sarah said, facing her sister as Milly also sank into a chair beside her. "I overheard Mr. Patterson talking to Mrs. Detwiler in the mercantile yesterday. They hadn't seen me come in. She was telling him what you'd said in the Ladies Aid Society meeting the other day. Folks in town are already calling us the Spinsters Club."

Milly winced but reached out and put an arm around her sister's shoulder. "We mustn't mind what people say, Sarah. People will always gossip." She hadn't missed the fact that Sarah had said *us,* and her heart glowed with love for her. Worried as she was, her sister was joining her in this project.

"Have you prayed about this?" Sarah asked. "I mean, I know we opened the meeting with prayer—that was a lovely prayer you said, by the way—but have you been praying about this? A lot?"

"Of course," Milly said. "I've been praying for months, ever since the war ended and those first few men started returning, and none of them were the single men on the Missing in Action lists. But I suppose we'd both feel more confident if we prayed now, right?" They had always prayed together, first as a family and now just the two of them, after losing first their mother and more recently their father. Milly had always found it a source of strength.

Sarah nodded. Milly took her hand, and they bowed their heads and sought the Lord's blessing on their enterprise.

Chapter Two

Nicholas Brookfield, late of Her Majesty's Bombay Light Cavalry, reined in the handsome bay he had purchased after leaving the stagecoach and studied Simpson Creek. A small town, more like a village really, consisting of one main street, with a sprinkling of buildings on both sides of the dusty thoroughfare. Signs proclaimed the presence of a saloon, a boardinghouse, a general store, a livery, a combination barbershop-bathhouse, and at the far end of the street, a church. Branching off from the middle of the main street was another road with several houses of various sizes, some sturdy-looking fieldstone or brick two-stories, others smaller and of more humble construction, wood and even adobe cottages.

He wondered if Miss Millicent Matthews lived in any of these, or if her home was out on one of the ranches he'd passed on the road into Simpson Creek. And for the twentieth time, he wondered if he was on a fool's errand. Had the intermittent fever he was prone to, and which had laid him low once again when he arrived in

Texas a week ago, finally seared his brain, rendering him mad? What else explained why he'd let curiosity take control and come here in search of the writer of that intriguing advertisement, instead of going straight to Austin to the job that awaited him?

He glanced at his clothing, deeming it too dusty from his travels to make a good impression on a lady. Pulling out his pocket watch, a gift from his brother when Nicholas achieved the rank of captain, he discovered it was only eleven. He would do well, he decided, to bespeak a room at the boardinghouse and visit the barbershop-bathhouse before paying a call on Miss Matthews, assuming someone in this dusty little hamlet would tell him where he could find her.

"Have there been any inquiries about our advertisement?" Prissy Gilmore asked, after all the ladies of the Simpson Creek Society for the Promotion of Marriage had settled themselves in a circle in the church social hall.

"Not yet," Milly admitted, as cheerfully as she could manage. "But it *has* been only two weeks. It would take time for a man to read the advertisement, compose a letter, perhaps have a tintype taken if he doesn't have one ready, and for that letter to reach the Simpson Creek post office." Afraid of discouraging her friends, she wasn't about to admit she had made a pilgrimage to the post office every other day this week, and her only reward had been the letter she now brought out from her reticule.

"However," she said, smiling as she drew it out of the envelope and unfolded it, "I do have this note from our Uncle William, who you will remember is the editor of the *Houston Telegraph*."

"*Dear Millicent and Sarah,*" she read, "*I hope this letter finds you well. I wanted you to know I am in receipt of your rather interesting advertisement copy and have published it (though I must confess with some trepidation as to what your late father would have thought of your scheme) in accordance with your request. I have to say this advertisement caused no small amount of talk in the* Telegraph *office and around the town. Word of it and of your group has spread to those cities with whose newspapers we share articles, so it may be possible that you will receive inquiries from as far away as Charleston, South Carolina, and even New York City.*"

Milly folded up the letter and stuck it triumphantly back in her pocket without reading the paragraph that followed, in which her Uncle William implored her to be very cautious in meeting the gentlemen who would write in response.

"So you see, ladies," she said, infusing every word with confidence, "our advertisement has made a stir. I'm sure we will begin receiving inquiries any time now—perhaps even in today's post!"

A pleased hum of excitement rose from the ladies sitting around her.

Maude Harkey raised her hand. "Milly, assuming these letters start arriving, we've never discussed how it will be decided who gets matched with whom. How will that take place?"

"That's a good question, and one I think the Society should decide as a group," Milly responded, settling her hands in her lap. "What do you think, ladies?" She watched as they all looked at one another before Jane Jeffries raised a timid hand.

"I think we should let the gentlemen decide," she announced, then ducked her head as if astonished at her own audaciousness.

"Yes, but how?" Milly prodded.

Jane shrugged.

"We could have a party," said Prissy Gilmore, who'd managed to avoid bringing her mother. "With chaperones, of course, so Mama won't have a fit—and the gentlemen could be presented to all of us. They could decide whom they preferred." She smoothed a wayward curl that had escaped her artful coiffure.

"Yes, but what if only one of them comes at a time?" Sarah asked. "Won't he feel awfully uncomfortable, as if he's on display like a prize bull at a county fair?"

"Well, he would be, wouldn't he?" Emily Thompson tittered. "Poor man. But perhaps it won't have to be that way. From the sound of that letter, it seems as if they might well come in *herds!*"

"Wouldn't that be wonderful? Then each of us could have our pick!" Ada Spencer said with a sigh, and everyone laughed at her blissful expression.

"Maybe the gentleman will express a preference as to the type of woman he's seeking," Maude Harkey said. "He might have a decided interest in short redheads, such as myself."

There was more laughter.

"Don't forget, ladies," Milly reminded them, "as more and more matches are made, the number of ladies looking over the applicants will be fewer and fewer.

Eventually there will be no more need for the Society, God willing, for all of us will be married."

"Amen," Ada Spencer said. "But the fact remains, we have yet to receive the first response to our advertisement. I hope we don't end up as the laughingstocks of Texas."

Her words hung in the air, and once more the ladies were glancing uneasily around at each other.

"I think we ought to pray about it now," Milly said. "And you've all been praying about it at home, haven't you?"

There were solemn nods around the circle.

"Very well, then," Milly said. "Who would like to—"

Sarah raised her hand. "I think when we pray, we ought to include something about God's will being done. I mean, it might not be God's will for all of us to be married, you know."

Milly opened her mouth to argue, then shut it again. The idea that the Lord might *intend* for her to go through life as an unmarried lady for whatever reason He had was startling, but it could be true.

"You're right, Sarah," she said, humbled. "Would you lead us in pr—"

Before she could finish her sentence, there was a knock at the door of the social hall. Then, without waiting to be invited in, a tousle-headed boy flung open the door.

Milly recognized Dan Wallace, Caroline's brother, and son of the town postmaster.

Caroline called out, "Dan, is anything wrong? We're having a meeting here—"

"I know, Caroline," Dan said. "But Papa said to show this gent where to go."

Caroline's brow furrowed, and Milly saw her look past her brother. "What gent?"

"He's waitin' outside. He came t' the post office. Says he's come in response to the advertisement y'all placed in that Houston newspaper. He's lookin' for Miss Milly, an' I knew she'd be here with you 'cause a' the meetin'."

Milly felt the blood drain from her face. It shouldn't be happening this way. A man couldn't have just *shown up*.

She looked uncertainly at the others. "But…but he was to have written a letter first," she protested, "so we could evaluate his application, then send him an invitation if we agreed he was a good candidate."

"Perhaps his letter got lost in the mail or delayed," Sarah pointed out, reasonable as always.

She supposed what Sarah had said *was* possible, Milly had to admit. Stagecoaches carrying the mail got robbed, or his letter could have fallen out of the mail sack and blown away, or gotten stuck to another going elsewhere…. But the man should have waited for a reply from them.

"I say an applicant is an applicant," Maude Harkey said. "He must have come a long way. Least we can do is see him and hear what he has to say."

Milly couldn't argue with that, she decided. They had prayed fervently that their advertisement would be answered, and it had been, though not in the way she had planned.

Now that the moment had come, though, she felt a

little faint. Her corset suddenly felt too tightly laced. It was hard to get a breath. She rose, wishing she had worn her Sunday best instead of this green-and-yellow-sprigged everyday dress, wished that she had time to pinch her cheeks…. Darting a glance at the others, she saw that all of them appeared to be wishing much the same.

"Well, by all means, invite him in, Dan," Milly said with a calmness she was far from feeling.

The boy looked over his shoulder at whoever stood beyond their sight and said, "You kin come in."

He was tall, taller by a head than Milly, which must put him at six feet or so, she thought absently, and so darkly tanned that at first Milly thought he was a Mexican. But then he doffed his wide-brimmed hat, and she saw that his hair gleamed tawny-gold in the light shed by the high window just behind him. His eyes were the blue of a cloudless spring sky, his nose straight and patrician. He wore a black frock coat with a matching waistcoat over an immaculate white shirt. He looked to be in his early thirties.

He was easily the most compelling man Milly had ever set eyes on.

He bowed deeply from the waist, and when he straightened, he smiled as his gaze roved around the circle of thunderstruck ladies.

"Good afternoon, ladies. My name is Nicholas Brookfield. I am looking for Miss Millicent Matthews." His eyes stopped at Sarah. "Are you Miss Matthews, by chance?"

"I—uh, that is, I'm S-Sarah Matthews, her s-sister…"

Sarah stammered, going pale, then crimson. She gestured toward Milly. "That's Millicent."

The woman she pointed to was nothing like the image Nick had formed in his mind of Miss Millicent Matthews, being neither blonde nor short. She was tall and willowy, her figure hinting at strength rather than feminine frailty. Her hair gleamed like polished mahogany, so dark brown that it was nearly black, her eyes a changeable hazel under sweeping lashes, her lips temptingly curving rather than the pouting rosebud he had always thought the epitome of female loveliness.

In that instant, Nicholas Brookfield's ideal image of beauty was transformed. Millicent Matthews was the most striking woman he had ever encountered. He couldn't imagine why he had thought, even for a second, that she was blonde. Why on earth had *this* woman needed to place such an advertisement? Were the men of Texas blind as well as fools?

"Mr. Brookfield, I'm sorry, we weren't expecting you. In the advertisement we placed, we indicated that an interested gentleman was to send a letter. Is it possible your letter got lost in the mail?"

Nick had wondered if the woman would confront him for not following directions, but she had given him a way to save face, if he wanted to use it. Nick wouldn't take refuge in a lie, however, even a small one.

He gave her what he hoped was a dazzling smile. "I'm afraid I didn't want to wait upon an answer to a letter, Miss Matthews, the post being so slow, you understand. I'm here in Texas to take up a post in Austin, but I happened upon your advertisement and found it so intriguing that I rode on to Simpson Creek, purely out of curiosity."

"'Purely out of curiosity?'" she echoed, narrowing her eyes. "Does that mean you're *not* interested in marriage, sir? That you just came to see what sort of a desperate female would place such an advertisement?"

"Milly," her sister murmured, her tone mildly reproachful. "We shouldn't make Mr. Brookfield feel unwelcome. We haven't even given him a chance."

So Miss Matthews could be prickly. This rose had thorns. Then he heard his words as she must have heard them, and he realized how offensive his half-formed idea of meeting the lady and her associates merely as a lark before settling down to a dreary job was.

"I'm sorry," he said. "I didn't mean it to sound that I was merely looking to amuse myself at your expense, ladies. I… I truly was impressed with your initiative, and decided I wanted to meet you."

His reply seemed to mollify her somewhat. "I see," she said, studying him. Her eyes seemed to look deep into his soul. "You're British, Mr. Brookfield?"

Nick nodded. "From Sussex, in southeastern England. But I've been in India the past decade."

"I—I see," she said again, seemingly uncertain what to do now.

Nick was increasingly aware of their audience hanging on to every word. "I—that is, I wonder if we might speak privately?" He couldn't think properly with all of them staring at him, let alone produce the right words to keep her from dismissing him out of hand.

Suspicion flashed in those changeable brown-gold

eyes. For a moment Millicent Matthews looked as if she might refuse.

Nick added the one word he could think of to change her mind, and infused it with all the appeal he could muster. "Please."

She glanced at the others, but they were apparently all waiting for her to decide, for no one said a word or twitched a muscle.

"Very well," she said at last. "We can step outside for a moment, I suppose. Sarah, will you take over the meeting? If you'll follow me, Mr. Brookfield…" She led him down the hall past the sanctuary.

Pushing open the pecan wood door, he walked outside with her, around the side of the church past a small cemetery and into a grove of venerable live oak and pecan trees behind the church. Fragments of old pecan shells crunched under their feet.

It was pleasantly cool in this sun-dappled shade, though the heat of the afternoon shimmered just beyond the influence of the leafy boughs. Insects hummed. A mockingbird flashed gray, black and white as it flitted from one tree to another. A curved stone bench curled around half of the thick trunk of one of the trees, but Millicent Matthews didn't sit down; instead, she turned to face him.

"Mr. Brookfield, before we say anything more, I feel compelled to point out that I'm merely the one who composed the advertisement. There are several other ladies to choose from, as you saw. I assure you, it's quite all right if you find you prefer another of them…"

So she had a sense of fair play and generosity. Nick liked that about her. But somehow he knew her suggestion was something he didn't even want to consider. It was incomprehensible how he could sense that already, but there it was.

"I know you will find this difficult to believe, since we've only just met, and we really don't know each other at all," he said. "I can well understand that it appears I'm making a snap judgment, and perhaps I am, but I would like the opportunity to get to know you better. I—I find you very attractive indeed, Miss Matthews, and that's the simple truth—"

He broke off, somewhat nettled as he noticed she appeared to have suddenly stopped listening. "Miss Matthews…"

"Ssssh!" Millicent hissed, suddenly holding up her hand.

Then he realized she was listening to something beyond the trees, up the road. Then he heard it, too, the pounding of hooves coming closer and a voice calling *"Miss Milly! Miss Milly!"*

"That sounds like Bobby…what can be the matter?" She jumped up, her brow furrowed, and began running toward the front of the church. Nick followed.

Just as they reached the road, a lathered horse skidded to a sliding stop in front of them and a wild-eyed youth jumped off, keeping hold of the reins. The other ladies, doubtless hearing the commotion, poured outside, too.

"Miss Milly! Miss Sarah! You gotta come home quick! There was Injuns—Comanche, I think—they attacked, and I think Uncle Josh is dead!"

Chapter Three

"Indians? Josh is dead? We have to get back there!"

Nick saw the color leach from Millicent Matthews's face until it was white as sun-bleached bones. He stepped quickly forward to catch her, but although she trembled, she stood firm. It was Sarah, her sister, who swayed and might have gone down if one of the other ladies had not moved in to hold her up.

"Sarah! Are you all right?" Milly asked, rushing forward to her sister, whom the other woman had gently assisted to the ground before starting to fan her face.

"Yes… I think so…everything went gray for a moment…" Sarah said. "I'm all right, really, Caroline. Help me up."

Still pale but obviously embarrassed at her near-swoon, she scrambled to her feet.

"We've got to get home!" Milly cried, now that her sister was standing. Her gaze darted around until it settled on a wagon whose horses were tied at the hitching post next to his mount, then back to her sister. "Sarah, come on, let's get you into the wagon—" She braced her sister with an arm around her waist.

Caroline said, "I'll help you get her into the wagon and go home with you. Dan, you run down and tell Pa and the sheriff to round up the men and come out to the Matthews ranch. And bring the doctor, just in case.... Quick, now!" she added, when it seemed as if the lad would remain standing there, mouth agape.

Then Milly seemed to remember him. "Mr. Brookfield, I'm sorry... I have to go. I'm sorry, but I won't be able to—that is, perhaps one of the other ladies..."

"Oh, but I'm coming with you," he informed her, falling into step next to her as she and the other woman helped Sarah walk.

"Really, that's awfully kind of you, but it's not your trouble. There's no telling what we're going to find when we get there," she told him, as if that was the end of the matter. Her eyes went back to her sister as the other woman clambered into the bed of the wagon and stretched an arm down to assist Sarah. "Careful, Sarah..."

"Which is exactly why I'm going," Nick said. "There's no way on earth a gentleman would allow you to ride alone into possible danger. There might be savages lying in wait."

She looked skeptical of him and impatient to be off. "Thank you, but I'm afraid you don't understand about our Comanche—"

He saw how she must see him, as a civilized foreigner with no real experience in fighting, and interrupted her with a gesture. "I have a brace of pistols in my saddlebags," he said, jerking his head toward his horse. "And I know how to use them, as well as that shotgun you have mounted on the back of your wagon seat. Miss Matthews, I have served in Her Majesty's army, and I have been tested in battle against hordes of murderous, screaming Indians—India Indians, that is—armed and out to kill me and every other Englishman they could. Let me come with you, at least until the men from town arrive."

His words seemed to act like a dash of cold water. "A-all right," she said, and without another word turned back to the wagon. She climbed with the graceful ease of long experience onto the seat and gathered up the reins. Before he could even mount his horse, she had backed up the wagon and snapped the reins over the horses' backs.

Milly's heart caught in her throat as the wagon rounded a curve and she spotted the smoke rising in an ominous gray plume over the low mesquite-and-cactus-studded hill that lay between there and home. Unconsciously she pulled up on the reins and the wagon creaked to a halt in the dusty road.

"Oh, Milly, what if it's true? What if Josh is dead? Whatever will we do?" Sarah moaned from the wagon bed behind her.

Please, God, don't let it be true, Milly prayed. *Don't let Josh be dead. Nothing else really matters, even if they burned the house.* She saw out of the corner of her eye that the Englishman had reined in his mount next to them, as had Bobby.

Braced against the side of the wagon bed, Caroline Wallace gave Sarah a one-armed hug, but she looked every bit as worried.

"We'll deal with whatever we find," she said grimly,

fighting the urge to wheel the horses around and whip them into a gallop. What *would* they do, with only a boy not old enough to shave to help them run the ranch? "And the sooner we find out what that is, the better. Here, Mr. Brookfield," she said, reaching around the slatted seat for the shotgun. "Perhaps you'd better have this at the ready."

His eyes were full of encouraging sympathy as he leaned over to accept the firearm from her. "Steady on, Miss Matthews," he murmured. "I'll be with you."

It was ridiculous to take heart from the words of a stranger, a dandified-looking Englishman who claimed to have been a soldier, but there was something very capable in his manner and comforting in his words.

"I'll go ahead, shall I, and scout out the situation?" he suggested. "See if it's safe for you ladies to come ahead?"

"And leave us here to be picked off? No, thank you," she responded tartly, gesturing toward the rocky, brush-studded hills. She could picture a Comanche brave hiding behind every boulder and bush. "We'll go together." She clucked to the horses and the buckboard lurched forward.

She couldn't stifle a groan of pure anguish when she rounded the curve and spotted the smoldering ruin that was the barn. Just then the wind shifted and blew toward the wagon, temporarily blinding her with smoke and stinging her eyes. Had the house been burned to ashes like the barn? Where was Josh? Or rather, Josh's *body,* she corrected herself, knuckling tears away from her cheeks.

Then the wind shifted capriciously again and she

saw what she hadn't dared hope for—the house was still standing. So was the bunkhouse, which stood across from it and next to the barn. Why hadn't they been burned, too? But the pasture beyond, in which some fifty head of cattle and a dozen horses had been grazing when they'd left for the meeting, was empty. There was no sign of the Comanche raiders except for a hawk's feather that must have fallen from one of the braves' hair, sticking incongruously in a rosebush by the house.

"They left Josh on t'other side a' the barn," Bobby whispered, as if fearing that speaking aloud would bring the Comanches back.

She couldn't worry about the loss of the cattle right now or how they would survive. She had to see Josh.

"Caroline, stay with Sarah, please," she said to the woman, who still crouched protectively in the bed of the buckboard by her sister.

"I say, Miss Matthews," Nicholas Brookfield said beside her, "please allow me to go first. There's no need to subject yourself to this if there's nothing to be done for the chap."

It was so tempting to accept his offer, to spare herself the sight of the old man perhaps scalped or otherwise mutilated, lying in his blood. But old Josh had been their rock ever since their father had died, and she owed him this much at least.

"No," she said, letting her eyes speak her gratitude for his offer. "But please, come with me."

Still holding the shotgun at the ready, he led the way around the barn.

At first, she thought the old man *was* dead, sprawled there in the dirt between the side of the barn and the

empty corral. He was pallid as a corpse, his shirt satu-
rated with dark dried blood. A deep gash bisected his
upper forehead, dyeing his gray hair a dark crimson.
A feathered shaft was embedded in each shoulder, pin-
ning his torso to the ground, and his left pants leg was
slashed midthigh. She caught a glimpse of a long, deep
laceration beneath. Not far away, a corner of the barn
still burned with crackling intensity. It was a miracle
flying sparks hadn't set Josh's clothes alight.

And then she saw that Josh's chest was rising and
falling.

"Josh?" she called, softly at first, afraid to trust her
eyes, then louder, *"Josh?"*

His answer was a groan.

She rushed past Brookfield, falling to her knees beside the fallen cowboy. "Josh, it's me, Milly. Can you
hear me?" Gingerly, she touched his face, not wanting
to cause him any extra pain.

Josh's eyelids fluttered and then he opened one
eye, blinking as he attempted to focus his gaze. "Miss
Milly…sorry… I caught them redskins stealin' cattle…
tried to drive 'em off with the rifle…" He squinted at the
ground on his right side and sighed. "Looks like they
got that, too. St-started…they started t' take my scalp…
dunno what stopped 'em from finishin'…"

"Thank God," Milly murmured. But Josh couldn't
hear her. He'd passed out again.

"Bobby, go get me some water from the well," Milly
called over her shoulder. "And tell Sarah and Caroline
to bring soap and a couple of clean sheets to make up
the bed in the spare room for Josh."

"And Bobby, bring me a couple of knives," Brookfield called out, pulling off his black frock coat and throwing it over a fencepost in the nearby corral. He rolled up his sleeves past his elbows, revealing tanned, muscular arms. "And some whiskey if you can find it. Or any kind of liquor."

Milly turned startled eyes to him and saw that he knelt in the dirt beside her, oblivious of his immaculate white shirt and black trousers. "Mr. Brookfield, what are you going to do?"

With his bare hands, he was digging into the dirt beside Josh's wounded shoulder. "Before he comes around, I'm going to cut off the arrowheads. There's no way we can pull the arrow shafts out otherwise without injuring him further."

"Are you a doctor, Mr. Brookfield?"

He shook his head without looking at her, still digging in the dirt.

"Shouldn't we wait 'til the doctor gets here to do that?"

He shook his head again. "You can't even move the man to a bed until we pull out those arrows. I've seen the regimental doctor remove a spear from an unlucky sepoy before, if that makes you feel better."

He didn't explain what a sepoy was, or if the sepoy had lived through the procedure, but she didn't have any better idea. And Dan Wallace might not find the doctor right away. They didn't dare wait.

"I suppose you're right—you'd better go ahead. But even if Josh comes around, we don't have any whiskey or any other kind of spirits. Papa didn't hold with drinking."

"It'd be to pour on the wounds mostly, though if he

regains his senses I'll be giving him some to drink," the Englishman answered, with that purposeful calm he'd exhibited ever since they'd received the awful news.

Just then Bobby dashed back, a pair of knives from the kitchen clutched in one hand, a half-full bottle of whiskey in the other.

Milly's jaw dropped. "Bobby, where on earth did you get that?"

Bobby scuffed the toe of his boot in the dust and refused to meet her eyes. "Mr. Josh, he had some in the bunkhouse. He didn't drink it very often," he added in a defensive tone, "an' never 'til the day's work was done. He never would let me have any, neither. Said I wasn't a man growed yet. He said I wasn't to tell you, but I reckon I needed t' break that promise."

"That's fine, Bobby," Nicholas Brookfield said, taking the bottle from him. "Now go hold one of the knife blades in the fire for a minute."

After the boy did as he was bid and returned with the knife, its tip still glowing red.

"Now you hold the hot knife, Miss Matthews—don't let it touch anything, while you, Bobby, hold Mr. Josh by the shoulder, just so…"

Obediently, she held the knife, watching as Bobby braced one of Josh's shoulders, holding it just far enough above the ground so that the arrow shaft was visible, while Brookfield sawed at the arrow shaft until he had cut it in two, then shifted the wounded man slightly so that he was no longer lying over the arrowhead and the tip of the shaft that was still embedded in the ground. Although Josh groaned, he did not wake up.

Brookfield and Bobby switched sides.

Caroline came from the house then, lugging a bucket of water that splashed droplets out the side with each step she took. "I thought it best to set Sarah to making up the bed in your spare room…" She stopped stock-still when she caught sight of Josh. "Heaven have mercy, he's in a bad way, isn't he? I was afraid she'd faint if she saw him like this."

Milly nodded, knowing Caroline was right. She'd felt dizzy herself, just looking at all that blood, but knew fainting was a luxury she didn't have. Josh needed her to be steady right now and help Nicholas Brookfield.

The Englishman had cut the other shaft away while she spoke to Caroline and was pouring the whiskey liberally over the wounds and his hands now. "I should have told you, but I'm going to need some bandages here as well. These wounds are liable to bleed when I pull the arrow shafts out."

Milly raced into the house, but Sarah had made the bed and had only just begun to rip the other sheet into strips for bandages.

"Milly, how is he? Is he going to make it?" Sarah's face was still pale, her eyes frightened.

"I don't know, Sarah. Hurry up with the bandages, will you? We're going to need a lot of them," Milly said, and dashed back to where Brookfield and Caroline waited for her. "She doesn't have them ready yet."

The Englishman frowned. "I have a handkerchief," he said, pulling a folded square of spotless linen from his breast pocket. "But we'll need something for the other side."

She knew she could send Caroline back to the house and hope that Sarah had some strips of cloth ready by now, but Caroline had sat down, facing away from the wounded man, and was looking a bit green herself. Brookfield looked at her expectantly.

"Wait just a moment," she said, and turning around so that her back was to Brookfield, reached up under her skirts and began ripping the flounces off her petticoat. She wondered what he must be thinking. Surely the well-brought-up young ladies of England would never have done such a thing, but then, they didn't face Comanche attacks, did they?

His cool eyes held an element of admiration when she turned around again and showed him the wadded-up flounce.

"Good thinking, Miss Matthews. Do you think you could kneel by Josh's head and stand ready to apply the bandage quickly, as soon as I pull the first shaft out? I'll move quickly on to the other one, then. Bobby, you hold his feet. He'll probably feel this to some extent, and he's apt to struggle."

Bobby nodded solemnly, so what could Milly do but agree?

Chapter Four

What a woman, Nick marveled, after they'd carried the still-unconscious old man into the spare bedroom and settled him on the fresh sheets. Not only had Milly Matthews not succumbed to a fit of the vapors while she watched him pull out the arrow shafts and the blood welled up onto the skin, but she quickly halted her sister from doing so as well. None of the English ladies of his acquaintance would have done as well as she did. His admiration for her grew apace, right along with his desire to get to know her better.

Now, of course, was not the appropriate time to express such sentiments. "We'll have to keep an eye on those bandages over the wounds, in case he continues to bleed," he told Milly. "And watch for fever." He knew he did not have to tell her that neither would be a good sign—though fever was almost inevitable. Right now, at least, only a very small amount of dried blood showed through on the white cotton.

"We'll set up watches," she said in her decisive manner. "I'll take—"

They all tensed when the sounds of pounding hooves reached them through the open window. Nick grabbed for the shotgun, which he'd gone back outside for as soon as they'd laid the old foreman down on the bed.

"Oh, my heavens, are they back to kill us, too?" Sarah cried, shrinking into the corner.

But Milly strode over to the window and flicked aside the homemade muslin curtains. "It's the posse from town. Maybe they'll be in time to catch those thieving Comanches and get our cattle back." From the slumped set of her shoulders, though, it didn't look as if she believed it.

A minute later, the men clomped inside, spurs clanking against the plank floor, bringing with them the smells of horses and leather and sweat. Milly went into the kitchen to meet them, and he heard her telling them about Josh's injuries and how "the Englishman" had pulled the arrows out of the foreman.

All nine of them were soon tramping back into the spare bedroom to see Josh for themselves—and to satisfy their curiosity about the foreign stranger, Nick assumed.

Milly introduced each one to him. They were an assorted lot, some were tall, some short, some had weathered faces and the lean, wiry-legged build of men who spent much time in the saddle. Others were paler and slighter, like shopkeepers. A couple seemed about the same age as Nick; three were younger, boys really, and the rest had graying or thinning hair. All of them nodded cordially to Nick, and all appeared dressed to ride except for the oldest, whom he had seen climbing out of a two-wheeled covered buggy.

"And last but not least is Doctor Harkey," said Milly, indicating the older man now bending over Josh and peering under the bandages. Doctor Harkey straightened as his name was called, and reached out a hand to Nick.

"You did well, it appears," he told Nick. "Doubt I could've done better myself, though of course only time will tell if old Josh will survive his injuries," he added, looking back at the unconscious man. "Are you a doctor?"

"Nothing like that, sir, but I'm thankful to hear you don't think I made things worse," Nick said.

"He was a soldier in India," Milly informed the doctor.

"I hate t' interrupt, but are we gonna stand around jawin' or are we gonna ride after them Comanches?" asked a beefy, florid-faced middle-aged man. "While we're talkin', those murderin' redskins 're gallopin' away with them cattle." He punctuated his words with a wide sweeping gesture toward the outside.

All the men of the posse straightened and started heading for the door.

Nick stood. "I'd like to go along, if you gentlemen don't mind. I can use their shotgun, and I have my pistols. That is, if you feel you'll be all right here, Miss Matthews."

Milly nodded, obviously surprised by his announcement.

Doctor Harkey stood up. "I'm staying here at least until the posse returns. Josh needs me more than they do."

The men of the posse looked dubiously at Nick. The

beefy man found his voice first. "That's right kindly of you, stranger, but y'ain't exactly dressed fer it," he said, eyeing Nick's blood-stained black frock coat and trousers. "And we didn't bring no extra horse."

"That's my bay standing out there next to the wagon, still saddled. And this suit is probably already ruined, so it makes no difference."

"We can get him some of Josh's clothes—they're about the same size," Milly said. "Bobby, run and fetch them."

The youth, who had been standing by the door, did as he was told, gangly arms flying, boot heels thudding on the floor.

"And he could use Papa's rifle," Sarah said, springing up from her seat. "I'll go get it." She excused herself as she pushed past the men.

The beefy-faced man turned back to Nick. "We'll wait five minutes, no longer, Brookfield. And I'll warn you, we'll be ridin' hard and waitin' for no one. This ain't gonna be no canter in th' park. You fall behind, you're on your own."

"You needn't concern yourself—I can keep up," Nick informed him coolly, holding his gaze until the other man looked away first.

Five minutes later, dressed in the old foreman's denims, work shirt, boots and floppy-brimmed hat, he was galloping across the field with the rest.

"He's quite remarkable, your Mr. Brookfield," Sarah said, as they looked through the window in the spare bedroom as the riders became swallowed in the dust in the distance. She had relaxed now that the doctor arrived and old Josh was sleeping peacefully. "Why, he just took charge, didn't he? I never would have imagined someone dressed like a greenhorn could act so capable."

"And that English accent," Caroline put in with a dreamy sigh. "I reckon I could listen to him talk for hours…"

"He's not *my* Mr. Brookfield," Milly corrected her sister. She did not want to admit to anyone, just yet, how impressed she had been with the way Nicholas Brookfield had jumped right into the midst of their troubles. She would not have expected any man who'd come to town with the simple purpose of meeting a gaggle of unmarried ladies to do as he had done, doctoring a gravely wounded man, and riding with men he had never met in pursuit of the savages. And she supposed if she had nothing else to think about, the Englishman's accent *did* fall very pleasantly on ears used to Texas drawls. But right now she had to wonder how they were going to survive, so she couldn't think about such frivolous things.

"Caroline, I can take you back to town in the buckboard, if you want," she said, changing the subject. "The horses are still hitched up."

"No, thank you, not with a bunch of wild Indians in the area," the postmaster's daughter said. "Besides, I'll just wait 'til Papa comes back with the posse and ride back with him. Meanwhile, I'll make myself useful around here. Sarah, why don't we go see what we can whip up for supper? Doc Harkey, you probably missed your dinner, didn't you?"

The old physician looked up from Josh's bedside. "I did, because Maude was at that meeting with y'all. She said she'd fix it as soon as she got home…but of course no one could've foreseen what happened. Anything will be fine for me, girls. I'm not picky. Josh'll need some broth tomorrow, but I imagine he won't be taking any nourishment tonight."

"While you two are doing that," Milly said, "I'll un-hitch the buckboard, then see if I can wash the blood out of Mr. Brookfield's clothes. I'm sure glad he could wear Josh's clothes. He must not know how the mesquite thorns and cactus would rip that fine cloth to shreds."

"Take a pistol outside with you," Sarah admonished, "just in case."

Milly was sure she had just nodded off beside the old cowboy's bedside when she was awakened by the sound of a cow bawling from the corral.

I must still be dreaming, because the Indians took all the cattle and most of the horses yesterday.

Then the door creaked open. The gray light of dawn—it had been midnight when she had sent the doctor to sleep in their father's bed—illuminated the dusty, rumpled figure of Nicholas Brookfield, while from the kitchen wafted the sound of her sister's voice mingling with the low voices of the other men and the smell of coffee.

"Did you…did you catch them?" she finally asked, though his weary eyes had already telegraphed the answer.

"No. We followed them until their tracks split up, each pair of horses following some of the cattle. We would've turned back sooner if the moon hadn't been full, but it was too dark to track. By that time we were considerably far from here, so we're just now getting back. But the good news is that either they missed some of the cattle and horses, or some managed to break away, because we found several along the way. So we rounded up a score or so of cattle and half a dozen horses."

Milly straightened, fully awake now. "That *is* good news. Better than I'd dared hope for." At least they wouldn't starve, although she'd hoped to sell the full herd to a cattle drover next spring. Now they might have to sell some of the horses to buy more stock. In time, more calves would be born, and the herd would grow again—if the Comanche left their ranch alone. But raiding Indians were a fact of life in this part of Texas, and probably would be for a long time to come. Until the Federal army managed to contain them in reservations or kill them, one took his chances with the Indians or moved elsewhere.

"How is he?" he asked, nodding toward the supine figure on the bed.

"He had a restless night," Milly answered, her gaze following his. "The doctor gave him some laudanum before I took over, and got some willow bark tea in him while he was lucid, for the fever, but he's been sleeping since then. He hasn't had any more bleeding."

"Thank God for that," he said, rubbing a beard-shadowed cheek.

"Yes. And you've done more than I could've possibly asked for, Mr. Brookfield," she said, giving him a grateful smile. "I smell breakfast cooking out there. Why don't you join the other men and eat, and then I'll hitch up the wagon and take you back to town. Or you could take a nap in the bunkhouse first, if you'd like. You must be exhausted."

"I'm not leaving, Miss Matthews," he informed her. "You're going to need some help around here, while your foreman convalesces."

"But…but you're not a cowboy," Milly said. "You said you had a position waiting for you in Austin. I couldn't possibly ask you to—"

"You haven't asked. I've offered. And I couldn't possibly leave two women to cope alone out here, with nothing more than a lad to help you," he said reasonably. "It wouldn't be right."

"But I could probably get someone from around here to help, until Josh is back on his feet," she said, not wanting to think about the possibility that Josh might not be able to resume his responsibilities. He wasn't out of the woods yet, and wouldn't be for a few days, Doc Harkey had said. He could still die if infection set in. "You know nothing of handling cattle and all the rest of the things a cowboy does."

"I can learn," he insisted stubbornly. "Bobby can teach me, and in time, Josh can, too. As for the men around here, it sounds as if they all have their own ranches to tend. Most of them thought you should sell out and move into town," he said. "Mr. Waters said something about making you an offer," he said.

Milly blinked. It didn't surprise her that Bill Waters saw this attack as a good time to persuade her to sell her property to him. He'd always wanted the Matthews property, because it abutted his land but had better access to Simpson Creek.

"Now, if you *want* to do that, I'd certainly understand," Nicholas went on. "But I got the idea you wanted to stay here. And in that case, you'll need me."

She stared at him while he waited calmly, watching her. Should she take him up on his offer? Could she trust him, or would he disappear as soon as he realized what a hard life he was signing up for, even temporarily? Was he just trying to impress her with his generosity, in an effort to woo her, to get her to let her guard down? Might he try to take liberties with her once she was depending on him?

"If you would feel more secure about allowing me to stay on and help you," he began, "you may dismiss what I said in the churchyard before all this happened, about getting to know you better. I know you have a lot on your mind right now besides courting, and if you only want me to serve as a cowhand, I believe you call it, and a guard to protect you and your sister, I'll understand."

"I... I don't know what to say," Milly managed at last. "What you're offering is...more than generous."

"Girl, I think you better take him up on it," a voice rasped from the bed beside them, and they both started.

"Josh, you're awake!" she cried. How long had he been listening? "How do you feel?"

"Like I been stomped on by a herd a' cattle with hooves sharp as knives," Josh said, smiling weakly. "With a little luck I reckon I'll make it, though. But it's gonna be a while afore I'm fit t'manage this here ranch an' keep young Bobby from daydreamin' the day away. This here Englishman's willin' to help you out, so I reckon you should accept an' say thank you to the good Lord fer sendin' him."

Chapter Five

Before Josh had begun speaking, Nick had watched the conflicting emotions parading across Milly's face—doubt, trust, fear, hope. Now, at the old cowboy's urging, the battle was over and trust had won—trust in old Josh's opinion, if not in Nick himself, as yet.

"Josh has never steered us wrong," she said, smiling down at the old cowboy and then back at Nick. "So I will take you up on your very kind offer, Nicholas Brookfield, at least until Josh is back on his feet."

He gave both of them a brilliant smile, then bowed. "Thank you," he said. "I'm honored. I shall endeavor to be worthy of the trust you've placed in me."

Milly looked touched, but Josh gave a chuckle that had him instantly wincing at the movement to his ribs. "Boy, that was a might pretty speech for what you just signed up for—a lot a' hard work in the dust and heat."

"I'll be very dependent on your advice, sir."

"I—I can't pay you anything for the time being," Milly said apologetically. "Just your room and board."

"My needs are simple," Nick said. "Room and board

will be plenty." He was only a third son of a nobleman, but he still wasn't exactly a pauper, so he had little need of whatever sum most cowboys were paid a month beyond their keep. He would have to write to the bank in Austin that was handling his affairs and notify them that his address would be in Simpson Creek, for now.

"I suppose you could have my father's bedroom when the doctor leaves…" Milly mused aloud.

"That won't be necessary," he replied quickly. "The bunkhouse will be fine for me."

Her forehead furrowed. "But…surely you've never slept in such humble circumstances," she protested. "I mean…in a bunk bed? I imagine you're used to much better, being from England and all."

He thought for a moment of his huge bedchamber back home in East Sussex at Greyshaw Hall, with its canopied bed and monogrammed linen sheets, and his comfortable quarters in Bombay and his native servant who had seen to his every need. Yes, he had been "used to much better," but he had also experienced much worse.

"Miss Matthews, I told you I was a soldier until recently, and while on campaign I have slept on a camp cot and even on the ground. I assure you I will be fine in the bunkhouse. Besides, I cannot properly be a cowboy unless I sleep there, can I?" he asked lightly, knowing it had been innocence that had led her to offer him her father's old room.

"But—"

"Miss Milly, you can't be havin' him sleepin' in the same house with you two girls," Josh pointed out, with a meaningful nod toward the kitchen, from where the sounds of conversation and the clinking of silverware against plates still floated back to them. "Once the gossips in town got wind a' that, they'd chew your reputation to shreds."

Nick could see that in her effort to be properly hospitable, Milly hadn't thought of how it would look for him to stay in the house.

"He'd best sleep out in th' bunkhouse, where the greatest danger'll be my snorin', once I get back on my feet," Josh said with a wink.

"It's decided, then," Nick said. All at once his long night in the saddle caught up with him and before he could catch himself, he yawned.

"Good heavens, I'd forgotten how exhausted you must be, Mr. Brookfield!" Milly exclaimed. "You've been up all night! Go on out to the kitchen and get yourself some breakfast, like I said, while I take some sheets out to the bunkhouse and make up a bed for you," she said, making shooing motions.

He remained where he was for a moment. "I suppose if I'm going to work for you, Miss Milly, you had better start calling me Nick," he said, holding her gaze.

He was delighted to see he could make Milly Matthews blush—and such a charming blush it was, too, spreading upward from her lovely, slender neck to her cheeks and turning them scarlet while her eyes took on a certain sparkle. Immediately she looked away, as if she could pretend by sheer force of will that it hadn't happened.

He saw Josh watching this little scene, too, but there was no censure in the old cowboy's gaze, only amusement.

"You'd best hurry on out to the kitchen like Miss

Milly said, Nick. The way those galoots out there eat, they're liable not to leave you a crumb."

Snatching up clean, folded sheets from a cedar-wood chest in the hallway, Milly followed Nick. Caroline Wallace was in the kitchen, pouring coffee. She and the handful of men standing around forking scrambled eggs from their plates nodded at her or mumbled "Good morning."

Threading her way through them, she found Sarah at the cookstove, talking to Doc Harkey.

"How's Josh?" Sarah had taken the evening watch, but she was no night owl, and had gone to bed when Milly relieved her. But Milly was never at her best in the morning or at cooking, so she was grateful Sarah was up with the sun and feeding the hungry men.

"Awake. I can tell he's going to make it, 'cause he's already ornery," Milly said with a laugh.

"I'll go in and have a look at him," Doc Harkey said, and waded through the throng of men toward the back hall.

Sarah looked questioningly at the armload of sheets Milly carried.

"Mr. Brookfield has very kindly offered to stay on and help us while Josh is laid up," she said, keeping her tone low so only Sarah could hear, and nodding toward Nick. He was talking to one of the other men while spooning clumps of scrambled eggs onto his plate to join a rasher of bacon and a thick slice of bread. "I'm just going to make up a bed in the bunkhouse for him."

"I see." Sarah's knowing eyes spoke volumes and she

grinned. "Well, isn't that nice of him? You have your very own knight in shining armor."

"Yes, *we* do," Milly corrected her in a quelling tone. "It is very kind of him, though he's never done ranch chores before. But he seems to think Josh can advise him and Bobby can show him what he needs to do."

"He seems like the kind of man who can do anything he sets his mind to," Sarah commented. "All right, you go make up the bed, but once these fellows go home, you go on to bed."

"Oh, I slept a little in the chair," Milly protested. "I'll be all right."

"I'm sure it wasn't enough."

"Thanks for handling breakfast," Milly said. "How did you ever manage?"

"The eggs were from yesterday morning, the bacon from the smokehouse. I'm sure I don't know what we're going to do after that. I found a few hens roosting in the trees, and that noisy rooster, but I'm sure the barn fire killed the rest of them."

"We'll make it with God's help, and one day at a time," Milly said, determined not to give way to anxiety. Only yesterday morning Sarah had been gathering eggs, while she had been planning a meeting to marry off the women in Simpson Creek. Now she had bigger problems to worry about.

"You're right, Milly," Sarah said, squaring her shoulders. "I guess we won't be eating chicken for a while until the flock builds up again."

"Or beef," Milly said.

"We'll have to send Bobby to look in the brush. Maybe some of the pigs made it."

* * *

Weariness nagged at Milly's heels by the time she finished making up the bed in the bunkhouse and trudged back across the yard. The men who'd ridden in the posse were in the process of departing, some saddling their horses, some already mounted up and waiting for the others. Caroline was riding double with her father.

At Milly's approach, Bill Waters handed his reins to Amos Wallace and headed out to intercept her.

"Mr. Waters, I want to thank you for taking charge of the men and doing your best to find our cattle," she said, extending a hand.

"You're welcome, little lady," he said in his usual bluff, hearty manner. "I'd do anything for Dick Matthews's daughters, and that's a fact. Wish we could've caught them thievin' redskins and gotten all of the cattle and horses back, instead of just some." He shrugged. "It's a shame this has happened, it surely is," he said, gesturing at the charred remains of the barn, from which a wisp or two of smoke still rose. "Now, I think you ought to reconsider my offer to buy you out. You could find rooms in town, take jobs…or move on to some big city somewhere. Don't you see it's the only sensible thing to do now that this has happened?"

"Thanks, Mr. Waters. We'll think about it," she said, as she had so many times before, ever since Pa had died. She saw by his exasperated expression that he knew she was only being polite.

"You need to do more than just think about it. Your pa would want me to make you see reason, I know he would!"

He was getting more red in the face as he talked. A vein jumped in his forehead. Milly fought the urge to pluck the hanky he had sticking out of his pocket and wipe his brow.

"The good Lord knows I'd hoped somethin' might grow between my boy Wes and you or Sarah, once the war was over. But it didn't work out that way."

Wesley Waters was one of the Simpson Creek boys who had not returned. Milly, Sarah and Wes had been friendly, but never anything more. But Milly believed his father hadn't wanted a romance between Wes and either of the Matthews girls nearly as much as he'd wanted a means of joining the Matthews land to his.

"Just tell me, how are you two going to cope out here, with Josh laid up and only that no-account boy t'help you?" He made a wide arc with his arm, including the whole ranch.

"We'll be all right, Mr. Waters. Mr. Brookfield has very kindly offered to stay on and help us while Josh is laid up."

He blinked at her. "That foreigner? What does he know about ranchin'? Beggin' yer pardon, Miss Milly, but have you been spendin' too much time in the sun without your bonnet? And that scheme of yours of in- vitin' men here t'marry is just plumb foolishness. Your pa would want me to tell you that, too!"

Temper flaring, Milly went rigid. "Mr. Waters, the way you're talking, I'm not sure you ever really knew my father after all. My pa always encouraged me to pray about a problem, then use my brain to solve it."

"And this is the solution your brain cooked up?" he said, pointing an accusing finger at Nick, who had just come out onto the porch. "Bringing an outsider—a *foreigner*—to Simpson Creek?"

Nick crossed the yard in a few quick strides. From where he had been, Milly knew he could not have heard Bill Waters's words, but he'd seen the finger pointed at him, for he asked quietly, "Is there a problem, Miss Matthews?"

She could have kissed him for coming to her side just then. "No, Mr. Waters was just fretting about his need to leave and go take care of his own ranch. But I assured him we'd be fine, with you to help us."

She saw Waters try to stare Nick down, but Nick returned his gaze calmly. "I'm sure Miss Matthews appreciates your concern," he said. "And I assure you I'll do everything in my power to ensure her safety and that of her sister." He offered his hand, which Waters pretended not to see.

"I'll count on that, Brookfield," he growled. "Good day, Miss Milly," he called over his shoulder as he stalked off to his waiting horse.

Bill Waters is nothing but a patronizing hypocrite, trying to hide his greed under a cloak of concern! thought Milly.

"What did he say to you? You're shaking," Nick observed, still keeping his voice low as Waters led the way out of the yard.

Milly was still stinging at Waters's condescending words, but she didn't want to repeat what the old rancher had said about Nick. Just then, she was saved from the necessity of talking about it by the arrival of the circuit preacher's buggy rolling into the barnyard.

"Reverend Chadwick, how nice of you to visit,"

she called, reaching the buggy just as the silver-haired preacher set the brake and stepped out of his buggy.

"Miss Milly, I was in Richland Springs. I was so upset to arrive back in town this morning and hear what had happened to you," he said, embracing her, then staring with dismay at the blackened ruin of the barn. "I came straight here. I didn't stop any longer than it took to water the horses," he said.

"Reverend Chadwick, a circuit rider can't be everywhere at once. We certainly understand that," Milly protested.

"And how is Josh?"

She told the preacher about their foreman's injuries. "I'm sure he'd be pleased to see you," she said. "Come inside. But before you do, Reverend, I'd like you to meet Mr. Nicholas Brookfield, who'll be helping us out here while Josh recovers."

Chapter Six

After introductions were made, Milly mercifully excused Nick and sent him to get some sleep. He'd thought at first he'd never be able to fall into slumber on the thin ticking-covered straw mattress in the middle of the hot Texas day.

The next thing he knew, though, the creaking of the door opening woke him as Bobby clumped into the room and started rummaging in the crate at the foot of his bed.

"Oh, sorry, didn't mean t'wake you, sir," the youth apologized, straightening.

"No need to apologize," he told the youth. "I never meant to sleep so long. And you'd probably better start calling me Nick, too," he told the boy.

Bobby looked gratified but still a little uneasy. "How 'bout Mr. Nick? Uncle Josh says t' be respectful to my elders."

"Fair enough." The angle of the shadows on the wall told Nick hours had passed even before he reached for the pocket watch he had left on the upended crate that served as bedside table and saw that it was four o'clock.

He'd slept the day away! Milly, her sister and Bobby had no doubt taken on tasks he should have been doing.

"What needs to be done?"

Bobby traced a half circle with the toe of one dusty boot, apparently also uncomfortable with the idea of giving an adult orders.

"I—I dunno, s—Mr. Nick. Mebbe you best ask Miss Milly."

"All right, I'll do that."

He found Milly in the kitchen, shelling black-eyed peas into a bowl in her lap. Sarah, her back to the door, was kneading dough. The delicious odor of roasting ham wafted from the cookstove.

"Oh, hello, Nick," Milly said. "Did you have a good sleep?"

"Too good," Nick said. "I want to apologize for lying abed so long when there's so much to be done."

"Horsefeathers," Milly Matthews responded with a smile. "You must have needed it."

Her lack of censure only made him feel guiltier, somehow. "Did you get some rest, ma'am?"

She shook her head. "I'll sleep tonight."

"As I should have waited to do. I only meant to lie down for an hour. This won't happen again, Miss Milly, Miss Sarah."

"Don't be so hard on yourself, Nick," Sarah admonished, looking over her shoulder.

"Thank you, but I intend to be more of a help from now on. What should I be doing now?"

Milly's hands paused, clutching a handful of un-shelled pods. "It's a couple of hours 'til supper—not enough time to get started on any rebuilding projects....

It might be a good idea if you and Bobby were to saddle up and go for a ride around the ranch so you can get an idea of how far the property extends and make a survey of what needs to be done. Oh, and you'll be passing the creek that runs just inside the northern edge. You and Bobby could take a quick dip and get cleaned up," Milly added, eyeing his cheeks and chin.

"A dip sounds good." Nick ran his fingers over the stubbly growth, imagining how scruffy he looked. He was glad he'd kept his razor in his saddlebag. He didn't want to look unkempt around this lovely woman he was trying to impress.

"Take your pistol with you," Milly called as he headed for the door. "You never know what you might meet out there in the brush."

"Do you mean Indians?"

She nodded. "Or rattlesnakes. They like to sun themselves on the rocky ledges that line one side of the creek. There's a little cave in those ledges. Sarah and I used to play there and pretend it was our cottage until we saw a snake at its entrance."

"Then I'll be sure and take my dip on the other side." He'd had enough encounters with cobras in India to have a healthy respect for poisonous snakes of any kind.

"Don't let Bobby dillydally in the creek," she admonished. "Supper's at six and Reverend Chadwick brought a big ham with him on behalf of the congregation."

"If Bobby wants to stay in the creek, I shall eat his share of the meat," he said with a wink.

Nick was as good as his word, riding into the yard with Bobby at quarter 'til the hour. By the time they'd unsaddled and turned the horses out in the corral, the grandfather clock in the parlor was chiming six times.

"Here we are, ma'am, right on schedule," Nick said, pronouncing it in the British way—"shedule" instead of "schedule." She watched him, noting the way his still-damp hair clung to his neck while he sniffed with obvious appreciation of the savory-smelling, covered iron pot she carried to the table with the aid of a thick dish towel.

"Your promptness is appreciated," she said lightly, although what she was really appreciating was the strong, freshly shaved curve of his jaw. Nick Brookfield was compelling even when tired and rumpled; when rested and freshly bathed, he was a very handsome man, indeed. She wrenched her eyes away, lest he catch her staring. "You can sit over there, across from Bobby," she said, pointing to a chair on the far side of the rectangular, rough-hewn table that had been laid with a checkered gingham cloth.

"How about Josh? Would you like me to take him his supper and help him eat first?"

"Oh, he's already eaten," Sarah said. "He's not up to anything but a little soup yet, but he took that well at least. Maybe tomorrow he can eat a little more and even join us at the table."

Milly was moved that Nick had thought of the injured old cowboy's needs before his own. She watched now as he seated himself gracefully, then waited.

"Nick, since this is your first meal with us, would you like to say the blessing?" You could tell a lot about a man by the way he reacted to such a request, Pa always said.

Nick hesitated, but only for a moment. "I'd be honored," he said, and bowed his head. "Lord, we'd like to thank You for this bountiful meal and the good people from the church who provided it, and the hands that prepared it. And we thank You for saving the house, and Josh, and please protect the ranch and those who live here from the Indians. Amen."

"Thank you. That was very nice, wasn't it, Milly?" Sarah asked.

"Uh-huh." Milly thought Nick sounded like a man accustomed to speaking to his Lord, but Pa had also said sometimes folks could talk the talk, even if they didn't walk the walk. "Here, Nick, take some ham," she said, handing him the platter, while she passed a large bowl of black-eyed peas flavored with diced ham to Bobby. He took a couple of slices, then passed it down to Sarah.

"We always pass the meat to Bobby last, because there'll be nothing left after he's had a chance at it," Sarah teased from her end of the table.

Bobby, who'd been watching the progress of the ham platter as it made its way down the table, just grinned.

"He's still a growing lad, aren't you, Bobby?" Nick said, smiling.

"I reckon I am," Bobby agreed. "Uncle Josh says I got hollow legs. Look, Miss Milly, I think my arms have growed some." After helping himself to a handful of biscuits, he extended an arm. The frayed cuff extended only a little past the middle of his forearm.

"*Grown* some," Milly corrected automatically, taking a knifeful of butter and passing the butter dish. "I suppose I'll have to buy some sturdy cloth at the mercantile next time I'm there and make you a couple of new ones. Josh probably needs a couple, too, though I know he'll say just to patch the elbows." She sighed. While making clothing was actually something she was good at, even better than Sarah, trying to find the cash to buy cloth or anything extra right now would be difficult. "Nick, what did you think of our land?" she said, deliberately changing the subject. She could fret about Bobby's outgrown shirts later.

"It seems good ranch country, to my novice eyes," he said, with a self-deprecating smile. "Much bigger than I thought. We didn't even get to the western boundary, or we would have been late returning."

"It's actually one of the smaller ranches in San Saba County," Milly said, but she appreciated how impressed he seemed.

"Is that right? Back in Sussex, you two would be prominent landowners. They'd have called your father 'Squire.' Most English country folk have very small plots and rent from the local noble or squire. I noticed there's fence needing repair along your boundary with Mr. Waters's land, by the way."

Before she could stop herself, another sigh escaped. "Yes, he won't repair it. He doesn't think there should be fences—'Just let the cattle run wild 'til the fall roundup, just like we always did,'" she said, deepening her voice to imitate the man. "I suspect he used to brand quite a few yearlings as his that were actually ours, before Pa put up his fence."

"Has he always been a difficult man?"

Milly shrugged. "He isn't really difficult, only set in his ways." He hadn't acted this way when Pa was alive, of course. And before the war he had cherished dreams of gaining the ranch by his son marrying Milly, or even Sarah. Milly supposed she couldn't blame the man for wanting to enlarge his property by persuading her to sell out—and only time would tell if he had been right that a woman couldn't manage a ranch.

Suppertime passed pleasantly. Nick Brookfield had perfect table manners and ate like a man with a good appetite, although not with the same fervor that Bobby displayed, as if he thought every meal would be his last. When it was over, he thanked them for the delicious meal, especially Sarah for the lightness of her biscuits, which brought a grateful warmth to her sister's eyes.

"Perhaps you should tell me what I should be doing tomorrow," he said to Milly, as Sarah began to clear away the dishes.

"I think I'll let Josh do that," she said. "Why don't you go visit with him now for a while? Bobby can see to the horses and the chickens."

"I will." He rose. "Would it be all right if sometime tomorrow I went into town? I need to pick up my valise at the boardinghouse, and let the proprietress know I won't be needing the room."

"Of course," she said. So he had taken a room at the boardinghouse before coming to meet her and the rest of the ladies, she mused. He'd intended to spend some time getting to know her. "Actually, we need sugar from the general store, if you wouldn't mind picking it up. Oh, and perhaps some tea? Don't Englishmen prefer to drink that?" At least, she thought she had enough egg money in the old crockery jar to cover those two items. She was going to have to scrimp until they had enough eggs to spare from now on.

"Coffee is fine, Miss Milly. You needn't buy anything specifically for me."

An hour later, he found Milly ensconced in a cane back rocking chair on the porch, reading from a worn leather Bible on her lap.

"What part are you reading?" he said, looking down at it. "Ah, Psalm One—'Blessed is the man who walks not in the counsel of the ungodly, nor standeth in the way of sinners, nor sitteth in the seat of the scornful,'" he quoted from memory.

Her hazel eyes widened. "Were you a preacher, as well as a soldier and occasional field surgeon?" she asked, gesturing toward the rocker next to her in an unspoken invitation to sit down.

He sat, smiling at her question. "No, but my second oldest brother is in holy orders, vicar of Westfield. They'll probably make him a bishop one day. Any Scripture I know was pounded into my thick head by Richard when I was a lad."

"And do you read the Bible now?" she asked.

He wished he could say he did. "I… I'm afraid I haven't lately."

He could see her filing the information away, but her eyes betrayed no judgment about the fact.

"And how did you find Josh? Does he need anything? Is he in pain?"

"He's not in pain, no, but he needs a goodly dose of patience," he said, appreciating the fine curve of Milly's neck above the collar of her calico dress. "He's restless, fretting over the need to lie there and be patient while he heals. But I think he's reassured that I can help Bobby handle the 'chores'—" he gave the word the old man's drawling pronunciation, drawing a chuckle from her "—and keep this place from utter ruin until he can be up and around again. Oh, and he says there's no need to sit up with him tonight, if you'll let him borrow that little handbell of your mother's he can just ring if he needs you."

"Hmm. That sounds just like him. I'd better check on him a couple of times tonight at least. I can just picture him trying to reach the water pitcher and tearing open those wounds again. That old man would rather die than admit a weakness."

Nick chuckled. "He said you'd say that, too."

They were silent for a while. Nick appreciated the cool breeze and the deepening shadows as the fiery orange ball sank behind the purple hills off to their right.

"Nick, why did you leave India, and the army—if you don't mind my asking, that is?" she added quickly.

She must have seen the reflexive stiffening of his frame and the involuntary clenching of his jaw.

"It's getting late, and I'm keeping you from your reading," he said, rising.

"I'm sorry, that was rude of me to pry. Please forgive me for asking," she said, rising, too. Her face was dismayed.

"It's all right," he told her. "I'll tell you about it sometime. But it's a long story." He'd known the question would come, but it was too soon. He wasn't ready to shatter her illusions about him yet.

Chapter Seven

As Nick tied his bay at the hitching post outside the general store, he saw two men standing talking at the entrance, one with his hand on the door as if he meant to go inside. Nick recognized one of them as Bill Waters, the neighboring rancher who'd pressured Milly to sell out yesterday. He'd never seen the other one, the one with his hand on the door.

"Hank, I'm tellin' you, the problem's gettin' bad around here," Waters was saying, "what with them roamin' the roads beggin' fer handouts and such. Why, a friend a' mine over in Sloan found half a dozen of 'em sleepin' in his barn when he went out one mornin'. He got his shotgun and they skedaddled away like their clothes was on fire."

The other man guffawed.

"We got t'nip it in the bud, before they try movin' in around Simpson Creek. That's why I'm revivin' the Circle. Bunch of us are meetin' at my ranch tomorrow night. Can you make it?"

Nick wondered idly who the men were talking about.

Beggars of some sort—out-of-work soldiers from the recent war? Certainly not the warlike Comanche. Poor Mexicans? And what was the "circle" Waters referred to?

"Excuse me," he said, when the men seemed oblivious of his desire to enter the store.

The unknown man glared at the interruption before taking his hand off the door and moving aside just enough for Nick to squeeze past. "I'll be there," the man said to Waters. "We kin blame Lincoln for this, curse his interferin' Yankee hide. I just wish I could shoot him all over again."

Nick nodded at Waters as he walked past him, but the man looked right through him.

"Good morning, Mr. Patterson," Nick said to the man behind the counter in the general store, recognizing him as one of the men of the posse. "Miss Matthews sent me for five pounds of sugar."

"That'll be thirty-five cents, please," said Mr. Patterson, measuring out the amount into a thin drawstring bag and wrapping it in brown paper.

Nick counted out the coins, glad he'd become comfortable with American currency before coming to Simpson Creek.

"Nicholas Brookfield, isn't it?" the shopkeeper asked. "How are you getting along out there? And how are the Matthews girls? And old Josh, is he recovering?"

"Nick," Nick insisted, pleased at Mr. Patterson's warm reception after the way Bill Waters had acted. He extended his hand and the other took it. "I'm well, thank you, and Miss Milly and Miss Sarah are doing fine. Josh is feeling better, though he's still in pain from his wounds, of course. I'll tell them you asked about them."

"You do that," the other said. He looked up, and raised his voice to carry to the far end of the store, where two older men were bent over a game of checkers. "Hey, Reverend—here's Nick Brookfield, that English fellow who's helping out at the Matthews ranch. Maybe he could tell you what you were wantin' t'know."

The white-haired minister who had come out to the ranch yesterday looked up, then rose and bustled over to him. "Mr. Brookfield, hello," he said, extending his hand.

"Nick," he insisted again. "I know Miss Milly and Miss Sarah would want me to thank you again for that very tasty ham."

"Oh, that was little enough. We were happy to do it," the old man said, beaming.

"What is it I may tell you, Reverend?"

"I was hoping," the preacher said, "that you might be able to suggest what else we—as a town, that is—could do for Milly and Sarah. I've known those two young ladies since they were babies, and I'm troubled about the situation they've been left in, especially after the Indian attack two days ago. I asked Milly, but I'm afraid she's determined to be self-sufficient, and I wouldn't want there to be something we could do to assist that she's ashamed to ask for."

Nick looked down for a moment, rubbing his chin. He wondered if he'd be overstepping his bounds to say what he really thought. Nothing ventured, nothing gained, he supposed. "I'd say their greatest need is for a new barn to replace the one the Comanches burned," he said. "Would there be any men who'd be willing and able to help them build one?"

Now it was the other two men's turn to be thoughtful. "Everyone would want to help, but they're pretty busy keeping their own ranches or businesses going…"

"But we could have a barn raising and put it up in a day!" Reverend Chadwick countered, with rising excitement. "Everyone could afford one day away from their own places."

"Yeah, we haven't had a barn raisin' in a coon's age," put in the man who'd been playing checkers with the preacher, who came forward now. Nick vaguely recognized the man who'd been introduced to him as the livery stable proprietor, although he couldn't remember his name. "Let's do it! Our ladies could provide the food, and we could all make a day of it."

"You'd all come out and put up a barn for them?" Nick was frankly floored that his tentative request for labor help was meeting with such an enthusiastic response. No wonder Americans had won their independence against the mighty British army—and maintained it in another war just a score of years later, if they always seized the initiative this way.

"Sure," Patterson said with a grin. "It's hard work, but at the end of the day there'd be a barn standing there, by gum. The ladies always have a great time visiting with each other at these things, and the children run around with each other and play, then nap like puppies in the shade. Usually the day ends with some fiddlin' music and a big supper."

"But what about the lumber needed?" Nick asked.

"Miss Milly and Miss Sarah don't have much in the way of ready cash…"

"Not many do, these days," Patterson said. "You may have heard Texas was on the losing side in the recent war."

Nick figured it would be impolitic to do more than nod his acknowledgment.

"We're gonna need lumber," the livery owner went on, thinking aloud.

"Maybe Mr. Dayton could be persuaded to donate it," Reverend Chadwick suggested. "Or at least offer it at a discount."

"Hank Dayton give something away?" snorted Patterson. "That'd be something new."

Hank Dayton. Had that been the man who had just been outside, talking to Waters? Nick had to agree—he didn't seem like the generous type.

"You never know. The good Lord still works miracles," Chadwick said with a twinkle in his eye. "I'll ask him. Failing that, perhaps he would at least extend credit 'til the Matthews ladies could pay him back, or we could hold a fundraising party…"

"When are we gonna have this barn raisin'?" Patterson asked. "The ladies'll need some time to organize the food and so forth."

"Shall we say a week from Saturday? When do you think would be good for Miss Milly and Miss Sarah, Nick?"

Nick shrugged. It wasn't as if Milly and her sister had a complicated social schedule of balls and dinner parties to work around. "The sooner the better, probably. Will you be coming out to tell her about it, sir?"

"No, I'll let you bring the good news, Nick. Just let us know if that date won't be convenient."

The proprietress of the boardinghouse hadn't been surprised that he would no longer need the room, having already heard of his new, temporary job—there certainly were no secrets in a small town. She'd probably already rented out his room. He gave her a quarter for keeping his valise for him, though, prompting a surprised thanks from the woman.

He couldn't help feeling a certain pleased anticipation as he drove the buckboard back to the ranch. Milly was going to be so surprised that the ranch would soon have a proper barn again! He was glad the preacher had left it up to him to bring the news.

On impulse, he stopped the wagon on the road home when he spotted a cluster of daisylike yellow flowers with brown centers growing alongside the road and picked a bouquet-sized handful for Milly. He wondered if this was violating his offer not to press her with courting gestures during their time of hardship. Yet had she ever actually said she would hold him strictly to that? He couldn't actually remember her saying it in so many words, so surely this small cheerful bunch of flowers would cause no offense.

It didn't. After unharnessing the horse and turning him out into the corral, he found Milly in the grove of pecan trees that stood next to the house. She wore a calico dress that had seen better days and was bent over a washboard set in a bucket of water, scrubbing stains from an old shirt. Wet garments hung to dry from low branches and across bushes. In spite of the shade, she

looked hot and tired. Beads of sweat pearled on her forehead. He strode over, holding the brown paper parcel
of sugar in one hand and keeping the hand holding the
bouquet behind his back.

Swiping one damp hand over her forehead to push
an errant lock of black hair out of her eyes, she caught
sight of him and stopped. She looked as if she felt embarrassed to be caught thus, but she smiled and said,
"Oh, the sugar! Thanks so much for getting that for us,
Nick. Were you able to pick up your things?"

"Yes," he said, putting the sack of sugar down on
the table at a safe distance from the tub of water, "and
I brought you these." He brought his other hand from
around his back and offered them to her. "They looked
so cheerful and appealing, I wanted you to have them."

Her eyes focused on the flowers, then locked with
his, and the color rose on her already-pink cheeks.

"Of course, they were just growing wild by the road,"
he added apologetically. "I don't know what they are.
But I didn't see any roses…"

Wiping her wet hands hurriedly on her apron, she
came around the table and took them from him, beaming. "They're *beautiful,* Nick! Thank you. That was so
nice of you! Brown-eyed Susans, we call them. The
only one I know who can keep roses alive around here
is Mrs. Detwiler, and I'm pretty sure she wouldn't share
hers. I think she counts and names each one," she added
with a laugh. "Why don't we take them inside and put
them in some water? It's almost dinnertime, and I'm
ready for a break," she added, rolling her eyes toward
the pile of laundry that remained. "And I happen to

know Sarah made some lemonade with the last of the old sugar. She's inside cooking."

He nodded his acceptance, happy that the flowers had pleased her. "Good. I have some news from town to tell both of you."

Milly looked curious, but led the way inside.

Sarah looked up from the stove when they entered, and sent him an approving look as Milly reached for an empty Mason jar to use as a vase.

"Now, what's this news?" Milly said, gesturing for him to sit while Sarah poured lemonade into glasses.

He told them about encountering Reverend Chadwick, Mr. Patterson and the livery store owner in the general store and about the conversation which had ensued.

Milly's eyes went wide. "They want to hold a barn raising? Here?"

Sarah grinned. "Well, here *is* where one is needed," she said wryly. "Everyone else around here who needs one has one. I think it's wonderful news, Nick."

"But Sarah, we don't have any money to pay for the lumber and nails and so forth!" Milly pointed out, her voice rising. Worry furrowed her brow.

"Reverend Chadwick thought he might be able to persuade the lumber mill owner to donate the lumber for the roof and stalls, or give you a discount—"

Milly interrupted. "There's about as much chance of that as a summer blizzard in San Saba County."

"Failing that, he thought Mr. Dayton could be persuaded to extend credit until you could pay him back, or maybe the town could hold a fundraising party." Nick was thinking of another option, too, that of offering her some money to help from his own funds, but he knew she would balk at that.

"We're *not* taking charity," Milly said in a tone of finality and with a stubborn jut to her chin. "Papa never would have considered it, and he always said never to go into debt. I'm afraid we'll have to tell them we can't accept this. Not 'til we can pay for it."

"But Milly..." Sarah began, looking distressed.

Milly Matthews was as proud as a duchess, Nick thought, but before he could say anything to try to persuade her, another voice spoke from the back hall.

"Your pa never planned on leavin' you two girls alone on this ranch like he did neither," said a voice from the hallway, and all three looked up to see Josh standing there, leaning heavily on a cane, his face pale with the effort it had taken to walk from his bedroom.

Milly sprang up, crying "Josh! What are you doing out of bed?" She rushed toward him, supporting him under the arm that wasn't holding a cane.

"I told him he could have dinner with us," Sarah muttered, going to his side, too. "Josh, you promised you'd wait 'til Nick came home, or Milly and I could help you!"

"Got tired a waitin'," the old man said, as Nick gently pushed Sarah aside and began helping Josh to the nearest chair. "'Sides, I heard Miss Milly spoutin' somethin' that sounded suspiciously like false pride to me, and I thought I'd better come remind her 'Pride goeth before a fall.'"

"You think we should *allow* the town to build us something we won't be able to pay for 'til only God knows when?" Milly asked, still with spirit, but Nick heard the tiniest note of doubt creep into her voice. "We'd never live it down—Bill Waters would see to that!"

"Oh, what do you care what that feller says?" Josh retorted. "He always seems t'have the ammunition to shoot off his mouth, but when he needed your ma to help him take care a his sick wife, he was glad to let her do that, and your pa lent him his prize bull fer his heifers whenever he asked. Ever'body needs help sometime, Miss Milly. You git back on yer feet, you kin help somebody else."

Milly sighed. "I… I suppose you're right, as always, Josh. Thank you."

"Anytime," the old man said. "Is that beans and corn bread cookin' on the stove, Miss Sarah? It's 'bout time fer dinner, ain't it?"

"Yes, and the beans are flavored with the last of the ham," Sarah said. "Milly, would you please go ring the bell to call Bobby in? I think he was out there cleaning out the chicken coop."

Chapter Eight

After the noon meal, Nick and Bobby went out to repair the fence line where the Matthews ranch bordered with Waters's land. Milly busied herself with finishing the wash, while Sarah took down the clothes that had dried, then hung up the newly washed shirts, dresses and sheets as Milly finished scrubbing them.

As they worked, Sarah chattered happily. "I think I'll make pecan pies for the barn raising, Milly. We still have enough pecans from last year. You know how my pecan pies always go quickly at church suppers. Even Mrs. Detwiler praised them at the last one. It's a good thing Mama planted those pecans she brought with her from East Texas when she and Papa moved here, isn't it?" She gestured up at the trees that shaded them now, with their boughs full of ripening pecans.

"Yes," agreed Milly. "We better hope there's a good crop of them this fall because it may be one of the few things we have to eat. I can't imagine how we're going to keep the men fed without slaughtering the remaining cattle and hens—and then how will we build up the herd and the flock again? We can't serve the men beans and corn bread every single noon and night."

Sarah's expression remained serene. "'Take no thought of what ye shall eat, and what ye shall drink, for your Heavenly Father knows you have need of these things'—isn't that what the Bible says?"

"Yes, but—"

"We have a vegetable garden." Sarah pointed in the direction of the rectangular patch in the back of the house. "It wasn't too badly trampled during the attack, and I've planted some more peas and beans. Bobby and Nick can help bring in meat. Remember how Papa would hunt deer every now and then, and rabbits and doves? I'm sure Bobby would just love an excuse to go tramping around in the hills and fields instead of doing ranch chores, and I reckon your Nick is a crack shot, too, from being in the army."

"He's not 'my' Nick," Milly said automatically, but her sister just laughed.

"I think *he* thinks he is," Sarah countered. "I just happened to be looking out of the kitchen window when he brought you those flowers. You had your back to me, but I could see his expression. His heart was in his eyes, sister dear."

Milly let the chemise she'd been washing sink back into the bucket of rinse water. "Sarah, he and I've been acquainted for what, three days? He couldn't possibly know his heart *or* mind in that amount of time. Just look at me," she said, with a despairing gesture at her damp, worn dress and the loose tendrils of hair that had come undone from the knot of hair at the nape of her neck, which were now plastered to her forehead. "This is how

I looked when he walked over and presented me with those flowers! Not exactly the belle of the ball, am I?"

Sarah just smiled. "It didn't seem to matter to him, from what I saw."

Milly sighed. "When I pictured a suitor courting me after I placed that ad for the Society, I pictured it so differently! I imagined parties where the applicants got to know all the ladies of the Society.... I'd planned to wear my best dresses and Mama's pearl earbobs, and have my hair done up just so.... I thought you'd be doing those things, too. And then, when an applicant and I decided we might suit one another, we would go on walks, and horseback rides, and picnics, and sitting in church together, and we'd sit on the porch and talk..."

"And then the Comanches attacked," Sarah said, her eyes warm with sympathy. "But you can still do those things, Milly. And you have Nick right here, where you can get to know him day to day, which will actually give you a lot more time with him than any of the other ladies will probably be able to have with their suitors."

Milly realized she hadn't considered that, but she wasn't ready to let go of her worry entirely yet. "But they get to prepare for their beau," Milly pointed out. "Nick came back sooner than I thought he would and saw me like *this*," she said, pointing at her face and her dress, "with my hair plastered to my forehead, with soapy water splashes on my oldest calico! I'm sure the lovely English girls he's known had milk-and-roses complexions and they surely weren't doing laundry."

"Then why didn't he marry one of them and stay in England or India?" Sarah countered calmly. "You've already forgotten he picked you out of the whole group, Milly."

"Yes, but I had one of my better dresses on then, and my hair wasn't falling down around my ears," Milly retorted, pushing another loose curl from her face with a wet hand.

"But that's the way he saw you first, and first impressions last. Enough of this fretting, Milly," Sarah said. "Nick will be gone 'til supper. As soon as we finish this laundry, we'll fill the tub and you'll have a nice bath. We'll wash your hair, put it up in papers, and you can put on a nice dress and use some of Mama's rosewater before he comes home. And tomorrow, why don't you take him into town with you—"

"What for? I already sent him for sugar."

"So you can spend time alone together," Sarah said, rolling her eyes in exasperation. "Come on, aren't you the brilliant woman who invented the Simpson Creek Society for the Promotion of Marriage? You said something about needing cloth to make Josh and Bobby new shirts, didn't you? And don't you need to check the Society's mailbox? There might be gentlemen wanting to meet the rest of us, you know."

Sarah's last sentence had been uttered as cheerfully as the rest, but it made Milly realized how self-absorbed she was being. She had started the Society for the betterment of *all* the single ladies, not just herself. Sarah deserved to find a beau just as she had.

"Why are you always so sensible?" Milly said, giving her sister a hug. "I'm sorry I'm such a complainer. And I will go into town tomorrow, with or without Nick. I'll bet that mailbox is chock-full of inquiries from bachelors."

* * *

Later, Milly hummed as she set the table for supper. She'd liked what she'd seen when she looked at herself in the cheval glass in the bedroom. The lavender-checked gingham dress showed off her slender waist and complemented her dark hair, which now curled softly around her shoulders. Better yet, the look of anxious fretfulness no longer clouded her eyes.

She *was* the founder and leader of the Simpson Creek Society for the Promotion of Marriage, and Nicholas Brookfield had picked her out from among all the other women. Now if only they were having something more exotic to eat than beans and corn bread for supper!

She heard the sound of horses trotting into the yard but forced herself to keep doing what she had been doing rather than allowing herself to run to the window. A *lady* did not allow herself to appear overeager, she reminded herself, and pretended to be busy rearranging the black-eyed Susans in their improvised vase.

She heard boot heels clomping on the porch. Nick. Would he notice she no longer looked the bedraggled laundress?

"I say, is it too late to provide something for supper?" Nick called through the window.

Milly went to the door and opened it. He was standing there, holding up a glistening stringer of ten bluegills and a sun perch or two. He grinned, clearly very pleased with himself.

"Where on earth did you find those?"

"Bobby and I had a spot of luck at the creek," he said. "We finished fixing the fence without much ado, and Bobby had stashed a couple of fishing poles and line and a trowel in that little cave. He's been taking the coffee grounds and dumping them on a patch of dirt under a big tree by the creek. He says it attracts earthworms, and sure enough, we found plenty with a little digging."

"You should see what a great fisherman Mr. Nick is. He caught twice as many as I did!" Bobby said, his look at Nick full of admiration.

"Oh, I don't know about that," Nick said modestly. "But it was great fun. Reminded of me of holidays in the Lake District, when I tagged along with my brothers when they'd go fishing. I'm sure I was a terrific nuisance, but Richard, my second eldest brother, always talked Edward, the eldest, into letting me come. There we were, just men, and our sister Violet couldn't make me come to her doll tea parties." His blue eyes sparkled.

"We could delay dinner a little to include their catch, couldn't we, Sarah?" Milly asked.

"Sure enough," Sarah agreed. "Assuming you gentlemen wouldn't mind cleaning them, of course." She went to a drawer and pulled out a pair of knives.

"Aw, Miss Sarah, I hate cleaning fish," groaned Bobby. "All those scales and guts and fish heads…"

But Nick accepted the knives and clapped Bobby on the shoulder. "Come on, lad, it's a necessary part of being a fisherman. *Ladies* should not have to deal with nasty things like fish heads, nor should they smell of fish. We'll clean them up in a trice, then go wash up while the fish are frying." He hesitated while Bobby trudged outside and Sarah returned to stirring a pot on the stove, then turned back to Milly. "If I may say so, Miss Milly, you look lovely," he said simply.

"Yes…you may say so," she said, feeling a flush of pleasure. He had noticed. "Thank you."

The fish, which Sarah had rolled in a batter of egg, corn bread and her own secret blend of spices before frying them, were devoured down to the delicate spine and rib bones.

"That was delicious. Thanks for catching them, gentlemen," Milly praised, giving Bobby an especially approving smile because it had been his idea.

Bobby beamed. "You're welcome, Miss Milly. And tomorrow night we're havin' venison," he proclaimed. "Me an' Mr. Nick are gonna go up in them hills and get that ol' buck I missed last fall when me an' Uncle Josh last went huntin'." He seemed to have no doubt that Nick's presence would guarantee success.

"You are? Uh…it would be wonderful to have some venison hanging in the smokehouse," Milly said, keeping her tone even. She didn't want to betray her disappointment that Nick would be out hunting when she had hoped to be going into town with him. It was much more important to let him provide meat that could feed the household many times than to have Nick's company for a jaunt into town she could easily do by herself, or postpone. "Well, good luck, then."

"That ol' buck is a wily one," Josh warned. "He didn't get that eight-point rack makin' foolish mistakes. You ever been huntin', Mr. Nick?"

Nick nodded. "Indeed, I have—red deer in the Scottish highlands—they're bigger than your American deer— and tigers in Bengal."

"Tigers?" Bobby crowed enthusiastically. "Boy howdy, Mr. Nick! Did you kill 'em?"

"One of them," Nick said. "The rajah's son got the other. A pair of them had been plaguing a village, eating their livestock, as well as one unlucky old man whom they caught out after dark on a path that led from one village to another."

"Oh dear," Milly murmured with a shudder as she imagined it. "Man-eating tigers?"

"And you weren't even afeared?" Bobby asked, his eyes glowing with hero worship. "I reckon you're 'bout the bravest man I ever did know, Mr. Nick!"

Nick looked embarrassed. "Of course I was afraid. My heart was pounding like a trip-hammer. But we couldn't let them go on killing people, could we? The honor of the Empire was at stake." He winked at Milly.

"I heard tell of a cougar like that 'round here," Josh put in. "Once they get the taste fer human flesh, they don't want to go back to jackrabbits and such…"

"Oh, please! I'll have nightmares!" Sarah murmured faintly.

"Don't you worry, Miss Sarah, that ol' cougar's long gone," Josh assured her. "And that buck sure ain't no man-eater."

"Nick, we could go tonight and camp out and everything—that would be the best way," Bobby told him eagerly. "Then we'd be right out there at dawn, ready to shoot."

"And leave these ladies unguarded at night? I don't think that would be a good idea, lad. We can leave just before first light, but not until."

Bobby's face fell. "Aw, there's not gonna be no Comanche attackin' durin' the new moon," he protested.

"B'sides, I'm here," Josh added. "I ain't sleepin' very well these nights anyways—I might as well sit up with a rifle."

Milly saw Nick hesitate, clearly loath to dismiss the old cowboy's ability to protect the sisters as he always had.

"But how quickly could you raise that rifle and shoot with your injured shoulders, Josh? For example...*right now!*" Lightning-fast, Nick drew an imaginary pistol and leveled it at Josh, and everyone watched as Josh pantomimed raising a rifle, wincing with obvious pain as he did so.

"I... I see what you mean," Josh admitted, his shoulders sagging. "I reckon I ain't quite up to it yet."

"Yes, it's temporary," Nick confirmed. "You'll be back to fighting trim before very long. But that brings up a good point, Miss Milly, Miss Sarah. You need more hands around here."

Milly's gaze flew from Josh to Nick. "More hands? Are you leaving after all, then?"

He shook his head. "No, not as long as you need me," he said. "But I think it would be wise to have someone on watch during the night, to keep an eye on the livestock, to make sure the Indians aren't creeping up on the house."

"But...but how would we pay them, even if we could feed them?" Milly asked. "Assuming there were any men available, which there aren't, Nick. Cowboys are usually unmarried men, and we started the Society because there *aren't* any of those around Simpson Creek."

Nick rubbed his chin. "I—we—didn't want it to be the first thing we told you, but when we went to repair the fence, we found the carcass of another cow."

Alarm lit both Milly's and Sarah's faces. "Could it have been an animal? We were speaking of cougars," Sarah said, with a visible effort to be calm.

"It was too neat to have been an animal," Nick said.

"But there's no tellin' if it was redskins or rustlers what killed that cow," Josh said.

"I should think if you let it be known you had positions open," Nick said, "even though for now you could pay nothing but their board, men riding through town seeking work would find their way to you. In time, they'd pay for themselves. If you had more cowhands, Bobby and I could go hunting at night, the livestock could be guarded and eventually you could enlarge your herd and pay wages."

"Well, we'd best start tonight on the guardin', not wait for any more hands," Josh said with finality. "You boys ride out after dinner and bring the herd into the corral. Like I said, I don't sleep much, so I'll sit up on the porch with the rifle. That way I kin come out and wake you so's you two can get that buck when he comes down to water. Then come mornin' I'll go sleep awhile."

Chapter Nine

He hadn't dared to expect that she would be sitting out on the porch again when he and Bobby herded the cattle into the opened corral at sunset. Yet there she was, sitting on the porch with Sarah. The women waved as Bobby jumped off his cow pony and slammed the gate shut on the lowing beasts.

"I'll put th' horses away, Mr. Nick," Bobby offered.

"Thanks, lad," he said, dismounting and handing over the bay's reins. "Next time I'll return the favor."

Sarah rose as he strode toward the porch. "Good night, Nick. I've left sandwiches for you men to take with you in the morning."

"Thank you, Miss Sarah."

He sank into the rocking chair Milly's sister had vacated. Milly resumed crocheting what looked like the beginnings of an afghan. For a few moments there was a companionable silence between them.

"I say, Miss Milly...did you want...that is, did you have something else in mind for me to do tomorrow besides hunting?"

"Oh, it was nothing important," Milly said, too quickly, and looked back at her afghan.

"Just a feeling I had from a look on your face," Nick said. A look that had flashed so quickly across those hazel orbs that he hadn't been sure he had seen it until her too-rapid denial confirmed it. "I thought perhaps you'd had some task in mind for me. Bobby and I can go track that buck any time, you know."

Milly shrugged. "No, it would be better for you to go hunting. I just thought I'd ride into town tomorrow and get cloth for those shirts I need to make…and perhaps call on Hank Dayton at the lumberyard and see what his terms would be for the lumber. I thought we could go together, but I can go on my own."

"With Comanches on the loose? I rather think not," Nick said. He flashed on an image of Milly alone, encountering savages on the road, and meeting Josh's fate or worse.

"I can't be afraid to ride into town alone the rest of my life. There might never be another Comanche raid."

But then again, there might be. "Could you still do your errands in the afternoon? Bobby and I will be back by noon, I should think, deer or no deer. The lad says it's best to hunt at sunrise, when they're seeking a place to bed down. They aren't active during the heat of the day, so I could still go into town with you—unless it's too hot for you to go then?" English ladies had never done their errands in Bombay in the afternoon, preferring to go in the morning or send their native servants in the interest of preserving their milk-and-roses complexions. And the rajah's daughter had never left the palace when the sun was beating down, sending her old *amah* to the bazaar for anything she needed.

"No, that would be fine," she said, coloring faintly. "Thank you. I can tell Bobby's tickled pink that you two are going. He thinks quite a lot of you, Nick."

And you? What do you think of me, Milly Matthews? Aloud, he said, "He's a good lad. I've actually learned quite a lot from him already."

Milly smiled. "If you get that buck, he'll be sure you hung the moon."

He laughed. "He's already planning to hang the antlers on the wall of the bunkhouse. Maybe he'll be the one to shoot it."

"Boys always need someone to look up to," she murmured.

"Yes, though I'm sure I won't replace his uncle. I can remember a crusty old sergeant major in India I felt that way about when I first arrived as a raw lieutenant fresh off the boat. I thought he knew everything about everything. He taught me a lot before…well, before he died." He wished he hadn't thought of McGowan and the massacre…. Too many good men had died in India, he thought. All for the sake of empire…

Her hazel eyes studied him in the growing darkness, as if she sensed the pain he felt at remembering James McGowan.

Clomping boot heels approaching from inside the house warned them their time alone was about to end. A moment later Josh joined them on the porch.

"Had me a nice nap, so I'm ready to go on watch now."

Nick had hoped for a longer time to talk with Milly, but perhaps it'd be easier tomorrow during their trip into town. "Yes, well, I'd better retire if Bobby and I are going to bring down that buck," Nick said, rising. "Good night, Josh, Miss Milly."

Nick and Bobby brought no venison home to the Matthews ranch the next morning, although Nick had bagged a wild turkey that had been startled out of the underbrush near them.

"We saw that old buck, but he was too far away to hit. We'll get him the next time, Mr. Nick says," Bobby told the women, who were admiring the slain tom Nick held up by his legs.

Nick forbore mentioning that the boy had tried the impossible shot anyway, spooking the buck so that creeping up on him upwind had been impossible.

"Well, I like turkey every bit as much as venison," Milly said, and the boy brightened.

"Yes, it'll be like Thanksgiving in August," Sarah added. "Bobby, if you'll start plucking the feathers, I think I can promise turkey for supper."

"Yes, *ma'am!*"

After the noon meal, Nick said he was going to go hitch up the buckboard, but Milly said, "Oh, why don't we ride? I haven't had a chance to ride Ruby—that's that red roan mare out in the corral, Nick—and I don't want her getting lazy."

"But, Milly, all the tack burned up with the barn," Sarah pointed out.

Milly shrugged. "Who needs a saddle?" She winked at Nick. "You won't disapprove of me riding bareback, will you?"

"Disapprove of my boss? Perish the thought, though

I'd be happy to let you ride my horse, saddled." Nick grinned, still dealing with the surprise of learning that his Milly was a daring horsewoman in addition to all of her other impressive qualities.

"No, thanks, I'd love the excuse to ride bareback. Fortunately, I was repairing the reins of her hackamore and it was in my room on the day of the attack, so it didn't burn up with the barn. Go ahead and saddle your bay, Nick, I'll join you as soon as I've changed my skirt."

Sarah's expression had become uneasy. "Milly, don't let Mrs. Detwiler see you," she moaned.

"Pooh, Sarah, that would be half the fun of it."

She came out to the corral minutes later, carrying the bitless bridle and wearing the divided skirt trimmed at each side with a pair of silver *conchas*. Nick had tethered the roan mare to the corral fence with a loop of rope around her neck. Now he stopped tightening his bay's girth and watched as Milly approached, noting how the riding skirt became her.

"You like it? Mother made it for me because she knew I'd have a more secure seat than if I rode sidesaddle. Not to mention that it didn't reveal my...ahem!... *limbs,*" she said in a conspiratorial whisper.

"You surprise me more every day, Miss Milly," he said, letting her see his admiration. "You're quite the intrepid lady."

She beamed at his compliment. "Josh taught me to ride when I was barely old enough to walk. Um...could we drop the 'Miss,' just while we're alone, Nick?"

Their gazes locked. "I would be delighted, *Milly.*"

While he finished saddling his bay, she bridled the well-mannered mare. Then Nick laced his fingers for her, providing a springboard for her left foot so she could mount.

By the time they reached the road, he'd decided her seat was as excellent as her hands.

"Does Sarah ride as well as you, Milly?" He tried to imagine an English lady cantering down the road bareback and couldn't. Texas women were full of surprises.

She shook her head. "She doesn't really like to ride very much because she had a bad fall once—from a sidesaddle. But she's a much better cook than I will ever be," she added loyally, with a self-deprecating roll of her eyes. "Her biscuits are so light they practically float away, don't you think?"

"Ah, well, one can't be good at everything, can one?" he asked lightly. If this woman learned to love him, he thought, eating less-than-perfect biscuits would be a small price to pay.

Once they reached Simpson Creek, their first stop was the post office. Caroline Wallace came running out while Milly was still dismounting.

"Oh, Milly, it's so good to see you! Still riding bareback like an Indian, I see. Mr. Brookfield, how are *you?* Is old Josh feeling better?"

Nick, tying the horses to the hitching rail, watched as Milly absorbed the other woman's conversational onslaught.

"Everything's getting back to normal, thanks, and yes, Josh is feeling much better. I can tell because he's getting ornery and trying to do too much."

Clearly unable to contain herself, the other woman could barely wait for Milly to finish answering her question. "Milly, can you imagine, we've had *two* applications to the Society!"

"We have? That's wonderful."

"I didn't think you'd mind me looking at them," Caroline said. "I figured, what with all you've had to deal with, it might be a while before you made it to town again. They'd both like to come up from Houston to meet us," she gushed. "I don't know if they'll be here in time for the barn raising, but wouldn't that be great if they were?"

"Yes, there's nothing like putting guests in town to work right away," Milly said drily.

"It seems to have worked out well for you," Caroline teased, with a meaningful glance at Nick. "Let me tell you about the letters." She brought them out of her pocket and unfolded one. "This one sounds just perfect for Emily—he's a widower from Buffalo Bayou—but I'm calling first dibs on this other one, a fellow named Pete Collier—if I like what I see when he arrives, of course, and if he feels the same. He says he's from Galveston originally, and he owns a pharmacy, but he's been looking to relocate. And he said he knew two or three other men who might be interested, depending on what he reports back to them…"

"Oh, so he's being sent to survey the prospects, is he?" Milly said with a laugh.

Nick imagined the pride Milly must be feeling that her idea was working. Now, he only needed to make sure Milly didn't find the new gentlemen more attractive than himself!

They went across the street to the general store from there, where Milly selected a bolt of sturdy tan broadcloth for the shirts she was going to make. "It might as well match the color of the dirt around here," she commented, politely rejecting a bolt of dark navy that the proprietor had brought down from the shelf first, "since it's going to absorb a lot of it while it's being worn…" Her voice trailed off as she stared out the window. "Oh, there's Mr. Dayton now, just going down the street," she said, looking out the window. "Mr. Patterson, will you save this bolt for me?" She dashed outside.

Nick edged toward the open door but remained within the building, wanting to unobtrusively overhear without being seen. Just as he had guessed, the man Milly was hastening toward was the same man who'd been speaking with Waters outside this store yesterday.

"Mr. Dayton, how are you? How's the family?" Milly asked, her voice friendly.

The paunchy middle-aged man stopped and shaded his eyes to peer at her. "Afternoon, Miss Matthews. Same as always."

"I hope y'all are coming to our barn raising," she said. "I haven't seen your wife in a month of Sundays, and from what I'm hearing already, the food's going to be the best this side of heaven."

"I'm sure Alice Ann will nag me into comin'," he said, looking less than pleased at the prospect. "As if I don't work hard enough all week long at the lumberyard."

Nick watched Milly's cheerful smile remain in place. "And that reminds me, I wanted to talk to you about the price of the wood for the barn. I—"

"I'll tell you right now I cain't jes' give that wood away," the man whined, his lips tightening. "The mayor's daughter's already been jawin' at me, tryin' to get me to donate it 'outa the goodness of my heart,'" he said, a sneer making his jowly features even more disagreeable.

"I completely understand, Mr. Dayton," Nick heard Milly say, still cheerful. "I was just wondering how soon you would require payment, so I could figure out if we could afford it. If we can't, of course, we'll have to wait to raise a barn when we can."

Nick saw the other man's face take on a wary look, as if he realized he might miss out on a sale altogether if he made his price too high.

"I can give you a couple weeks, ma'am, and then I'm gonna need payment in full. I got mouths t'feed, y'understand."

"Of course," she said, her voice losing none of its warmth. He marveled at her poise.

Just then he saw another man join them—Bill Waters.

"How do, Bill? Didn't know you'd be comin' inta town today," Dayton said. "Now, Miss Milly, I didn't mean t' speak too hasty," he said. "Seein' Bill here, I might could work somethin' out to help you out, under certain circumstances…"

Nick straightened. There was something in the man's tone he didn't like.

"Oh? And what circumstances would those be?" Milly's voice had cooled, but the lumberyard owner didn't seem to notice.

"Why, I'd give that wood to you as a weddin' present."

Milly sounded puzzled. "But I have no wedding planned, Mr. Dayton. Did you mean if I married a man I met through the Society for the Promotion of Marriage?"

"Naw, I'm not talkin' about that fool business. That's jest about the featherbraindest idea any female ever came up with. Why you'd want to find a stranger to get hitched with, I don't know, since I happen to know you're standin' right next to a fine man who'd give you anythin' your little heart desired if you was to marry him."

Nick heard Milly gasp, even as his fists involuntarily tightened. So now the old man thought he could persuade Milly into marriage, if he couldn't get her to sell the ranch?

"I—I don't know what to say," she managed at last.

"Why, 'yes,' of course," the lumberman said, misunderstanding her struggle for words. "Seems to me you'd be the luckiest female in San Saba Country to get hitched t' a man like my friend Bill Waters."

Nick thought Milly might leave them without another word, but the remarks had evidently sparked her ire. "Oh, Mr. Dayton, I just know you're teasing me, isn't he, Mr. Waters? Why, Mr. Waters is older than my father was when he died! Excuse me, gentlemen, I have purchases to pick up inside." She turned back toward the store, still laughing as if she'd been told the most humorous joke ever.

"Well, maybe you ought t' see if her sister has more sense," Dayton said in a purposely carrying voice as Milly put her first booted foot on the boardwalk. "I hear that Sarah girl kin cook at least."

The two men guffawed. Nick fought the urge to go knock both of them flat, but a display of brutish behavior would neither impress Milly nor help her in the long run.

Her composure slipped as soon as she was inside the

store. Nick could see she was fighting tears. He wanted to gather her into his arms and hold her and kiss away her distress, but they weren't alone and he didn't want to embarrass her. And he wasn't even completely sure if she would welcome his comfort.

"Steady on," he said, daring to put a hand on her shoulder. Beneath his fingers, her muscles bunched in suppressed rage. "Those two are mere blowhards. I've seen their ilk before."

"Those hateful old coots," Milly whispered. "As if I'd marry Bill Waters to get free lumber for our barn!"

On the way home, he told her about the partial conversation he'd overheard between the two men when he'd entered the general store yesterday, and asked what group of people they'd been talking about.

"Probably former slaves," Milly guessed. "They were freed because of Lincoln's Emancipation Proclamation during the war, but most of them left their owners with nothing, just the clothes on their backs and no idea of how to earn a living."

"Did your father own slaves?" he asked carefully. England had abolished the trade over fifty years ago, but he'd seen plenty of racial bigotry among the British in India.

"Heavens, no," she said, then added, "he never would have, but hardly anyone else did around here either. Most slaves in Texas were in the cotton-growing areas, not on ranches. Oh, goodness, look at the time," she said, when the grandfather clock in the store chimed three. "I suppose we'd better head home..."

Chapter Ten

After breakfast Sunday morning, Milly, Sarah and Nick climbed onto the buckboard to attend church in town. Ordinarily, Josh and Bobby would have come along, but Josh still wasn't feeling up to bouncing over the rutted road, and Bobby had offered to stay home with his uncle. Milly suspected Bobby was happy to have the excuse not to attend. Bathing, wearing his good shirt and pants and sitting still for the sermon were not high on his list of favorite activities.

One could never have guessed Nick had been wearing cowboy clothes the last few days and doing menial chores like fence mending and livestock tending, she mused, trying not to steal too many sidelong glances at the Englishman beside her. He was once again the picture of a refined gentleman in his black frock coat, trousers and white shirt and tie. Thank goodness she had been able to wash the bloodstains away!

She knew she also looked well in her Sunday best dress of light blue silk-and-cotton *Merveilleux,* which had been made from a bolt of fabric sent to her mother by Aunt Tilly from New Orleans before the war. They would be the cynosure of all eyes as she walked into church beside him.

But their fine apparel wasn't what made her heart light and joyous this morning; rather, it was the memory of his pleased reaction to her invitation to attend church with her. She had told him church attendance wasn't obligatory for ranch employees—the Matthewses had no rule that cowhands must attend Sunday services if they would prefer to take their ease in the bunkhouse or elsewhere.

"Oh, but I would be most honored to escort you to church, Milly," he'd said with that enchanting accent of his and that smile that lit up his blue eyes. "I never missed Sunday services at home in Sussex or in India when I could help it, though my army duties sometimes prevented me."

"I imagine our little church in Simpson Creek will be somewhat different than what you're used to at home," she'd responded, imagining stained-glass windows of rainbow hues, walls darkened by age and a minister in formal robes.

"I imagine so," he said. "The church at Greyshaw was built in Norman times, about 1250, but it's fairly small, too, having been only the chapel of Greyshaw Castle beside it."

"Built in 1250?" she'd echoed wonderingly. "Why, that's over six centuries old!"

"Yes. My brothers and I used to joke that the vicar was every bit as ancient," Nick recalled with a grin.

"I'll bet your mother had her hands full keeping the three of you in line," she'd said.

He looked away just then, as if something she'd said had troubled him. She didn't want to ask him about it in front of Sarah, though, and in any case, they were drawing near to the church.

Every head turned as Nick followed Milly into a pew about midway toward the front of the church, while Sarah went forward to the piano. Now he understood why Milly's sister played hymns so often on the piano at home. Here and there he recognized men he'd met at the general store, who nodded at him, or ladies who'd been present at the Society meeting the day he'd met Milly. Many of the latter waved discreetly at the Matthews ladies as they passed and smiled shyly at him. Only one older woman narrowed her eyes as he and Milly passed her pew. Could this be the infamous Mrs. Detwiler? He noticed Waters and Dayton sitting together in the front of the church, with their families spread out on either side of them. Apparently they saw no conflict in their bigotry and church attendance.

Milly's idea that the Simpson Creek church was "somewhat different" from the Greyshaw chapel had been an understatement, Nick thought as he settled himself by Milly. Yet somehow the simplicity was very appealing. A white frame building with a wooden floor, the church had no stained glass, only clear windows open because of the heat. Even so, many of the ladies wielded their fans.

The piano at which Sarah sat looked time-worn. A simple polished wooden cross graced the wall from the floor nearly to the ceiling at the front of the church. It drew the eye because of the lack of other beautiful things to compete with. Perhaps that was as it should be, Nick thought.

A man took his place at the front of the church and raised his hands for silence. "Good morning, Simpson Creek residents!" he said. "Our first hymn will be number twenty-six, 'Blest Be the Tie that Binds.'"

Fabric rustled and wooden pews creaked as everyone got to their feet and Sarah played the opening chord. Nick and Milly had taken the last two spaces in the pew, so there was only one hymnal left. Milly opened it and held it out to him. Deliberately he allowed his fingers to brush hers as he took it from her and held it so they could both see, enjoying the flush of color that rose in her cheeks and the way she cleared her throat, missing the first line of the old hymn.

After that, however, her alto voice, rich and true, blended with his tenor as they sang this song and two more before everyone sat down for the sermon.

Nick forced his mind away from the pleasant rosewater scent Milly wore. As a preacher, Reverend Chadwick lacked the resonant voice and polished speaking style Nick had always associated with men of the cloth, but sincerity shone from his shiny, perspiration-beaded face as he spoke of the Sermon on the Mount and how the townspeople should apply those truths to their living today. Nick felt blessed and encouraged half an hour later when the white-haired man closed the service in prayer.

"Oh, and before you leave," the preacher added, holding up a hand, "I want to remind everyone of the barn raising at the Matthews ranch next Saturday morning, bright and early. I'm sure you'll all want to come and help build, not to mention help out in the delicious meals that the ladies will prepare. And if anyone is able to spare any cash, Miss Priscilla Gilmore is accepting donations to help pay for the lumber." He indicated a pretty strawberry blonde, who flashed a vivacious smile.

That said, he walked down the aisle to the door to shake everyone's hands as they left.

"Your sermon was inspiring, Reverend. I'm glad I was here," Nick told him.

"And we're glad you're here, too, Mr. Brookfield, and especially pleased that you're helping Milly and Sarah," the other man said, pumping his hand with enthusiasm. "Please do come back."

In no apparent hurry to go home, people gathered in front of the church. Nick followed Milly to where her sister was chattering with a trio of ladies.

"Your piano playing was excellent, Miss Sarah," he complimented her, when there was a break in the conversation.

"Thank you. I guess all those years I tortured Milly and our parents with my practice are finally paying off," she said with a modest smile.

"Hello, Mr. Brookfield, Sarah... Oh, Milly! I just can't wait for the barn raising! It's going to be so much fun!" exclaimed the bright-eyed strawberry blonde as she dashed down the steps to join the group.

"It's nice of you to collect money for us, Prissy," Milly said. Nick thought he could detect a hint of uneasiness in Milly about the subject. "I'm not sure anyone has any to spare, but we appreciate the thought—"

"Oh, but you just have to know how to appeal to those who can give," the other girl said with a blithe confidence. "For example, the food's going to be free, of course, but at the supper, we're going to auction off the pies and cakes. That'll bring in the money, sure enough—every one of those men has a sweet tooth. And we're posting notices about the barn raising and party to all the neighboring towns."

"Goodness, Prissy, you have been busy!" Milly praised. "Maybe we should have made *you* president of the Society for the Promotion of Marriage."

The other girl laughed. "Oh, no, I'd never have thought of your scheme in a million years! But wait, I haven't told you everything! We're going to charge a nickel a dance with any of us ladies, even for the husbands with their wives, though we'll make the husbands pay only once."

"Prissy! Are you sure Reverend Chadwick will approve of that?" Milly asked.

"Who do you think thought of it?" the other girl retorted with a wink. "He says all these men are free enough with their spare change when they come into town to buy tobacco and visit the saloon. Next Saturday they can contribute to a good cause instead."

"I've heard again from that man from Buffalo Bayou I told you about *and* the pharmacist from Galveston," Caroline Wallace announced, joining the group. "Both of them will be arriving in time for the barn raising and have been invited to meet our Society members there. I'm so excited I could squeak!"

Nick thought her excited voice already sounded a little squeaky, but he hoped the coming applicants were everything Miss Wallace wished for.

Nick's back was to the steps, but he could tell by the

way the girls straightened and their smiles faded that someone disagreeable was approaching. Sure enough, when he glanced over his shoulder, he saw the sour-faced elderly woman bearing down on them. Her expression, Nick decided, looked as if she had just drunk a cup of curdled milk.

Miss Wallace and Miss Gilmore edged away.

"Good morning, Mrs. Detwiler," Sarah called out in a determinedly cheerful way. "How are you this morning?"

"Mrs. Detwiler, may I present Nicholas Brookfield, who's been helping us out at the ranch?" Milly said, glancing at Nick a little desperately.

He guessed what Milly wanted. "Mrs. Detwiler, I'm honored to make your acquaintance," he said with a bow that would have done credit to the Prince of Wales, and bestowing a smile on her that would have melted Queen Victoria at her stuffiest. "I'm told you raise the prettiest roses in the county, possibly all of Texas."

But Mrs. Detwiler was not to be charmed. "I don't know who told you that, but I hope they told you they weren't for your bouquets," she snapped, then turned. "Miss Matthews, I have a bone to pick with you."

It was hard to tell which sister she was addressing, for she glared at both. "Me?" Sarah volunteered. "Did I hit some wrong notes in the hymns this morning?"

"Not you. Your sister. Milly Matthews, I asked Reverend Chadwick to speak about this to you discreetly, but he says *he* sees nothing wrong with it, so I suppose it's up to me. I saw you yesterday, riding that horse of yours bareback like a heathen hussy. It was scandalous, that's what it was, especially in the company of a man," she said, sharing her glare with Nick. "I told your mother when you were a girl she was wrong to let you do so, but you're much too old to carry on like that now."

Nick could tell by the way Milly's chin lifted that she was holding in her anger.

"Oh? I'm sorry, I didn't see you, or I would have said hello and introduced Mr. Brookfield then, though I *thought* I saw your curtain flutter as we rode by," she said.

Nick saw the woman's face darken at the implication she had been spying on them.

"I'm sorry my bareback riding offended you," Milly went on, "but I'm afraid the saddle burned up with the barn. Mr. Brookfield did offer me his, though," she added, as if attempting to be strictly accurate.

"Well, you should have accepted it, or better yet, taken your wagon," Mrs. Detwiler told her. "I'm sure an Englishman is used to more seemly deportment than what you displayed yesterday, aren't you, Mr. Brookfield? Come now, be honest."

"I find the women of Texas, and especially Miss Milly, utterly refreshing in their conduct, madam," he told her, keeping a smile pasted on his face with some effort. "She has an excellent seat, that is, she's quite the horsewoman," he added, afraid the woman would deliberately misunderstand his words.

Stymied, Mrs. Detwiler redoubled her attack on Milly. "It's not just the fact that you're riding bareback, Milly Matthews, but the indecorous *attire* you wore—that split skirt. I was scandalized! Your poor mother must be have been rolling in her grave."

Milly's spine became even more rigid, if that were

possible. "My mother is in heaven with Jesus," she said, enunciating every word. "And she sewed that skirt for me."

Mrs. Detwiler tsk-tsked. "Well, I have done my duty and can say no more if you choose not to listen. Good day, Mr. Brookfield."

He gave her a bare nod as the woman stalked away with a rustle of black bombazine, then turned back to Milly. There was a sheen in her hazel eyes as her gaze followed Mrs. Detwiler, and her lip quivered.

"That spiteful woman!" Sarah hissed, taking Milly's hand. "Don't pay any attention to her."

"I know I said having her see me would be half the fun, and I don't care what she thinks of me, but I won't have her criticizing our mother! She was rude to her when she was alive, too." She swiped angrily at a tear that escaped down her cheek. "I'm sorry, Nick. I'm not normally such a crybaby. You've seen me cry two days in a row now!"

"Stiff upper lip, Miss Milly," Nick advised, wishing he could kiss her tears away.

She blinked at him. "How do I..."

He thought she was going to ask how on earth she was to regain her composure after the old woman's verbal attack, but then he saw that she was taking him literally, struggling to assume the expression he'd suggested. The result made her giggle, and soon all three of them were laughing.

Milly was smiling again. "It's impossible to cry when you're concentrating on keeping your upper lip straight, isn't it?"

"That's the spirit."

Chapter Eleven

The next five days passed in a flurry of preparation for the barn raising. The men spent the time outside completing the clearing of the old barn's remains and scything the yard in addition to the usual chores of caring for the livestock and providing meat for the table.

Milly and Sarah were fully occupied inside, cleaning the house from one end to the other. The barn raising and party afterward would take place outside, but the women would put last-minute touches on the food in the kitchen and nurse babies and lay small children down to nap in the bedrooms away from the heat of the day. Even if the critical Mrs. Detwiler didn't come, they wanted their home to be at its best for the rest of the women to see, a place they could be proud of.

In the evenings, Milly sewed new dresses for her and her sister, using their mother's beloved old Singer sewing machine and bolts of sprigged muslin they had found among their mother's possessions. Clearly she had set them aside to make dresses for her daughters, for pinned to the primrose yellow one with peach colored flowers was a scrap of paper with "Sarah" inscribed on it, while the vivid green one with cream colored flowers was labeled "Milly." Next to the bolts, they'd found yards of satin, wide grosgrain ribbon, buttons, lace and a couple of yards of sheer white lawn which she'd apparently bought at the same time.

Milly had sketched designs for the dresses when she'd first organized the Society for the Promotion of Marriage, thinking she'd have advance notice before they met anyone, and had gotten as far as cutting out the pattern pieces. Then Nick had appeared without warning and the Comanches attacked the same day. She'd had no time for sewing until now.

After consulting Sarah, Milly made her sister's dress a demure one with a ruffled yoke trimmed in lace and a matching ruffle at the hem. She used the grosgrain ribbon to fashion a sash at the waist and part of the lawn to make a ruffled apron with a band of the yellow muslin to form the ties.

After finishing Sarah's dress Wednesday night, she hung it from a peg on the wall and threw herself into the construction of her own, ever aware that Nick would see her in it. Her dress would have ruffles at the hem and the sleeves, as well as a lawn insert over the top of the bodice trimmed with lace, a sash of the wide grosgrain ribbon and a green-trimmed ruffled lawn apron.

"Ohh, Milly, it's beautiful," cooed Sarah, coming into the room, but she was staring at her own dress hanging on the wall. "I love it! You're so talented. But you didn't have to make my dress first," she added worriedly, seeing that Milly had only begun to stitch her own dress. "It doesn't matter what *I* wear—there won't be any beau there for me."

"Pooh, I have plenty of time to finish my dress, especially if you'll let me off the pie-making detail Friday if it's not done yet."

"It's a deal," Sarah said with a laugh. "I know you hate rolling out pie crust anyway."

"You've got that right," Milly said, relieved. "And who says there won't be a beau there for you, Sarah? What if Caroline and Emily and those two new men who are coming don't take a shine to one another, but one of them turns out to be perfect for you? You'll want to look your best."

Sarah shrugged. "I don't think there's much chance of that, but I do love parties and wearing something new."

"Well, you better try it on," Milly said, nodding toward the dress, "just in case it needs alterations."

"It fits perfectly," Sarah said a couple of minutes later, when Milly had helped her button up the back of the dress. "Don't change a thing. Oh, I nearly forgot what I came to tell you—Nick's sitting out on the porch. Josh is with him and talking his ear off, but I think he's looking for you, Milly. He looked up when I came out to bring them coffee, and he looked *so* disappointed when he saw it was only me. You've been working so hard on your sewing in the evenings, you haven't been out there at all after supper this week, you know."

The information made Milly warm inside. "You think he's looking for me? Hmm…" Would she have time to finish the dress if she went out to sit with him now, or was it better to keep sewing and make him miss her all the more?

No, she wasn't into playing coy games. She *wanted* to spend time in Nick's company, to listen to that exotic English accent, to drown in the depths of those blue eyes when their gazes met.

"I think I have time to take a little break from my labors," she told Sarah with a wink. She could always come back after Nick bid her good-night and sew by the light of the lamp until she got too sleepy to thread the needle.

It rained at dawn on the day of the barn raising, right after the men had lowered the sides of beef onto the hot coals in the barbecue pit they had dug, but it stopped by the time they were gathered around the breakfast table.

"I don't think that rain'll hurt none," Josh opined. "It's washed away the dust, and that ain't a bad thing."

"Yes, and it's already clearing to the west," Nick said, looking out the kitchen window. "Ah, there's Mr. Dayton now with the lumber," he added as the creak of a wagon axle confirmed his words. "It appears he's brought his family with him."

Milly could already hear the six Dayton children clamoring to get down, and groaned. "Oh, dear, we're not even dressed for the party yet," she said, with a gesture at her own everyday shirt and waist. She'd thought she'd have time after breakfast to don her beautiful new green dress—completed at midnight the night before—before the first wagons started rolling in. But there would be no leisure to dress once Alice Ann Dayton crossed their threshold. Probably because of her husband's tyranny, the woman attended social events so rarely that she never stopped talking once she arrived at one, following her unfortunate listener around reciting a never-ending litany of her ailments and her noisy brood's misbehavior. They should have figured Dayton wouldn't make a second trip from town to get his family, but they hadn't expected him quite so early.

"Scoot," Sarah told her quickly, motioning Milly toward her bedroom. "I'll keep Mrs. Dayton and the children occupied while you get ready, then you can do the same for me."

"And Bobby and I'll go out and help Dayton unload his lumber," Nick said, rising.

Milly blew a kiss to her sister and made good her escape.

The wagons started arriving thick and fast about an hour later, for the men were eager to get a good start on the barn before the sun rose too high. Nick was glad they'd set up the tables and chairs under the trees the night before, for he and Bobby were kept busy assisting the drivers, unhitching the teams and turning them out in the corral. Men brought their tools—hammers, saws, shovels, brace and bits and more chairs. Their women flocked toward the ranch house, laden with picnic baskets, covered dishes and pitchers, most accompanied by excited offspring yelling at the top of their lungs. Nick kept an uneasy eye on the children lest one of them dart in front of the dancing, nervous horses he led toward the corral.

The ladies of the Society for the Promotion of Marriage arrived in one big buckboard driven by Caroline

Wallace, all chattering like magpies and eyeing the clumps of men as if to see if any strangers had arrived.

Nick would have thought that Dayton, as the lumberman, would take charge of the building, but he seemed content to sit and rock on the porch and watch the women bringing dishes into the house. Instead, Mr. Patterson from the mercantile and Mr. Wallace from the post office began organizing the building of the frames.

"I've never built anything, but I'll be happy to do whatever's needed," Nick told Patterson as soon as he had unhitched the team of the last wagon to arrive.

Patterson grinned. "You reckon you're better at sawin' or hammerin'?"

Nick shrugged. "I've never done either, but let me try my hand at sawing." Another man was already sawing planks laid atop a pair of sawhorses and he figured he could watch and learn.

"Well, pick up a saw from that pile a' tools over yonder and Andy'll tell you how long to cut 'em," Patterson said, nodding toward the livery owner with the saw. As Nick walked away, Patterson cupped his hands and yelled toward the porch, "Hey, Dayton, you gonna do any work today or are you only supervisin'?"

"Seems like I done enough by loadin' up this lumber and bringin' it out here," Dayton grumbled, keeping his seat.

"St. Paul said those who do not work should not eat," Reverend Chadwick, who'd been swinging a hammer like a much younger man, retorted, with a meaningful nod at the tables under the trees. "I caught a glimpse of the bounty that we have to look forward to at midday, Hank, and I don't think you'd want to miss that."

With a put-upon air, Dayton trudged out and grudgingly picked up a hammer. But every time Nick looked up from his work, it seemed Dayton was drinking water under a tree, and once Bill Waters arrived at mid-morning, the two seemed to spend more time talking in low tones to each other than accomplishing any actual work.

After a bit of instruction from Andy Calhoun, he learned how long the planks needed to be and how to saw them most efficiently and pass them over to where the frames for the sides, front and back were taking shape. Soon the whistle of his saw joined the sounds of the shovels digging holes into which the new upright beams would be lowered. Moments later the pounding of hammers rang out as men joined boards together with wooden pegs and the precious nails that had been salvaged from the wreckage of the old barn.

Nick found himself actually enjoying the physical labor and camaraderie of working as one with the men of Simpson Creek. He'd done a lot of hard work since coming to the Matthews ranch and by morning he knew his shoulders and back would ache, but he thought he had never been so content.

He enjoyed still more the occasional glimpses of Milly as it grew closer to noon. Wearing a becoming green dress he'd never seen before, she was a whirlwind, bustling to and fro from the kitchen to the tables carrying out dishes, directing other ladies and placing the additional chairs around the tables. He caught her eye once and she smiled and waved. He hoped she'd stop and talk, but she only dashed back into the kitchen. At least he could look forward to sitting with her when they stopped for the noon meal.

* * *

"Miss Milly, this is a good time to break for dinner, I think," Patterson said, coming to the porch just as Milly left the kitchen, carrying a cloth-covered bowl of biscuits fresh from the oven. "The upright beams are in place, and we've got the four frames all ready to be pegged into them this afternoon."

"Excellent," she approved. "Y'all have worked hard this morning." Milly yanked the rope connected to the cast-iron bell hanging from a post by the step and the clanging soon had men laying down their tools all across the grounds. Her eyes found Nick, who'd rolled his shirtsleeves up his arms and was now wiping his face under the floppy-brimmed hat with his handkerchief. He looked up at her then and grinned.

As the bell's clamor died away it was replaced with the sound of hoofbeats as around the bend, two men rode up on horseback.

"Sorry to be so late," announced one of them, a stocky man with graying dark hair. "We meant to make it here last night, only we took a wrong turn outta Austin, which lost us some time, then we couldn't hardly find anyone in town to direct us here." He took a look around. "I guess that's 'cause most everyone is here."

"We finally asked the saloon keeper," the other man put in, dismounting from his horse. He was a younger man, with tow-colored hair and a ready smile. "Pete Collier's my name, from Galveston, and that there's Ed Markison, from Buffalo Bayou. We're here to meet the single ladies."

Chapter Twelve

"Wel—" began Milly, stepping down off the porch, but she didn't even get to finish the word before Caroline Wallace dashed past her and went forward to the two men.

"Welcome, gentlemen, I'm Caroline Wallace, and my brother Dan will take your horses...*won't you, Dan?*" she called to the boy, who'd already begun ambling toward the food-laden tables. "This is Milly Matthews and her sister, Sarah, and this is their ranch—"

"Ah, so it's your barn we've come to build, ladies?" Ed Markison, the older man, said gesturing toward the beginnings of the new building.

Milly, amused at the way Caroline had made sure hers was the first face Pete Collier laid eyes on, nodded. "Yes, and we're very grateful for your coming to help. We're just about to sit down and eat, and—"

"So you've come at just the right time," Caroline finished, then looked over her shoulder at the other ladies of the Society who were hovering uncertainly on the porch. "These are the rest of the ladies of the Society for the Promotion of Marriage," she said. "This is Emily Thompson—she's a widow, just as you are a widower, Mr. Markison..." she said, and identifying each lady in turn, including Sarah, who smiled shyly and excused herself to go back into the kitchen to get another platter of food.

Nick had arrived at Milly's side in time to witness Caroline's maneuvering, and he winked at Milly. There was something in his eyes that seemed to say, *Isn't it nice that we've already found one another?* Oh, she hoped she was right about that!

"Figures these yahoos managed to get here just in time to eat," Milly heard Hank Dayton mumble to Bill Waters. She winced, fearing the newcomers had heard his churlish remark, but they seemed fully occupied gazing at the ladies.

"We're mighty pleased to make your acquaintance, ladies," Pete Collier said, bowing to all of them, but his gaze returned to Caroline. "Might it be possible to sit together while we eat, so we can begin to get to know you?"

Milly guessed Caroline wanted that, too, but to her credit, she didn't try to secure any extra privileges for herself. "Oh, but we ladies will serve while the menfolk eat. Then we'll eat while y'all get back to work."

Collier and Markison looked disappointed, and so did Nick. "I'd hoped you could sit with me," he whispered, and his voice made her all tingly inside.

"But we'll all be sitting down together at supper, when all the work is done," she said, raising her voice to include the two newcomers. "And afterward, there's to be dancing."

"I reckon we'll just have to wait for the pleasure," Markison said good-naturedly.

Reverend Chadwick stepped forward. "If the wonderful smell is any indication, the ladies have made sure dinner will be delicious," he said. "Why don't I say the blessing?"

If the good-natured groans as the men left the table were anything to go by, dinner had been a resounding success. Milly suspected many of them would have preferred to stretch out in the shade of the pecan trees and nap, but much remained to be done before a new barn would stand where the old barn had been.

"I can't remember when I've been this full. You Simpson Creek ladies are the best cooks ever gathered in one place," Nick said to her as he rose from his place at the table, where he'd been sitting between Reverend Chadwick and Mr. Patterson. "I don't believe I shall need to eat more for a week."

"Ah, but then you'll miss Josh's barbecue for supper, and that would be a shame," she said, nodding toward the barbecue pit, where sides of beef another rancher had donated were already sending their savory aroma wafting into the air. Josh, fretting at his inability to take a more active role in constructing the barn, had declared he would take charge of roasting the meat while the rest of the men worked.

"Try not to let him overdo, will you?" Nick urged softly, glancing toward the wiry old cowboy, who was getting stiffly to his feet at the moment from another table. "When he's not tending the roasting meat, he's been walking around all morning, making suggestions. I'm afraid he's tiring himself out."

"Sarah said she'd try to get him to go take a rest inside this afternoon and let her take over, but you know how stubborn he can be," she whispered back. "He hates being on the sidelines. It was either let him tend the barbecue or we'd find him up on a ladder trying to hammer the new roof."

His smile was sympathetic. "Very well, then, I'll see you later," he said, and rejoined the other men for the afternoon's work. Milly's gaze followed him, watching him help several men lift one of the frames to fasten it to the upright beams.

"The new gentlemen seem like nice fellows," Sarah said, as she gathered up a load of dirty plates to wash. She nodded toward Markison and Collier, who were taking up hammers.

"Yes, and they already seem smitten with Caroline and Emily," Milly observed, grinning as they watched the two ladies staring at the newcomers and giggling together.

"Who'd have thought Caroline was such a flirt?" Sarah remarked, laughing. "She really swooped in and took charge of that Collier fellow, didn't she?"

"Not that he minded," Milly said. "He can't take his eyes off her."

"And the widower seems very pleased with Emily, too."

Milly thought she heard a note of wistfulness in her sister's voice, and studied Sarah more closely. "Dearest, you don't…that is, you and the other ladies—Prissy, Maude, Ada, Jane—y'all aren't feeling left out, are you?"

"Oh, no," Sarah insisted, a little too quickly. "I can't speak for them, but as for me, I—I'm very content to wait for my turn—*if* it comes. Help me get the rest of these dishes and silverware back to the kitchen, so we'll have enough for us."

Milly joined the others who were picking up stacks of dishes and covering platters of food to keep the flies off. They had to work around Waters and Dayton and three other men, who had remained at the table, talking with lowered voices, their heads all close together. They stopped talking and sat back to allow Milly and the others to pick up their dirty dishes, making Milly feel almost like she was intruding.

"We're just takin' our time digestin' that fine meal, ladies," Bill Waters said. "You don't mind, do you?"

"No," Prissy Gilmore said in her outspoken way, with a pointed look at the other men who were already hard at work. "As long as you don't mind us ladies taking over the table in a few minutes."

"Those pies were mighty fine, Miss Sarah," Bill Waters said, balancing his chair on the back two legs, his hand joined over his rounded abdomen. He pointedly ignored Milly. "Yessir, Miss Sarah would make some lucky man a fine wife. Can you imagine enjoyin' pie like this every evening?"

There were chuckles from the other men, and one of the others murmured, "Too bad I'm already hitched."

Milly could tell Sarah hated their attention by the dull flush of color. "Oh, I wouldn't bake pies for my husband every day, Mr. Waters. I wouldn't want him to get fat." She didn't look at his belly, but her mean-

ing had been plain enough, so the other men guffawed
as if she had said it.

"Guess she told you, Waters."

Milly and Sarah took their armloads of dishes and
walked off without saying another word until they
reached the sanctuary of the kitchen. For the moment,
they were alone, but the other ladies would soon be
joining them there.

"The *nerve* of those men," Milly fumed. "If I wasn't
a lady, I'd tell them to go home. They came only to eat,
after all. They've hardly lifted a finger to help the other
men. Why, Josh has done more, keeping the spits turning, than all of them combined."

"We'll just pretend they don't exist," her sister said,
laying a comforting hand on her shoulder. "But, Milly,
what do you suppose they're up to? Whenever I'd bring
a new platter to their part of the table, they were talking about 'the circle' and 'ridding Simpson Creek of
the trash the Yankees sent us.'"

Milly stared at her, startled. Wanting to be near Nick,
she'd made sure to be the one to take and refill platters and cups at his table, and hadn't heard any of this.

"I don't know what this 'circle' is, but I've heard
them say nasty things about the homeless former slaves
I've occasionally seen wandering the roads."

"Those men said they were going to make sure they
didn't 'roost here,'" Sarah said. "And they were saying
nasty things about Nick and the two new men, too—
about not letting Simpson Creek be taken over by foreigners and 'Johnny-come-latelies,' and making sure
they knew their place."

Milly felt a shaft of anger stab through her. "Well,

they're the *only* ones who don't like Nick, then. Did you see the way the other men were talking to Nick like they'd known him all their lives? Those are the men who really represent Simpson Creek, I think. And they seemed to be making Mr. Markison and Mr. Collier welcome, too." She'd enjoyed the way the men of the town seemed to have made Nick one of their own. She'd heard them talking about plans to make the town safer in case of Indian attack, and had looked forward to asking him about it.

When they went back outside to bring in another load, their tormentors were saddling their horses.

"Good riddance," she muttered under her breath, then immediately asked forgiveness for her lack of charity and patience.

No sooner had the men disappeared, however, it seemed heaven was giving her another chance to display these virtues, for a pair of horses pulling a buckboard came lumbering around the bend and pulled to a creaking stop. It was driven by George Detwiler, Junior, who tended bar at the local saloon, and the old lady he helped down from it was none other than his mother, Mrs. Detwiler.

Lord, I said I was sorry, she protested inwardly. She'd been secretly glad this morning when her critic had failed to show up when the other ladies had arrived, and assumed this was Mrs. Detwiler's way of tacitly emphasizing her disapproval of Milly. But now here she was, and being handed down a covered dish that looked suspiciously like a cake.

Smoothing her features to hide her dismay, Milly

went forward to welcome the older woman. Where was Sarah when she needed her sister's diplomacy?

"Hello, Mrs. Detwiler," she said. "How nice of you to come. When we didn't see you this morning, we feared you might be ill—"

"You didn't care enough to send someone to check, though, did you?" the older woman retorted. "No, I couldn't very well come until my son could take an hour away from the saloon to drive me, could I? Since no one else offered to bring me," she added, with a resentful glance at the rows of parked buggies and wagons.

Milly didn't suppose she asked anyone for a ride, just waited for someone to read her mind. "I'm sorry, you're right, of course. We *should* have thought to send Nick or Bobby to fetch you." Which would have required pulling one of them away from their tasks here. "I'll see that one of them takes you home, though, whenever you're ready."

Mrs. Detwiler sniffed. "As if I'd let that young rapscallion Bobby drive me anywhere. We'd probably end up overturned in a ditch. And as for that Britisher, you called him *'Nick'*? Not 'Mr. Brookfield,' as is proper? My girl, if you behave in this fast, loose way, how do you expect to gain the favor of a real gentleman?"

Too late, Milly saw the trap she'd fallen into. "Mr. Brookfield is an employee of the ranch now, and as such, he asked that I call him by his Christian name. He calls me 'Miss Milly,' of course." *Please, God, help me keep my temper!* "But I'm glad you managed to get here, in spite of the difficulties, and how nice of you to bring…what is it, cake?"

Mrs. Detwiler sniffed. "Of course. Everyone clamors

for my chocolate cake at social events. And even if the town's duty to its widows has been forgotten, I believe I know *my* duty to support the community. I could hardly stay home at my ease when all of Simpson Creek has gathered to help you. George, dear, you may pick me up whenever you are able tonight, if I have not come home already," she told her son, who was turning the wagon in a wide circle to return back the way he had come. "My son, of course, cannot stay—not everyone is able to just drop their usual tasks for a daylong party."

Milly glanced back at where the men were muscling yet another frame to the upright beams, a strenuous job requiring teamwork. Hardly a party game.

"Come and eat," Milly said, gesturing at the food-laden table. "We ladies are about to have our dinner, now that the men have eaten and gone back to work."

Chapter Thirteen

The sun was setting, illuminating the new barn in rays of red and gold. In the next few days, Nick and Bobby would spend many hours painting it, but for now it stood in unadorned, simple splendor. The scent of newly hewn wood filled the air and mingled with the savory odor of the barbecue.

"I reckon we should pray again before we sit down to this feast. Isn't it wonderful having the ladies and gents and children all together this time?" Reverend Chadwick smiled, and standing in front of their places at the tables, everyone bowed their heads.

"Almighty God, this morning we purposed to 'rise up and build' and we thank You for blessing our efforts. Behind us stands a completed barn where this morning there were but a few ashes left from the old one. We thank You for giving our men strength and safety in this effort, and for the tasty dinner we had at noon, and the equally delicious supper we're about to partake of, courtesy of our ladies—and Josh. Amen."

There was a din of people settling into their chairs,

the hum of conversation and the clinking of spoons against crockery as people passed the serving dishes piled high with barbecued beef, pinto beans cooked with bacon, hot biscuits, corn bread and slabs of butter. Amid the noise Nick turned to Milly. "So this dress is what kept you from the porch in the evenings all this week?" he asked in a low voice designed to carry only as far as her ears. "It's very becoming."

"Thank you." His compliment had her flushing with pleasure.

He had no idea how handsome he was, she thought, his skin bronzed by the sun, making his eyes seem that much bluer. Like most of the men, he'd dunked his head under the pump after the work was done to cool off, and now a loose lock of drying golden hair fell forward onto his forehead.

It would have been unladylike to confess how often her eyes had strayed to him all afternoon, watching the smooth play of his shoulder muscles under his shirt as he strained with the other men to help lift the skeletons of the barn frames with ropes. He'd climbed a ladder to help pound the rafters in place, then the roof's tin covering. Next came the boards to the sides of the barn. Agile as a cat, he'd scrambled up the frames with the others to join the higher boards and trusses in place. She'd savored his appreciative smile when she'd taken a bucket of freshly pumped cold water out to the men, and watched a mug passing from hand to hand to where he'd been straddling the ridgeline, and the muscles of his throat as he lifted the mug to swallow the water in a few quick gulps.

Had he been born with such grace?

As if reading her mind, Andy Calhoun leaned across the table and drawled, "Nick, I thought you said you was a soldier, but you was shinnyin' up them frames like you'd been buildin' things all yore life."

Nick grinned. "I'm afraid I was the despair of my father, for as a boy I'd much rather climb a tree or help the fellow who came to repair the roof on the dower house than play cricket or chess with the sons of Lord Swarthmore."

Cricket? Dower house? What did these words mean? Milly wondered as she passed yet another steaming platter of savory barbecue. She'd have to ask him later.

"Your pa knew one a' them English lords?" the other man asked, clearly awed.

"Actually, my father was a lord himself—a viscount, actually," Nick admitted, almost as if it was something to be embarrassed about.

"Then why don't we call you 'Lord Brookfield,' or somethin' like that?"

"I'm a third son, not a lord. I'm just an 'honorable.' My oldest brother Edward inherited the title, while my middle brother Richard went into the Church. So it was the Army for me," he finished, as if that was his only logical destiny, "where my climbing skills came in handy once when the maharajah's young son managed to clamber up onto the upper reaches of an ancient banyan tree but was too scared to climb down."

Calhoun whistled. "And now you're here in Simpson Creek, Texas, buildin' a barn for Miss Milly and Miss Sarah. Ain't life interesting?"

Nick tipped his head back and laughed, a merry sound that sent tendrils of warmth curling around Milly's heart. He turned to look at Milly next to him for a moment, then back at the other man. "Indeed it is, Andy. Indeed it is."

Andy's questions seemed to break the ice for the others, and Nick could hardly get an uninterrupted bite due to all the questions he was asked. It gave Milly a warm feeling to see how completely the Englishman had come to be accepted among the townspeople. Everyone liked Nicholas Brookfield, which made her feel as if her growing love for him was not ill-judged. Everyone, she reminded herself, except those such as Waters and Dayton.

"I surely did like the idea you mentioned at noon about building a fort, Nick," Mr. Patterson, sitting up the table a couple of places, said during a momentary lull in the conversation. "I don't think it would attract the Federals here, like Waters was afraid of. I don't know when we'd all have time to work on it, but I do think it's a good idea."

There were nods of agreement from several men up and down the table.

Then Mrs. Patterson spoke to her husband on his other side, distracting him.

"Fort? What fort is he talking about?" Milly asked.

Nick looked a little uncomfortable.

"Why did Mr. Waters say it would bring the Federals?"

Nick sighed. "Possibly I've overstepped my bounds, and if I have, you need only to say so. I—I'd hoped to talk to you about it after the party. We were discussing the likelihood of another Comanche attack, since everyone thinks they might get more bold after getting away with it the last time. This time the Comanches hit only one ranch—yours—but they tell me in times past, they've raided many ranches, sometimes an entire town, burning, looting, killing, taking captives."

Milly couldn't suppress her involuntary shudder at the thought of being snatched away by savage Indians. It was said that the ones who were killed at the scene of a raid were the lucky ones. She glanced involuntarily at Josh, who was holding fort at another table about his secret barbecue sauce recipe. He was still moving stiffly, still wasn't up to taking on a cowboy's work yet.

"A fort would give people a place to take refuge when the Comanches are raiding, a place where the men could defend their families," Nick explained. "Properly placed, a lookout at a fort would be able to give warning when the Comanches were coming. We'd have a big bell up there to toll the warning. A fort might even serve as a deterrent. Who would want to attack such a community?"

"Where would you put such a thing?" Milly asked, though she had already guessed.

"Subject to your permission, of course, atop that hill behind us."

She'd been right. Milly swiveled in her seat to look behind her at the hill that overlooked the ranch, and the road from town that ran along the southeast side of it.

"A fort? On Matthews property? Made of what? Why there?"

He answered her last question first. "As a former soldier—" A shadow passed over his eyes as he said the words. "I can tell you it's a commanding position. From that position, one could see what's coming in all directions. It's not far from town, and there's a deer trail up to the top," he went on, pointing, "that could be widened enough for wagon traffic. You and Sarah and the townspeople could take refuge there, and the men could fire at the Indians from the safety of the walls." He paused a moment, as if to let her take it in. "And as for the materials, it's a very rocky soil, isn't it? Limestone, I'm told. If all that loose rock could be gathered up, I imagine most of the fort could be made of freestone and some sort of mortar. The other men agreed that would work."

"You seem to have thought it all out," she said faintly, her mind whirling at the implications.

"Not completely, no, and as I said, I should have spoken to you first. It must seem incredibly cheeky of me to be speaking of a use for part of your land when I'm only your ranch hand."

She raised her eyes to that blue, intense gaze of his, her heart pounding. "I think you know you're becoming more than that."

He blinked. "I... I hope so, Milly. Then you're not dreadfully angry at me? Still, it would have been proper to ask you first, but at the noon meal, one of the gentlemen began talking about the likelihood of another Indian raid and the need for some sort of protection in the area...and I... I mentioned what I'd been thinking about."

"No, I'm not angry," she said. "It's a lot to consider, yes. And to discuss with Sarah, and Josh, and the rest of the town. But why did Mr. Waters think such a thing would bring the Yankees here?"

"He said if we built a defensive fortification it would

look like we were planning to mount a resistance against their occupation—a rebirth of the Confederacy. And he said that would make the 'blue bellies' come down on San Saba County like a wagonload of anvils. The last thing anyone around here wants, according to him, is Federal troops occupying Simpson Creek."

Milly pursed her lips. Would building a small fort— a place that would usually stand unoccupied—bring the Yankees to her town? It seemed unlikely, but memories of the war were still raw and bitter. It might even lead to ill feelings and reprisals toward Sarah and her for allowing a fort to be built in the first place.

"But before you spend another moment worrying about it," Nick added, "I should tell you the consensus is that most of them couldn't figure out when they'd find the time to work on such a project." He sighed again. "It's not like a stone fort could be erected in a day, like a barn." His hand sought hers under the table and gave it a quick squeeze, then let hers go before anyone could notice. "Why don't we agree to talk of this later?" he suggested. "It's much too serious a topic for such a festive occasion."

For the next hour, everyone ate and talked and laughed. Even Mrs. Detwiler, seated down at the far end of Milly's table, had lost her sour expression. Sarah was keeping the old woman busy talking, no doubt asking her opinion about everything she could think of. God bless her sister for her big heart!

Then it was time for dessert. All through the meal, the children had been eyeing the plates of cookies, cakes and pies sitting on a separate, smaller table—especially Mrs. Detwiler's chocolate cake and Sarah's pecan pies.

Now several of the adults were staring at them with open interest, too.

Milly stood and rapped on her plate with her fork to get everyone's attention while Sarah came to her side.

"I'd like to thank everyone for coming," she said. "Your generosity in pitching in to build a barn for us— well, there are not words enough to tell you how appreciated that is…" She stopped then, feeling the sting of happy tears in her eyes and a thickening in her throat that made further speech difficult. "I—that is, my sister and I," she said, putting an arm around Sarah's waist to draw her closer, "we thank God for all of you and will keep you in our prayers every day. If there's ever anything we can do for you, you have but to ask. I know no one wants to hear a long speech right now, so I'll just say it again—thank you from the bottom of our hearts."

There were cheers and applause and whistles and stamps as her voice trailed off, but she held up a hand. "I'm told my friend Prissy has some instructions about the desserts…"

Prissy marched forward then, smiling broadly and waving, always pleased to be the center of attention. "I'd like to echo Milly's thanks to everyone for coming and giving of their time and effort to build a barn, and to feed those who did the building," she said. "Milly and Sarah are trying their very best to keep their papa's ranch going. But we're not done, ladies and gentlemen. That wood you've been hammering and sawing all afternoon has yet to be paid for. We don't want to build a barn, then leave Sarah and Milly with a big debt for all that wood, do we?"

"*Noooooo*," everyone chorused.

"Then we are going to have to help these girls defray the cost, aren't we?"

"*Yes…*" the diners agreed, though less enthusi-astically.

"Good. I'm glad you agree. For we're about to auction off all these sweet goodies you see at the table." Everyone groaned, but Prissy went right on. "For example, who's making the first bid for this dee-licious chocolate cake, baked by our very own Mrs. Detwiler?"

Milly shared an amused glance with Nick and Sarah as the old woman preened at the attention. But bidding—led by Prissy, who was in her element as auctioneer—was brisk, and eventually Mrs. Detwiler's cake went for three dollars to a cowboy from the Waters ranch who was flush with his month's pay.

Then Sarah's pies were auctioned, one at a time. Nick gallantly started the bidding at two dollars on the first one, and kept the bids rising by adding two bits each time someone else bid. Then, once the last bidder had bid five dollars, he graciously conceded. He did this for all three of the pies she had made, and finally won the bidding on the last one. Other pies and cakes fetched lower amounts, but it all added up, and finally, the reverend purchased the cookies for two dollars and dispensed them to the children.

Prissy came forward again. "Well, we've raised sixty dollars, folks, but we still have a long way to go. You can hear our musicians tuning up over there for the dancing we've been promised," she said, nodding toward a couple of fiddlers and a man strumming a guitar. "Now, there's nothing more fun than dancing to good fiddle music, is there? But we're going to make you fellows pay for the pleasure this time—just a little. We're charging two bits a dance, except for husbands with their wives—they have to pay only once."

Groans and protests erupted, but Prissy's smile didn't dim in the least. "Quit your bellyachin', fellows. You know the ladies are worth it, and it's for a good cause. Place your coins in the bowl here on the table."

Chapter Fourteen

The moon had sunk low in the sky and all but the oldest children were asleep in or under wagon beds when one of the fiddlers announced the last dance.

"Morning's going to come all too soon, even though Reverend Chadwick's agreed to delay the service an hour. Now, we've saved the best for last—we're going to make this final one a waltz, folks."

A pleased chorus greeted this announcement. They had danced reels, schottisches, polkas and square dances—the latter entirely new to Nick, of course, with its allemande lefts and rights and do-si-dos, but he'd caught on quickly with the generous help of the partiers—but there had been no waltzes.

"So husbands, take your wives' hands, and you courtin' fellas, find a lady to dance with."

"My dance, I believe?" Nick said, crossing to where Milly had just danced an energetic reel with one of the cowboys who'd come from nearby ranches. He hadn't liked seeing the fellow claim her for the reel, but to be fair, he'd danced at least half of the other dances with

Milly. He realized she had a social duty to dance with some of the other gentlemen present.

During these times he danced with the other ladies, not only the ladies of the Society, but those whose husbands were not enthusiastic dancers, earning him much gratitude.

"But I was hopin'—" the fellow started to protest.

"I'm sorry, Hap, but I did promise Mr. Brookfield the last dance," Milly apologized. "Look—Miss Spencer has no partner. Perhaps you should ask her."

As Hap loped away in the direction of Ada Spencer, Milly gave Nick a smile of relief and welcome.

"I'm so glad you reserved this last dance," she whispered. "He's a nice boy, but he must have stepped on my feet three times—and you know in a reel, partners aren't dancing that close most of the time. I'd probably be limping after a waltz!"

"Ah, so it's only to escape injured feet that you're glad to see me?" Nick teased, assuming a mock-aggrieved expression.

"Silly! You know that's not the only reason," she told him as the musicians strummed the opening strains of "Lorena."

Nick was glad that small-town Texas folk ignored the custom of wearing gloves at dances, for he savored the warmth of her smaller hand in his as much as the glow of her eyes as they whirled gracefully around the makeshift dirt dance floor. Other couples danced past them—Caroline and Pete Collier, Emily Thompson and Ed Markison, Sarah and one of the other cowboys, Mr. and Mrs. Patterson, but he and Milly might have been the only couple dancing. He wanted the dance to go on forever, so he could go on holding her, moving with her, like this.

"You waltz very well," she told him, making him glad of every one of those tedious weekly dances he'd attended in Bombay. They had been held to allow the daughters of the married officers to mingle with the "griffins" as the new junior officers of the company were called, for most of those who were "old India hands" were either married themselves or, more rarely, confirmed bachelors.

"Thank you. And so do you, Milly," he said. He wondered if she had learned to waltz before the war and had danced this dance with a favorite beau. Oddly, the thought didn't trouble him. She was dancing with *him* now, and from the look in her shining hazel eyes, she was very pleased to have it so.

The other couples had dropped out by now, and they had the floor to themselves. Everyone watched them, and the fiddlers and guitar player prolonged the music. When the music faded away, there was a burst of applause.

Even in the flickering light of the hanging lanterns, he could see her blush, suddenly self-conscious, as if she had totally forgotten the rest of the world while she was dancing with him. The thought pleased him immeasurably.

Surely it was time to advance his courtship?

"I'm going to help the men hitch up their wagon horses," Nick told Milly, with a nod toward the corral, where Bobby—who'd been too young and bashful to take part in the dancing—was already doing that.

"Perhaps we could spend a few minutes together on the porch once all the guests have departed?"

She blinked, and a slow smile curved her lips. "I'd like that," she said. "And now I'd better help the ladies round up their dishes and their older children."

It was over an hour before the last wagon rolled out of the yard and disappeared around the bend in the road toward town.

"Good night, Miss Milly, Miss Sarah," Josh said. "It sure was a fine party."

"Thanks in large part for your delicious barbecue," Milly said.

Sarah agreed and added, "Please, won't you share your recipe with me?"

"Mebbe," Josh said, a twinkle in his eye. "If you'll bake me another a' them pecan pies. I didn't get nothin' but one skinny piece this time. C'mon, Bobby, help this old cowboy get over to th' bunkhouse. I've stiffened up, settin' too long watchin' the dancin' and jawin' with old Mr. Preston."

"Oh, Milly, that reminds me," Sarah said, "Mrs. Preston told me they'd decided they were too old to be ranching anymore, so they're moving to San Antonio to live with their son and his family—and they're *giving* us their flock of chickens, a half-dozen pigs and twenty head of cattle!"

Nick saw Milly's mouth fall open in astonishment. "But that's wonderful! How nice of them, when they could easily sell them. I… I wish I'd known that, before they left, so I could thank them."

"That's probably why they told *me,* sister. I imagine they figured you'd insist on paying them somehow,"

Sarah said, with loving exasperation. "They told me Papa had helped them take care of the stock while Mr. Preston was laid up with a broken arm, so they wanted to do this for us."

How true, Nick thought. If the old wife had announced the gift to Milly, she *would* have tried to decline, unless she could pay for the livestock. And that would be more debt on top of the what they owed for the lumber, for there was certainly no way the money raised by the pie-and-cake auction and the dances, could have covered all the cost of the barn lumber. His Texas rose surely had stubborn streaks of pride and independence!

Milly had had no idea how much she and her sister were loved by the town, Nick thought, having watched the surprised joy in her eyes today as Simpson Creek turned out en masse to help them. Nick smiled to himself. Miss Milly Matthews was going to be one surprised lady when she went to give Dayton the money that had been raised, and tried to bargain for time to pay off the balance, for she was going to learn that a mysterious benefactor had already paid it!

Nick and Milly sat down together, not in their respective rocking chairs as usual, but this time on the porch swing. They spoke of inconsequential things until light no longer shone from within the house or the bunkhouse. Milly had kept a lantern to light her way into the house, but she had turned it down so it emitted only a faint glow between them. The only sound came from the sleepy hooting of an owl in a nearby tree and the crickets chirping in the grass.

"I enjoyed your Texas hoedown—at least that's what Josh called it—very much, Milly," he told her, wondering how to broach the subject on his mind. "The whole day, actually. Everyone was so friendly and kind."

At least after Mr. Waters and Mr. Dayton and their cronies left, he thought, and later, the dour Mrs. Detwiler, who seemed to have it in for Milly. The crabby old woman could be avoided, but those men seemed right bad apples and Nick wished Milly and Sarah's land didn't border on Waters's.

"They like you very much, too, Nick. Everyone's been telling me how impressed they were at how hard you've been working around here, but especially today. And the ladies like your accent," she added with a giggle.

"Do they now?" he said, amused, but also touched at his acceptance by the townspeople. *Would they still like him if they knew everything about him?* "But if I stay around for very long, I might start drawling and saying 'y'all,' you know. How would you like that?"

She laughed, but suddenly she became still, as if she'd realized the deeper meaning of his words.

"I'm wondering if we might amend our agreement, Milly."

"Wh-what do you mean, exactly?"

"We agreed I was here to help while Josh is laid up, nothing more. But holding you tonight as we waltzed was like a wonderful dream, a dream I wanted to come true. I'd like to court you, Milly. I know we had agreed to postpone it until Josh had recovered, but I... I don't want to wait any longer—if you're willing, that is."

He held his breath for the endless seconds it took her to answer.

"Yes, Nick. My answer is yes. But...how do we begin?" she said, her voice sounding a little breathless.

He took a deep breath, praying he was not being too bold, but nothing in her eyes made him think so. "For one thing, we could kiss to seal the deal, rather than shaking hands."

"Ahh," she said, and tilted her face to his.

Her lips were the sweetest he'd ever tasted. And he could tell from her drawn breath that she'd never been kissed before.

Better not rush your fences, lad. Taking his lips from hers, he gazed into her face. Surely all the starlight in Texas had taken up residence in her eyes.

"Could we... I'm sorry, I'm afraid I'm being very forward, but might we do that again?" she asked, her voice tremulous.

His heart sang within him. "It would be my pleasure, dear girl," he said, and lowered his head again, intending to make this kiss deeper and much more leisurely...

Just as his eyes nearly closed, out of the corner of one eye he caught a movement in the shadows by the barn.

He jerked away from Milly and was instantly on his feet, instinctively standing in front of her.

"What is it? Nick, what's wrong? Why—"

"Quiet! Milly, get inside, now!" he commanded in a whisper, motioning for her to move quickly. To his relief, she obeyed, and he followed her.

Once inside, he reached for one of the two rifles in their horizontal racks over the coat pegs. "I saw something—someone—creep into the barn. I've got to find out who it is. You stay here."

"An Indian?" she whispered, her eyes enormous in the dark kitchen.

"I don't know," he admitted. "I didn't see more than a quick movement."

"But you can't go out there by yourself!" she cried, still keeping her voice down, but seizing his wrist with a shaking hand. "If it's a Comanche, he won't be alone! Go get Bobby—"

He blew out the lantern.

"Milly, *stay here!*" he barked. "Lock the door behind me, then grab the other rifle and have it ready. Don't make a sound!" He went back outside before she could say anything more, praying she would do as he said.

Chapter Fifteen

Milly huddled in the dark kitchen, clutching her rifle, staring out through the window at the hulking shape of the barn into which Nick had disappeared, sure he was wrong to have gone alone, sure she should run out to the bunkhouse and wake Bobby and send him to the barn to help Nick—maybe even Josh, too. She was sure that any minute now, she would hear a blood-curdling war whoop, followed by Nick's cutoff scream. Then the rest of the Comanches would erupt from the trees and attack the house...

Then she saw him walking back to the house, briskly, but his gait did not appear alarmed. She dashed to the door to let him in.

"It wasn't a Comanche," he said.

"Then who w—"

"Come, and bring the lantern. I'll show you."

Her hands still trembling, she relit the lantern and followed him out into the night once again. The lantern cast wobbling circles of light on the ground as they walked.

Once inside the barn, he took the lantern from her and held it high, illuminating four men huddling in the corner of the rearmost stall. They were of differing ages, but similar in height and build, and alike in the darkness of their skin, the whiteness of their wide eyes and the raggedy condition of their clothes.

"Miss Millicent Matthews, may I present Elijah Brown and his brothers—Isaiah, Caleb and Micah." He pointed at each of them in turn.

All of the men pulled off their hats, three of which were tattered and floppy-brimmed, while the youngest wore a forage cap, and inclined their heads with a dignity that nevertheless betrayed their apprehension.

"We're sorry t' have give you a fright, Miss Matthews, we surely are. We was jes' lookin' fer shelter for the night, that's all, I promise you, ma'am," the one called Elijah said.

All eyes were on her, including Nick's. And as she stared back at them, she saw how thin they all were, especially the one in the middle—Caleb, had that been his name? His clothes, or what was left of them, hung from his tall frame as if he had once been almost stocky.

"But…how did you come here?" she asked.

"We been wanderin' the roads, ma'am, lookin' for work, but so far we ain't found none. We saw this barn goin' up today, and Isaiah wanted us t' offer to help in exchange fer supper, but I didn't think that was a good idea, what with all th' folks that was here. Some folks don' like havin' us 'round, y'understand." The last thing he said with an apologetic but matter-of-fact air.

"Miss Milly, might we give them something to eat?"

Nick asked. "Elijah says they haven't had anything in two days except for some pecans they found."

There was food left from the party—half a pie, a dozen or so pieces of fried chicken, a basketful of biscuits, a dish of green beans. Sarah had covered them and left them on the cast-iron stove, saying it would be their Sunday dinner, but how could Milly say no? Hope shone from the dark eyes trained on her.

"Of course," she said. "Nick, would you come back to the kitchen with me and help me carry things?"

He followed her back to the house. "Milly, I think the answer to our problem is in that barn," he said softly, once they were back in the kitchen.

She turned to him. "What problem? What are you saying?" It was late. There were four strangers, homeless former slaves, in her barn, and she didn't have time for riddles.

"You need help to run the ranch properly, these men need jobs. Why not let them stay? I imagine they'd work for their board alone, like we do, until you could afford to pay them."

She felt her mouth drop open. "I... I don't know," she said at last. "I—I'd have to think about it...and ask Sarah, and Josh..." She had no experience with other races; she'd never had occasion to even speak to a person with dark skin. Before the war, there had been few slaves in ranching country except for one or two on the bigger spreads, mostly kept as cooks and household help. Most slaves had lived in the rice-and cotton-growing plantation areas to the east and south.

She remembered the men whispering at the table today, and the conversation Nick had reported overhearing between Waters and Dayton, about how "the circle" was going to take care of the problem posed by just such men as Nick had found in the barn.

Aware that he was waiting for an answer, Milly turned back to the leftover food on the stove. "I...we'll have to see," she said. "Meanwhile, let's take this food out to them."

Was there a flash of disappointment in those blue eyes?

Milly pulled open a drawer in the cabinet and took out four tin forks from the supply of eating utensils used during spring roundups and picnics. She wasn't about to risk the loss of any of Mama's silverware. Then she felt guilty for her suspicion. She had no reason to think these men were thieves, no matter what the likes of Waters and Dayton said.

"Thank ya, ma'am," Elijah Brown said as the men eagerly took the dishes and the forks from them. "We'll be movin' on once we've et. We'll leave th' dishes and forks right here when we go. We don't wanna be no trouble."

"But it's the middle of the night," she said. "You can sleep here at least."

She thought she saw wetness in the man's liquid brown eyes, but he blinked before she could be sure. "That's right decent a' you, ma'am. Thank ya."

"I'll bring them some spare blankets from the bunkhouse," Nick said, and she saw approval lighting his gaze. He followed her out. "I really think it's the perfect solution, Milly," he said, as they stopped halfway between the bunkhouse and the house.

"I'll think about it," she repeated, wishing he

wouldn't try to rush her about this. "And pray about it. I have to see what the others say. Tell those men...you can tell them not to leave in the morning until we've made our decision."

"Very well," he said, and left her, striding toward the bunkhouse without another word.

Vaguely disappointed, she went into the house. Why couldn't he tell her he understood her hesitation? Hadn't he just kissed her? Hadn't they just agreed to begin courting?

In the morning, over breakfast, she told Sarah, Josh and Bobby about their visitors, and Nick's idea, while Nick ate his eggs and biscuits and said nothing.

"Well, what do you think?" she said into the thoughtful silence.

Sarah shrugged. "I don't know, Milly.... Whatever you decide is all right with me."

Milly shot her sister an exasperated look before turning to the old cowboy. "Josh, what do *you* think? Is it a good idea?"

Josh leaned back in his chair. "Well...we could give it a try. Tell 'em they could stay on a trial basis, see how it works out. We *do* need help around here, like Nick says. I ain't never worked around them folks, though..." He grinned crookedly and chuckled. "Might be worth it just to put a stick in Bill Waters's spokes."

Milly sighed. It was all very well for Josh to be gleeful about aggravating their cantankerous neighbor, but she and Sarah would bear the brunt of any reaction, not Josh.

She was going to get no real help in making the decision, she saw, other than the feeling she had gotten while lying awake praying until nearly dawn this morning.

If you do this for the least of these My brethren, you do it for Me.

She sighed. She needed to decide, so they could all get on with getting ready for church. "All right, Nick, I suppose we can—" she began, but shut her mouth again as the sound of hoofbeats reached her ears.

It was Waters and a trio of his ranch hands, she saw from the window, and by the time she got to the door, they had stopped in front of the house, sending a cloud of dust flying through the air. The men were all armed, with rifles tied to the backs of their saddles and pairs of pistols in their belt holsters.

"What can I do for you, Mr. Waters?" she said, hearing someone coming to stand behind her and knowing without looking that it was Nick. "We were just getting ready for church."

"Sorry to disturb you, Miss Milly, but we're out lookin' for that band a' ex-slaves that's been robbin' folks blind around these parts. I found 'em roastin' a steer on my property, bold as you please, and I wanted to make sure they weren't botherin' you, too."

By an effort of will, Milly kept her eyes from straying to the barn behind the men, lest she give away the four men's presence. If what Waters said was true, the men in the barn had lied to her about being hungry. But they hadn't looked at the food like men who'd just eaten beef steaks. *Please, God, don't let them come out of the barn right now or even peek out.* "No, they haven't bothered us," she said with perfect honesty.

"That's good. Well, you go on to church, then, but

if you happen to see 'em on the road, you tell them to git outta San Saba County, or there's white men who'll teach 'em a lesson they might not live to regret, them and anyone fool enough to shelter 'em." He touched the brim of his hat automatically, the gesture of respect mocking after the threat he'd just uttered.

Chilled to the bone despite the heat of the sun, Milly stepped back inside without a word while the riders wheeled and galloped away.

"I'm sorry," she said, as soon as she'd closed the door. "I'm afraid they can't stay after all. You'd better tell them to move on."

He looked thunderstruck. "You're going to let that… that blowhard tell you what to do?"

She flinched at the incredulity in his voice. She'd hoped he wouldn't question what she said. "You heard Waters," she said, her hand outstretched in a plea for his understanding. "Surely you can understand I—we—have no choice. Those men might be in danger if they stay, and we can't chance having trouble here. Why, they might even burn the ranch down."

Josh and Bobby and Sarah were silent, watching as Milly pled for his understanding.

"Or they might understand that it's your choice to employ whom you please, Miss Milly," Nick said evenly, while his eyes flashed blue sparks of ire. "People like Waters are cowards, and they thrive only as long as they can intimidate others into doing what they say."

It was a challenge, and she knew it, but as much as she wanted to quench the anger in his gaze, she couldn't give in. A part of her was angry that he'd placed her in this position and made her choose. Her heart ached in realization that saying no would probably toll the death knell over what had been beginning between them.

"You're right, it *is* my choice to employ whom I please, Nick, and I'm telling you I can't risk what you're asking me to do. You're a foreigner here, and you weren't here to see the hatred and violence that ran rampant here between the men like Waters and the men who disagreed with them about slavery and such."

His eyes were hard as flint. "I've seen bigotry before, Miss Matthews. There was plenty of it in India, coming from the British and aimed at the very people whose country they'd taken over. They called the sepoys—the Hindu and Moslem Indians who served in the army—'blackies' and treated them with contempt, even though they couldn't have held on to their comfortable life of privilege without them. I've seen the Indians themselves and their mistreatment of the 'untouchables,' the lowest caste, and I tell you I can't stomach it. But as you've reminded me, it's your decision to make."

There was nothing she could say to quench the contempt in his eyes, she thought, blinking against the sting of tears. "I'm sorry," she said again. "Does that mean you won't stay either?" She held her breath, afraid of his answer.

It was an eternity before he answered, and when he did he didn't look at her. "I've made a promise to you, and I'll keep it," he said at last. "I'll stay until Josh is able to work again. Then perhaps I'd better go back to Austin and take that job at the embassy, if it's still open."

She realized that he was telling her that anything

would be better than this, for he'd already expressed his distaste for that tedious position.

"Very well," she said.

"I'll tell them," he said, and left the house, letting the door slam behind him and leaving his breakfast half-eaten on the table.

When it was time to leave for church, there was no sign of him.

Chapter Sixteen

Josh stated he felt well enough to attend church, and whistled from the back of the wagon all the way there. Bobby, as usual, tried to wiggle his way out of going, but his uncle insisted that if he was going, Bobby was going, too. So the boy finally clambered aboard, his cowlick firmly wetted down and wearing his Sunday clothes.

Milly was grateful that their presence kept Sarah from speaking to her about the confrontation with Nick. Her feelings were too raw, too uncertain to talk about it. She already dreaded the end of the service, when someone was sure to ask her why her handsome British "cowboy" hadn't come to church with her this time.

She felt like a wooden puppet as she entered the church, greeted others, sat down with her sister, Josh and Bobby and sang the hymns. She was just going through the motions.

Nicholas Brookfield had nothing but contempt for her now, and as soon as Josh was completely back on his feet, he would leave. He thought her a coward for not being willing to employ the four homeless men because of Waters's threats.

But you just don't understand the risk, she argued with him in her mind. *I'm responsible for the welfare of my sister and the employees I already have, Josh and Bobby. How can I continue to feed them if the Matthews ranch is nothing but a smoking ruin? Where would Josh, as old as he is, get a new job? Where would Sarah and I live, in a tent?*

"My message today," began Reverend Chadwick, "is taken from the sixth chapter of Micah, verse eight, 'What doth the Lord require of thee, but to do justly, and to love mercy, and to walk humbly with thy God?'"

Inwardly, she groaned. How could refusing to give those men jobs be "doing justly"? Employing them would be showing mercy, but what if it caused them to come to harm at the hands of the mysterious "circle"? Surely it was better to let them move on to somewhere where their lives would be safer?

Even if she wanted to change her mind, though, those men were already gone—she knew this because she had peeked inside the barn while Bobby was hitching up the wagon. There was no sign of them, though the dishes and forks were neatly stacked in a corner of the stall on top of the folded blankets.

I'll show mercy next time, Lord, I promise, and act justly, I promise. I'm sorry I did the wrong thing this time. But how am I to make this right with Nick? Is it too late for that, too?

"Don't worry, it's all going to work out," Sarah whispered to her, as they stood to sing the final hymn.

Milly gave Sarah a grateful look. She was always so

perceptive. Milly had pretended to pay attention to the sermon, but her sister had sensed the presence of the turmoil within her.

Now she had to run the gauntlet between the church door and their wagon. *Please, Lord, don't let anyone ask me about Nick...*

"Now, where's that handsome gentleman I saw you waltzing with just last night, Milly Matthews?" Mrs. Patterson cooed. "My, he is a good-looking man! And I just *love* the way he talks, don't you?" She aimed the remark not at Milly but at Mrs. Detwiler, to whom she had been speaking when Milly and her sister drew near.

"I...uh..." What should she say?

"Evidently *foreigners* think it's all right to lie abed on the Lord's Day after a party," Mrs. Detwiler sniffed. "As for the way he talks, why, I don't know what's wrong with plain *American* speaking. It was good enough for me when my George walked this earth."

"We let Mr. Brookfield get some extra rest today," Sarah said, stealthily squeezing Milly's elbow. "It seemed only fair, since he was up on top of those rafters as much or more than any other man there. I noticed several of the men were missing this morning."

"Yes, my husband, for one," Mrs. Patterson said. "He's so stiff and sore this morning he could hardly get out of bed. I reckon he did too much, trying to keep up with the younger men like Mr. Brookfield. I told him the Lord would understand if he didn't come to church this morning."

Mrs. Detwiler was neatly caught. She could hardly continue to criticize Nick for not being there if Mrs. Patterson's husband had stayed home, too.

"Good seeing you ladies," Milly said. "We must be getting home to start dinner."

But they were unable to make it to the wagon without encountering Caroline Wallace and Emily Thompson, who were accompanied by their two new beaus from the coast and looking happy as butterflies in a field full of bluebonnets. Fortunately, they were so wrapped up in their own joy that they accepted the same excuse Sarah had given the other two women at face value.

"Pete, Mr. Markison, Emily and I are going to have a picnic on Simpson Creek this afternoon," Caroline burbled. "Why don't you and Nick join us?"

"Oh, and you, too, Sarah, naturally," Emily added quickly.

Milly saw Caroline flush with embarrassment at her inadvertent gaffe.

"Oh, thanks, but after all the excitement yesterday I think I'd just like to rest," Sarah said imperturbably.

"Me, too, I'm afraid," Milly said. "Thanks for asking us. Another time, perhaps."

"We'll count on it."

After that, they made their escape to the wagon, where Josh and Bobby were already waiting.

"I'm sorry Caroline left you out of the invitation," Milly said, as she steered the horses back out onto the road. "She never seemed so giddy and thoughtless before."

Sarah patted Milly's hand and smiled. "She's not thoughtless, Milly, just excited. I'm pleased for her that it's going well so far. I wasn't feeling left out, I promise you."

Milly sighed and clucked to the horses to urge them

into a trot. "You're a much better person than I am, Sarah." Although she, too, was pleased for the other ladies, her heart had ached that she couldn't accept their invitation—she wouldn't have had an escort either.

When they drew up at the ranch, she spotted Nick up on a ladder already slapping paint on the barn.

"Where did you get that?" she asked, pointing to the bucket from which he was brushing white paint onto the raw timber.

Nick had turned around when the wagon pulled into the yard, but now he turned back to his work. "Mr. Patterson brought it when they came yesterday. I thought he'd mentioned it."

"No. How thoughtful of him," Milly said, wishing Nick would turn around again, disappointed that he evidently hadn't gotten over his anger at her while she'd been gone to church. But she was a fool to have hoped he would, she told herself. "We'll call you when dinner's ready," she said, trying to sound bright and cheerful.

"I'm not hungry," came his curt reply.

Milly exchanged a look with Sarah.

"Well, come down from there and have some lemonade at least, and rest this afternoon," Sarah urged. "It's going to be too hot to be out here painting this afternoon. You'll have a sunstroke."

Nick turned half-around, then. "Thank you, Miss Sarah, but after a decade in India, I'm used to the heat." He might have been speaking to a stranger, he was so polite. "You needn't worry."

"But it's Sunday!" Milly protested, before she could stop herself. But she was once more speaking to his back.

"This needs to be done, Miss Milly," he said, plying

his brush. "It would be a shame to let termites or rain damage such a new building."

"I'll be right out to help you, soon's I eat, Mr. Nick!" Bobby called, full of eagerness to help his hero and oblivious to the tension stretching between the man on the ladder and the woman on the ground.

"Let him go, Milly," Sarah whispered. "He'll come in when he's ready."

But he did not come in until supper, ate silently and quickly, then excused himself to go to the bunkhouse, muttering something about a headache.

"It ain't surprisin' he's got a sore head, bein' out in the sun all day like that," Josh commented, looking after him with shrewd eyes.

Nick had just asked her to partner him in the Virginia reel. In the illogical way of dreams, the Englishman showed no sign that he remembered their earlier disagreement. He wore the gray dress uniform of a Confederate officer, complete with a saber dangling from a sash around his waist. He laughed as he bowed to her from the line of gentlemen that faced the ladies while the fiddler played the introductory notes of the tune.

"Miss Milly, Miss Milly!" Bobby's urgent shout pierced the pecan wood door and the fragile bubble of her fantasy.

What on earth? Another Comanche attack? But no war whoops pierced the stillness outside. Throwing a wrapper around her nightgown, Milly dashed to the door of her bedroom, rubbing the sleep out of her eyes as she went.

Bobby stood there clutching a lantern, the light transforming his worried face into that of a nightmare creature.

"What is it, Bobby? Is Josh w—"

"Naw, it's not my uncle, it's Mr. Nick. He's sick, Miss Milly, and shaking so hard I'm afraid he's gonna fall outta bed. And he's talkin' outta his head. Uncle Josh says you better come."

While he'd been speaking, Sarah's door had opened across from hers and Milly saw her sister standing there, taking in every word. "You go ahead, Milly," she said. "I'll get out some willow bark and start brewing a tea and bring it out to the bunkhouse as soon as it's ready."

Pausing just long enough to throw her shawl over her wrapper, Milly dashed after the boy, running to keep up with his long-legged stride. What could have struck Nick down so quickly? He'd worked too hard out in the heat all day, of course—could this be sunstroke, striking so many hours later?

Josh already managed to light a couple of lanterns in the bunkhouse, banishing the shadows to the far corners of the room and underneath the bunks. He'd been bent over one of the cots, but when he straightened and turned at the sound of the door banging open, his weathered, worn face was as apprehensive as Bobby's had been.

"Miss Milly, he wuz sound asleep when me 'n' Bobby came in t' bed down, but a few minutes ago he woke us up complainin' about the cold, and beggin' fer blankets," Josh said, shaking his head in amazement at a body needing blankets on a July night. "We piled every bit a' covering we could find in here on him, but it didn't seem to warm him at all. Then he was shoutin' about a tiger about t' spring on him, an' mumblin' some outlandish foreign gibberish." He took a step backward, sagging into the chair behind him, and Milly could see the cot on which Nick lay.

Even before she reached his bedside, Milly saw the sheet over Nick fluttering from his trembling beneath it, and heard a rhythmic clicking. She thought it was the legs of the bed shaking against the floor planks, but then she realized it was it was Nick's chattering teeth. His face was pale and his skin bumpy with gooseflesh.

"Nick!"

His eyes were slitted open and seemed to track the sound, but there was no recognition in them. "Ambika…" he said, and mumbled some unintelligible phrase.

Ambika? What—or who—was Ambika? Was he speaking some tongue he'd learned in India?

"Sarah's coming with some willow bark tea," she murmured over her shoulder to the old man and the boy. "Hang on, Nick." *Oh, Sarah, hurry!* She collapsed onto her knees next to the bed. *God, save him! Don't let him die!*

Chapter Seventeen

She appeared to him in his dream—Ambika, youngest daughter of the rajah. Her name meant Goddess of the Moon. She was the most beautiful woman he had ever seen, with her thick, lustrous, raven-black hair like a river of silk. Aptly named, she could be mysterious as the moon, too, favoring him with one of her rare smiles and letting him see the gleam of her fathomless dark eyes in one moment, pouting and veiling herself the next in the filmy, iridescent fabrics trimmed with pearls and sparkling gems. She wore anklets and bracelets with tiny golden bells, so her walk was as musical as her voice.

She'd promised him much with her eyes, and even knowing it could never work, he'd fallen in love with her. But now, in his dream, she was watching his ceremony of disgrace, just as she had on that day. He thought he heard her laughing at him, and not even her veils could muffle the acid scorn in it. *"No wonder they call you Mad Nick..."*

Mad Nick.

Millicent Matthews was there in his dream, too, but she was not laughing. Instead, she stood opposite Ambika, with the assembled ranks of the Bombay Light Cavalry between them. Compassion and sorrow etched her face. She seemed to be reaching out to him, stretching her arm as one did to a drowning man, but even though he extended his arm to her, he could never seem to make contact. He was being swept away, not by water, but by rows and rows of uniformed soldiers, mercilessly pushing him onward.

Maybe someday he'd stop dreaming of a woman who, in the end, had only caused him pain.

As she watched, he stopped shivering and the pallor of his face was gradually replaced with flushing. She reached out a hand to touch his forehead and yanked it back, alarmed at the intensity of the sudden heat. He was burning up! Where was Sarah with that tea?

"We got t' take them blankets off him, Miss Milly, so he kin cool off, afore he gets so hot he has a fit," Josh told her, and she yanked the coverings away until Nick was once again covered only by a sheet.

"Fetch me some water, Bobby!" she said, and when he ran back in with a bucket from the well she drenched the bandana hanging on his bedpost and sponged Nick's sweaty face. He yelped in alarm at the first cool, wet touch of the cloth, then sank back, eyes closed, still shivering as he submitted to her ministrations. She sponged his face, then uncovered one arm at a time, then the other, wiping them down with the cool wet cloth as she had seen her mother do when Sarah had come down with a fever as a child.

Sarah arrived an eternity later, carrying a cupful of the tea, and with Bobby helping to raise him up, they managed to ladle the tea into him, spoonful by spoonful. Eyes screwed shut, he grimaced at the taste, but in some recess of his heated brain, he must have known they were trying to help him, for he allowed them to continue until he had taken the entire cupful.

"Bobby, you'd better ride for the doctor," she said. The boy nodded wordlessly and pulled on his boots.

Nick raised his head off the pillow and muttered something that sounded like *"Kwine...ih v'lees..."*

"What, Nick? What are you saying?" Milly asked. More Indian words?

But he said nothing more, his head falling back on the pillow once again. While she waited, she prayed silently. *Please, Lord, save him! You sent him to help us, didn't You? So You wouldn't let him die of a fever when we need him so badly, would You?*

Then she realized how bossy her prayer sounded. Surely it was wrong to talk to the Almighty like that.

Lord, I'm sorry for speaking to You that way. I'm just so afraid for him! Please save him, I beg of You! If he dies, I don't even know how to notify his family... But Your will be done...

Across the bed she saw Sarah, her eyes closed, her lips moving. She was petitioning Heaven, too.

An hour passed, and as she watched, ever so gradually the dry hotness of his skin became damp, then wet. Great pearls of sweat rose on his forehead and dripped down his cheeks. When she touched him, he felt cooler, though still overwarm, and she saw that the sheets on top and beneath him were drenched with sweat.

"We've got to change these sheets or he'll get chilled again," Milly muttered. "Sarah, could you please get some dry sheets from the house?"

As soon as her sister returned, with Josh insisting on helping despite his stifled grunts of pain, they turned the unconscious man on his side, first to one side of the bed, pulling out the drenched sheet beneath him and replacing it with a fresh dry one and repeating the process until he was once more surrounded by clean, dry sheets. He never woke. When he was once more lying on his back, Milly stared, hypnotized by the regularity of his chest rising and falling beneath the covering.

By now, Josh was snoring in his bunk. Sarah's head nodded forward as she fell into slumber, then jerked herself upright, blinking as she struggled to regain full alertness.

"Sarah, go back to the house," Milly told her, gently touching her sister's shoulder. "I'll send Josh if I need anything."

Sarah shook her head. "I couldn't sleep," she insisted, her words belying the yawn that escaped from her right afterward.

"Well, at least curl up on one of those empty bunks over there," Milly said with a wry smile. "You almost fell out of the chair just then."

Sitting in a cane back chair by Nick's bed, Milly had nodded off herself when, some time later, she woke to hear his voice calling her name.

"Yes, Nick?" she said, leaning toward him and feeling his forehead. Once again, it was hot and clammy to her touch. His eyes were open, and he shivered, but there was a spark of recognition in his red-rimmed blue eyes.

"*Lareea*. Need *kwine*…quinine," he corrected himself, jaws clenching in an obvious attempt to keep his teeth from chattering again. "My v'lees."

She didn't understand the first word, or the last, but finally comprehended quinine. "Quinine? You need quinine for what's ailing you?" Where was she to get that?

"In my v'lees," he said again. "Under…th' bed…"

Kneeling, she felt underneath the bed, her hand coming in contact with something solid and made of leather, and pulled it out by the handle. It was the leather grip he had brought with him from the boarding house. Ah, he'd been saying *valise!*

"In…s-side," he said, motioning for her to open it. "Bottle…quinine. Drops…put a few drops in water…"

She did so, finding a small amber bottle with a stopper atop some papers. She grabbed a cup that was sitting on his bedside and poured a glass of water, then carefully tipped the bottle to allow a few drops of the quinine to mix with the water before swirling it around. He drank it down as if his life depended on how fast he could swallow, and for all she knew, it did. Then she almost giggled at the awful face he made as he drank the last sip.

"Nasty, dr-dreadful stuff…bitter…"

The effort of drinking the quinine water seemed to exhaust what little energy he had left, and he sank back on the pillows, his eyes closing once more in sleep.

"Milly, it's morning," Sarah's whisper and her gentle touch on her arm, roused Milly from sleep in the chair by Nick's bed.

Milly jerked herself upright, conscious of needles

of pain from her stiff neck. Startled that she had fallen asleep when she'd meant to keep vigil, she immediately turned to look at Nick. The Englishman still slept, one arm atop the sheet, the sound of his breathing regular and unlabored. His color looked all right, though a little pale, but just to reassure herself, she reached out a hand and touched his forehead. His skin was dry and warm, but not overly so.

Outside in the yard, the rooster announced the rising of the sun.

"Why don't you go back to bed in the house for a while?" Sarah said, still whispering. "You can't have slept very well, all scrunched over like that."

Milly stretched, yawning, pushing an errant strand of hair from her braid out of her face, and reached a hand back to knead her stiff neck. She looked at Sarah, then back to Nick, hesitating.

"Josh is awake, and he can watch over him for a while. I'll check on him every little bit. Go on, now."

Milly looked around. "Where's Bobby? Didn't he ever come back from the doctor's?" The boy's bunk was empty.

"Doc Harkey's at a ranch between here and San Saba, delivering a baby. Bobby left a message to come when he could. He's out spreading hay for the horses."

Surrendering, Milly started for the door.

"Th-thank you, ladies…"

They whirled to see that Nick was awake, his eyes open.

"I'm sorry, we didn't mean to wake you," Milly said, going back to the bedside. "How are you?"

"Weak as a cat, I'm afraid…but it would have been

worse without your help," he said, his voice raspy. "The quinine's…only thing that helps."

"Do you know what caused your fever?"

He nodded, eyes closing with the effort, then opening again. "Malaria…"

"Malaria? Malaria caused your fever?" Milly said, catching sight of the alarm that flooded her sister's face.

Nick had evidently seen it and interpreted Sarah's expression, too. "Not…not c-catching," he said. "It's…a souvenir of my…time in India…returns every now and then t' remind me. Not…often… The quinine helps… shorten the attack somewhat… But it's not over… there'll be more…"

"So how can we help you recover? What do you need?" Milly asked.

"W-water…" Nick's eyelids drooped, as if the few words he'd said had exhausted him.

She poured a fresh cup of water from the pitcher; then with Sarah helping to prop him up, Milly helped him sip it. He drank thirstily until the cup was empty.

"Th-thanks," he said again. "Sleep now…"

He was asleep as soon as Sarah lowered his head to the pillow.

It was three days before the cycle of chills, fevers and sleeping, followed by lucid intervals, was over and Nick, assisted by Bobby, felt well enough to leave the confines of the bunkhouse for a chair on the porch, where Milly waited in one of the rocking chairs.

He felt a great deal better now that Bobby had brought him hot water and assisted him to wash and shave, but his legs felt about as strong as pudding. He hated to have Milly see him this way, pale and leaning on the boy. What a bad bargain she must think she had made, depending on him for help with the ranch!

And how beautiful she looked in her simple calico everyday dress, her face lit from the sunlight on her right, her dark hair gleaming with reddish highlights.

"Thanks, lad," he said, as he sank into the rocking chair. "I'm much obliged to you."

"Aw, 'tweren't nothin', Mr. Nick…" the boy mumbled.

"Nonsense. I wasn't fit for the company of a lady before you helped me clean up," Nick insisted, and the boy smiled shyly.

"You're welcome. I—I'd better get on with my chores. Holler when yer ready to go back to bed, or you need anything," Bobby said, clumping down the steps. He strode back across the yard to the corral.

"Would you like some coffee?" she said, indicating the pot and cup on the low table between them.

"Indeed, I would," Nick said, savoring the excuse to just sit there and watch her as she poured the steaming brew into the cup, then handed it to him before pouring a cup for herself.

He closed his eyes in bliss as he swallowed. "Ah… that's wonderful stuff. I'm getting quite fond of your Texas coffee, Miss Milly. It's making me forget all about tea."

"It's Arbuckle's brand," she said. "It's new this year— the first coffee that comes pre-roasted. It's actually made by Yankees, but we drink it anyway," she murmured with a wry smile. "Each bag comes with a peppermint stick—Bobby always begs for that."

Nick cleared his throat. "I... I'm sorry you had to see me like that, Milly—when I was delirious with the fever, I mean. These malarial attacks don't happen often. In fact, it hasn't happened for so long I didn't recognize the signals and thought I was only overtired from the heat. If I'd recognized it, I'd have drank some quinine water and perhaps have succeeded in heading it off."

She looked surprised. "Becoming ill is nothing to apologize for, Nick. I...we...just felt sorry for you, and wished we could do something to make it go away more quickly."

He winced inwardly. Sorry for him was not at all the way he wanted her to feel.

"You said you got this malaria in India," she went on. "What causes it? Why don't we have it here?"

He shrugged. "I don't think even physicians know exactly. But it seems to be prevalent in marshy areas, so I should think it's too dry here for that."

She nodded her understanding, then took a deep breath. "Nick, I... I just want to say I'm sorry for the quarrel that we had Sunday, about the ex-slaves. You were right, and I was wrong. I was being a coward."

He looked down at his hands for a moment, then back up at her. "It's all right. I was wrong, trying to impose my wishes on you. You know best what the realities are here after all."

"It's good of you to say, but no, I was totally at fault. I realized it, sitting in church. I let my fear of confronting men like Bill Waters make me afraid to do the right thing. And we *do* need help around here."

"Yes, my falling sick rather proved that point, didn't it?"

Milly sighed. "Of course it did. I... I don't suppose it would be possible to find those men and bring them back?" she asked, with a tentative smile.

He felt the grin spreading over his face. "When I sent them on their way, I told them about the cave over by the creek, and the fish they could catch there with the poles we left in the cave. With any luck they're still there. Bobby could go out there and tell them you're willing to offer them jobs."

Chapter Eighteen

Bobby returned with the men riding in the back of the wagon, all smiling broadly. Once it had pulled to a stop between the barn and the house, they clambered out, the other three waiting while Elijah approached, hat in hand, to where she still sat on the porch with Nick. Sarah came out to join them, wiping her hands on her apron, and behind her hobbled Josh.

"Miss Milly, Bobby told us 'bout you offerin' us jobs as hands, and I want to say for all of us, we're right grateful. We're gonna show you how grateful by workin' hard for you, ma'am. You just have to tell us what you want, and me 'n' my brothers, we'll do the best we kin for you and your sister. We ain't never ezactly been cowboys, but we've tended livestock. We'll learn quick, I promise you."

Milly smiled at Elijah and his brothers beyond him. "Welcome to our ranch. This is my sister, Sarah," she said, nodding at her. "And our foreman, Josh. You already know Nick Brookfield. It's we who should be grateful that you were willing to come back. I—I'm sorry I sent you away the other night. I—"

But Elijah held up a hand. "'Scuse me for inter-ruptin', Miss Milly, but you don't have t'apologize. We understand givin' a job to folks like us ain't somethin' you do lightly, an' bless you for givin' us a chance." His eyes were understanding and kind.

"Thank you," she murmured, feeling she'd just ex-perienced a profound moment of grace. "Josh and Nick will be giving you your orders, showing you the ropes and providing you with tools. You'll sleep in the bunk-house," she said, pointing to it. "You'll eat…" Milly stopped to consider. The kitchen table was a little small to accommodate four more men. "I think we'll need to move the table onto the side porch, and combine it with the one in the bunkhouse. That'll work until the weather gets cold, at least."

Elijah looked a little uncomfortable at this. "Miss Milly, you don't need to do that," he said. "Me an' my brothers, we could pick up a pot o' beans or whatever in the kitchen and take it out to the bunkhouse. It ain't fittin' for us to eat at the same table as our boss."

There was a muted chorus of agreement from his brothers.

"Nonsense," she said. "Our other hands don't eat in the bunkhouse, so neither will you. Perhaps some-day this ranch will be a bigger operation and the hands will have to eat in the bunkhouse, but right now that's hardly the case."

"But ma'am…"

Sarah, behind her, spoke up. "I'm the cook, and I agree, much less work for me that way. And none of you other men object, do you?" Her gaze took in Josh, Bobby and Nick.

Bobby looked surprised to be asked, but shook his head with the other two men.

"Thank ya, ma'am. We ain't met with such kindness since…since I don' know when," Elijah said, his eyes suspiciously wet before he looked down again.

But all the thanks Milly needed was the warm glow of approval in Nick's blue gaze.

"Then that settles it. Why don't you get settled in the bunkhouse. Josh, would you be able to show them where the sheets and blankets are? Bobby, please help me move the tables onto the side porch."

"And what am I to do, Milly?" Nick said, rising.

"Your job is to sit right there and rest," she told him. "Tomorrow will be time enough for you to start earning your keep again," she added with a wink.

Over dinner, they learned more of the four brothers. Once again Elijah, as eldest brother, served as the spokesperson. They ranged in age from twenty-five to nineteen. All of them had been slaves on a large cotton plantation in eastern Texas, but none had been aware that they'd been set free by Lincoln's Emancipation Proclamation until General Gordon Granger brought the news to Texas in June. None of the men were married. Elijah had had a wife, but she had died in childbirth. Isaiah had been sweet on a girl, but she'd been sold away from the plantation and after that the two younger brothers, Caleb and Micah, had been reluctant to set their affections on any of the female slaves on the plantation.

"I told 'em there'd be time enough for that later, once we're settled down, with jobs and a place to live and such," Elijah said, with an air of wisdom far beyond his years.

They were curious about the history of the Matthews ranch, too. Josh was clearly in his element while telling the story of the Comanche attack that had nearly cost him his life—which led naturally enough into Nick telling them about his plan for building a stone fort up on the hill.

"Sure, we'll help you build that," Elijah said. "Sounds like a good idea, case them Injuns come raidin' again." He ran a hand over his head full of tight black curls. "I don't fancy *my* scalp decoratin' no Comanche spear."

"We'll work on that only when we have time to spare from our other chores," Nick told them. "One of the local families is donating their stock to the ranch, and they're bringing them tomorrow, so we'll need to get them settled in."

"Mr. Nick, mind if I ask you where you come from, sir?" It was Isaiah, speaking up for the first time. "I ain't never heard nobody speak like you do. Are you from some furrin' country?"

Nick's brow furrowed for a moment in confusion, and Milly was about to explain that Isaiah meant *foreign,* but he must have figured it out then, for he explained he was from Britain, by way of India, a country on the other side of the globe. The man's eyes grew wide. "I bet you got some stories to tell, Mr. Nick."

Nick laughed. "Indeed, I do. I imagine we'll find time to swap yarns, as Josh puts it."

"Then how'd you end up here, Mr. Nick?" Caleb asked.

"You two stop bein' so nosy," Elijah said. "I 'pologize for my brothers, Mr. Nick. I reckon we've been so busy findin' our way in the world, I ain't properly taken the time to teach 'em manners, like mindin' their own business. Please forgive 'em for askin'."

"I don't mind," Nick assured him. "But it's rather a long story," he said, glancing at Milly. "Perhaps we'd better tell it another time."

It had been a good day, Nick mused at sunset the next day as he washed up at the pump before supper. He'd gone to bed right after supper the night before, still weak from the effects of the fevers, but today he felt much stronger and he'd been able to properly pull his weight.

The Prestons had come as planned, bringing the cattle, pigs and chickens, and now six new pigs contentedly wallowed in the pen Bobby had built for them while Nick was ill. There had been a few minor skirmishes between the old hens and the new, but the pecking order had been rearranged, and Milly and Sarah were already discussing how many eggs to leave the hens to set upon, and how many to use for cooking or selling.

The twenty head of cattle were rangy longhorns, like the ones already at the ranch, but in addition there was a vigorous young bull, which would more than replace the old one the Indians had slaughtered.

Even over the sloshing of the water, Nick could hear the cattle lowing as they explored their new enclosure. He thought of the stockier breeds of cattle back in England, and wondered what kind of cattle they might produce if they were bred with the hardy Texas cattle. Perhaps Edward could be persuaded to ship him some from England, he thought. Ah, but he was getting ahead of himself, wasn't he?

"Mr. Matthews must be pleased as punch to see this," Josh said, staring out at the corral and the pasture beyond as he joined Nick at the pump. "Why, this is like the glory days before the war."

"You believe those in heaven can see what's going on on earth?" Nick asked, smiling. "So do I." He hoped that Milly and Sarah's father was happy he had come into their lives.

"'Course I do," Josh said. "I don't think we stop carin' 'bout the ones we loved when we go through them pearly gates." He rubbed his bristly chin. "You know, with a little luck, it won't be but a couple of years before we can send Matthews cattle along with some trail drive to Kansas, mebbe even head up the drive ourselves." He looked wistful at the thought.

"Sounds like you'd like to be a part of that," Nick observed.

Josh whistled. "Trail drives are hard on a young man, and I sure ain't young no more," he mused, rubbing his lower back. "Between the river crossin's, the Injuns, the rustlers and the stampedes, not to mention snakes, it's a dangerous trip, and that's a fact. But Bobby would be jest the right age by then."

Both men watched as the lowering sun illuminated the figure of one of their new hands as he threw out flakes of hay for the horses in the corral.

"That was a good thing you done, persuadin' Miss Milly to give them men a chance," Josh said. "Didn't want to pressure Miss Milly to set her mind a certain way because a' what *I* believed. But I reckon now that those men are free, they need work same as a stove-up ol' cowboy like me does. Mind you, not ever'body in Simpson Creek's gonna think so."

His words confirmed Nick's suspicions. "You think there will be trouble from men like Waters?"

Josh rubbed his chin again. "Oh, Sheriff Poteet will probably discourage any *real* mischief from those fellas in that 'Circle'—" his face wrinkled with contempt as he said the name "—but there might be some unpleasantness. Some folks jes' ain't happy 'less they kin hold someone else down. And it's likely the Circle knows about it already."

Nick was surprised. "But how?"

"Mr. and Mrs. Preston seen 'em when they was here, and they probably mentioned it t'somebody, innocently enough, and that person told somebody, who told somebody…" His hand made circles to indicate the speed at which gossip traveled. "And the Waters hands might see the Browns out mending fence and tendin' cattle…"

"I… I see."

"I'm just tellin' you so you kin keep your eyes open, that's all."

"Should I—should we—discuss it with Miss Milly, do you think?"

"Naw, I wouldn't go worryin' her," Josh said. "Just be watchin'. And while I'm handin' out free advice, young man," he added with a grin, "it's my opinion you oughta git busy courtin' Miss Milly in earnest."

Nick was startled at the older man's frankness. "What makes you say so?"

"I've been knowin' that young lady since she was knee-high to a horned toad and I saw the way she fretted over you when you were sick. Any fool kin see she loves you, Nick, so I'd get crackin' if I were you."

Without another word, Josh walked into the house. Nick stared after him. Clearly, the old cowboy approved of him or he'd never have urged Nick to step up his courtship. What Josh had just said had sounded more warm and fatherly than any of Nick's real father's infrequent attempts at conversations. The fourth Viscount Greyshaw had been distant as the clouds, decreeing that his third son should go into the army simply because he already had an heir and a second son in the Church. The army had suited Nick very well until recently, but he had often wondered how his father would have reacted if Nick had had other ideas. He already knew that if his father had been alive when Nick had been stripped of his colors and drummed out of the army, he would have disowned him.

His brother Edward hadn't done so, of course, but Nick suspected he was relieved, nonetheless, that his disgraced younger brother had decided to put an ocean between them rather than return to England. One shouldn't have to be embarrassed by a family connection to Mad Nick Brookfield. It was bad enough that his mother, after giving her husband three sons and a daughter, had become legendary for her indiscretions.

Nick shook his head as if to clear it. What was done was done. Mad Nick had been left behind in Bombay. He was Nicholas Brookfield, and he was going to take Josh's advice about stepping up his courtship of Milly.

Chapter Nineteen

"Good morning," Milly said to the postmaster sorting mail behind the counter. "Is Caroline around?"

Amos Wallace looked up, but the normally friendly man didn't smile at her as he usually did and return her greeting. "She's in the back office. Caroline!" he called over his shoulder. Then he went back to his sorting, almost as if Milly was a stranger.

Caroline emerged from the office before Milly could think much about his demeanor. "Come on back, Milly," she said, beckoning and opening the swinging half door. "I was hoping you'd come in today."

Milly followed her into the small office and sat in the chair next to the roll-top desk. "Why? Are there any new letters from prospective suitors?"

"Yes, three!" Caroline grinned, pulling them out of a pigeonhole. "And they all sound like good candidates. Shall we convene a meeting of the Society?"

"Wonderful! Let's see, today's Friday…how about Monday for our meeting?"

"That's when the Ladies Aid Society meets," Caroline reminded her.

Milly felt a guilty twinge as she realized she hadn't even thought about the Ladies Aid Society since the Indian attack, but quickly dismissed it. She'd had quite a lot to contend with since Josh was laid up.

"All right, Tuesday, then. Help me pass the word."

"As president, you should take these and give them a preliminary look," Caroline said, handing the letters to Milly.

Milly put them in her reticule, intending to study them later.

"How are things going with Mr. Collier?" Milly asked, and was delighted to see her friend blush.

"Pete's coming for supper tonight!" Caroline's voice fairly squeaked with excitement. "Ma and Pa met him at the barn raising, of course, but this will be the first time he's had supper at our house. I'm going to cook chicken and dumplings and black-eyed peas and peach pie, all my specialties. Ma's going to help me a little," she admitted. "I have trouble getting it all done at the same time."

"That's the way, show him what a good cook you are," Milly approved. "I've always heard that's the way to a man's heart."

"And how's that handsome Englishman of yours?" Caroline countered with a grin.

"Better now, but we had quite a scare," Milly said, and told her about Nick's attack of malaria.

"How frightening," Caroline commented. "And this could happen again?"

Milly nodded. "I'll know what to do next time,

though. Apparently taking quinine shortens the attack. This time it caught him unaware, though, and he was delirious and couldn't tell us what he needed." Then she remembered the delicious news that she'd come to share with Caroline before going on her other errands.

"You look like the proverbial cat that swallowed the canary," Caroline said, studying her. "I take it it has nothing to do with the subject of nursing a man with a fever."

"Nick asked me to dinner at the hotel this Saturday night," she said. "He made a reservation—or as he said it, 'I've bespoken dinner at seven, if that's agreeable to you, Miss Milly,'" she said, imitating his accent as best she could. She couldn't stifle a giggle. "I couldn't bear to tell him no one's probably ever needed a reservation for supper in the entire history of the hotel."

"Oh, how sweet," Caroline gushed. "Well, it certainly seems as if he'd like to move things along—"

Just then Mr. Wallace entered the office. "Caroline, if you're going to take off the last part of the afternoon, I need you to get back to work," he said, his voice uncharacteristically brisk. His gaze avoided Milly.

Now Milly was sure something was wrong. Usually Mr. Wallace had plenty of time to crack a joke with her, to ask her how the ranch was doing. Now he wouldn't even look at her.

Caroline jumped up. "Sure, Pa, Milly and I were just talking," she said. "What do you need me to do?"

"Your ma needs you to run down to the mercantile and fetch some sugar," he said.

"Sure, Pa. Milly, I guess I'll see you later…"

Milly rose, too. "Actually, I have something to buy

there, too," she said. "So I'll walk with you. Have a good day, Mr. Wallace," she called, but he'd already gone back to sorting the mail and offered her no reply.

"Caroline, what's wrong?" she asked, as soon as they'd crossed the street and were heading toward the mercantile. "Did I come at a bad time?" Suddenly, she guessed what her friend was going to say and she felt sick at heart.

Caroline sighed and looked down at her feet, her feet slowing. "Papa's heard about the new hands you hired for the ranch."

"I… I see…" Milly said. Josh had been right—the news had gotten around. "Does he think I should have turned them away?" she said, guiltily aware it was exactly what she had done at first. "Caroline, the ranch needs cowhands, and there hasn't been anyone else passing through, looking for work—especially since I can't pay anything but board right now. I—I didn't realize your father felt that way."

Caroline's eyes were startled. "It's not that—you know we never had any slaves, before the war. It's just that he knows how men like Waters feel about it…"

"Caroline, your father's not a member of the Circle, is he?"

Her friend looked confused. "Circle?"

"That group Waters and Dayton are part of, that wants to keep any of the former slaves from settling anywhere in San Saba County."

"No, I'm sure he's not. He just doesn't want any trouble…"

"And I'm sure my new cowhands won't cause any

trouble," Milly said, a trifle stiffly. "They just want a home and honest work."

"Please don't be angry with *me*, Milly," Caroline said, putting a hand on her friend's shoulder. "I don't feel that way. In time, he'll see it's no problem, but don't be surprised if other folks act like he did."

Once inside the store, Caroline immediately bought the sugar she'd been sent for and left, while Milly went to the back to where the bolts of fabric were kept. She needed to buy enough denim to make shirts for the four brothers, for she'd learned that the ragged, threadbare ones they wore were the only ones they possessed.

Mr. Patterson, when he was measuring the cloth and wrapping it up for her, acted the same way toward her Mr. Wallace had—brisk, businesslike, treating her as if she was a stranger.

"What's wrong, Mr. Patterson?" she asked, once he'd handed her her wrapped package. Was she to be treated this way by everyone in town? "Is it our account? We should be able to pay it by the end of the month." She knew it wasn't their bill that made him so taciturn, but she wanted to hear what he would say.

"Nothing's wrong. End of the month will be fine, Miss Milly," he said, but he wouldn't meet her gaze either.

"Do you disapprove of the new ranch hands I hired, Mr. Patterson?"

His grip tightened on the pencil he was using to figure the cost of the fabric. "None a' my business, Miss Milly."

"But you *do* disapprove. Yet you never owned slaves either."

His eyes met hers for the first time. "It has nothing to do with that. It's just that ex-slaves living here will probably lead to more of them coming, and then an office of the Freedmen's Bureau here, sooner or later, and Yankee carpetbaggers to run it. They'll say they're here to make sure the former slaves are treated fairly, but these Freedmen Bureau fellows are scoundrels, Miss Milly. Opportunists. Swindlers. We don't need that in Simpson Creek."

"All that will happen because I hired some help?" she questioned, her tone ironic.

His gaze softened, and he was once more the kind man she'd known all her life. "It could. You just be careful, Miss Milly."

She thought at first he was warning her about her new employees, and she was about to insist she could trust them, when he went on.

"You be careful around men like your neighbor and his cronies. They aren't pleased about those men living out on your ranch."

After the last two encounters, she wasn't looking forward to speaking to Mr. Dayton about what they owed for the barn lumber, but it couldn't be helped. She didn't like owing any money to anyone, even Mr. Patterson, but owing a large sum to a surly man like Dayton was especially onerous.

How they were going to come up with the money to pay the balance, she had no idea. In time the ranch would once more be self-sufficient, making money from the sale of cattle, horses, chickens and eggs, but for now they were cash-poor.

Lord, You've promised to meet our needs. Help me

to figure out a way to earn some money, she prayed as she trudged along the dusty street between the mercantile and the lumberyard.

Her mind not on her steps, she dropped the hem of her skirt which she'd been holding out of the dust, then nearly tripped as her booted foot caught and partially tore a flounce. Ah, well, it wouldn't be a difficult repair…

I can sew. And mend.

Suddenly she reversed her steps and nearly ran back into the mercantile and up to the counter where she found Mr. Patterson was dusting the shelves.

"Mr. Patterson, I have an idea for making some money," she said, "if you're willing to allow me just a little more on the ranch account."

He looked up, waiting, his expression a bit wary.

"Would you be interested in selling ready-made dresses in your store? I hear a lot of mercantiles are doing that now, not just selling the fabric to make them. I could make them up in a variety of sizes. Oh, and if you're willing, I could leave a card with my rates for alterations and mending, and a basket. Folks could leave clothing that needs mending here, and I could pick it up, mend it and bring it back for them to pick up."

The mercantile proprietor took off his glasses and dusted them on his shirt before answering. "We could try it, I suppose, and see how it goes…. I won't charge you for the fabric now, but take the cost out of the profit when they sell. But you'd have to pay me back eventually if they didn't sell," he added, his brow furrowing.

Even his doubt couldn't quash the flow of confidence she was feeling. "They'll sell," she told him. "Ever since

Mrs. Ferguson's eyesight failed, there's been no town seamstress. I just wish I'd thought of this sooner! Very well, I'll take that bolt of blue-figured calico and that green gloria cloth. I'll have these ready within the week, I promise."

Now when she walked to the lumberyard, her feet seemed to have wings. Surely selling dresses would enable her to pay off the debt for the lumber a lot sooner.

She found Hank Dayton in the lumberyard, planing the sides of a stack of planks.

"Good morning, Mr. Dayton," she said, though it was nearer to noon. "I've come to find out what we owe you after the amount raised at the barn raising was taken out." She was going to offer him one or two of the steers, if he was willing to take them in lieu of cash.

He wiped his sweaty brow with a rumpled, yellowed bandana, then stuffed it back into his pocket. "Nothing," he said, then spat into the wood shavings as if the answer left a bad taste in his mouth.

She blinked. "Nothing? How can that be? I know how much was raised that night, and from the price you quoted me, we must owe you about a hundred dollars at least."

He narrowed his eyes at her. "You gone deaf, Miss Milly? Must be all that sweet-talkin' that British fella's been doin' to you, when you ain't doin' things like hirin' those shiftless beggars I heard about. You don't owe me nothin'. Not one red cent." From the scowl on his face she decided he found the fact vastly disappointing.

"But how can that be?" she demanded, ignoring his jabs about Nick and the new hands. Not for a moment would she believe this man had just decided to wipe the debt off his books out of the goodness of his heart.

"Look, you got any questions, you talk to that foreigner about it," he snarled. "Meanwhile, I got work t' do."

He was as good as telling her to leave, but she stood her ground. "Are you saying Mr. Brookfield settled the balance of our debt?"

"Yep," he said, using the plane with such savagery that it seemed he wanted to shave the wood down to paper. "Your fancy 'cowboy' came in and paid what you owe. Said I wasn't to tell you how it was paid—only I thought you oughta know. Around here we got a word for women who let men they ain't married to pay their debts."

She actually felt the blood drain from her face as the meaning of his ugly words sank in. And then it rushed back, filling her cheeks with heat.

"How dare you say such a thing, you sneaking sidewinder?" she said, taking refuge in one of her father's old phrases. "He meant to be kind and generous, and you want to make it sound horrible! Well, you just hand me the money he gave you and I'll give it back to him, and we'll pay you with a couple of the new steers the Prestons gave us. You can sell them or butcher them, I don't care. Will that make us even?"

"Now, I cain't do that, Miss Milly," he said with a smirk. "I got bills t'pay, too. That money's already spent, y'see."

Her hands fisted at her sides in frustration. "I see, all right. Good afternoon, Mr. Dayton."

Chapter Twenty

She found Nick up on the hill with the four new cowboys. Driving the wagon up the narrow track to the top, Milly was amazed to see they'd already laid out a perimeter for the stone fort and had gathered a pile of rocks of various sizes as high as her shoulder. Right now they were taking a break in the shade formed by an outcropping of limestone, passing around a couple of canteens of water.

"This is amazing!" she marveled, forgetting for a moment her encounter with Dayton.

Nick grinned up at her. "It's a good start, isn't it? I think it's getting too hot to do more today, but if we can use the wagon, it'll be easier to gather up the rocks the next time we can work on it."

"Sarah just asked me to tell you dinner's ready. She didn't figure you could hear the bell up here. You can ride down in the wagon bed."

While the four brothers went ahead to the pump to wash up, Nick helped her unhitch the horses and turn them out in the corral. She used the moments alone with him to tell him what Dayton had said.

Nick's blue eyes blazed with fury by the time she finished the account. His hands clenched into fists just as hers had. "The blackguard! I believe I'll pay him a call this afternoon and make him pay for his blasted cheek! Texas doesn't allow dueling, does it?"

"No…" she said, though she knew there were lawless towns farther west where quarrels were commonly settled with guns.

"Pity. I'll have to settle for giving him a proper drubbing, then."

She put up a hand. "No, you mustn't do that. Don't you see, it'll only make things worse. Then he'd have to retaliate. As it is, no one with any sense will believe his nasty insinuations. Anyone who would doesn't have the brains God gave a goose."

Her words caused his lips to curve into a half smile. "I'm so sorry, Milly. I never meant for what I did to help to cause you any embarrassment. I… I suppose it *could* look like…" He reddened. "Like an inappropriate gift."

"Only to the evil-minded. Just ignore Dayton and his sort," she pleaded. "We won't need to do more business with him anytime soon. I *do* want to thank you for what you did, Nick—for paying off the balance," she said. "It was more than generous of you."

"You're welcome," he said. His eyes retained some of their storminess. He gave a deep sigh. "I wanted to be an anonymous benefactor. Blast the man!"

Then Milly caught sight of Sarah beckoning from the side porch. "I think we're holding up dinner. We'd better go wash. But not a word about what Dayton said, please,

Nick. I don't want to upset Sarah, too." She would tell Sarah later about the way Mr. Wallace and Mr. Patterson had acted toward her, though, in case Sarah went into town and was treated likewise.

"Very well, if you'll promise not to tell her about my paying off the lumber bill—at least in front of me. I didn't do it to be thanked, you see."

She stared up at him, hardly able to believe how unselfishly *good* he was.

Over the meal, she told Sarah and the others about her idea of selling ready-made dresses at the mercantile.

"What a great idea, Milly," Sarah praised. "I've heard lots of ladies at church wish they had your skill with a needle and your eye for decorative touches."

"I'll start on them right after the shirts I'm going to make for you men," she said, then told them about the denim she'd purchased for that purpose.

"Is it Christmas?" Micah wondered out loud. "Sure looks like summer out there to me, but I ain't never had new clothes 'less it was Christmas."

Everyone chuckled.

Sarah's eyes had gone thoughtful. "I wonder if I could interest Mr. Patterson in selling my pies, too? What do you think, Milly?"

"I don't see why not," Milly replied. "Maybe the hotel restaurant would buy them, too."

Nick raised his glass of cold tea. "I'd like to propose a toast," he said. "To the Matthews sisters—entrepreneurs extraordinaire!"

"That was delicious!" Milly said, putting down her knife and fork after taking the last bite of tender roast beef. "Sarah's a great cook, but it's nice to eat supper elsewhere for a change...especially when I'm with only you."

Nick studied her across the restaurant table. Milly Matthews looked delicious tonight, too, in an entirely different sort of way. She wore a dress of some rose-colored silky fabric and a lacy shawl around her shoulders. She'd put her hair up, allowing him to appreciate the graceful length of her neck. A cross pendant dangled from a simple, delicate gold chain. A faint hint of rosewater wafted from her skin, a more appealing scent than any of the exotic musky perfumes he'd ever smelled in India.

He wanted to kiss her tonight. Surely the sparkle in her eyes ever since they'd left the ranch together indicated that she wouldn't take that amiss? He'd head out of town on the road back to the ranch, then stop the wagon and kiss her.

"Would you folks care for dessert?" the waiter asked, breaking into his thoughts.

"Oh, no, I couldn't..." Milly murmured.

"That's a shame, ma'am, 'cause the cook made a Boston cream pie that looks absolutely delightful."

Milly groaned. "It's tempting..."

"The lady will have a piece. And we'd like coffee," Nick said. The waiter had been perfect, there when he was needed, friendly without being obsequious, a distinct contrast to the hotel proprietor, who'd pretended not to hear when Milly had called "Good evening" to him as they'd walked through the lobby toward the restaurant. Apparently he'd heard about the ranch's new employees, too.

"Mmm, you really must try this," Milly said, holding a forkful out to him after the waiter had come and gone again.

It was sweet, but not nearly as sweet as looking into those mercurial green-gold eyes and watching her rosebud lips open involuntarily as she fed him the morsel of pie. Did she know how irresistible she was?

"Nick…" Milly began, as if she had something on her mind.

"Yes?" he murmured, unable and unwilling to remove his gaze from her eyes and mouth.

"Nick, what is 'Ambika'?"

He couldn't have been any more astonished if Milly had asked why he'd been called Mad Nick.

"How…how do you know that name?" he asked, when he could find his voice.

Something in his face must have told her the word had unpleasant memories attached to it, for she said, "So it's not a *what,* it's a *who?* I'm sorry…it's just that you called that name, over and over again, when you were delirious with fever. I wrote it down—at least, the way it sounded to me… I'm sure I misspelled it—so I could ask you about it some time. I—I was just curious, that's all. You don't have to tell me if you'd rather not."

Of course he'd rather not. He'd rather the name had never intruded into this romantic dinner. Her eyes, which had reflected the candle's dancing light, were anxious now. Troubled.

He could lie, he knew. Make up some innocuous story about Ambika, say she was the colonel's children's *amah,* or something like that. The real Ambika would remain thousands of miles and oceans away.

But he couldn't lie to this woman he had begun to love. He was planning to kiss her tonight and perhaps even begin to talk about their wedding.

He could answer her questions, tell her the truth... just not all the truth.

"Ambika was the youngest daughter of the maharajah—the prince, that is—of the Bombay area."

"And you knew her? You were friends?"

"We were acquainted, yes. Though one could hardly say a princess could be a friend of a lowly British captain. Her father was allied with the major general, and so the rajah often brought his family to joint social events." *Please, Milly, leave it at that.*

"Was she...very beautiful?"

Beautiful didn't begin to describe Ambika's sultry, sloe-eyed appearance.

He shrugged, as if Ambika's looks had held no importance to him. "I suppose you could say so, yes. A lot of the lads in my company fancied themselves in love with her."

"What about you?" Her changeable hazel eyes were merely curious, not probing or accusatory, yet he knew the truth could wreck their growing feelings for one another. And he could not do that.

He laughed. "I? Well... I was taken with her for a time, I suppose...she was pleasant to look at and all that...and enjoyed talking to young officers.... But I never for a moment thought...that is to say, she was a princess, destined for an arranged marriage with some rajah somewhere, whoever her father decided he needed an alliance with..." He shrugged, trying to imply that's all there was to it, an infatuation that was soon over.

"You called out her name, Nick. Several times."

As much as he willed himself to, he could not continue to look Milly in the eye. He shrugged again. "I dream of India, sometimes…and of people I knew there. The dreams I have when the malaria fevers come… Milly, they're weird, outlandish. I suppose I was remembering her…but last night I dreamed of the major general," he said, as if Ambika was just another person his dreams dredged up from his soldiering time. "It was the oddest thing," he said with a chuckle that sounded forced even to him. "In my dream, he was working alongside Elijah, Isaiah, Caleb and Micah, building the fort on the hill…"

Just as he'd hoped, she was distracted. "Yes, dreams can be strange—"

"As I live and breathe, it's Mad Nick Brookfield!" said a voice coming from across the room where an archway separated the hotel lobby from the restaurant.

It couldn't be.

Nick looked up, praying he had imagined the voice calling his name, a voice he'd thought never to hear again.

Of course he had not imagined it. Captain Blakely Harvey stood in the entranceway, transfixed, a smile curving beneath his bushy mustache. As their eyes met, Harvey started forward, eyes alight, extending a hand. "It *is* you, isn't it?"

Nick wished the man would suddenly be miraculously transported to the steppes of Russia, but when it didn't happen, there was nothing for it but to rise and greet him.

"Harvey, whatever are you doing here?" he asked. Harvey wasn't in uniform.

"I could ask you the same," the other man retorted. "And in fact I will. I came to Texas to visit my dear uncle the ambassador. I expected to see you there, naturally. But when I arrived, you were nowhere in evidence. I asked the old man about it, only to learn you had never taken up your post in Austin, but had instead sent him some crazy message about visiting the countryside before you settled down to your duty. And now I understand why," he said, his gaze sliding in an oily fashion over Milly. "In fact, your rusticating in this dusty little town makes perfect sense now."

Out of the corner of his eye, Nick saw Milly dart a glance at him. Doubtless she was wondering why he didn't have the good manners to introduce them.

"Fair lady, I will introduce myself since Nick apparently isn't about to," the other man said, giving a low bow. "I am Blakely Harvey, late of Her Majesty's Bombay Light Cavalry, just as Nick is."

Milly darted an uncertain glance at Nick, then looked up at Harvey. "I'm Milly Matthews, sir. How…how nice that you've come to visit Nick. You two must have many memories in common."

"Don't we, indeed?" Harvey said with a chuckle. "I look forward to reminiscing with him while I'm here."

Nick had had enough of this charade. He stood. "Miss Matthews and I were just leaving, Harvey. And you may as well tell your uncle I will not be assuming my post, and I apologize for not writing him to that effect sooner. Now that you know that, you may as well leave Simpson Creek."

Harvey's eyes dueled with his for a long moment. "Leave this delightful hamlet on the same day I've arrived? My dear boy, how inhospitable of you! Why, you must know I've gone to no end of discomfort to reach here, taking the stage as far as I could before hiring a hack—though the miserable bony thing that conveyed me the rest of the way here could hardly be called such, or even horseflesh," he said. "No, I'm afraid I will need to rusticate myself for a few days, to recover from the journey. Surely there's some amusement to be had in this charming little town, perhaps other beautiful ladies to meet, Nick, old boy?"

"There's hard work 'to be had' here, but since you were always averse to that, I know you'd be too bored to remain," Nick said, taking a step forward so that there were only inches between them. The other man was shorter, so Nick had to look down to lock eyes with Harvey, but he did so now. The other man looked away first.

"And if you're really fortunate," Nick went on, "you might meet up with our neighboring Comanches. Their hospitality rivals even that of the Punjabis," he added, referring to the fierce tribesmen of the region northeast of Bombay. "Good evening, Harvey. Nice seeing you again."

Chapter Twenty-One

Milly held her tongue until the wagon passed the last house in town; then, as if she could hold back her curiosity no more, she broke the uncomfortable silence.

"Nick, why were you so unfriendly to that man? You two were in the army together. I mean, I suppose he *was* a little forward toward me, but…" Her voice trailed off.

He said nothing, trying to figure out what to tell her without telling her too much, until at last she sighed and ventured, "You don't have to tell me. It's none of my business."

He didn't want Milly, *his Milly,* transformed into this timid woman. "I'm sorry," he said at last. "Blakely Harvey and I were never friends. He's a double-dealing scoundrel and a womanizer, and I didn't like him even breathing the same air as you. I only hope he'll take the hint and depart in the morning." He didn't really think he could be so lucky, though.

"I… I see…" she murmured. "May I ask why he called you Mad Nick?"

He stared between the horse's ears ahead of him,

wondering what to tell her. There was no way he could answer her question with complete honesty—he'd rather be struck dead by a bolt of lightning, here and now.

"Oh, I suppose it was because I was a 'neck-or-nothing' rider when I was a griff—a newcomer to India—and because I'd take any dare, risk any gamble, both on campaign and during the silly games we played to stave off boredom…" That much was true, but it wasn't the madness that had finally made the nickname irredeemably his.

"Oh. I could tell you didn't like it, when he called you that."

That, my lovely Milly, is the understatement of the century. He could hear the puzzlement in her voice. Perhaps she thought he wasn't a good sport, that he was overreacting to good-natured teasing. He'd a thousand times rather she think that than know the truth.

"Well, we needn't speak of him again," she said, as if that settled the matter completely. "It certainly was a delicious supper, Nick. I had no idea the cook at the hotel could produce a meal like that. Thank you for taking me."

She was trying, Nick thought, but there was no way to bring back the light, intimate atmosphere that had been present at their table in the restaurant, when Nick had been thinking of kissing her tonight. He knew the time wasn't right now. Seeing Harvey, with his smirk, appear out of his nightmares had poisoned the air too much.

There would be other nights, he thought. He loved Milly no less now that he did before Harvey had materialized at the hotel, and he wanted a future with her just as much as ever. Maybe more.

He could see the hill in front of the ranch as a hulking shape in the distance.

"I'll have to be careful not to go on too much about that roast beef in front of Sarah," Milly mused aloud, clearly trying to fill the silence, "or she might think I don't appreciate her cooking… Nick, was that a gunshot? There…there it is again! And do you smell smoke?"

Then there was a volley of gunfire, and the wind brought the smell of smoke unmistakably to their nostrils.

The horse had been ambling along at a slow trot, but now he started and whinnied in alarm, even as Nick reached back and grabbed the rifle that was kept in the wagon. He flapped the reins over the horse's rump to hasten him along. "Get on there!"

"Oh, dear God…" Milly cried, clutching him as the horse lurched into a gallop. "It must be Comanches again! Sarah! Nick, hurry! If they've hurt her…"

It was fortunate the road was level, for the horse slowed his pace only slightly as they careened around the bend.

Nick saw several things at once—horses with riders disappearing around the next curve in the road, Josh and Bobby, illuminated by flames forming a ring around the trees, firing at the riders, while Sarah, a shawl clutched around her, screamed from the porch.

And he saw the ring of fire around the trees, and the four new hands, who had formed a bucket brigade from the pump to the circle of fire.

Nick tossed the reins to Milly, then jumped down from the wagon, and ran into the barn to where the shovel was kept. The fire wasn't high, but it had been a typical hot, dry summer, and in moments the fire could spread and engulf the grass, and then the trees. In a minute he was back, frantically beating at the fire with the shovel and digging at the loose dusty ground and throwing dirt on it, while the other men threw buckets of water. Josh and Bobby had given up firing at the departed riders and appeared at his side, carrying buckets, which they'd filled with the loose dirt they'd scooped up in the corral.

Between them, they subdued the fire in a few minutes. Milly came out to join them, Sarah at her side, each of them clutching lanterns, and silently they all assessed the damage.

The grass inside the ring was singed, as were some of the lower leaves on the trees, but blessedly, the trees had not caught on fire, nor had the fire spread to the house nearby.

"Who was it?" Milly demanded. "Not Comanches."

"No," Josh agreed. "Them fellas wore white hoods over their faces. I was sleepin' sound, but Isaiah was on watch and heard 'em ride up. They were real organized, Miss Milly, 'cause one a them threw a rock inta a window of th' house, while the others poured somethin' out of a jug in a ring 'round them trees and then set the torches they were carryin' to it. We snatched up our guns, and while that fire was flamin' up, they ran their horses round the bunkhouse, yippin' like wild Injuns while we shot at 'em. 'Bout the time you drove up, they must've had enough, 'cause they took off."

Nick hadn't noticed the damaged window, but now he looked up and saw it was the parlor window that had been broken.

"Here's the rock," Sarah said, producing it from a pocket in her wrapper. "And the message that was tied onto it," she added, handing a crumpled piece of paper to Nick.

Milly held up the lantern so they could read the scrawled message:

SAN SABA COUNTY FOR WHITES ONLY! YOU HAVE BEEN WARNED!

"What's it say, Miss Milly?" asked Elijah. "We…we never had any book learnin'."

Milly's eyes were full of unshed tears as she faced the oldest Brown brother. "I—I don't want to say such awful words. This is the work of that Circle. I guess a circle of fire is some kind of symbol."

Elijah's voice was respectful but insistent. "I reckon we better know the whole truth, ma'am."

Her voice shaking, her body visibly trembling, she read the ugly message as Sarah came to stand by her side. Nick put his arm around Milly.

The four brothers eyed one another, their faces both alarmed and angry.

Milly and Sarah exchanged glances full of silent understanding. "I… I'll understand if you want to leave, and we'll find a way to pay you something for what you've done so far, Elijah. But if you're willing, we want you to stay. Papa didn't raise us to bow down to bullies."

"Especially bullies who won't even show their faces," Sarah added, and both women turned to Elijah.

"You're runnin' a risk, Miss Milly, Miss Sarah," he said, his face sober. "But I reckon you know that. We could keep runnin', but before long we have to make a stand, I figure, 'cause we got a right to exist and earn an honest livin'. As long as you're willing, it might as well be here."

"We are. I only wish we'd have been a little quicker

getting home," Milly said. "I'd like to have pulled that hood right off that coward Bill Waters."

Sarah shuddered. "I'm just thankful you got home when you did, so Nick was able to help put out the fire before it did any real damage to the pecan trees. Thank God the wind was out of the west so the house didn't catch."

"We're blessed," Milly agreed. "Thank You, Lord."

"Amen," chorused the four brothers.

Nick added a prayer of thankfulness in his heart, combined with a request for continued protection.

"Yes. And thank you, Isaiah, for being on watch," Sarah said, and he nodded.

"Should I ride back to town for the constable—I mean, the sheriff?" Nick asked. He thought he might also pay a late visit to Blakely Harvey. No doubt he was staying at the hotel. Perhaps he could be a little more persuasive about the benefits of Harvey leaving Simpson Creek early next morning.

"Not tonight," Milly said with a sigh. "There's nothing he could do tonight, anyway. We can leave a little early in the morning for church and pay him a visit—if you think it's even safe to leave the ranch, Nick."

But Josh answered before he could. "I reckon it'll be safe enough here—bullies like to strike in the dark, not in broad daylight. We'll stay and guard it. Don't be too surprised if Sheriff Poteet don't get all het up about the fire, though. He 'n' Waters've been amigos for years."

Nick saw Milly's eyes widen with dismay and felt an aching sympathy for her. First the Comanches, and now the two sisters faced not only social disapproval but the threat of violence because they had dared to employ four ex-slaves. Surely the shoulders he now held an arm around were too fragile to handle all this! He wanted to take her away from all this, to some place where these threats could never reach.

"No one on this ranch should go anywhere—on the ranch or off it—alone," he said instead. On a Texas ranch, it probably went without saying that no one should go anywhere without being armed.

"Sounds like liquored-up cowboys jest out indulgin' in tomfoolery," the sheriff drawled the next day, when they stopped in to see him on the way to church.

Milly felt a spark of irritation at his casual dismissal. "Drunken cowboys don't ride around with hoods over their faces, carrying torches," she retorted. "Would you have called it tomfoolery if the wind had shifted and our house had caught fire? As it is, we nearly lost our pecan trees and had to put out a grass fire."

"But the house didn't catch fire," Sheriff Poteet said in that same maddeningly condescending tone, as if she'd been silly to bring up the possibility.

Nick had been a solid presence at her back since she entered the sheriff's office. Now he touched her shoulder lightly and stepped forward. "Any further such 'tomfoolery' will be met with appropriate force, Sheriff. The Matthews ranch will be defended. If you hear of anyone who was involved in last night's incident, Mr. Poteet, perhaps you ought to warn them of that."

Milly saw the sheriff's eyes narrow in his weathered face as his gaze shifted to Nick. "Ain't you takin' a bit much on yourself, Brookfield? Last I heard, you were jest workin' for Miss Milly and Miss Sarah."

"I can assure you, Mr. Brookfield speaks for me in this matter, Sheriff," Milly said.

Poteet ignored her. "Miss Milly and Miss Sarah have brought some of this on themselves, and that's a fact."

"Indeed, sir?" There was a wealth of contempt in the two icy words Nick uttered.

"Yep, they surely have. You're a foreigner, and I don't expect you t'understand these things, but no one approves of those shiftless beggars she's given shelter to. I'd say those fellows in the hoods were only expressing the feelings of the community."

"Those shiftless beggars, as you call them, were honest men looking for work," Milly said. "I was in need of help on the ranch. My problem and theirs were solved when I gave them jobs. Now it remains to be seen if you're going to do *your* job, Sheriff, which is to uphold the law."

Poteet leaned forward, his small eyes cold in his middle-aged face. "Your papa must be rollin' in his grave t' hear you talkin' like a blue-belly Yankee."

The injustice of his remark took away her breath and left a seething anger in its place, so much so that she didn't dare speak. Didn't the Bible say in the book of Romans that Christians should be subject to the higher powers, and render them respect? But how could she respect a lawman who wouldn't uphold the law?

Nick stepped forward. "This conversation is over. If you won't be responsible for the safety of the Matthews ladies and their ranch and its other inhabitants, I will be."

Chapter Twenty-Two

Visiting the sheriff—and telling Sarah, who had been waiting in the wagon outside, about it—had been hard for Milly, but walking into church and finding Blakely Harvey sitting in the back row next to Ada Spencer nearly put Milly over the edge.

Milly saw Nick tense beside her at the sight of the man, and guessed he would have liked to turn on his heel and walk back out, but he took Milly's arm as if nothing were wrong and headed toward their usual pew. He gave no acknowledgment of Harvey's smirking nod, but Milly could see Ada waving animatedly at her, obviously pleased as punch with the new acquaintance she had made. Milly forced a smile onto her face and waved back. If they'd been earlier, she knew Ada would have beckoned her over to introduce Harvey, but since they had arrived just as church was about to begin, Milly and Nick took their places quickly, while Sarah hurried forward to sit at the piano.

"Of all the blasted cheek," Nick muttered, his voice pitched low so as to reach only Milly's ears.

Milly sent him a sympathetic glance as she sang the first line of the hymn. There would be no escaping Ada and her new friend after the service, of course—and no way to warn Sarah that Nick's fellow Englishman was not cut from the same cloth as Nick.

Sure enough, Ada, with Blakely Harvey in tow, practically ran up to Milly before she and Nick had even descended the church steps.

"Milly, can you imagine? What are the odds that I'd meet *another* Englishman, just walking along our streets, taking his constitutional?"

Just as she said these words, Mrs. Detwiler passed by. She gave the foursome a hard stare. As she stalked by, she muttered, "Blasted foreigners are taking over this town. You'd think they never heard of the Revolutionary War!"

In spite of himself, Nick began to chuckle, and Harvey joined in. For a moment Milly had hopes the scene would be carried off without open hostility.

"Why, Mr. Brookfield, Mr. Harvey says he knows you!" Ada exclaimed. "Did you know he was here in town?"

Nick gave a rigid nod at Harvey, who hadn't lost his smirk, before replying to the excited Ada. "Yes, we discovered his presence at the hotel restaurant last night."

The spareness of his reply ought to have given Ada a hint, but just then Harvey squeezed her arm and bestowed on the dazzled woman a smile of distracting charm.

"And I just know you're tickled that he's here to visit, aren't you?" Ada gushed. "It'll be wonderful for you, won't it, having another Englishman here in town, and not only that, but he tells me you and he were in the army together!"

"Ah, but alas, since he can't stay very long, it'll be a transient pleasure," Nick murmured.

"Well, I'm already trying to change his mind about *that*," Ada admitted with a coy wink. "Simpson Creek is a wonderful place to live, isn't it, Milly? Wouldn't it be nice for your Nick if there was another Englishman living here?"

Milly could see Ada thought she had a good chance of persuading Harvey to stay.

"Ah, but what would I *do* here, dear lady?" Harvey said with a fond smile that virtually begged for Ada to find him a reason to stay. "I'm a diplomat, not a cowboy, and my uncle, the ambassador in Austin, declares he would be lost without me. I merely came to catch up on old times with M—with Nick, here."

He had so nearly said Mad Nick, and not by mistake. Milly knew he was toying with Nick like a cat does with a mouse trapped between its paws. Only Nick was no mouse, she thought with rising irritation.

"Sarah, hello! Let me present my new friend to you, who's also Nick's old friend," Ada bubbled, as Sarah joined them. And so Milly and Nick had to hear the whole story over again and to watch in silence as Harvey trained his dazzling smile on her sister.

And Sarah agreed that it was wonderful that Nick had a fellow countryman here, and how pleased she was to meet him.

"Mr. Harvey, you must—" Sarah began.

Milly knew her sister, so she knew what Sarah was about to say—"come have dinner with us, for I know you'll want to spend more time with Nick. Bring Ada, too, of course"—and she knew she had to act quickly and decisively.

Standing next to her sister, Milly moved her foot discreetly and quickly, and under the cover of their long skirts, brought it down on Sarah's foot—not sharply or painfully, just firmly, so that Sarah could not mistake it as an accident.

Sarah faltered.

"Must what, Miss Sarah?" prompted Harvey. He may have been aware some message had just been conveyed between the two sisters, though he couldn't know how, for they weren't looking at each other and their hands weren't touching.

"Ah...continue to enjoy your time here in Simpson Creek," Sarah finished, a slight flush appearing on her cheeks. "Hadn't we better be getting home, Milly? I've got to get dinner in the oven. Nice to meet you, Mr. Harvey. We'll see you later, Ada," she said, and headed toward the wagon without another word.

"She's right, we do need to be getting home," Milly said. "Ada, don't forget about the meeting on Tuesday afternoon at the church."

"I won't. Blakely, why don't you come for dinner at my house. Ma and Pa would be thrilled to meet you," Ada said. "They didn't come to church today because Pa's rheumatism was acting up."

"I'd be delighted, Miss Ada," Harvey said, giving her a courtly bow. "Nick, old boy, why don't you join me for supper again tonight at the hotel? We can catch up on old times then," said Harvey.

Milly saw Nick hesitate, then nod. "That would be

most…agreeable," he said, and it was as if the word agreeable was a polite euphemism for something else. "Shall we say seven o'clock?"

"Perfect. Very well, then. Miss Milly, Miss Sarah, it was a pleasure meeting you. I'm sure our paths will cross again while I'm here."

"Nick, why did you agree to meet with him?" Milly asked, after they had left the church and Nick had explained to Sarah that Harvey was not someone whose acquaintance she should cultivate.

"I'm hoping to persuade the cur to leave town without further ado," Nick said darkly, and from the way he clenched the reins, Milly was rather afraid he meant to use his fists, if necessary. Blakely Harvey must be a villain, indeed.

As it happened, however, Nick returned from town before Milly had even left the porch to retire for the night.

"How was your supper with Mr. Harvey?" she called, as he dismounted his horse. From the tension on his face, it didn't appear to have gone well, but she couldn't see any scrapes or bruises to indicate Nick had had to resort to fisticuffs.

Even in the deepening twilight, she could see his face darken. "It didn't happen. He failed to appear. The hotel proprietor said he returned to the hotel in late afternoon, then left again a short while later."

"Do you think he's avoiding you?"

"Possibly. Perhaps the wisest thing he's ever done," Nick said, but she could see he was frustrated.

"Well, come inside when you've unsaddled your horse and I'll fix you something to eat, then," Milly said.

"Wait, there's something else," he said, when she would have turned and gone inside. "This was sticking in the dirt at the bend in the road," he said, pulling something out of his pocket and holding it out to her.

It was a crude doll made of straw tied to a straight stick by means of some twine. The doll's body had been painted black.

"There was straw stacked around the stick like a pyre," Nick said. And there had evidently been a circle of fire lit around it, then stamped out. "I was meant to find it, I think."

They stared at each other.

Milly looked around the group of women Tuesday when the Spinsters' Club—as everyone in town insisted on calling it, rather than by its proper name—reconvened. She couldn't help but wonder if any of the ladies' fathers or brothers were part of the Circle that had left the threatening symbol near her house Sunday night. None of them mentioned Milly's new cowhands, or seemed as if they were uncomfortable in Milly's presence, but perhaps they didn't know of their relatives' participation in the hateful group.

She had to stop being so paranoid, she told herself. The group had formed for the purpose of finding husbands, and she needed to concentrate on running the meeting.

"These candidates sound very promising," Milly announced. "I'm going to pass around the three letters so you can all read them. There's a rancher from Bastrop, a bootmaker from Grange and a physician from Brazos County. Only one of them, the rancher, enclosed his picture…"

There was a pleased sigh as Prissy Gilmore, sitting beside Milly, received the picture and studied it. "Why, he's a handsome fellow and no mistake. I'll bet those eyes are blue as bluebonnets, too…"

"None of the others sent pictures," mused Sarah. "I wonder what that means?"

Caroline shrugged. "It worked out well enough without a picture for you, Milly, and for me and Emily."

"Maybe the men can't afford to have them taken," Jane Jeffries suggested in her tentative way.

"Or they're not only not handsome, but are fat, bald and homely!" chuckled Maude Harkey, a little nervously.

"You know, that man could have had that picture taken years ago," pointed out Caroline Wallace. "He might be considerably older now."

"Perhaps some men just don't want to be judged by a picture," Milly suggested.

"That might not even be *his* picture," opined Ada Spencer, pointing to the daguerreotype of the rancher. "We only have his word for it, after all." A smug smile spread over her face. "I'm glad I found Blakely on my own."

"Oooh!" crowed Prissy. "So things are going well with you two, then?"

Ada blushed and grinned. "So far, yes. He has such refined manners! And that accent! Why, he could charm the doves out of the trees when he talks!" Her blush deepened.

Ada wouldn't think so highly of her visiting Englishman if she'd heard Nick's opinion of him. Ought she to try to warn Ada? She doubted the woman would listen.

"But what will you do when he goes back to Austin? He's only visiting, isn't he?" Maude Harkey asked.

"We'll see," Ada said mysteriously. "He went out riding with Bill Waters the other day to see some ranch land that was for sale. He's thinking about buying up quite a bit of land and becoming a cattle baron, he says."

Milly could barely stifle a groan. Even with as little as she knew about Harvey, she didn't relish the idea of having him around permanently—and especially not as a friend of Bill Waters. Even if Nick hadn't said anything negative about the other Englishman, there had been something about Harvey that was too slick, too polished to be real. She hadn't liked his overbold manner, or the way his gaze wandered where it shouldn't. She hoped Ada wasn't being too trusting in the Englishman's company.

Milly gently steered the club back to its agenda.

"Ladies, if we might go back to the subject of what we're going to do about the men who wrote these letters—would we like to pick one of us to start writing each of them, or should we invite them to Simpson Creek to meet us all at some social event?"

"Why don't we do both?" suggested Jane Jeffries. "One of us could write to each of the men and tell him a little about us, and invite him to whatever event we plan—with the understanding that he'd be free to pick any of us once we've all met—those who don't have anyone yet, I mean."

"Let's see, how many of us haven't met anyone yet?"

Prissy said. "Jane, Maude, Sarah, Hannah, Bess, Polly, Faith and me. Are we not to count you, Ada?"

Ada shook her head. "You can leave me out. I'm sure I've found *my* Prince Charming," she said.

Milly was equally sure she hadn't. She *had* to warn her, she decided, before the other woman lost more than her heart.

Maude said, "Let's draw straws, and the short straw holders don't write the letters—though they might be the ones picked when the men actually come, right?"

"True," Prissy agreed, and went to find the church broom to pull some straws. When the drawing was over, Sarah was one of the winners.

"Slowly but surely, we're putting the Spinsters' Club out of business," crowed Maude.

"Not really," Bess Lassiter said. "My sister's going to be eighteen this fall, and she says she wants to participate, too."

"And my cousin's coming to live with us from San Antonio," Faith Bennett put in. "Her fiancé died at Palmito Hill," she said, referring to the last pitched battle of the war, which had taken place on Texas soil. "And while she's not in a mood to think about courting again just yet, I know she will be one day."

"And my friend over in Lampasas heard what we were doing and wants to come for a visit so she can take part," put in Hannah Kennedy.

"Our success is perpetuating the club," Prissy remarked, as each of the three winners blindly selected a letter. Sarah picked the letter written by the doctor.

"Well, we have yet to celebrate our first wedding," Milly pointed out, "but it seems likely we will be soon."

Which of them would be married first? Would it be her?

"I have a suggestion," Prissy said. "We wouldn't have to plan anything on our own if we invite them to the Founders' Day Celebration."

"Perfect!" Maude cried. "It's not 'til October, which is far enough away that we can expect at least one reply letter from each, and possibly more, and each will have time to travel here."

"And it should have cooled off a little by then," Jane added, fanning herself. The intense heat was typical for August in Texas.

"And there are activities all day, from the speeches in the morning, the box lunches at noon, games in the afternoon and the square dance at night," Sarah said. "Sounds perfect to me."

"Founders' Day it is, then," Milly concluded. She knew Nick would be glad to see them come out, for he had accompanied them on the road for their safety. "Ladies, we are adjourned." She turned to Sarah. "Wait for me by the wagon with Nick, will you?" Milly whispered, as the ladies dispersed. "Ada, may I speak to you?"

"Oh, Milly, can it wait 'til another time?" Ada said, already halfway to the door. "Blakely's coming to take me on a ride. And here he is now," Ada said, as the door to the social hall opened from the outside. Harvey stood there, smiling in his smirking way.

Chapter Twenty-Three

"You saw Harvey go in?" Milly asked Nick, when she and her sister came out to the wagon. She'd already told Sarah what Nick had said about the man.

He nodded. Yes, he'd seen the blasted scoundrel go in and come out with Miss Spencer, wearing a doting, besotted expression on his face as if he were half-blind with love. Only Nick knew the expression was as false as anything else about Harvey.

"Did you two speak? Did he apologize for not showing up for your supper together?" she asked, as Nick reined the horse in a wide circle to head the wagon back down the road toward home.

He shook his head. "I left my calling card at the hotel Sunday night, so he cannot claim to have forgotten entirely about our engagement, and he's made no attempt to come to me to apologize. Anyone at the hotel could have told him my direction. So when he walked by me on his way into the church, I gave him the cut direct."

Milly's brow furrowed, and he realized she must not have understood the British term. "Sorry, my Englishness is showing, I fear. I meant I ignored him. He seemed content to do the same to me."

Then Milly told him about Harvey's riding around with Waters to look at property, which had him stifling the urge to disparage the man's parentage aloud. What kind of game was Harvey playing? Was he trying to torment Nick by making him think he would settle here, or would he actually do so? Having him living anywhere near would be like having a cobra in the room, but not being able to see it, never aware when it would strike.

"Nick, I tried to speak to Ada alone back there," Milly said, breaking into his worried thoughts, "to warn her, but she rushed off with Harvey instead. Should I keep trying?"

"Are you good friends?" he asked.

Milly was thoughtful. "Not like Caroline and I are. More like acquaintances, I'd say. We've known one another ever since we first learned our ABCs in school, but then Mama died at the beginning of the war, and we were busy helping Papa, and she's been taking care of her parents…"

"She probably won't listen to you," Nick said, aware he sounded cynical, but it was the truth, from his experience.

"I've got to try, don't you think?" she said, her hazel eyes troubled. "She's clearly head-over-heels about him. If Harvey's as much of a snake-in-the-grass as you say…"

"Oh, he is," Nick said, "every bit of it." *And more.* "You can only try, but often people hear only what they want to hear. So what did you ladies discuss at your meeting?" he asked, wanting to distract Milly from her worries.

He listened while Milly and Sarah chattered about the men who'd written letters and how three of the ladies had been selected to write back and invite them to come for Founders' Day. Nick was glad to hear that Sarah was one of the ones picked and that she, too, was pleased about the prospect in her quiet, unassuming way. Sarah deserved to be happy, too, he thought. He only hoped the man to whom she would write was worthy of her.

"That meeting went on way longer than I would have thought it was going to," Sarah fretted after glancing up at the sun's position. "Goodness, our men must be thinking we've taken off and left them to starve!"

"Oh, I think Josh could warm up last night's beans and make some biscuits, if he had to," Milly commented drily. "He wasn't born eating your cooking, you know. Once we get done with dinner, though, I'm going to start working on a dress for the mercantile."

"The new men seemed real pleased with their shirts," Sarah said. "Bobby said they couldn't stop looking at their reflections in the bunkhouse mirror, as if they thought they were wearing royal robes."

"Maybe they never had any clothing before that wasn't someone else's castoffs," Milly mused aloud.

Nick could tell she was gratified by the new cowhands' appreciation, and his heart warmed again with love for her.

When the wagon reached the turnoff that led to San Saba, however, they encountered a mounted troop of blue-coated soldiers about to turn in the direction of the county seat.

Seeing the long blue line of cavalry, Nick felt a moment's nostalgia. Once he had ridden at the head of a troop like that, all smartly dressed in the uniform of Her Majesty's Bombay Light Cavalry. Now, if he could encounter them again, it would be he who was given the cut direct.

Out of the corner of his eye, he saw Milly stiffen. He supposed her suspicion was natural, given that blue coats had been a symbol of the enemy even earlier this same year. It would take time, Nick supposed, for Texans and other Southerners to feel part of the Union again. His own country had had its civil wars, the Wars of the Roses and between Cavaliers and Roundheads, but that had been long ago.

"Afternoon," said the commanding officer at the head of the double line of mounted troops, touching his brimmed hat with a gloved hand. "I'm Major McConley of the Fourth Cavalry."

"I'm Nicholas Brookfield, and this is Miss Milly Matthews and Miss Sarah Matthews. May we be of any assistance?" He felt the heat of Milly's glare as soon as the words were out of his mouth.

The major shook his head. "Thank you, no, we're out on patrol. We've had reports of Quanah Parker and his braves raiding over by Chappell. You had any trouble with Comanches?"

Briefly, Nick told him about the raid that had taken place the day he arrived, and about the carcass they'd found after that.

"No problem since then, eh?"

None caused by Indians, Nick wanted to say, wishing the soldiers could do something about the threats made by the Circle, but he knew Milly wouldn't want him to give these Federals any reason to linger.

"Keep your eyes peeled meanwhile," Major McConley advised. "I'm sure they'll be raiding every chance they get now to build up their food stores before they move to the Staked Plains for the winter." With a final salute, he motioned the troop forward, and they rode past toward San Saba.

It was sobering to remember that whatever their problems were with white troublemakers, the potential still existed for an attack by Indians that could be far worse.

Milly let her breath out in a great whoosh. "I thought sure he was going to ask who was building a fort up there and why," she said, nodding at the hill in the distance where they had begun their fortress.

Nick doubted the major could have noticed the low rectangle of rock from the road, and even if he had, it might not have occurred to him what the building was to be. Nick thought it was even possible that the major might have approved of the citizenry doing what they could to protect themselves. He couldn't be sure, though—perhaps Milly's suspicions were based on Texan experience with the occupying troops.

Milly's mention of the barely begun fort, coupled with the major's words, made Nick thoughtful. They had wanted to build their fort on the ideal high ground, but so far all they had been able to accomplish was to establish a rocky perimeter. Their duties of tending the livestock and keeping the fences mended, as well as the difficulty of working under a hot summer sun that rivaled Bombay for intensity, had kept them from accomplishing very much. There was still so much more work to do before it would be tall enough to keep anyone safe within it. At the barn raising, several men had been interested but so far no one had shown up to help build it.

It might be due to their disapproval of the four ex-slaves, or perhaps the men thought a fort overlooking Matthews land might not help them in town all that much. Perhaps it was merely that everyone was busy with their own affairs. Nick had no way of knowing for sure.

At the present rate, though, with just the six able-bodied men on the ranch working on it, it might be a year before the walls were high enough to protect anyone. It wasn't just a matter of building four high, stout stone walls. They needed parapets near the top of the walls where men could fire at attackers through slits in the walls as he'd seen in medieval castles in England. But they couldn't assume the Comanches would wait until the fort was done before they attacked again.

When they reached the ranch, the news was even more sobering. Over dinner, Elijah announced that Caleb had been shot at just as he succeeded in untying a calf he'd found lying helpless on its side, its legs tied together. The young man hadn't been hit, or seen who had fired at him, but the shot had come from the area where Waters's ranch bordered with both the Matthews ranch and the road. He had returned fire in that direction, then jumped on his horse, hightailing it back to the ranch.

"The calf was obviously tied up and left there for you to find," Nick speculated, "so someone could get a shot off at whoever found it. I'm thinking they were counting on it being one of you brothers, rather than Bobby or I."

"I think so, too," Elijah growled. "And I don't like it. There's somethin' else they've been doin' and we didn't tell you about it—didn't want to worry you, Miss Milly, Miss Sarah—but now I reckon we better."

"Oh?"

Elijah nodded. "Three-four times now, we found nooses hangin' where we'd be sure t'see 'em. Little ones, like doll-sized, and big ones. Hangin' from tree limbs, mostly…but we found one right in the barn."

Sarah gasped in horror.

Milly clutched at Nick's arm. "So you think it was one of the Circle, trying to terrorize the Browns into leaving?" Sarah asked Nick.

"Yes, and I think they'd seen me leaving with you ladies on the way to town."

"But we can't prove it was someone from the Circle shooting at Caleb, can we?" asked Milly, frustrated. "If the shot came from where Waters's land borders with ours *and* the road, it could have been anyone—even a Comanche—shooting from the road. At least that's what Waters and his Circle cronies will say—that Caleb was too scared to see where the shot had come from."

"I wasn't scared. I was mad, Miss Milly," Caleb said. "I wanted to hit whoever the buzzard was who shot at me."

"And end up being hanged as a murderer?" Isaiah asked. "They'd claim you shot an innocent man who hadn't fired his gun, and you know it."

Caleb was silent.

"Well, I'm tired of living like this," Milly said with some heat. "The Comanches have always been a danger around here from time to time, but with the new threat posed by the Circle, I feel like none of us are safe away from the house and that when we go to town, we leave the ranch more vulnerable," Milly said. "I'm beginning to feel like we're prisoners on the ranch, especially you fellows," she said, nodding toward the four brothers. "I'd like for it to be safe for you to go to town if you wanted to without people acting nasty toward you, or worse."

Elijah nodded. "Yeah, Miss Milly, it's like we're still not free, no matter what Mr. Lincoln said, God rest his soul."

Nick could only agree. He wanted peace, not only for the sake of those living on the ranch and in the town, but so he could court Milly and move toward marriage.

"Let's all ponder the problem this afternoon, then put our heads together after supper and see if we can come up with some solutions."

Take that, and that, and that, Milly thought, slicing through the chalk line she'd traced on the length of cloth.

"Easy, there," murmured a familiar English voice from the doorway of her sewing room. "Who are you slicing up?"

Milly whirled around and straightened, seeing Nick leaning against the doorway with negligent grace, holding a glass of cold lemonade in each hand.

She felt herself flushing in embarrassment that he had so accurately guessed her thoughts. "Bill Waters, Blakely Harvey and the Comanches, alternately," she confessed. "Not very Christian of me, is it?"

"It's very *human* to be angry at those who are trying to hurt you," he said, handing her a glass. "Especially those who are supposedly civilized and should know better. Anyway, I was thirsty and thought you might be, too."

"Thank you," Milly said, raising her glass in salute before drinking down a cool, refreshing sip. "Did you come to discuss strategy?" How handsome he was, smiling at her from the doorway, his teeth flashing white in his suntanned face, his eyes sparkling with a compelling blue warmth. Did he have any idea how he affected her?

"No," he said. "Strategy can keep 'til after supper, as we said. I came for this." In three short strides he closed the distance between them and drew her near. And then he was kissing her, with a sweetness combined with that same fierce intensity that she had been using to slice through the cloth only a minute ago. He kissed her as if Sarah wasn't just down the hall in the kitchen, white to her elbows with flour. His kiss was warm and tender and full of promise, and for a long moment she wanted him never to stop. But at last he did, and let go of her, but he gazed down at her as if she was the most beautiful woman in the world.

"W-why did you do that, just now?" was all she could think to say, and then wished she hadn't opened her mouth and said something so idiotic. Perhaps if she'd had the sense to remain silent and had gone into his arms again instead, he would have given her more of those wonderful kisses.

"Because, my dear Milly, because we both needed it," he said in that completely English way of his. "Because we've been so busy, not only with the tasks of everyday living, but with big problems. A man who's in love with his lady would naturally want to kiss her, but each time, a problem reared its ugly head."

"You are?"

His brow crinkled in puzzlement—or maybe he was just teasing her, to get her to say it. "I am what?"

"A man in love with his lady? With me?"

He smiled that slow, dazzling smile that set her heart to pounding. "I am, indeed, Milly Matthews. I'm in love with a lady who uses her imagination to solve a problem—a group of unmarried ladies who have no men to marry, I mean—a lady who stands her ground, who doesn't resort to the vapors when faced with danger. Yet she feels guilty for pretending a piece of cloth is her worst enemy as she slices through it. I just thought that lovely woman should know how I feel, and I decided to come take the time to tell her so."

"Ohh…" she said, completely unable to say more. "Oh, Nick. I love you, too. I—I just feel guilty that I've involved you in something much more than what you bargained for. You didn't ask to be confronted with murderous savages—red or white."

"No," he admitted. "I came to Simpson Creek on a lark. But having found you, Milly, I'm not about to let you go, or let problems, big or small, frighten me away. We'll solve the problems, Milly, I know we will, with God's help. And then I want to marry you and raise children just as spirited as their mother."

He spoke with such sincerity that she knew he meant it, and would see his hope become reality.

"And with the quiet strength of their father," she said. "Let's kiss on it, shall we?"

Chapter Twenty-Four

"The way I see it, Waters and the rest of his associates are counting on that trapped feeling Milly mentioned at dinner," Nick said to the solemn group gathered around the table after supper. "They're treating you like a hawk does a hare, swooping over it often enough that it doesn't feel safe in its refuge or out of it, so at last it becomes too anxious to stay. It flees, which leaves it vulnerable to the hawk. In this case there is one hawk using another to help it—between the Comanches and the Circle, we don't feel completely safe on the ranch or off of it, am I right?"

Slowly, everyone nodded.

"There are people who could be allies in town, but the hawks have isolated you from them, so you feel reluctant to go to them for help for fear they'll refuse, and they feel some distrust of you, too. If we can break that isolation somehow, if we could prove we are more valuable to the town than any of these men in the Circle, we would have allies who would come to our aid, and the Circle wouldn't feel free to attack. And the town could become safer from the Comanches. But it will mean postponing something we've started here at the ranch, at least for now."

"What?" Milly asked for all of them.

He explained.

Milly sighed after he finished. "I suppose you're right," she said. "But how are we to get them to agree to this?"

"Here's how I propose to do it," Nick began. "First, we have to think of a way to speak to as many people as we can at one time. When is almost everyone gathered together all at once?"

"At church," Milly and Sarah said in unison.

Nick smiled as if he were a teacher and they were clever pupils. "Do you think Reverend Chadwick would support our plan?"

"Sure, he'd back our plan, all right," Josh agreed. "He don't like folks treatin' other folks badly, no matter what the reason is."

"The success of the plan," Nick went on, "depends on us getting to Reverend Chadwick and soliciting his support secretly, so that the Circle is taken by surprise. Do you think he would let us use the church to hold our meeting directly after Sunday's service?"

"Yes, I think he would," Milly said. "But how do you propose we ask him, without tipping our hand, so to speak?"

"I'd suggest sending Bobby to town in the morning, ostensibly to buy some item at the mercantile you might need, but in reality his main purpose will be to deliver a letter to Reverend Chadwick, outlining our reasons for having this meeting right after church, and not announcing 'til the end. We'll ask him to give Bobby an answer either immediately, or if he wants to pray and think about it, we could send Bobby back next morning. No one's likely to bother Bobby riding to and fro."

The youth grinned from ear to ear at being selected for such an important mission.

"It could work," Milly murmured, her elbow propped on the table, her fingers rubbing her chin.

"If we must, we can mention meeting that cavalry detachment on the road, and what the major said about the Comanche raids likely increasing before winter. That tacitly reminds the townspeople you have the option of involving the cavalry to help against the Circle, if they won't help, without actually saying so. But I think we should avoid that if we can."

"And if they will help, you think that will break the power of the Circle?" Sarah asked.

"Yes, especially if the Brown brothers would be willing to assist," he said, turning to them. "And may I say, I for one wouldn't blame you if you chose not to participate," Nick said, his gaze directed at Elijah, Isaiah, Caleb and Micah.

When he had finished explaining this part of the plan, the brothers each looked at one another. Then, slowly, they nodded.

"It'll make the Circle's fool notions about them look downright silly," Josh said.

"Exactly," Nick agreed. "Especially if the men of the Circle are taken by surprise and react without time to think."

Josh cackled with glee. "You mean, if they shoot off their mouths? Bill Waters is good at that."

Nick nodded, smiling at the older man's enthusiasm. "It will show the town who's for the town's good and who's out only for their own good."

"I'll write the letter," Milly said, rising and going to the parlor, where she found a pen, ink and paper in their father's old desk.

Reverend Chadwick, however, didn't send an answer back with Bobby. He came himself, driving his buggy into the yard at noon with Bobby leading the way on his horse.

"Reverend, you're just in time for dinner," Sarah called, wiping her hands on her apron while Milly was still staring from the doorway.

"Good! I was hoping a hungry man could find a bite to eat after that hot, dusty ride. You got some sweet tea, too?" Reverend Chadwick asked as he climbed down from the buggy.

"Of course."

"Sarah, Milly, I had no idea you were faced with such dilemmas," he said, striding toward the porch, raising a hand in greeting to Nick and Josh, who'd heard his arrival and come out of the barn and bunkhouse. "Oh, I heard bits and pieces of that ugly nonsense Bill Waters and Dayton and their friends have been spouting, of course—people don't always lower their voices quickly enough when I come in the room," he added with a wink. "But I hadn't realized things had come to such a pass that your men were being shot at. It's a terrible business, terrible," he added, as Milly ushered him to a seat at the table, and Sarah handed him a glass of cold tea. "I suppose some of the good people of Simpson

Creek have allowed themselves to become persuaded of the silly fables men like Waters tell about folks like your four new cowboys," he said, speaking frankly since the Brown brothers were just now riding in from the north pasture and couldn't hear him. "If we don't put a stop to it, the town will only be further and further divided, and then how could we fight off the Comanches? Besides, I don't want men like Waters gaining the whip hand over this town. Mayor Gilmore's getting along in years, and when he steps down, I don't want Bill Waters taking his place if I can help it."

Five days later, Reverend Chadwick lowered the hands he had raised in benediction. "And now, before we go our separate ways," he announced, "I have been asked to call a meeting of the townspeople."

As a hum of speculative conversation rose in the pews around them, Milly's gaze locked with Nick's. Taking his hand, she gave it a little surreptitious squeeze and felt his reassuring squeeze in return. The moment was at hand.

"Who asked for this meeting? I don't know anything about a meeting," Prissy's father called toward the pulpit, confusion creasing his features and causing the ends of his bushy mustache to twitch.

"I haven't heard anything about it either," Bill Waters declared from the back, rising.

"The Matthews sisters and Nick Brookfield have requested it, and having heard what they wish to discuss with all of you, I support it," Reverend Chadwick said with quiet dignity. "I suggest we pray once more and ask the Lord to bless this meeting and that His will be done," he added, and bowed his head, praying aloud for exactly that.

Bill Waters hadn't sat back down while the reverend was praying, and now Dayton stood, too. When Milly had arrived at church she'd been dismayed to see that Blakely Harvey was once more sitting by Ada; now he looked as if he was about to get to his feet, too—as were several other men sitting in the back rows.

"I'm not interested in hearing anything those three would have to say," Waters shouted.

"Ain't no law can make us stay, is there?" Dayton demanded.

Reverend Chadwick unclasped his hands, palm upward. "Of course not," he said in his mild, resonant voice, "but I think you'll find the subject matter particularly of interest to you. So I'd encourage you to remain, gentlemen."

Muttering and eyeing one another, Waters and Dayton and the rest sat back down.

"The Matthews sisters have chosen Mr. Brookfield as their spokesman," Chadwick went on. "Nick, would you come to the front, please?"

"A blasted foreigner's going to speechify at us?" one of Waters's cronies protested, and received an indignant look from Harvey.

Milly watched proudly as head high, his posture ramrod-straight, Nick strode toward the pulpit. He was so brave—he had not taken the easy way out, either with her or with the town, and now her heart swelled with even more love for him.

Nick cleared his throat. His gaze touched hers briefly, then he looked out over the congregation. "It's been my pleasure to have gotten to know many of you since I came to Simpson Creek a short few weeks ago, and I thank you for your welcome," Nick said. "Most of you will remember that the day I arrived was quite a dramatic one, a day in which the Misses Matthews's foreman nearly lost his life in a Comanche raid. I'm told some of you have suffered similar attacks in the past, and even lost family members. We were blessed that no one was killed this time." He paused and let his gaze roam the pews. "So I know you will understand that the choice I'm about to put in front of you could be a matter of life and death."

He had their attention now, even that of Waters's bunch, who had relaxed since the Englishman didn't seem about to accuse them of anything.

"At the barn raising, some of us men talked about building a fort atop the hill overlooking the ranch. As a sentinel post, it's a perfect place to build it, but my thoughts have changed on it somewhat."

"What are you saying?"

"Yeah, spit it out, Englishman!"

"I think that should be the second fort, the lookout fort. The first fort should be erected right here in Simpson Creek."

Now a hum of conversation rose again, and after a moment, Reverend Chadwick raised his hands for quiet.

"Comanche raids usually come without much warning, correct? And I'm told that the raids are expected to grow more frequent in the fall as the Indians steal what they need before they travel to their winter quarters."

How clever of Nick to cite the informed opinion of the cavalry major without identifying him, Milly thought, because many of the townspeople were predisposed to discount any opinion coming from a bluecoat.

"Many of you, I think, have wondered how it would be possible for you to reach the safety of the fort atop the hill if a band of braves suddenly appeared—and you're quite right—you might not have time. However, you *could* make it to a fort right here in Simpson Creek. Therefore, I am proposing we build a fort in town, and because we believe so deeply in this project, the men of the Matthews ranch will start work as soon as the site is chosen, and we'll work right alongside everyone else—or alone. We'll be there either way, because we value the town of Simpson Creek and want safety for its citizens." He paused to let his words sink in, and during this time Milly looked around her. Faces were thoughtful, heads were nodding. She could hear them reminding each other how some communities had "forted up" in abandoned garrisons during the war when the Comanches had roamed the state almost unopposed.

Nick has them, she thought.

"I did say 'the men of the Matthews ranch,' did you notice? I meant *all* of us—Josh, Bobby, me—and our four new hands, Elijah, Isaiah, Micah and Caleb Brown."

Silence cloaked the room as everyone looked at everyone else—and then all gazes were trained on Waters, Dayton and the others of the Circle to see what their reaction would be.

They were silent, impassive, their arms crossed, as if by remaining immobile they could stop what was coming.

"I think it's only fair when a person is being talked

about that he be present, don't you?" Nick went on. "Gentlemen, will you come in?"

The door that led from the pastor's study to the sanctuary opened, and out walked Elijah, Isaiah, Caleb and Micah Brown, eyes wary but heads held high. They had gone in there through the outside entrance during the service, Milly knew, and had been waiting there ever since.

Several people gasped aloud.

"How dare you?" shouted Waters, eyes bulging, his face red with fury. "We don't let those people in our *church!*"

Reverend Chadwick, who had been standing to the side of the front pew, raised an arm now. "These men are here with my permission, and I warn you, I'll take any insults or harm offered them as a personal affront. This is a church, and a church is sacred ground."

Glaring, with his hands on his hips, Walters drawled, "I got a question for Miss Milly."

Milly stood, wondering what he had in mind, and faced the older man. "I'm listening, Mr. Waters."

"You 'n' Miss Sarah, you pay them boys up there?" He pointed a stubby, age-spotted finger at them. "Real money, that is?"

Milly felt hot anger knot her stomach. She knew what Waters was about now.

"No. At the present time, we can't afford to." *Like many of you, the war left us cash-poor,* she wanted to say, but Waters had made it personal, and she would not take refuge in an easy excuse, however reasonable it was. "They get room and board. But as the ranch begins to prosper again, we plan to—"

"My cowhands make twenty dollars a month," Waters shot back. "And now you're proposing to have them labor to build the town a fort—hard work for men just getting room an' board, I'd say. How's that different from them bein' slaves? My pa had a few slaves once. That's all we 'paid' them, too—room an' board."

Milly felt her face flush. "I don't pay Nick anything either," she argued. "Or—"

Waters interrupted with a suggestive snicker.

Milly's hands clenched at her side, but she knew she had to retain her dignity to keep the high ground. "And Josh or Bobby haven't been paid either, ever since the war began. You wouldn't call them slaves, would you?"

"Reverend, may I say something?"

It was Elijah who had spoken. Everyone stared. Waters ground his teeth as if enraged by Elijah's effrontery.

"The difference between us and slaves is we *want* to be workin' for Miss Milly and Miss Sarah," Elijah said. "And we're *willin'* to help y'all folks with buildin' that fort—if you're willin' to have us help."

Elijah stepped back into line with his brothers, and Nick once again took hold of the pulpit and began to speak. "But the problem with having these four strong young men building a fort for everyone's safety is that because of the bigotry and prejudice of a few, these young men who are willing to work hard to make Simpson Creek a safer place to live might not be safe themselves—on the road to and from town, or while they're here building. And everyone here knows I'm speaking of the Circle."

Chapter Twenty-Five

Bill Waters jumped to his feet, shaking his fist. "You've got a lot of gall, Englishman, coming here and accusing us of anything!"

"I'm not accusing you of just 'anything,' Mr. Waters. I'm accusing you and your associates in the Circle of hiding under white hoods and attempting to terrorize these men who only want to live and work like the rest of us. You've set fires and left hangman's nooses where these men would find them. When that didn't work, you attempted murder—"

Waters was the picture of outraged innocence. "Attempted murder? I don't know what you're talking about."

Milly left her pew and dashed up to the pulpit before she even realized she was moving. "You know exactly, Bill Walters, but I'll tell those who don't—I'm speaking of the bullet that was fired at Caleb Brown when he was in the southeastern part of our land last Tuesday. Fortunately, your assassin failed."

The hum in the room became an excited buzz.

"You're a liar, Milly Matthews. Becoming an old maid has addled your brain," snapped Waters.

"Careful," warned Nick, his soft voice a lash. "You're speaking to a lady."

Waters smirked and crossed his arms over his barrel chest. "All right, I'll put it more politely. Miss Matthews, you've been lied to by that boy and you've imagined all the rest. Perhaps you've been overly influenced by that foreigner next to you."

"Brookfield, you don't know what it's like, dealin' with people like them," Dayton snarled, pointing at the brothers, his face flushed. "You lily-white English only know folks as white as you. You never had a passel a' helpless fools let loose on you after a war."

Nick's blue eyes blazed in his sun-bronzed face. "It's true, we freed our slaves some time ago, and without a war." He stood his ground at the pulpit while the hum of conversation rose to a wasplike buzz, then died down as the congregation waited to hear what else would be said. "And as for lily-white…can you mean *me?*" he asked, and rolled up his sleeves, revealing forearms as tanned as any Texas rancher's there.

Several ladies and men chuckled. His humor had brought them back to him, Milly thought.

"Yes, I'm English, and I wasn't here during your Civil War. But the British Empire extends all over the world, and in India, I assure you, white Englishmen were distinctly in the minority—a few thousand in a vast country of brown-skinned people. Yet for the most part, we respected them and worked alongside them, helping bring modern civilization into that country."

Milly, who'd been sitting sidewise so she could see

both Nick and the reactions of the Circle, saw Blakely Harvey step into the aisle now.

"Oh, yes, Nicholas Brookfield *respected* the Indians—if *respect* is what you'd like to call his ah…*liaison* with the rajah's lovely daughter, the Princess Ambika," he said, his voice silky. "But the army called it inappropriate and 'conduct unbecoming an officer' and he was drummed out of the regiment in utter disgrace. That's how he came to be in Texas, good people. I daresay he wasn't welcome back home in England. And you'd consider letting him advise you what you should do?"

Milly saw Nick's face drain of color and his gaze fly to her. He flinched as if the words had been a physical blow.

So he hadn't trusted her enough to tell her the truth about Ambika, the woman whose name he had called in his delirium. *"We were acquainted, yes… I was taken with her for a time…"*

Yet Harvey was saying his relationship with the Indian woman had been much more. A shameful amount more. If Nick lied to her about this, what else had he lied about?

Could she love him now?

Love rejoices in the truth. Love bears all things, believes all things, hopes all things, endures all things.

Milly looked Nick in the eye and mouthed the words, *I love you.*

There would be time to hear his side of things, time to hear the complete story, but right now, the important thing was to stand with this man who loved her. And she believed in his love, whatever he had done.

She saw Nick straighten. "There is more to this story

than what Mr. Harvey insinuates, of course. But the person who has a right to hear it first is the woman I love, Miss Millicent Matthews, and I pledge here and now that she will."

Silence gripped the church.

Reverend Chadwick stepped forward and let his gaze roam about the church. "Let he who is without sin among you cast the first stone."

Milly saw men, and even some women, drop their gazes and stare down at their feet.

Nick cleared his throat. "Mr. Harvey called you 'good people,' and he's right about that, at least. You are good people. And we're asking, good people, for you to let Elijah, Isaiah, Caleb and Micah Brown work alongside us *in safety* to build that fort for the common good of us all, earning their right to be as respected as any of you. Which means telling the men of the Circle that you won't tolerate, silently or openly, their hatred and violence."

There was utter silence as Nick stood there with Milly next to him, as each person in the church eyed his neighbor, then Waters and Dayton and the other men who stood with them at the back of the church, then looked back at Nick and Milly—and at Reverend Chadwick as he came back to the pulpit to join them.

"Well, what do you say?" the pastor asked. "Are you the 'good people' that Nick, here, called you?"

Mr. Patterson stood up. "I don't know about the rest of you folks, but I went to war, and I've had enough of killin' except to defend myself and my family. I vote yes—let's build the fort, and the more folk that want to pitch in—" he gestured at the four brothers up front "—the quicker we'll have us a fort."

Mr. Wallace stood up now. "Haven't we lost enough in this war? I lost my son. Waters, you lost yours, too. Why, Miss Milly had to organize a group of ladies just to bring more young men to this town! Ain't you hated enough for a lifetime without hatin' anybody else? I vote yes, too."

"Anyone wants to make life safer from them Comanches, I'm all for that," the town's milliner announced.

One by one, townspeople stood and aligned themselves with Nick and Milly.

Then Mrs. Detwiler rose ponderously to her feet, and Milly had to stifle a groan. Would the old woman say something awful that turned the town against Nick again? *Please, God...*

But when Mrs. Detwiler began to speak, Milly thought she could indeed believe in miracles.

"Bill Waters, you gonna hold on to your stiff-necked ways 'til the Comanches stampede through here again?" the old woman demanded. "Not me!"

That seemed to be the final straw for Waters, who raised his arm and made a disgusted, dismissive gesture with his hand. He turned on his heels and walked out and the others of the Circle stomped out after him. Harvey went as well, leaving Ada looking stricken.

Mrs. Detwiler gave a sniff of satisfaction, while Milly tried to make up her mind whether to laugh or cry happy tears.

Then the old woman pointed at Sheriff Poteet, who'd been sitting midway back, his arms stretched out over the back of the pew. "Sheriff, did you know about any a' these goings-on?" she demanded.

He dropped his arms and sat up straight. "Ma'am?"

"You heard me, young man."

Milly had to stifle a smile, for Poteet was only perhaps a decade younger than Mrs. Detwiler.

"Well..." He drew out the syllable as far as it could go. "Miss Milly did come to me a few days ago about that fire some yahoos lit around her pecan tree...and she did say they was wearin' hoods over their heads, but shucks, ma'am, that didn't give me no proof who they were..."

"And you didn't even investigate, did you? Same as when someone stole some a' my prize roses, or the pie I had cooling on my windowsill. You just couldn't be bothered. From now on you better shape up, Sheriff Poteet, 'cause this town pays your salary. Otherwise we're liable to vote that foreigner in as our new sheriff—he's shown a lot more gumption than you."

"That won't be necessary, Mrs. Detwiler," the sheriff said, meek as a lamb.

The old woman harrumphed at that, as if not fully convinced. "And furthermore, I'm one to put my money where my mouth is. You know that big old field in the back of my house? Mr. Detwiler bought us a big piece of land behind our house, planning to build homes for our children one day. But he was always too busy being the parson, and the Lord took him home before he ever got the chance. Bein' as it's near the center of town, I'm thinking that lot would be a good place to build a fort—if y'all agree."

Reverend Chadwick started to clap, and in seconds, everyone was clapping and cheering their approval.

When the applause finally died down, Mrs. Detwiler's face was pink with pleasure. Milly couldn't recall seeing her smile.

Nick bowed from the pulpit. "Bravo, Mrs. Detwiler. Your generosity will inspire all of us. I propose we name it Fort Detwiler."

Again, there was thunderous applause.

Mrs. Detwiler beamed. "Generous? Not me—I just want to be closest to the fort, that's all. I'm an old woman, and I can't run so fast."

Everyone laughed.

"It's not necessary to name it after me, young man, but thank you for the thought. And now I reckon we'd all better get home for our dinners and rest up, 'cos bright and early Monday morning, I expect to see all you menfolk hard at work with these young men—" she pointed at the Brown brothers "—building that fort."

After the meeting was brought to a close with another prayer from Reverend Chadwick, Milly, her heart in her throat, approached Mrs. Detwiler to thank her for what she'd done. To her astonishment, the old woman hugged her, and begged Milly's forgiveness for the way she'd treated her ever since Milly had thought up her scheme to bring bachelors to town for the unmarried girls.

"I was just pure jealous at your daring, don't you see, Milly? I never had such spunk in my whole life, and I was coveting yours. Now I've got to admit I'm proud to know you. And don't worry, you and your young man will work out any problems about the past. None of us come to our spouses straight from heaven, you know. None of us is perfect," she said.

"Thank you," Milly said, and burst into the tears she'd been trying so hard to hold back. Nick handed her his handkerchief.

Then Sarah came forward and invited Mrs. Detwiler to come home with them for supper.

"Thank you," she said, "but two of my sons are coming in from Deer Creek this afternoon. In fact, they're probably already at the house wonderin' why I'm not home from church yet. But I'll take a rain check, sweet girl."

Chapter Twenty-Six

No one spoke of Blakely Harvey's embarrassing revelation on the way back to the ranch. Everyone but Milly and Nick seemed eager to fill the silence. The Brown brothers voiced relief at the town's willingness to work with them and reject the Circle. Sarah chattered about Mrs. Detwiler's amazing turnaround as if oblivious to Milly's distracted quiet.

Milly had told him she loved him while he stood alone in front of the church, giving him a flash of hope that her love for him had not died in the instant that Harvey had coldly attempted to destroy his reputation. Perhaps in that moment her generous heart had overridden her self-respect and motivated her to support him in case of public censure. But now that she had time to think, she might not be so quick to ally herself with a man who was, despite his high moral pronouncements, nothing but a liar after all.

"I'll unhitch the horses," Nick said aloud as they pulled up in front of the barn. He was not surprised when Milly lingered with him rather than following

Sarah into the kitchen to help put dinner on the table as she usually did. The other men went into the bunkhouse.

Once the wagon horses were in the corral, by tacit agreement she followed him into the cool dimness of the barn. He turned to face her with the same feeling a man must have when turning to face a firing squad.

"Do you…do you hate me, Milly? Do you want me to leave?" *Or merely abandon any pretense that I am worthy of you?*

She blinked at him. "*Hate* you? No, of course I don't hate you. How could I hate you? Didn't you see me mouth the words 'I love you'?"

He held up his hands, palms upward. "Yes, of course I did, and I thought perhaps it was a noble gesture, not abandoning me publicly in front of the wolves—the Circle, that is—and the townsfolk. I thought once we were alone, you might tell me that you've reconsidered how you feel, now that you know what I've done—"

She flew at him now until she was practically toe-to-toe with him, her face upturned, her eyes blazing. "You British idiot! You thought I was being *noble?* Is that what a proper English lady would do? Well, Texas women are different! We don't give up so easily on someone we love. I came in here to hear the truth from you, not some silly self-sacrificing *nonsense!*"

She was magnificent when she was angry, but he didn't want to chance making her angrier still by telling her so.

"I love you, Nicholas Brookfield, and that's not going to change," she went on. "But now I believe you have something to tell me—or so you promised back there in church."

He nodded and gestured toward a pair of old chairs. "Why don't we sit down?"

He waited while she settled herself, took a deep breath, then said, "Yes, it's true that I had feelings that were inappropriate for the maharajah's daughter Ambika. It will not excuse me to say that she collected the hearts of naive British officers like some women collect jewelry, or that she had claimed Blakely Harvey's affections before she turned her efforts toward me. Nor is my shame any the less though I can say we never…that is to say, didn't actually…" He broke off, his face flushing. "Oh, Milly, none of this is proper to say to you…"

She leaned forward, her eyes full of compassion. "I believe I understand."

"We were alone together in her bedroom when we were interrupted by the intrusion of a servant girl who came in to clean the room, not knowing I was there with the princess. Princess Ambika flew into a rage, striking the poor terrified girl again and again."

His eyes closed as he relived the incident in his mind, remembering how the silky, enthralling woman had been transformed in an instant into a screaming, brutal virago. "She would have killed the poor girl then and there had I not intervened, restraining her and telling her I could not allow anyone, even a princess, to beat a helpless servant. Then she turned on me, screaming and telling me to be gone and take the worthless girl with me. I left the palace, vowing never to return except in the course of duty, and never alone. I saw that the servant girl was given employment in the army compound in the household of a colonel's wife. But the colonel's wife reported she soon disappeared. I assumed the girl had returned to her village, but then she was found murdered. A knife left by the body bore the royal insignia."

He heard Milly gasp, and felt her hand on his shoulder, felt its warmth even through his shirt. He took it for a moment, squeezed it to show he was grateful for her touch, then rose to his feet, unable to sit still any longer.

"I thought living with my guilt was awful enough, but Ambika was not finished with her revenge. No one shames a maharajah's daughter, it seems, and escapes unscathed—though of course my guilt in knowing I'd had a part in the servant girl's death hardly qualifies as unscathed."

Milly had risen behind him. "Ambika is the one who got you thrown out of the regiment," she guessed.

"Yes, her father called my commanding officer to the palace and berated him for allowing an officer to attempt to despoil his daughter—as if that were possible!" He gave a bitter laugh. "The maharajah was demanding my head—quite literally."

Again, he heard her gasp. "Hadn't you told him the truth?"

"Of course, but try to see it as he must have—after all, the maharajah could command thousands to attack, and the army had been through the massacre at Calcutta some years before. What was one stupid fool of a captain more or less?"

"But in the end, that's not what happened."

"No. Obviously, I stand before you with my head very much attached to my shoulders. In the end, the general made a very brave decision not to let a maharajah decide the fate of one of Her Majesty's soldiers, and settled for drumming me out of the regiment in disgrace. I was forbidden to tell the truth to anyone, for my own safety and the preservation of relations between the British government and the maharajah. But Blakely Harvey, back in Ambika's good graces, spread the story of my foolishness among my fellow officers. For the most part, they thought me an idiot allowing the fate of a serving girl to matter. That's when the nickname 'Mad Nick' took on a life of its own. Harvey's gossip wasn't traced back to him, though. He paid no price for it."

"No wonder you despise him," she breathed.

"God forgive me, yes. And to have him show up here…" He shrugged. "Just to be on the safe side, for they didn't trust the maharajah not to have me permanently silenced, the general hustled me out of Bombay in the dead of night and put me on a ship."

He fell silent, drained by the confession.

"Is that it? Is there anything else I need to know?" Milly asked.

"What more could there be?" he asked, genuinely confused.

"I just want there to be complete honesty between us," she said simply. "The subject of your family came up once, and you looked distinctly uncomfortable, Nick. I… I didn't want to pry, but I think it's better I know everything that could affect us in the future."

"Oh. Well, I suppose it does explain why I was such a fool with the maharajah's daughter," he said, realizing it just that moment. "I suppose I never thought about it…. My mother was a lovely woman who decided after my sister, her fourth child, was born that she had been dutiful to the viscount, my father, long enough. She threw over the traces, as it were, and became something of a scandal. She finally left my father. He divorced her, and I never saw her again before she died."

"How old were you when she left?" she asked quietly.

"Fourteen. Father was never quite the same after that. He'd always been a bit distant, the proper Victorian noble who believed children should be seen and not heard, but after that, he may as well have lived on the moon."

He didn't realize he was shaking with suppressed tears until she circled around him and took him into her arms.

"I love you," she said, after a while. "Broken places and all. We may argue from time to time, but I will never, never cause you not to trust me or doubt my love."

He stared at her. "You're more than I could ever deserve," he said at last.

"None of that," Milly insisted, putting a finger to his lips. "You were wonderful today," Milly told him. "And so brave—like a general leading his troops into battle."

"I had you fooled, then," he said wryly. "I was shaking in my boots—for me and the Browns," he told her. "I wasn't sure if the Circle fellows would pull out guns or if the townspeople would tar and feather me. But they came through for us, didn't they?"

"Especially Mrs. Detwiler!" she said, shaking her head in wonderment. She still couldn't believe it. The old woman who'd reminded her of a dragon was now a friend.

"Simpson Creek's going to be a different place, thanks to you," she murmured. "I feel so much safer."

He sighed. "My dear Milly, you give me too much credit. The Comanches are still out there, and they could still attack here at the ranch. I promise you, though, we'll have a fort on top of the hill next year, but until then…"

She loved hearing him speak of next year, as if he assumed he'd be there with her for all the years to come. They'd be married by then, she thought. They hadn't spoken of a date yet, but she knew they would.

"I've told you before the Comanches have always been a possible threat," she said calmly. "Until you build that fort, we'll do what we always do—pray for the Lord's protection."

"Your faith is strengthening mine, Milly Matthews," he said, gazing into her eyes. "It's just one more reason I love you."

The compliment and his declaration swelled her heart with joy. "And your goodness is making me a better person, Nicholas Brookfield. I would not have been brave enough to hire the Browns on my own, or to take on the whole town as you did today. So we will help each other grow in faith, I think. What's that verse in the Proverbs—'Iron sharpens iron'? And then it goes on to speak of one friend sharpening another?"

He smiled. "We were friends first, Milly, and I always hoped the woman I married would be my best friend, too. I can hardly believe I'm daring to ask this after what happened today, but will you marry me?"

"Yes. Oh yes, I will marry you!"

Cupping her chin, he kissed her, tenderly and thoroughly.

"When?" she asked, as he lifted his lips from hers.

He was thoughtful. "As soon as the fort is finished? Will that give you enough time?"

Milly nodded, already thinking of the wedding dress she would sew.

"I should write and invite my brothers and sister to come. Richard, the vicar—he'll adore you. He'll tell you you're much too good for me," he said, a fond smile curving his lips. "I imagine he never expected me to marry a woman who lived her faith like you do."

"Perhaps he could take part in the wedding ceremony. I imagine Reverend Chadwick wouldn't mind."

Chapter Twenty-Seven

The rest of August and September flew by. Every morning, as soon as the chores were done, the men would ride into town to work on the fort. They always left two of the men home with Milly and Sarah for their protection.

Milly worked at dressmaking mornings and afternoons, alternately her wedding gown and the dresses she was making for the mercantile. Each dress sold almost as soon as she brought it in, Mr. Patterson informed her. Milly was pleased to see her creations on the ladies of the town, and there were usually garments to be altered or mended waiting for her at the store, too.

While Milly sewed, her sister baked, both for the hotel and the mercantile. Both were pleased to watch the amount of money growing in their bank account.

At midday, Milly and Sarah interrupted their endeavors to drive the wagon into town, accompanied by one of the men, while the other kept watch over the ranch. While Sarah delivered pies and cakes to the hotel restaurant, Milly took her dresses to the mercantile, along with more of Sarah's baking. Then they took Nick and the rest of their men their noon meal, and sat down with them to eat.

The other ladies of the town were doing likewise for their men. Members of the Spinsters' Club stopped by to chat with Milly and Sarah about the wedding preparations and the upcoming Founders' Day celebrations. Caroline and Emily flirted with their beaus, who were working right alongside the rest of the town to build the fort. Sarah and the other Spinsters compared their letters and speculated about the men who had agreed to come meet the ladies on Founders' Day.

Dr. Nolan Walker, the man from Brazos County with whom Sarah had been corresponding, had written her three times. His letters were short, and he mostly responded to what Sarah had written about her doings, but he didn't offer many details about himself. The fact didn't seem to bother Sarah much—"Men just don't write long detailed letters," she told Milly. He claimed to be looking forward to meeting Sarah, and Sarah was satisfied with that, reminding Milly that he might decide he liked one of the other Spinsters better, anyway.

Her sister's calmness about the matter was typical of Sarah, Milly knew, but she thought it was a good thing Nick had just traveled to Simpson Creek and not corresponded with her first. She knew she would have plagued him with questions. Typical of all those in love who want others to feel that same joyous emotion, Milly hoped that the man from Brazos County would be the right man for Sarah.

Milly wasn't surprised that Bill Waters never came to the work site. Dayton and a few of the others participated from time to time, but when they did, they ignored the Brown brothers. There was no changing some people's hearts, Milly mused, but if they helped build the fort and caused no trouble, that was all that mattered.

It did her heart good to see how the rest of the town had come to accept Elijah, Isaiah, Caleb and Micah, greeting them as they rode into town and at the site. Mrs. Detwiler had made them her own personal concern, plying them with extra sandwiches and cookies. As a result, the Brown brothers had lost much of the wary tenseness that had marked their expressions and had begun to smile, laugh and exchange pleasantries with the townsfolk. They even seemed to walk taller.

Ada came to the work site but rarely, and was either accompanied by Harvey, who apparently considered himself above manual labor, or spoke of meeting him soon for some outing. There was a strained quality to her. Milly wondered if she was still unsure of the Englishman's affection.

A detachment of the Fourth Cavalry, led by the same Major McConley whom Nick and Milly had encountered before, paid a visit when the fort was halfway done. The arrival of blue-coated soldiers alarmed some in Simpson Creek, but after talking to the mayor, Nick and several others at the building site, McConley reassured them that the Federals had no argument with the citizenry being ready to defend themselves against Indian attacks. He even suggested features to include in the fort.

The fort rose in height, foot by foot, behind Mrs. Detwiler's house, as summer faded into fall. It was clear it would not be completely finished by Founders' Day, though it was nearly so. The stone walls stood two stories high, interspersed with narrow windows to fire through at the second-story level. These were reached by a stairway. There was no complete ceiling between the first floor and second floor, only narrow walkways. The heavy, metal-reinforced double doors had just been fitted into place. It could be bolted from the inside. There was a well in the center of the fort and a stone fireplace against the back wall. Beans and rice had been stockpiled against an interior wall in case of a prolonged siege.

By the week of Founders' Day, only the roof, which was to be tin so that flaming arrows could not set it afire, was not in place. The interior was big enough that everyone in town would fit inside, and all those who could reach the fort in time from the nearby ranches.

Milly was thankful as the building's completion drew near, but prayed the fort would never need to be used.

Founders' Day dawned bright and sunny. The intense heat of summer had metamorphosed into cooler nights and pleasantly warm days.

"I'm sure glad the original settlers didn't found this town in the middle of the summer," Milly remarked as she settled herself on the driver's bench of the wagon next to Nick. Sarah was already sitting in the wagon bed along with Josh; Bobby and the Brown brothers had mounted their horses and would ride alongside as they drove into town for the festivities.

"There's a nice breeze," commented Sarah, lifting her face to it as the wagon left the yard. She looked lovely today in a dress of cream-colored crossbar lawn sprigged with orange and yellow flowers. It had a lace-insert bodice and a matching shawl for later if it grew cool. A very fitting dress for Sarah to wear to meet her prospective beau, Milly decided, for naturally she had made the dress. It would accent Sarah's lovely golden hair.

Even if her sister wouldn't admit it, Sarah was nervous, Milly thought, though only someone who knew her well would have guessed it by the way she kept playing with her topaz earbobs and pendant necklace.

Milly wore a new creation, too. Her two-piece dress featured a shaped peplum and alternating wide and narrow stripes of moss green sprigged with autumn leaves and solid burned orange. She couldn't wait to see everyone.

Turning onto the road, Nick snapped the reins to quicken the horses' pace, then, after he had transferred the reins to one hand, Milly saw him rub his forehead.

"What's the matter?" she asked. "Are you all right?"

He nodded. "Bit of a headache, that's all. Sarah made me some willow bark tea for it before breakfast, before you came into the kitchen."

"You didn't tell me," Milly said, feeling a frisson of worry skitter up her spine. She'd spent longer than usual over her toilette, wanting to look perfect today at the festivities, for they were going to announce their wedding date, the Saturday after Thanksgiving, and invite everyone to the ceremony. "Are you sure you'll be okay? It's not—"

"Not malaria," he finished for her. "No, don't worry, Milly darling. Most times a headache is just a headache, even for me. I have my quinine, just in case," he said, pulling out a small flask from his shirt pocket.

"Most men who carry one of those would have whiskey in it," she said with a chuckle.

They went to the fort first, for the festivities were

to begin with a dedication and blessing of the unfinished fort by Mayor Gilmore and Reverend Chadwick, respectively. A midday picnic on the church grounds would follow and then games for the children—a fishing contest on the banks of Simpson Creek, foot races and sack races. Supper was to be a barbecue sponsored by the hotel, and for those who still had stamina after all that, the day would end with a concert put on by the Fourth Cavalry Regimental Band—a neighborly gesture, Milly thought—and end with fireworks at dark.

Dr. Nolan Walker had written he would probably arrive in town by noon, so Sarah had arranged that he would meet her at the midday picnic. But Prissy Gilmore dashed up to them as the ceremony was beginning.

"He's here! They're all here, all three of the candidates! I just happened to be leaving our house when these three nice-looking strangers came riding by, and asked if I could direct them to the church, so of course I did, and then I found out who they were! And then we ran into Jane and Maude, so of course I introduced them and said I'd come find you!"

"Well, are you going to tell me what he's like?" Sarah demanded, grabbing Prissy's hand. "Is he good-looking? Does he seem nice?"

Prissy grinned. "Rather handsome in a craggy sort of way, I'd say, and yes, he seems nice…"

"But what? There's something you're not telling me, isn't there, Prissy Gilmore? What is it?"

Prissy looked mysterious, her gaze straying sideways. "Well…there *is* something surprising about him…"

"What's that?"

"I'm not going to tell you. You'll just have to come

meet him," she said, grinning like the cat that swallowed the canary.

As Milly watched, Sarah's face went pale, then flushed as she clutched Milly's hands in hers. She was shaking. "Oh, Milly, this is it! Wish me luck!"

"Oh, I do…" Milly began, but Prissy was already pulling Sarah away with her.

"Come on, Nick, I want to see this man," she said, urging him after them.

"Easy, there," he said, pulling back. "Why don't we give your sister some privacy? I'm sure she'll introduce us to her beau, if she approves of him. Let's stay right here as we planned, and listen to the mayor and the reverend's speeches, and by the time we get to the churchyard, Sarah will be ready to introduce us to him, I reckon," he said, winking as he gave a fair imitation of a Texas drawl on those last two words.

Milly was torn, but she knew Nick was right, so she settled down to watch the fort dedication.

Sarah was standing by herself, clearly waiting for them, when they arrived at the church grounds. Even from a distance she looked mad as a wet cat.

Milly hurried forward.

"I'm so angry I could spit, Milly!" Sarah cried. "Can you imagine? Nolan Walker's a *Yankee!* That's what Prissy was calling 'surprising'! Of all the nerve—"

"But… She said he was nice…" Milly began. "Didn't he seem like a nice man?"

"Milly! There's no way I could consider getting to know a…a blue belly! A man who could have been the one who shot my Jesse! He *lied* to me, Milly!"

"Did he…are you saying Dr. Walker claimed to have

fought for the South in his letters?" Milly asked, desperately trying to make sense of her sister's words. She'd never seen Sarah so furious.

"No! He mentioned being an army doctor, and tending the wounded, and that he'd even had to fight alongside the other men at times—he just didn't *bother* to tell me he'd worn blue, not gray—as if that wasn't important!"

"Sarah, dear, perhaps you should give him a chance..." Milly began uncertainly, taking hold of her sister's flailing hands. Sarah hadn't mentioned Jesse since that day in the church when Milly had first thought up the Spinsters' Club, so Milly had assumed Sarah had begun to accept her fiancé's loss, especially after she'd agreed to write to Dr. Walker.

"Not on your life! I'm not about to take up with any Yankee! Not after my Jesse died in the war and I'll never even know what happened to him! I couldn't bear to spend a moment in that man's company, from the moment he opened his mouth and started talking in that horrible Yankee accent! This is how he talks—'Hello, Miss Matthews, I'm glad to meet you,' she said, mimicking an accent that sounded flat and nasally to Milly.

Sarah burst into tears, and went into her sister's waiting embrace, sobbing. "I told Prissy she could have him, if her standards were so low, or he could just ride back out of here on that horse of his!"

Chapter Twenty-Eight

Milly looked from her sister's tear-stained face to Nick. After proffering a handkerchief, he hovered by the two of them as if not certain what to do. Milly didn't know either. Ought she to encourage Sarah again to give the man a chance, against her sister's strongly held convictions, or just let her be?

Sarah finally wiped her eyes and cheeks. "I—I'll be all right," she said. "Don't worry about me. I don't want to spoil the day for you. I said all along we might not suit one another." She shrugged. "If you don't mind, though, I'm going to sit with you two rather than the others."

Sarah made a vague gesture toward the group standing next to the church, which included the three candidates, Prissy, Maude and Jane. Since Maude and Jane were each standing close to one of the men, Milly assumed the man standing by himself must be the rejected Yankee. Milly couldn't see him well, but from where she was standing Dr. Nolan Walker appeared tall and reasonably well-favored, and had hair that might have been brown or auburn—she couldn't be sure from this distance. Prissy approached him and seemed content enough in his company. As Milly watched, he offered Prissy his arm and the group of six strolled over to a spot on the lawn where Maude spread out a large tablecloth. So Sarah's loss, or rather rejection, might well be Prissy's gain, Milly decided, but then she saw Walker aim a glance in Sarah's direction. Even from so far away, she thought she could read regret on his face.

Milly urged Nick and Sarah over to an area near the bluff overlooking the creek, deliberately picking a spot to have their dinner that was as far away from the three couples as possible. They were soon joined by Josh, Bobby and the Brown brothers, who'd been visiting with some cowboys from the ranch beyond Waters's property, and Milly had been pleased to see the ready acceptance they were given.

They made short work of the delicious dinner Sarah had packed—fried chicken, biscuits and homemade jelly, apple pie and cold tea.

"I'm full as a tick on an ol' dog's ear," Josh said, when nothing was left but chicken bones and crumbs. He patted his stomach as he stretched out backward on the blanket.

"Me, too. Miss Sarah, you sure are a good cook," Micah said, and the others joined in the praise.

Nick put down his chicken leg, hoping Milly hadn't noticed how little he'd eaten, or how many times he'd surreptitiously rubbed his thumping head. He didn't want to spoil this special day. Perhaps if he stole away for a few minutes he could drink his quinine without any of them becoming the wiser. He still wasn't sure it was a malaria attack—those had always been heralded by headaches, but as yet he hadn't had any of the premonitory chills.

But the eyes of the woman who loved him missed little. "What's the matter, Nick?" Milly whispered so that the others wouldn't hear.

"That headache's being a bit stubborn about going away," he told her. "Don't worry about it. I'm sure it will fade in time."

"Nick, are you sure this is not your malaria?"

"I don't think so," he tried to tell her, but even to his own ears he didn't sound sure.

"We can go home, you know."

"I don't want to spoil the fun for the others," he protested. He'd been relieved to see Sarah laughing along with the others at some joke Josh had made.

"We don't have to," Milly argued. "We could take two of the horses, and whoever rode them could come back in the wagon."

"No, we wanted to invite people to our wedding, didn't we? I don't think it's the malaria, but just to be sure, I'll go ahead and take a draft of quinine. Let me just get a cupful of water from the church pump to wash that bitter taste down, and I'll be right as rain."

"Englishmen are every bit as stubborn as American men!" Milly retorted in exasperation. "At least let's go inside while you drink it, and get you out of the sun for a few minutes," Milly said, rising to her feet. "Sarah, we'll be back in a while. We're going to get a drink of water and then go around and tell folks about the wedding," she said.

But Nick's hopes of a few peaceful minutes alone

with Milly in the cool dimness of the sanctuary were to be frustrated. When they walked inside, Nick's eyes made out a huddled form in a front pew even as the sound of weeping reached his ears.

It was Ada Spencer. He had to smother the urge to groan aloud.

Milly rushed forward. "Ada? Ada, what's wrong?"

The woman started. Obviously she had been sunk too deep in distress to hear their quiet entrance.

Nick took in the other woman's disheveled hair and red-rimmed eyes as Ada looked up.

"What is it?" Milly asked gently. "Where's Mr. Harvey? Did you two have a quarrel?"

"He's gone," Ada said dully. "He left town about an hour ago…"

"But why?"

"Did he hurt you, Miss Spencer?" Nick said, stepping forward. "I promise you, if he did, we'll hunt him down and see that he's punished."

The woman shook her head, a weary gesture that spoke volumes. "No…not like you mean," she said, her voice raspy and cracking. "He didn't do anything I didn't agree to. But when I told him I was expecting his child, and I wanted to know when we were going to marry, he said he was leaving and going back to his post in Austin—maybe even back to England."

"We'll find him and bring him back," Nick said, promising himself he'd force the scoundrel to make an honest woman of Ada Spencer, even though he was sure Ada was better off without him, even if it meant bearing a babe on her own.

"No!" the woman cried, startling both of them with

the vehemence she was able to summon. "I don't want anyone that doesn't want me! I'll go away somewhere—tell everyone I'm a widow! But you can't tell anyone what he did, Milly, swear you won't…" She buried her face in her hands as a new paroxysm of sobs erupted from her.

Milly knelt by Ada's side and gathered the woman into her arms. "Of course I won't, Ada dear, but you mustn't think of leaving. No one in town will condemn you—"

Ada raised her head and opened her mouth, surely about to argue.

And then a shattering scream split the air from outside.

"Oh dear heaven, what can that be?" cried Milly. Ada jerked bolt upright, her sorrows momentarily forgotten, and all three of them ran to the door as the screaming went on and on.

When they reached the outside, it was all too plain what had caused someone to scream—a winded horse stood there, its flanks heaving. A man slumped over the horse's neck, his back pierced with multiple arrows. He was tied on the saddle by a rope binding his hands around the horse's neck and tying his feet to the stirrups.

"It's Blakely!" screamed Ada, and fell over in a faint.

"Milly, stay with her!" Nick shouted, and ran to the horse. Everyone else who had been picnicking had jumped to their feet, but seemed riveted to the spot with horror.

He was certain Harvey must be dead, but when he reached the horse, he saw the man was still breathing.

"Harvey, can you hear me?" Nick hoped the man had passed out, for surely he must be suffering untold agony if he was conscious.

To his astonishment, the man turned a milk-white, blood-spattered face toward him. "Comanches…coming…they killed Waters…" he managed to say, and then his eyes rolled back as a last breath rattled through him and he died.

And Nick heard the pounding of hooves in the distance.

"The Comanches are coming! We've got to get to the fort!" he shouted. He ran back to where Milly was stooping over Ada, trying to slap her awake, and with one swift motion moved Milly aside and scooped up the unconscious woman.

"Milly, can you run?"

Wordlessly, her eyes wide, she nodded. "But where's Sarah?" Her eyes searched the lawn.

Both saw Sarah at the same time, running toward them alongside Elijah. The other Brown brothers, Bobby and Josh flanked them. Sarah's gaze met Milly's, and she beckoned for Milly to hurry, then ran to the street.

Milly took off, running alongside Nick.

All around them, parents snatched up their little ones, the children wailing in confused protest at their suddenly interrupted fun. Women screamed and men drew their guns as they ran. They became like a sea of ants, all streaming toward the fort in the middle of town.

Then over all the cries and turmoil came the whoops and shrieks of the charging Comanches on their mounts splashing across Simpson Creek behind the churchyard.

A panic-stricken woman collided with Milly, and

Milly nearly fell, saved only by Nick's extended hand. Arrows and bullets whooshed and whined past them as they fled, past the livery, past the mercantile, past the hotel, past the general store… Dear God, surely they must be near the fort!

Nick heard Milly panting for breath, and he breathed a prayer as he ran with his unconscious burden. *Please, Lord, let Milly make it to safety, and Sarah. Take my life if You will, but save this woman and the others.*

Some men had already reached the fort and the wagons parked outside it, and had grabbed rifles to set up a covering fire at the Comanches galloping so closely behind the last of the townspeople. Their firing slowed the attackers' charge long enough, Nick thought, as he ran inside with Ada and Milly, for the townspeople to make it to safety—at least those who hadn't been felled as they ran. He'd seen at least a couple go down, but he'd dared not stop to help them.

As soon as he laid Ada down inside the fort in Milly's care, he dashed back outside, grabbing the rifle that Josh tossed to him from the wagon. Together they fired at the front line of the mounted Comanches until the last men ran inside. Then they, too, jumped inside, and rammed the door bolt home.

Men were already perched on the inside second-story walkways, firing out of the narrow windows as the whoops of the Indians and the whinnies of their horses circled the square stone fort. Nick joined them even as the first chills racked his body. The malaria would have to wait.

Below him, he saw that Milly had turned over the care of Ada to Mrs. Detwiler, who was already clucking over her charge as if a hundred murderous savages weren't whooping outside. As the older woman sponged her face with a damp cloth, Ada blinked and raised her head, only to bury her face against Mrs. Detwiler's body as war whoops floated in through the windows, joined by a bloodcurdling scream and thud outside as a settler's bullet found its target.

In a moment, Milly had joined him at an adjacent window, firing with a rifle he didn't recognize. *Lord, save us and make me always worthy of this brave woman!* Looking to both sides, he saw Josh, Bobby and the Brown brothers, all firing out at the attackers. Between Elijah and Caleb stood the Yankee Sarah had rejected, shooting a Winchester carbine out the narrow window with deadly accuracy.

He could hear Reverend Chadwick and several others below, praying aloud for their deliverance, and added his silent prayers to theirs.

Where was Milly's sister? Then he spotted her, one of several women huddled over wailing, terrorized children against the walls as flaming arrows rained in with hissing sounds from the roofless top of the building. These embedded themselves harmlessly in the dirt floor, where the fires soon hissed out. The echoing yelps and screams rose upward to rattle around inside Nick's skull with the hammer and anvil already jammed inside there. He stiffened his body to try to control the chills that threatened the accuracy of his aim.

Just a little longer, Lord. Let the fever hold off a little longer... As he watched, their coppery skins and contorted, screaming faces became the faces of warring Punjabis and the town's buildings became the northern plains of India. He fired again, and had the satisfaction of seeing a Punjabi—no, a Comanche—about to loose a flaming arrow fall off his horse with a hoarse cry instead. As he looked, his blurring vision caused the crumpled body on the ground to become two.

And then, blessedly, they heard a bugle in the distance, and more pounding hooves. As Nick watched through blurry vision, horsemen in blue galloped around the corner, heading straight for the fort, as Comanches scattered left and right, fleeing the oncoming cavalry.

Chapter Twenty-Nine

When Nick woke, he was lying in a strange bedroom and Milly was sponging his forehead with water that felt blessedly cool.

"Where am I?" he asked, staring up at the lovely face of his beautiful Milly.

She smiled down at him. "Ssssh! I don't want her to know you're awake just yet, so I can have you all to myself. You're in Mrs. Detwiler's spare bedroom, and she's out in the kitchen making broth for you. She wouldn't hear of us taking you home in the wagon until you came around. But I wouldn't be the least bit surprised if she insists you stay longer. I think it's been a long time since she had anyone to ply with calves' foot jelly and tea."

"I… I take it the Comanches have been routed?"

She nodded. "Put to flight, the few who survived the crossfire between our fort and the cavalry."

"Thank God," he said soberly, to which she said, "Amen."

"It'll be a long time before they try to attack Simpson Creek again, the major said, now that we have a fort," Milly continued.

"Have the others been back to the ranch yet? Is it all right?" he said, hardly daring to hear the answer. If Waters had been killed and his ranch burned, it was always possible the Matthews ranch had been hit, too, and the livestock stolen.

"Untouched. We've been so blessed."

"Indeed, we have. Thank You, Lord." He straightened up in the bed. "The last thing I remember was hearing the cavalry bugler sounding the charge, and the cavalry galloping into sight."

Milly grinned now. "That's when you swooned."

He glared at her with all the ferocity he could muster—which wasn't much, considering the headache he still had. "I did not *swoon,* woman, I'll have you know. Men do not swoon. Females swoon."

"Very well, you fell unconscious," she said reasonably, but mischief still danced in her eyes. "Whatever you did, you slept nearly around the clock. It's Sunday now."

"Did we…lose very many townspeople?" Nick had guessed from Milly's calm demeanor that Sarah and their ranch hands must be all right, so now he could ask about the others.

Her expression sobered. "Doctor Harkey. He didn't make it to the fort. He must have been behind us."

"That's a shame. Poor Maude…"

She nodded. "Blakely Harvey, of course… And the major said they found Bill Waters and a couple of his hands killed and the ranch house burned to the ground."

Nick nodded, unable to find anything to say. No one

deserved to die that way. He only hoped Waters and Harvey had had time to cry out to God before they died.

"Other than those, no one was killed, though several got arrow or gunshot wounds, and there's an assortment of cuts and bruises."

"And the town's without a doctor, because Doctor Harkey is dead."

Milly shook her head. "In God's providence, no, it's not. Remember, the Yankee who was corresponding with Sarah was a doctor? Right now he's busy as a barefoot boy on a red ant bed, as Josh would say."

"How does Sarah feel about that? Before the attack, I'm sure she was hoping he'd ride back out of here when the day was over."

Milly grinned. "I'm sure she realizes he's a very essential man to have around right now. I think she's worried he'll decide to stay, though, now that the town needs a doctor." She chuckled. "I met him, and I liked him. I think he might just turn out to be exactly what my sister needs. If Prissy Gilmore doesn't snap him up, that is."

"It'll be interesting to watch."

She nodded. "He's been to check on you, though of course you wouldn't remember it. He's brought some more quinine from Doctor Harkey's supply. He expects taking the quinine when you did will considerably shorten this attack."

"I feel quite a bit better already."

From somewhere beyond the bedroom a clock began to chime.

"Church will be over soon," Milly remarked. "We'd better get you shaved for the visit."

"Visit? Who's visiting?"

"The mayor was planning to stop by after the service at church—they were going to give thanks for the town's deliverance," she said. "He says the town's going to proclaim you a hero. I believe he's commissioning a medal to be made."

"I? As I recall, every man in the fort was firing at them, and the bravest woman I know, too," he said, reaching up to cup her cheek.

"If it weren't for you, that fort wouldn't have been there just when we needed it. And we'd still have been giving in to the demands of bullies wearing hoods and making threats."

He smiled, warmed by the love and admiration he saw in her eyes. "And all because one plucky woman decided to advertise for husbands." He raised his head and met her lips. "I love you, Milly Matthews. Being your husband is going to be an adventure."

* * * * *

SPECIAL EXCERPT FROM

When a rookie K-9 cop becomes the target of a
dangerous stalker, can she stay one step ahead of this
killer with the help of her boss and his K-9 partner?

Read on for a sneak preview of
Courage Under Fire *by Sharon Dunn*,
the next exciting installment to the
True Blue K-9 Unit *miniseries, available in*
October 2019 from Love Inspired Suspense.

ookie K-9 officer Lani Branson took in a deep breath as
e pedaled her bike along the trail in the Jamaica Bay
ildlife Refuge. Water rushed and receded from the shore
st over the dunes. The high-rises of New York City,
ade hazy from the dusky twilight, were visible across
e expanse of water.

She sped up even more.

Tonight was important. This training exercise was an
pportunity to prove herself to the other K-9 officers who
aited back at the visitors' center with the tracking dogs
r her to give the go-ahead. Playing the part of a child lost
 the refuge so the dogs could practice tracking her was
obably a less-than-desirable duty for the senior officers.

Reaching up to her shoulder, Lani got off her bike and
essed the button on the radio. "I'm in place."

The smooth tenor voice of her supervisor, Chief Noa
Jameson, came over the line. "Good—you made it ou
there in record time."

Up ahead she spotted an object shining in the settin
sun. She jogged toward it. A bicycle, not hers, was proppe
against a tree.

A knot of tension formed at the back of her neck as sh
turned in a half circle, taking in the area around her. It wa
possible someone had left the bike behind. Vagrants cou
have wandered into the area.

She studied the bike a little closer. State-of-the-a
and in good condition. Not the kind of bike someone ju
dumped.

A branch cracked. Her breath caught in her throat. Fe
caused her heartbeat to drum in her ears.

"NYPD." She hadn't worn her gun for this exercis
Her eyes scanned all around her, searching for movemei
and color. "You need to show yourself."

Seconds ticked by. Her heart pounded.

Someone else was out here.

Don't miss
Courage Under Fire *by Sharon Dunn,*
available October 2019 wherever
Love Inspired® Suspense books and ebooks are sold.

www.LoveInspired.com

Love Inspired®

Inspirational Romance to Warm Your Heart and Soul

Join our social communities to connect with other readers who share your love!

Sign up for the Love Inspired newsletter at **www.LoveInspired.com** to be the first to find out about upcoming titles, special promotions and exclusive content

CONNECT WITH US AT:

Facebook.com/groups/HarlequinConnection

 Facebook.com/LoveInspiredBooks

Twitter.com/LoveInspiredBks

LISOCIAL2